PRESCHOOLED

A Novel

Anna Lefler

Full Fathom Five digital is an imprint of Full Fathom Five, LLC

For information visit Full Fathom Five Digital, a division of Full Fathom Five, LLC at www.fullfathomfive.com

Cover design by Cow Goes Moo™

ISBN 978-1-63370-071-0

First edition

A portion of the author proceeds from this book will be donated to the Los Angeles Regional Food Bank, a nonprofit organization whose mission is to end hunger in the Los Angeles community.

For Madison and Henry
And for hardworking snack-parents everywhere

1
Justine

There was a season in Santa Monica, and within it a time of day, when the air was so silken, the light so honeyed and ethereal that it almost, *almost* made up for the lack of street parking. It was under this blue bowl of ocean air that Justine circled the block for a third time in search of a spot where she could legally abandon her car. She could not be late to new-family orientation. Margaret Askew, owner and headmistress of Garden of Happiness, would take a dim view of a parent tardy to the first event of his or her preschool career. After all the mom reconnaissance Justine had conducted to secure a place for her daughter behind the school's exclusive picket fence, she was not about to christen the experience with a hairy eyeball from the woman she'd heard referred to as "the Leona Helmsley of the preschool world."

But where was Greg? He said he'd call when he was close so they could walk in together. She dialed him from her cellphone. "Dude. Orientation starts at six o'clock."

"Get off my back, woman. I was stuck on a conference call." Justine heard the smile in his voice and the NPR background chatter on his car radio. "Who's with Emma?"

"My mom."

"She's checking all the expiration dates in our fridge, isn't she?"

"As we speak. Hey, are you here yet? I don't want to walk into this thing alone. It's bad for my street cred."

"Your *what*? I hope you haven't already fallen in with some rough mommy-gang."

"I'm just saying. You've only got fifteen minutes to make it here from Century City."

"Challenge accepted. Bye."

As she continued the hunt for parking, she thought back on the school tours, applications, interviews, and intelligence-gathering that had led them to Garden of Happiness. She couldn't say exactly when the quest for admission to the ideal preschool had taken on the urgency of, say, finding a government safe house after turning state's evidence, but she knew where it had started:

Tumblepants Toddler Music Jamboree.

Justine made a point of staying on the fringes of the mommy clusters she observed every Tuesday morning at Emma's music activity class. She had heard enough talk of residual C-section fat pouches, episiotomies gone awry, and recalcitrant lactation glands to reinforce her belief that it took more than some shared war stories from the birthing trenches to turn a stranger into a real friend. After leaving her job to become a full-time mom, she had filled her days with errands and projects, working within the baby's nap schedule, determined to continue as a productive member of society even though she no longer drew a paycheck. With Emma a few months shy of two years now, Justine felt she had a pretty good handle on the transition from the methodical world of law firm marketing to the lawless frontier of motherhood. That all changed one Tuesday morning during a frenzied rendition of "Old MacDonald Had a Farm" when one of the other moms casually asked how her preschool interviews were going.

"You're already interviewing?" Justine shielded herself from the maracas her daughter was wielding like nunchuks on the mat next to her. "Come *on*, I knew we were getting close, but I thought I had a little more time before those hijinks started."

The mom, who happened to be the wife of one of Greg's law partners and a former lawyer herself, adjusted her glasses, which were made of clear plastic with the exception of the nosepiece and gave the unsettling impression that a random piece of metal had been clamped onto her face. "I know I've said this before, but there's a payoff to being in a top-tier baby group: you are *in the loop*. We calendared the admissions deadlines while we were still learning to use breast pumps." She held up a finger. "Yes, that sounds like overkill, but the fact is we live on the Westside, where preschool isn't something you just walk in and *sign up for*." She gave Emma a once-over. "The unfortunate news for you is that, according to our group facilitator, there are more boy spots available this year than girl spots, at least in the schools that matter. You'll have to work around that while you're playing catch-up."

Another mom—whose diminutive Guatemalan nanny stood sentry behind her strapped to a $400 diaper bag that appeared to be twice her weight—chimed in to the conversation. "Listen, do yourself a favor and go straight to the school whisperer. Starting this late, you're going to need her."

"'The *school whisperer*?'" Justine said. "Are you serious?"

"A school application consultant?" she uptalked. "The *LA Times* did a big piece on her last year—she helps with your written answers and preps you and your kid for interviews?" She looked at the partner's wife, then back at Justine. "Oh my God—it's so lucky you talked to us!"

Justine stewed as she drove away from the mall. She had heard of those high-powered baby groups, of course, but hadn't been interested in joining one. She didn't feel the need to discuss Emma with strangers or disturb their private routine of outings, naps, songs, meals, and tickles. *Those women are preschool extremists*, she told herself when she and Emma arrived at home. Still, she couldn't resist calling one school on the moms'"hot" list. When the administrator informed her that "families in the know" placed their children on the enrollment waiting list one to two years prior to preschool eligibility (or, as she would later tell Greg, "before they had crowned at Cedars-Sinai"), Justine felt the resurgence of her old competitive drive, which had been mothballed along with her briefcase since leaving her job. She wasn't about to let a little mom-on-mom hazing and front-office attitude bully her daughter out of the running before she'd even started. No, she and Greg would decide which schools interested them enough to apply and, after that, may the best toddler win. The admissions quest was *on*—and Justine would be undertaking it without a consultant, whispering or otherwise.

Months later, just when it seemed Emma would spend her preschool years languishing on various Westside waiting lists, Justine received a call from her first-choice school: Garden of Happiness. They had a spot for Emma...if Justine could deliver the tuition check by the end of the day.

"The school with all the rules?" Greg said when she called to give him the news. "Didn't you think that place was annoying?"

"I think *all* the schools are a little annoying—for the *parents*. But Emma seemed most comfortable at Garden of Happiness, and that's going to matter a lot when the time comes for me to drive away and leave her there. Besides, everyone I've talked to says that no one helps parents cope with preschooler behavior better than Margaret, even if she's not what you'd call warm and fuzzy."

"There's an understatement," Greg said with a laugh. "But I see what you're saying. The whiff of totalitarianism aside, they do seem to know what they're doing at that school."

Justine delivered the tuition check within the hour.

After waiting for a cigarette-smoking woman in workout wear to coax her sheepdog into her Volvo and drive away, Justine pulled into a curbside parking spot and hurried toward the school. When she reached the gate, she lingered on the sidewalk, hugging her purse to her chest as she looked over the fence into the front play area. Created from the yard of the converted house that comprised the school's main building, the play yard held a water table, a fleet of sturdy riding toys, and a large, plastic log cabin complete with shutters and a chimney. Justine pictured Emma setting up her imaginary life in the cabin, flipping the whole-wheat pancakes that were part of her well-adjusted family's balanced breakfast before settling in for the day's work at her successful home-based business, all while responding to the dozens of daily comments on her wildly popular blog.

"You must be new."

Justine turned to see a woman leaning against the fence on the far side of the gate. She wore boxy jeans, clogs, and a linen blouse with a leather messenger bag slung across her chest. Her expression was matter-of-fact.

"You're a parent at Garden of Happiness?" Justine said.

"Oh, yeah. Getting ready to start lap number two with son number two." She stepped forward and offered her hand. "I'm Bette."

"I'm Justine, admissions survivor."

"Good one," Bette said without smiling. "I'd be careful with jokes like that. Margaret has ears like homeland security." She twirled a finger in the air as though the surrounding trees were laced with concealed listening devices.

Justine glanced over her shoulder, but all she saw were other parents arriving for orientation. "So this is your second child at the school. I'm surprised you need to go through orientation again."

Bette frowned and lowered her voice. "Oh, I don't *need* to. I'm being *forced* to. Don't get me started."

"Ah. Got it." Justine was beginning to understand why this mom hadn't been among the parent volunteers she had encountered during the admissions process. It was easier to picture Bette piloting a get-away car than a welcome wagon.

"Something wrong?" Bette said. "You seem even more stressed out than the other rookies."

"I'm just worried about being late."

"So, you're here by yourself? Single mom?"

"What? Oh, *no*. Not that there's anything wrong with that, of course. I'm waiting for my husband so we can walk in together."

"Join the club." She looked over Justine's shoulder. "And here he is now." Bette crossed her arms. "Took you long enough," she yelled past Justine, making her wince.

"Actually, I'm right on time," the man said.

Justine couldn't say whether her body or her mind reacted first to the familiar voice behind her. She was pretty sure, however, that it would be bad form to sock a dad in the stomach at new-family orientation, even if she had been harboring the desire to do so for the last eight years.

She turned, and there was Harry. Or, as he had become known to Justine and her best friend Ruthie, The Crapwizard. It had been Ruthie who had coined the term "lovestupid" to describe Justine's state of mind when her relationship with Harry ended, arguing that "lovesick" bestowed a noble, Jane Austenish tone on its collateral effects that was undeserved. "The Crapwizard" on the other hand, had been a collaborative effort.

He wore jeans with a slim, open-necked pullover and his brown hair fell across his forehead with a casual roguishness Justine knew was anything but accidental. As much as she hated to admit it, the years looked good on him. Then again, everything looked good on him—a fact of which he was obnoxiously aware. Justine started to smooth her hair and adjust the strap of her orange silk top, then brought the traitorous hand back down to her thigh with an audible *slap*.

"Let me introduce you guys." Bette stepped forward and gestured at Justine. "What was your name again?"

"We've already—" Justine began.

"Harry Rivers," he cut in, giving her a meaningful look. "Excellent meeting you." They shook hands and for a moment she thought she might get swept up in some gaggy soft-focus montage of their time together in Berkeley—late nights studying in coffee shops, early mornings in his apartment, feeling his abs through his T-shirt as they roared across the Golden Gate on his motorcycle. *Screw that*, she thought, *this isn't some Lifetime television movie.* She seized his hand and squeezed it as hard as she could. She knew she couldn't hurt him—he was a sculptor, after all, with the strength that came from working with metal and stone—but she wanted to.

"Justine Underwood," she said. "*Such* a pleasure." The look in his eyes shifted and she knew he was gauging her thoughts.

Turning back to Bette, she took in the aviators nestled into the dirty-blond pixie cut, the absence of makeup, and gruff manner. Within a nanosecond, her mind had processed this data and classified Bette as "sporty." This fell at the opposite end of the spectrum from "vixen," which, knowing Harry, is what she would have expected. She knew she shouldn't categorize people, but the fact was, she could not have come up with a more unexpected candidate for marriage to Harry if she'd had a year to think about it. (As for her own classification, her aversion to tight clothing alone ruled out potential vixendom. She preferred to classify herself as "feminine," with a sufficient arsenal of Cinemax skills to repel any attempted application of the deadly-bland "wholesome.") From the corner of her eye she saw Harry flip his hair with a toss of his head—a habit that had grated on her when they were together and which was even less appealing on a man in his early thirties.

More parents flowed through the school gate. Justine checked her watch—three minutes after six o'clock and still no sign of Greg.

"We should get in there before the flying monkeys take attendance," Bette said. "Do you want to walk in with us or what?"

"You can always save the hubs a seat," Harry added with the smile she had struggled to wipe from her mind in the months after he left Berkeley for Chicago—a period Ruthie had dubbed the "Five Flavors of Grief:" Thin Mints (denial), Do-Si-Dos (anger), Tagalongs (bargaining), Trefoils (depression) and, finally, Samoas (acceptance). It had taken three metric tons of bath salts, a one-night-only Bill Murray film festival, and some good, old-fashioned ladyballs to propel Justine off the sofa and back into the world after his departure.

Thank God she was over him.

"You guys go on in," she said. "I'm sure he's just parking."

"Suit yourself," Bette said, then turned to Harry, who seemed to be waiting for a further response from Justine. "Move it," she said, shooing him through the gate and looking back at Justine to roll her eyes.

Justine watched them disappear around the corner of the building—the last parents to go in for orientation. The sidewalks were empty now. She started digging through the used tissues, sparkly barrettes, and baggies of crumbling fish crackers that had overtaken her purse since becoming a mom. She found her phone under a bottle of hand sanitizer. Its screen lit up with a text from Greg.

> *Got called back to work. Just found out the other side going to court in the AM with an ex parte motion— must prepare. Be home late. Sorry to miss it. Represent!*
> *G*

"Are you frickin' *kidding* me?" Slinging her purse back on her shoulder, Justine dashed through the wooden gate and across the empty play area toward the yellow door. Behind it she heard a round of soft applause. They had started without her.

Orientation began with an informal "mixer," which translated into roughly twenty well-heeled couples milling around in the sand among the play structures while trying to look like the kind of people who begat geniuses—or at least exceptional offspring who would someday exhibit a genetically superior ability to accessorize. On the wooden deck at the edge of the sand was a table loaded with fruit trays, cookies, cheeses, and other snacks, along with iced juices, sodas, and waters. The sandy play area was surrounded on three sides by the school—the former house in front, three classrooms on the side, and one more in the rear, the top floor of which was Margaret's private office. On the fourth side was a five-story office building. The school's neighbor on the other adjacent lot was a 1950s apartment house whose tenants had attempted to restore their privacy by shrouding their balconies with a rain forest's worth of climbing vines and hanging plants.

Many of the parents seemed to know one another already and gathered in lively groups among the slides and push toys, pulling in a teacher to answer questions or chatting among themselves. Justine worked her way through the crowd, gathering bits of information and making conversation. After thirty minutes of forced socialization, she was not only on the verge of dehydration, but had foolishly outed herself to two helicopter parents as a follower of the Ferber sleep training method.

"I don't understand," said the mom. She exchanged a disapproving glance with her husband then turned back to Justine with what Justine imagined was the same expression Jeffrey Dahmer had received during group "share time" in prison. "You just *ignore* her? And let her *cry* herself to sleep?"

"No, see, there's an actual scientific process and—"

"We could never do that to Denim," the dad said with a firm

shake of his head. "His therapist has explained to us that he's an extraordinarily sensitive child—"

"And gifted," the mother interjected.

"Yes, exactly," the dad continued, "which is both a blessing and a curse. Denim's exceptional nature causes him to experience the world around him on a much deeper level then an ordinary child. As his parents, we bear the responsibility of shielding him from negative stimuli of all kinds."

"Geez, I wouldn't call learning how to doze off 'negative stimuli,'" Justine said. "I mean, we all have to figure out how to do it, right?"

The husband and wife exchanged another look. "We need to go talk to Margaret about Denim's dietary restrictions now," the dad said, touching his wife's elbow as he turned to go.

"Good luck," the mom said. The couple distanced themselves from Justine as though they had seen her name on some internet parenting watch list.

"She only cried for fifteen minutes," she called after them. "She's a fast learner." The knot of tension behind her eyes began to throb. She walked across the play area, the heels of her new sandals sinking into the sand, and stepped up onto the deck. Grabbing a bottle of water from the refreshment table, she took several deep swallows and wished once again that Greg were there with her, not because his networking skills were any better than hers, but because she knew he would be as amused and/or appalled by the night's encounters as she was. Later, they would find ways to work snippets from the night into their evening routine, such as, "Due to my extraordinary level of giftedness, I find this mint toothpaste to be an assault on my senses."

Right now, though, she didn't feel like laughing. If phones weren't verboten on school grounds, she would pull hers out then and there and text Greg, "*I am bombing preschool orientation.*"

Okay, maybe "bombing" was too strong a word, but the sense of quiet triumph that had buoyed her for the past few days evaporated the moment she heard Harry's voice. Before his appearance, she had been primed to accomplish her goals for the evening, which included asking questions that showed she was an informed/caring mom but not a smothering/soul-scouring/nightmare mom, sorting the potential mom friends from the emotional remoras and mean girls, and, most importantly, making a stellar impression on Margaret, thus reinforcing that her decision to accept Emma into the school had been a shrewd—albeit last-minute—one. Trying to do all this while avoiding a heinous former boyfriend in the play yard, however, had put her off her game.

She took another drink. As she lowered the bottle, she saw Harry starting across the play area toward her, alone. Before she could pretend to be otherwise *occupado*, he was standing next to her.

"Hey," he said. He plucked a cluster of grapes from a bowl on the food table and ate one, munching with obvious contentment.

Her mind scrambled for some *Cosmo*-approved response that would simultaneously make it clear that she had not given him a second thought in the last eight years and drive home the fact that leaving her had been the worst decision he'd ever made (including the time he let that Macy's salesman talk him into buying a pair of "man capris"), while also hinting that she had probably received a Nobel Prize—or at least a Grammy—since he last saw her and was now way too B&I (busy and important) to give the time of day to a femme-pants-wearing ex.

"Hello," she said. *Nailed it*, she thought and looked away.

"Same school. What are the chances?" He ate another grape and took stock of the crowd.

"Insert obligatory 'it's a small world' observation here," she said and reached for a tortilla chip.

"A lot of people would get uptight in this situation, but I say let's not be uncomfortable. We can just be normal, right?"

Had he always talked like this? And where the hell was the dip? "How very...*European* of you," Justine said as she foraged across the food table, her chip poised in the event of guacamole.

"What does *that* mean?"

"Oh, you know, disregarding the messier parts of past relationships to preserve some facade of friendship. Highly evolved and all that."

"But haven't we always been friends?"

A blue pottery bowl of guacamole appeared behind a tower of mini burritos like a mirage in the desert. "The *best*," she said and jabbed her chip into the green mound. "Feel better now?"

Harry gave her a wary glance. "Better in what way?"

"You know, you get to be the good guy who took the high road. You came over here to smooth things and now you can check me off as 'handled' and go on about your business. That's got to be satisfying."

Harry chuckled, but not before the irritation showed in his face. "Wow. Well, I guess you've got me all wired, then."

"Just keepin' it real."

Harry scowled. "I hate that expression."

She popped the last bite of chip in her mouth, shrugged, and then checked the time on the red rooster clock hanging under the eaves outside the classroom.

"Oh my God," Harry said. "I'd forgotten about your eyes." He stepped toward her. "I never could find the right word for that color. Somewhere between blue, gray, and green." He brought his face close to hers, studying one eye, then the other. "Why do they make me think of the desert?"

"I don't know," Justine said, wiping the salt from the corner of her mouth. "Maybe you spent your honeymoon there."

Harry opened his mouth as if to say something, then looked past her toward the main building. "There's Bette waving us in. Mixer's over—time for the lecture."

She saw Bette gesture at him to hurry up and he took the few steps down into the sand. "So great seeing you," he said and headed toward the back of the little house without waiting for a reply.

"I guess we're done talking about my eyes," she mumbled and hitched her purse up on her shoulder.

When Harry reached the kitchen steps, Bette's voice cracked across the play yard. "Come on, let's get this over with."

"Ah, the little woman," Justine said, then trudged through the sand and into the school to find a seat.

Forty-five minutes later, she doubted she would ever walk upright again.

The parents were perched on rows of miniature plastic chairs in the school's main space—the former living room of the original house. Justine had been trying to find an arrangement of her limbs that would compensate for her current fourteen-inch ground clearance. Nothing she did, however, had any effect on the pains rocketing up the backs of her thighs to her rump, which, thankfully, had lost all sensation twenty minutes earlier. Around her, there was a constant rustle in the audience as the other parents contorted their bodies in the toddler-sized seats. Many fanned themselves with the meeting handouts to circulate the air, which was saturated with the cumulative scents of the adults' Euro-posh grooming products and the school's signature blend of hand sanitizer, library bindings, and modeling clay.

At the front of the room stood Margaret in plaid slacks, a crisp, pink blouse, and loafers. Next to her on a projection screen was the image of a small girl eating lunch at one of the school's tables.

"This adorable child is doing something wrong. Who can tell me what it is?" She looked out at the audience, whose heads just reached the level of her braided leather belt. "Uh-oh, parents, we already covered this rule."

The parents murmured and Justine studied the picture of the little girl. Velcro shoes, check. Elastic-waist shorts for quick potty access, check. Hair pulled back for ease of play, check. What rule had been broken?

"It's the juice box, parents." Margaret pointed at the screen. "That's a no-no." Behind her, the school's four teachers shook their heads in synchronized condemnation. In the third row, a woman with a side-swept ponytail struggled to keep her waifish arm aloft under the weight of a massive men's Rolex. Margaret gestured to her. "Yes?"

The mom dropped her arm into her lap with visible relief. "It's because it's not organic juice, right? That's why it's not allowed?"

Margaret studied the woman with an expression that suggested she might be reconsidering her admission status. Then, with a pinched smile, she addressed the room at large. "Who would like to help this new mom?"

"Oooh, juice box infraction," Justine said under her voice to the woman next to her, whose bangles and prayer beads rattled as she took furtive notes on her iPhone. "Tough call." The woman gave Justine a leery frown, then went back to tapping on her phone's screen.

"Correct." Margaret bestowed a quick nod on another mom in the audience who had apparently cracked this portion of the preschool code. "It's too tempting for little fingers to squeeze a juice box. And when you squeeze a juice box, what does it become? A squirt gun." She waited, motionless except for her eyes, as she searched for other wayward parents. "Moving on," she said at last.

Justine studied the back of Harry's premeditated bedhead two rows in front of her and wondered what brought him back to his hometown, which he'd always disparagingly referred to as "La-La

Land." When it came to surprises, she preferred the kind that arrived in pretty, recyclable paper to the kind that came wrapped in radioactive memories with half-lives of a thousand years. She also preferred that her exes got uglier as time passed. Was that too much to ask? Almost a decade later, Harry had not developed even the suggestion of thickness around his waist and, if anything, his shoulders were broader than the last time she'd sized them up.

He turned suddenly, motioning toward Margaret with his eyes and giving Justine a conspiratorial smile—one that she alarmed herself by returning without thinking. *Stop that*, she thought. Being in the same school with this guy didn't mean she had to participate in some cute, watered-down version of their old connection. Besides, she already had a reliable flirtationship with her barista. Nor could she picture herself in one of those groovy California arrangements where exes and their spouses bobbed around together in a hot tub on the weekend, talking about how busy they all were while pretending to be above it all. No, if she were going to manage this unwanted intrusion of her past into her present, old-fashioned avoidance was the best approach—and one she could throw herself into with gusto. Chances were their children would not be in the same group, and, in any case, it would most likely be Bette she interacted with, not Harry. She felt her shoulders release a bit. Now that their strained re-introduction was behind them, they would likely cross paths only occasionally, almost as if he weren't at the school at all. She could handle that.

"Last thing, new parents." Margaret waved a stack of white envelopes. "We have a little program here that we call 'Garden Gnomes.' Each new family is paired with a senior family at the school, similar to a Big Brothers Big Sisters program." She began handing out the envelopes. "Your Garden Gnomes will be your go-to school contacts, starting with a family playdate where everyone can make friends before school starts." Margaret read the front of another envelope and handed it to Justine.

As the parents around her began coaxing their bodies back into post-evolutionary stature, Justine opened the envelope and read the letter inside. It was a brief note, stating simply that her family's official Garden Gnomes were Bette and Harry Rivers. The response this news caused Justine to deliver under her breath would not have been Dr. Seuss-approved.

2
Margaret

Margaret waited until the last new parent disappeared down the sidewalk, then shut the school's outside door with a satisfying *thunk*, thumb-flipping the lock as she had done thousands of times in the eleven years since opening Garden of Happiness. *Thank goodness school is starting,* she thought as she made her way down the breezeway in the fluorescent glow of the office building next door. One more week in her silent, empty house and she would have been driven to crafting. Margaret was *not* a crafter. Then again, after a summer that had seen her husband move out and her daughter leave for college in Oregon, she wasn't sure *who* she was anymore. This new and distasteful sensation was most acute when she was away from her school. At least when she was inside the Garden of Happiness gates, she could feel like *some* aspect of her life was still proceeding according to plan.

In the main building, the last squat chair had been stacked, its feet dragged across the gritty linoleum with prejudice by an investment banker who made no effort to hide his pique at being assigned such a menial task. *That woman doesn't know who I am,* his posture had telegraphed as he pushed a teetering tower of chairs against the wall with an angry *clunk*.

Margaret had observed this, a smile playing at the corner of her mouth. She knew exactly who this man was. He was just another little boy who didn't want to put the blocks back in the bin after playing with them. And across the room, rubbing her temples, her fingers glittering with wedding diamonds, was the grown-up version of a little girl who relied on a trip to the nurse's office to avoid her classwork. Margaret had studied all the parents during orientation, tagging each of them like a preschool game warden. *Instigator. Teacher's pet. Bully. Diplomat.* She saw them all, year after year. She could predict their misbehavior in any scenario, could recite the high points of their childhood parent-teacher conferences with routine accuracy.

Relationship management was quite simple, really, once a person realized—as she had early in her teaching career—that adults were merely children with more dangerous toys. "Children need rules," she often said. "A world without rules is terrifying to a child." To Margaret, it made no difference if the child in question was five... or fifty-five.

She snapped off the lights in the main room, leaving only the undulating glow from the fish tank. Crossing the large circular carpet with its pattern of children in cultural dress embracing one another in global peace and harmony, she approached the rabbit cage. She reached under the low table and pulled a basket from behind a bag of food pellets, her nose twitching at the tang of the wood shavings. Inside, a towel was speckled with stray curls of cedar. She shook it over the cage and refolded it to cover the basket's bottom.

"Looks like we've got our work cut out for us this year, wouldn't you agree, Ozone? Another group of delightful children saddled with sincere but misguided parents. They will all certainly benefit from our help." She brought her face close to the cage and peered at its occupant. Ozone the bunny blinked back at her with that caffeinated look rabbits wear around the clock. "Ready to go upstairs for the night?"

"I always suspected you liked that poofball better than you liked the rest of us," said a man behind her. Her husband's appearance in the doorway startled her, but she didn't let it show. She was not about to give him the satisfaction of seeing her off-balance.

"I know I locked the outside door," she said as she loaded the spotted bunny into the basket, "which begs the question, Eddie: how did you get in?" In the half-light from the fish tank, he looked twenty years younger. She was confronted by the jarring memory of the rangy man with the ready smile in her college philosophy class whom she had noticed long before he noticed her. She reached for the wall and flipped the switch, flooding the room once again with institutional fluorescence, restoring his slight paunch and the retreating hairline that framed his handsome face. Better.

He squinted, then waved a metallic keychain. "I still have this."

Margaret glanced at the object dangling from his hand. "You entered my school using an Egyptian ankh? I'm sorry to disappoint you, but it's not a mystical door out there, just a regular one." She lifted the bunny's basket to her waist.

"The ankh is the *keychain*, Margaret," Eddie said with a tight smile. "I mean I still have a key to our school."

Margaret looked up. "*Our* school? I think those incense fumes have left you disoriented." She took solid, proprietary steps in her loafers as she walked past him and into the kitchen.

He followed as she set the basket on a low table. "Look," he said, taking a deep breath. "I know we haven't seen each other since we dropped Leticia off at her dorm a month ago, and I know my showing up here has the potential to be unpleasant, but my goal—" he cleared his throat, "—my goal is to ease the continuing journeys of our soul vessels on the calmest waters possible."

Margaret picked up a cookie from a plate of leftovers and threw it at Eddie. It bounced off the front of his shirt, leaving a short, chocolate skid mark.

His mouth fell open as he looked down at the smudge. "Did you just throw a Mint Milano at me?"

"It appears you have piloted your 'soul vessel' into hostile waters," Margaret said, dusting the cookie crumbs from her hands. "Luckily for you, the teachers finished off the baklava—it's harder than it looks to get out of cotton."

"You are unbelievable, you know that?" Red splotches appeared on his neck.

"Calm down, Eddie. You don't want to boil your chi, or whatever it's called." She moved around the kitchen, stacking napkins and wiping countertops.

Eddie rolled his neck and huffed loudly. "You know what? I'm going to make a conscious decision to break free from my old emotional script here. You are reacting to *your* reality and that's okay. I am creating a new reality for myself." He shook out his shoulders.

Margaret turned to him, sponge in hand. "Let me make this easy for you. Why are you here?"

Eddie clamped his mouth shut and they stared at each other for a moment. "Fine," he said. "I am here as a courtesy to inform you that, although your lawyers did not include this school in our divorce settlement, it is, in fact, half mine. As such, you are required to buy out my half if you wish to retain it as your sole property once the divorce is settled." He crossed his arms.

Margaret gasped and took a step toward him. "I *instructed* the lawyers not to include it. This has always been *my* school—we agreed on that from the start. You can't have forgotten our conversation that day with the realtor."

"I haven't forgotten it, but you've got a slight misinterpretation there. We agreed the school would be yours to *run*, not yours to *own*. Big difference."

"Do you really think I'll let you walk away with half the value of a business I've spent more than a decade building *on my own?* You've never even shown any interest in it."

"That's how it works. We're both entitled to half. Of everything."

"Is that what your guru told you? That it's okay to neglect your business until it atrophies, then gouge your wife out of her life's work and paddle away in your woo-woo canoe?" She stalked across the kitchen and stood next to the table, stroking Ozone.

"Why do you feel the need to mock the evolution of my beliefs?" Eddie said. "What am I supposed to do with that? I invited you to learn with me, to walk with me on the path of enlightenment, and all you've ever done is insult me."

"Eddie, you're a dentist with irritable bowel syndrome. You won't leave your car with a valet if his hair touches his shirt collar. Do you see how ridiculous this is? You can't think that I would participate in your tie-dyed mid-life crisis."

"I'm not getting into this with you, Margaret. I'm past it. Like I said, I came here because I thought you deserved a heads up that my lawyers *will* be including the school in the settlement. I'm not trying to be cruel, but we bought it together and it has to be split."

Margaret looked down at the linoleum. She planned to upgrade the floors to bamboo within two fiscal years—sooner if the fundraising proceeds exceeded expectations. On the desk in her office sat a binder that contained a timeline for these projects and more; plans that stretched beyond the next decade of the school's future. The notion that Eddie would dare to interfere with her vision for Garden of Happiness was absurd. Then again, it was typical of him to try and save face by making empty threats before accepting the inevitable. She had seen the same pattern of behavior when he shopped for cars. After exhausting all of his "negotiating tactics," he was a man who paid sticker price and then congratulated himself on screwing the dealer. She shook her head, frustrated with herself for getting drawn into his posturing. The truth was that Eddie would never make good on his threats about the school. He didn't have the grit.

She held out her hand, palm up, and stared at him.

"What's that?" He shifted in his canvas shoes. "What do you want?"

"Here's what you're going to do," she said. "You're going to conclude your little power play. You're going to give me my key. And you're going to leave."

"Am I?" He wrapped his fingers around the keychain and jammed his hand into the pocket of his loose cotton pants.

She withdrew her hand, making a mental note to call the locksmith the following morning. "You know, petulance is bad for your karma."

"Wow," he said. "How foolish of me to think you'd be civil about this, even for Leticia's sake."

"What's next, Eddie? Are you going to throw a tantrum? Stop wasting my time." She motioned toward the open kitchen door. "Run along."

"With pleasure. I'm sure you and the rabbit will be very happy together...as long as he stays in his basket." He walked out the door, leaving it open to the dark sand pit beyond.

Once he was gone, Margaret paced around the kitchen, stopping at the counter in front of the plate of cookies. "Now he can tell himself he stood up to me," she said to Ozone, "and that will be the last of that." She took the biggest cookie from the plate and bit off the top. "Ugh, these are stale," she said through her mouthful.

As she dumped the cookies into the wastebasket, she noticed the plate—a melamine piece Leticia had made with a mail-away kit when she was seven. Margaret could see her at the breakfast table, laboring over the round piece of vellum with her markers, the tip of her tongue poking from the corner of her mouth in concentration. "I'm all done, Mommy!" she'd said, and held up the paper circle. On it was a stick-figure family—Leticia, Margaret, Eddie, and a brown scribble of terrier named Rufus, all surrounded by pink hearts.

Margaret washed the plate, then yanked open a cabinet and slid it into the bottom of the stack where it would not ambush her again. "I've got to take these things home," she said to herself, referring to the family belongings that had found their way into Garden of Happiness over the years. They were scattered throughout the school—handmade picture frames, lumpy clay vases, and even some of the sturdier toddler toys. That was what you did when you started a school from scratch—you used what you had. Even the library was built around Leticia's original book collection. Margaret had always enjoyed reading to a circle of wriggling preschoolers, often beginning a book before realizing it was the very copy she had read at her daughter's bedside while holding her small, restless hand. Now that she and Eddie were divorcing, these sentimental discoveries were like unexploded land mines, waiting to be tripped and send Margaret reeling.

She told herself she didn't miss Eddie himself, but his presence, which had made the family feel calm and complete. If she were going to embrace this belief, she needed to be on guard against the sensory memories that lived on in seemingly innocuous locations—the scent that lingered in the leather of his desk chair, or the round tones of the wind chimes he had hung in the backyard sycamore tree. She resented the feeling that their family memories would always be off-limits and that she would never find true contentment in her home again.

She wasn't the only one who felt this way. Margaret had seen the relief in Leticia's face a month earlier when she left—practically fled—for college in Portland. What had been an intimate, mostly effortless mother-daughter relationship for eighteen years had unraveled as Leticia struggled to find a footing between her warring parents. Sullen and withdrawn, she kept any college jitters she may have had to herself. When Margaret saw the mound of new twin bed linens, pillows, and colorful milk-crate shelves one day on the floor of Leticia's room, she realized she had been excluded from her daughter's preparations to escape what she had heard her refer to as, "the effed-up reality show that has become my family."

And then Leticia was gone and Margaret's home of more than twenty years offered her no more comfort than a stranger in the supermarket. The first night Margaret was alone in the house, she took her pillow down the hall to the guest room, where she arranged and rearranged herself on top of the polyester bed spread, the streetlight shining in the window all wrong. Most nights, she wandered to the sofa with a book that remained unopened, or to the brick steps of the back patio where she would listen to the night sounds of the neighborhood before making another agitated attempt at sleep. As the weeks passed, her intimate belongings made their way to the guest room, but she had yet to slip her feet between the sheets. Peeling back the guest bed spread would complete her transition from wife and mother to solitary female, a guest in her own house. As tough as everyone seemed to think she was, this was too much for Margaret to bear.

Margaret set Ozone's basket on the deck by her feet, then pulled the kitchen door shut behind her. "Can you smell that with your rabbit nose, too? Another school year." She took a deeper breath and surveyed the shadowy play area across the sand to the decks. "At least when I'm *here* I feel like myself." She hoisted the basket under one arm and walked past the classrooms, checking the locks as she went.

Margaret's office was at the back of the school, built above one of the classrooms. Most parents started and finished Garden of Happiness without ever seeing its interior, and the new children seemed to absorb without instruction that the last thing they wanted was to be summoned up those wooden stairs for an audience with the school's ultimate authority. At any given time, Margaret might be sitting at her desk in front of her window, observing from above as the children swarmed the play structures and the parents flowed in and out of the yellow door. "There she is, looking down on us from preschool Valhalla," it was reported to Margaret that a parent had once grumbled after glimpsing Margaret's signature black shag through the window.

Margaret reached the top of the stairs and entered her office, shutting the door firmly behind her. It was a good-sized room; in the center was a large, denim sofa peppered with red throw cushions. In front of the sofa was a low table that held a Baccarat crystal apple and the most recent copy of the Garden of Happiness student yearbook. This edition was Margaret's all-time favorite and had been designed by a famous architect whose sons by his second wife were currently enrolled in the school. The book was exquisite, with a hinged white-birch cover into which the school's name and year had been laser engraved. *No other school has a book like this*, Margaret had thought when she was presented with her copy. Yes, it was expensive, but the parents had been more than happy to pay the hundred-dollar suggested donation for their keepsake copy. Certainly no one had complained to *her* about the price.

She lifted Ozone from the basket and settled him on a thick, chenille blanket on the sofa, then walked to the small refrigerator in the kitchenette, returning with a carrot stub. She poked it between the rabbit's front paws, then moved to her desk, which ran almost the entire length of the front wall. Set under the countertop was a bank of locked file cabinets that held the student-family records—detailed accounts of eleven years' worth of families that had passed through Garden of Happiness, including Margaret's personal observations on mothers who shirked volunteer duties, fathers who networked inappropriately in the sandbox, children who telegraphed the beginnings of what would become lifelong neuroses, and the measures Margaret had taken in response. Also handwritten inside the folder flaps in Margaret's precise chalkboard print were individual tallies of donations made by each family to the school.

"Let's see if there's any word from our girl," she said to Ozone. She sat in her desk chair and opened her email inbox, but did not find a message from Leticia. Just before she powered off the computer with a sigh, she noticed an email from Seth, her divorce lawyer. She clicked it open.

Margaret,

Please see forwarded message below from Eddie's lawyer. We'll talk about this.

Seth

Seth,

Regarding the Askew divorce, we need from your client an appraisal of the Garden of Happiness property in order to calculate a buyout market value.

Eddie has indicated to me that the preschool is the largest asset of the marital estate, given that the Askews used most of their community assets to buy the property eleven years ago. As we await the appraisal by a vendor of your choice, we will consult with real estate brokers for a second independent assessment of the value of the property.

We look forward to receiving your appraisal by the end of next week.

Regards,
Rachel

"No!" Margaret shouted, and shoved her desk with both hands, propelling her chair backward with a force that made Ozone freeze with fear. The chair collided with the coffee table, sending the crystal apple rolling and the yearbook sliding onto the floor with a *crack*.

She jumped up and walked to the back of the room where the windows faced the alley and, blocks away, the waves swept under the pier's neon-pulsing Ferris wheel. Unlatching the window, she pushed it upward and stood sucking in the ocean air, arms rigid at her sides. *I am not crying*, she thought. She watched a man wielding a trash picker make his way down the alley, fishing cans and bottles from the bins with the spindly rod. When she slammed the window, the rabbit flinched, his carrot falling to the floor with a *thump*.

"For heaven's sakes, Ozone," she said, replacing the stub between his paws on the way back to her desk. "Don't be such a drama queen."

She sat back in her chair and rolled to the desk, placing her fists on each side of the keyboard. "So, Mr. 'Good Vibrations' is on the offensive now." If there was one thing she hated, it was when people did not behave according to her predictions. But that didn't mean they couldn't be dealt with. "I've got news for you, Eddie," she said aloud after reading the message again. "You've taken enough from me. I won't allow you to take any more."

She powered off the computer and swiveled toward the coffee table. She returned the crystal apple to its place and retrieved the yearbook from the floor. It had landed on its edge, snapping the laser-cut cover in two.

3
Justine

Of all the roles Justine had imagined Harry occupying in her life, Garden Gnome was pretty far down the list - at least fifteen spots below podiatrist. As she flipped on her headlights and pulled away from the curb to drive home, she tried to get comfortable with the idea. "Harry is my Garden Gnome," she announced to the car. It sounded like the title of a song by some emo band wearing pretentious glasses and ironic knee socks. And there was nothing she could do about it. She had already cornered one of the teachers to ask if the assignments could be changed. The woman's expression as she shook her head had made clear that this was the kind of inquiry that could land a new parent on secret probation before school even started.

Her cellphone rang and Greg's private line glowed on the screen. She slipped in an earbud to answer it. "Hey, how's it going?" Greg despised legal fire drills, especially those that kept him at his desk all night. "Did you get your thing done?"

"Almost," he said. "The case keeps getting uglier. My schedule is going to be crazy for a while with this one."

"Don't forget to block out the night of our anniversary dinner—I had to make those reservations two months in advance."

"Got it. Nothing will interfere with the celebration of the Big Six."

"Are we calling it 'the Big Six?' That doesn't sound very big."

"Are you kidding? This is California—I should be leaving my second wife by now."

"*Nice*," she said with a laugh.

"Where are we going?"

"Giorgio's. Mom will sit with Emma."

"Perfect. I've been craving that ravioli with the truffle oil since the Big Five. Everything go all right tonight at the preschool fiesta?"

Justine glanced at the letter crumpled next to her in the passenger seat. "Um, yeah, I think so. Oh my gosh, there was this one couple you wouldn't believe—"

"Hang on a sec." The sound became muffled, but she could still hear his voice. "Make it half pepperoni. Don't worry, I won't let any of my meat products come in contact with your section." Laughter erupted in the background and Greg came back on the line. "Sorry. What were you saying?"

"That's okay. Are you almost finished there?"

"Kind of. We've got a couple hours to go. Keith and Simone are still here, too, so we're getting some food."

Justine's eyes narrowed. *Simone*. Disdainful vegetarian of the lustrous, waist-length hair and pneumatic bustline, whose default expression was that of a person who had just lost a hand of strip poker—intentionally. Justine's time at the law firm had overlapped Simone's by only six months, but in that short period she had gotten the clear impression that Simone relished her unofficial position as resident legal hottie, and when it came to her male colleagues, she was both an enthusiast and a collector. It was as if she had arrived at the firm with the same mindset as a lottery winner strolling into the Mall of America: there were tantalizing acquisitions behind every door and she had cash to burn.

"I didn't know Simone was on the team." Justine banged her palm on the steering wheel, blasting the horn at a driver trying to snake her turn at a four-way stop.

"She wasn't, but she had some time and volunteered to help us out. Turns out she's got experience with maritime law, which is where our team was weakest."

Justine lowered her voice. "I know you can't talk right now, but I'm sorry you got stuck with her after you told me how terrible her brief was on that other partner's case."

"Well, she's saving our bacon tonight."

Justine heard a female voice in the background.

"Correction," he said into the phone with a warm chuckle, "we only get Simone's specialized help if it's *tofu* bacon."

Justine tapped the steering wheel with her thumb. She knew Greg didn't ponder other people's agendas the way she did, but was he truly unaware when a woman was playing up to him, or did he make a conscious decision to sit back and enjoy the ego stroke?

"*Anyway*," she said, "orientation was quite the sociological odyssey. We were also assigned our very own Garden Gnomes."

"Excuse me?"

"Margaret matched us up with another family and we have to get together with them before school starts."

"And the encroachment on our free time begins. Don't you think Emma would be just as happy at a school that doesn't require week-end networking? It's *preschool*—not *med school*."

"We've already talked about all this. Besides, the tuition is paid and, judging from that contract, Margaret's favorite word is 'non-re-fundable.' I was only telling you about the family playdate because you'll never believe who I ran into tonight—"

"Just a second," Greg interrupted and the sound became muffled again. "Listen, we've hit a new snag in our argument and I need to deal with it. Sorry to cut you off, but the sooner I get back to it, the sooner I can leave, okay?"

"Sure." *It will keep*, she thought as she turned onto her street and drove up the block toward home.

"Baja Beverly Hills" was the term they had coined for their neighborhood. Their remodeled 1920s-era house was three doors outside the city limit, and marked by the transformation of the pavement from patched and pockmarked to smooth and seamless. "That's so Beverly Hills," Ruthie had commented on her first visit. "Even their streets have had work done."

She walked up the thirty brick steps to the front door and turned, as she always did before sliding her key into the lock, to see the view of Century City and beyond. She caught the delicate zest of the lemons hanging on the tree next to the door, still warm from an afternoon spent roasting in the early-autumn sun. Inside, her mother's enormous Vera Bradley tote bag sat on the step in the arched doorway between the foyer and living room.

"Oh, there you are." Her mother, Barbara, flipped off the bathroom light, wiped her nose with a tissue, then folded it and tucked it into the front pocket of her khakis. "A 'Lois' called. Something about a book club meeting. It's on your machine." Justine could tell she had just fluffed her curly, salt-and-pepper hair and applied a fresh layer of Clinique Watermelon, her signature lipstick.

She gave her mom a hug and picked up the familiar scent of roses on her white, cotton sweater—the fragrance of the sachets she had used in her closet for as long as Justine could remember. Growing up in a quiet pocket of South Pasadena, her mother's closet had been one of her favorite places to hide and play in the shady, bungalow-style home. When her parents divorced more than a decade prior, there had been no question that her mother would continue living there. Now, on every visit to her grandmother's, Emma, too, would find an opportunity to slip away to the "rose room."

"Thanks, Mom. Everything go all right with Emma?"

"Why shouldn't it have? I may not be some fancy Beverly Hills nanny, but I still remember a thing or two about taking care of a child. Did you have fun at your school get-together?"

"It was interesting." Justine winced at her choice of words. Her mother, always on the lookout for crime, marital strife, and biohazards, would no doubt replace a vague word like "interesting" with a more specific term. Like dysentery.

"What does *that* mean?" Barbara heaved her tote onto her shoulder.

"Nothing, I just met some new families and…what?" Her mom was standing almost toe-to-toe with her. "What's that look for?"

"What happened to you?"

"Nothing *happened* to me. It was school orientation."

Her mother retrieved her reading glasses from their chain, stuck them on the end of her nose, and leaned in closer.

"Mom, stop it," Justine said, pulling away. "You're creeping me out."

"Oh, come off it. Something obviously went down at that school tonight." She let the glasses drop back to her chest. "Why are you holding out on me?"

"Let's not get all *Cagney & Lacey*. I'm not holding out on you. I'm just tired."

Barbara studied her face for another moment. "You don't look right, but I guess you'll sing when you're ready." She nodded toward the front door. "Is Greg coming up behind you?"

"No, he got called back to the office—there was an emergency with one of his cases."

"He missed Emma's orientation?" Her mother's eyes widened. "You sure you don't have anything to tell me?"

"He wasn't happy about it, Mom." Justine tried not to let on that he hadn't sounded unhappy about it at all.

Her mom crossed her arms. "I've got all night, kid."

"Geez. Okay, thank you for sitting." Justine gave her a hug and opened the door.

Half an hour later, after changing into her nightgown, brushing her teeth, and scrubbing the day's makeup from her face, she moved through the house, tilting the white plantation shutters to let in the night air. She padded down the short, coved hallway, her shearling slippers almost silent on the wood floors, and slipped into her daughter's bedroom. Leaning over the side of the crib, she stroked Emma's auburn wisps and tucked Scooter the plush turtle under the covers. Emma made a rhythmic motion with her mouth as if she were nursing, a habit that always triggered in Justine's memory the physical sensation of those tender newborn months. She laid the back of her hand against Emma's warm, pale cheek before sinking into the rocking chair.

As the parade of pastel fish swam by on the nightlight, she settled into the cushions. She needed to talk to Ruthie. No one could understand the impact that Harry's surprise reappearance had on Justine better than her best friend.

Good old Ruthie. Justine didn't know what she would have done without her after Harry left for Chicago. It was Ruthie who had been waiting on the front steps of her apartment building when she returned from saying good-bye to him. Ruthie, who listened to hours of weepy reminiscences and still managed not to refer to Harry as "dungbastard" and "Mr. Head Game"—at least for the first day. And Ruthie, who brought a shopping bag full of DVDs and knew just when to segue from *Blazing Saddles* to *Pretty in Pink*. She had been skeptical of Justine's involvement with Harry from the start, reacting to Justine's repeated swooning with a level of enthusiasm usually reserved for the guy with the limp ponytail who was always trying to squirt a lotion sample into her hand at the mall. It still puzzled Justine how her friend's vision had been so much clearer than her own. She knew Ruthie would go straight into *Mad Max* mode when she heard that Harry was back in Justine's world. After years of dormancy, "dungbastard" was no doubt on the verge of resurrection.

She closed her eyes, let her head fall back against the rocker cushion, and tried to do a Buddhist relaxation exercise she'd read about in a magazine at the car wash. Maybe it wasn't Buddhist, though, but Raja...or Tantric? Then again, she always associated the word "tantric" with marathon Sting sex, which she figured was the opposite of relaxing—at least for the first five hours or so.

Fucking Harry.

When Justine spotted him for the first time that night on her friend Soraya's graduation cruise, she had immediately pegged him for a non-starter. *No way*, she'd thought. Too pretty. Too cocky. She was the girlfriender of the wry diamond-in-the-rough, not the unabashed frat boy. But as the party boat crisscrossed the bay, she found herself pressed against him, refusing to yield her spot as everyone jammed close to the rail to admire the lights of the Golden Gate Bridge against the backdrop of black sky.

Two hours later, they had covered everything from her fascination with Alcatraz to his fear of Barbra Streisand. At the end of another hour, they had traded confessions (she was wearing a second-hand party dress, and he was a compulsive flosser) and had moved on to trading sips of a suspicious, bright-green cocktail they agreed smelled like a dog's ear infection. He was nothing like she expected and, as she watched him talk, she silenced the warning voice in her head and chided herself for having stereotyped him at first glance. By the time the boat returned to dock, she was willing to overlook the shamanesque man-necklace that hung down his chest on a narrow, leather cord, chalking it up to some kind of misplaced Sundance catalog irony. One-night stands were not her style, but when she stepped onto the wooden planking and felt his hand steadying her at the small of her back, she knew she would be making an exception.

She also knew—but tried to ignore—that she already wanted it to be more than that.

The next morning, she woke alone in the bed, hating the feeling before she opened her eyes. What time had he slunk out, shoes dangling from the crooks of his fingers? She rolled over and told herself to shake it off. She had known what she was getting into, after all, and now she had to get through the morning after. The empty Saturday loomed ahead and already her mind was replaying scenes from the night before. She was wishing she had some kind of distraction when she became aware of an aroma. Was something on fire? No, it was...breakfasty. When Harry appeared in the doorway in his T-shirt and boxers, she had to pull the covers up to her nose to hide her grin.

"I made English muffins, but the only thing you have to go on them is mustard and whipped cream." He smiled and pushed his hair around on his head.

"Good luck getting anything out of that whipped cream can," she said.

"Hey, you're probably busy today, but let's do something."

"Yeah? Like what?"

"We will confabulate over a real breakfast. I know a joint down Telegraph Avenue."

"I have to warn you—restaurant breakfast brings out my inner lumberjack."

He smiled and motioned with his head toward the bathroom. "Is it all right if I take a quick shower?"

"Sure. There's a clean towel there on the shelf."

"Excellent." He crossed the room and, as he peeled off his T-shirt, she watched his shoulder blades glide up and down, having apparently been designed specifically for that function by a team of German engineers. He disappeared through the doorway and she felt herself tumble down a lovely rabbit hole—one that was much too deep for her warning voice to penetrate.

"Hey. Are you awake?" Justine felt a hand on her shoulder and opened her eyes, squinting against the harsh hallway light that threw Greg into silhouette. She lifted her head off the rocker's cushion and cleared her throat.

"Wha—what?"

"Sorry. Did you pick up the dry cleaning today?" He was still in his suit pants and dress shirt. "I have to go to court in the morning. I need a white shirt."

"Sshh, don't wake Emma," she whispered, getting up from the rocker and shooing Greg out of the room. "I hung your shirts in your closet." She shut the door behind her. "Did you get everything done tonight?"

"Yeah, but I'm beat."

Hands in his pockets, Greg shifted from foot to foot. Justine noticed he didn't have the round-shouldered droop he usually displayed after a marathon workday. "Actually, you seem pretty perky."

"Hardly," he said with a snort. "You coming to bed?"

"In a minute. What's that?" She pointed at his shirt pocket.

"Oh, yeah." He pulled out a piece of orange paper and handed it to her. "It's a coupon. For dry cleaning."

"Um, oh-*kay*." She turned it over in her hands. "Thanks."

"Don't thank me. It's from Simone. She said she saw it and thought of you."

4
Ruben

Ruben's Rush T-shirt clung to his chest with sweat, but not because he was struggling to dislodge the double stroller from the elevator doors. No, the sweat had appeared in a sudden, clammy sheen ten minutes earlier when he realized his notebook was missing. Now he needed to get back to the condo and find it before his wife, Deandra, got home from work.

No matter how he pulled and tugged at the stroller, its rubber wheels only wedged themselves tighter between the metal doors. "Strong I am in the Force, but not that strong," he grunted, acknowledging to himself that the emergence of his Yoda voice usually signaled that a situation was about to deteriorate further. He adjusted his grip and, with a final heave, sprung the stroller into the hallway.

"There's your problem." Mr. Benveniste, resident of unit 4C and known condo crank, dropped a sack of garbage down the trash chute before slamming it shut. "Those kids are too old to be in a stroller. What are they, eight?" He didn't bother to wait for Ruben's reply, but walked back into his unit, banging the door closed behind him.

"No, they're *three*," Ruben said in the direction of the door. He checked under the stroller's bonnet to make sure the twins were still asleep. "When they say 'it takes a village,' I guess they're talking about a village full of Bengay-scented curmudgeons," he mumbled.

The twins were nestled together, their black hair spiked with perspiration. Harris' hands sat palm-up on his knees, while Lily clutched a long magnolia leaf in her fist like a fan. *Thank God*, Ruben thought, and started down the hallway at a rapid clip. It would be easier to look for his notebook if they were napping.

He'd discovered the blue spiral was missing when he went to write down the new bit he had just thought of for his standup act. But now the idea was slipping away from him. He arrived at his door and stopped, trying to remember the joke. "Guerrilla, urban guerrilla, guerrilla mom." He mashed his palms against the early sprinklings of gray hairs at his temples, but came up with nothing.

Forgetting a joke, however, was the least of his problems.

He dropped to his knees and began rooting through the stroller's basket for the third time. "When your wife goes back to a job she hates so you can stay home and write a sitcom script," he said through clenched teeth, "it's probably best not to lose your official script-writing notebook." He pawed through the remaining drifts of crushed Cheerios and Starbucks napkins before giving up.

"Crap." He stood and checked his watch, fighting the panic that was prickling in his stomach. "Please let it be in the condo."

Slipping his key into the lock, Ruben opened the door and eased the stroller onto the foyer's tan marble floor. He palmed his keys into the hammered, silver bowl on the side table—a wedding gift from Deandra's Thai grandparents—and thumbed through the stack of magazines and catalogs next to it. No sign of the notebook.

As he turned the corner into the living room, he picked up the scent of his wife's perfume—a blossom-heavy Kors fragrance that never failed to remind him of their Mexican honeymoon—a split-second before he saw her standing barefoot on the fuzzy area rug.

It wasn't only Deandra's presence in the condo that startled him, it was the expression on her face. Eyes pinched, mouth pursed, nostrils flared—the effect was formidable, erasing every trace of her usual feminine softness. Any hope that this look was directed at her loathsome boss or one of her coworkers, whose names he could never keep straight, evaporated when he saw his notebook. Splattered against the cushion with one page partially torn out, it appeared to have been shot into the sofa with a cannon.

Ruben's mouth went dry. He took a step toward his wife.

Deandra pointed toward the splayed notebook, her chin wobbling as she spoke. "There's *nothing in there.*"

Ruben held his palms toward her. "Okay, hold on."

"And that kind of freaked me out at first, right? Because that would mean you hadn't written anything since I started back at HealthShield. Nothing in two whole months." She took a deep, halting breath. "But then I realized how silly that was—the idea that you could be home all that time and make *no* progress on your script. Right? *Silly.*" She licked her lips and Ruben stood, mesmerized. He had never seen her like this before. "I mean, obviously you do your writing in a *different* notebook. Or on the laptop?" She pointed at the sofa again. "And that notebook is just for *fun?*" She smiled with such insincere force that Ruben thought she might crack a tooth.

The adolescent boy in him wanted to lie his face off and tell the scary lady that—yes!—there was another notebook containing a killer sitcom script and he was days away from handing it off to his friend Vince at the network, who would then "put it in the right hands." The grown man in Ruben, however, looked at the woman he loved, the one who had been his ally from the moment he made her laugh that night at The Comedy Store, and knew that he had to tell her the truth.

Eventually.

"Here's the thing," he said, "but first I have to tell you how great that outfit is on you. Is it new?"

"A joke, Ruben? Now?"

"Sorry. Listen, it's not what it looks like."

She stared at him.

"Okay, it *is* what it looks like, but not for the reasons you might think."

"Oh, good," Deandra said, crossing her arms and swinging her black, silk curtain of hair behind her. Ruben watched it flow past her shoulder and noted that, even in the midst of a crisis, this motion elicited its usual, evolutionary response in him. "I am excited to hear what will no doubt be a compelling explanation."

Ruben sighed. "You just need to know that, no matter how bad this looks, I've tried everything, okay? I've worked in every crevice of this condo, including the hall closet. I've tried writing at the coffee shop and sitting in the car." He moved around the room as he spoke. "I don't know if you've heard me out here, but I've been watching Vince's show in the middle of the night, studying the episodes I recorded and trying to figure out what my problem is."

This is all Vince's fault, he thought. *Telling me my stuff is "subtle and writerly."* He cringed at the memory of how eagerly he had latched onto Vince's praise.

"Go on," Deandra said.

"Well, that's what I've been doing." Ruben tugged at his shaggy hair. "And then things started to get a little weird."

"'Weird?' What do you mean 'weird'?"

"First I started stretching before I sat down to work, which hurt like a mother, by the way." He cleared his throat. "Then I became dependent on designer water—you know, the kind that's supposed to make you more creative." He hesitated, unsure how much he should divulge. "I even...meditated."

Deandra raised an eyebrow. Ruben saw her jaw muscle flex.

"The thing is, I've been working every single day and I don't know what the hell is going on, but I think I've lost it. I've lost my funny.

I'm like a golfer with the shanks. It's the only superpower I've ever had and it's just...gone." He stopped pacing and faced his wife. "But you have to know, Dee, I've been giving it my best shot."

For a moment, Deandra didn't move. Then her shoulders drooped. "For two months, I've been sitting on the freeway twice a day and dealing with that shrew at the office who's out to get rid of me. That's her goal, did you know that?" She looked past him to the window, where the vertical blinds sliced the afternoon sun into tall, slender pieces. "It might as well be printed on my business cards: Temporary Minion. But that was the deal we made. You would quit the escrow company, I would go back to work until you wrote your script and got your TV job." She stopped talking for a few moments, her eyes still on the window. "Today was the worst. She blew up at me about the *font* on a *memo*. Stood me up in front of the whole office and lectured me on *attention to detail*. I had to get out of there. I only looked in your notebook to get some idea of how much longer it would be until the script was finished." She blew her nose with a violent *honk* and looked back at him. "And when I found nothing in there but a few scribbles, I kind of flipped out."

Ruben opened his mouth to explain further, but she stopped him with a wave of her hand.

"I just feel like an idiot, you know? All this time while I was thinking things were going great, you were guzzling smartwater and praying for the planets to align." She dug her toes into the carpet. When she looked up again, her face had softened. "I had no idea you were struggling like this. Why didn't you say something?"

"I thought I could work through it on my own. Without worrying you."

God, he would have loved to talk with her. The truth always seemed more manageable when it sat between the two of them under Deandra's calculating gaze. For reasons Ruben had never understood, this woman believed in him. He found her unwavering support—something he had never in his life experienced—exhilarating, and he was determined never to give her a reason to withdraw it. Of course, some days were more challenging in this regard than others.

"And you couldn't talk to your comedy buddies about it?" she said. "Try to get some advice?"

"Yeah, right. Whine to the guys in the clubs about how I'm afraid I've lost my funny? Why don't I tell them I'm impotent, too?"

"I'm just trying to understand this, all right?" She stepped over her work pumps on the floor by the coffee table and walked to the foyer to check on the twins still sleeping in the stroller. Satisfied, she went into the kitchen and continued talking across the breakfast bar. "And you never considered getting a book on sitcom writing?" She filled a tall, green glass with tap water. "Or taking one of those classes?"

"One of what classes? The ones in the catalog where they teach secrets to instant wealth and train retirees on how to use 'The Facebook?' If it were that simple, I wouldn't have gotten vibed out in the first place."

Ruben was encouraged, however, that Deandra seemed to be shifting her approach from ass-kicking to assisting. Secretly, he harbored the belief that there was a fundamental distinction between him and his wife, that he was a "creative" person and therefore at the mercy of the mysterious ebb and flow of inspiration, while Deandra was a "regular" person—naturally equipped to handle the regimen of the workaday world. Could it be that she sensed this distinction as well? That she was beginning to appreciate how difficult it had been for *him* these past months? He felt a tentative tingle of relief.

"I'm sorry, but I don't know what 'vibed out' means. I don't have the luxury of using metaphysical excuses at my office job." She took a sip of water and watched him over the top of the glass.

"All I'm saying is that I haven't been sitting around doing nothing. I know we're both banking on this opportunity and I've been trying. Every frickin' day."

Deandra took another swallow of water, then lowered the glass, her eyes still on him. "There is no *try*, Ruben. There is only do."

Ruben's mouth fell open. "You did *not* just Yoda me."

"Oh, I believe I did." She brushed past him and walked back into the living room.

Ruben followed her. "Jedi mind shit? *Really?*"

Deandra plunked her glass onto a coaster. "I have no doubt that you can do this. I've *never* doubted it. It sounds to me like all you need is a little help with your methodology."

"I'm blocked, Dee. I think all writers go through this at some point."

Deandra tilted her head to the side and studied him, working her jaw back and forth. Ruben had the uneasy feeling that she was picturing him as a troublesome, stopped-up toilet and considering her plumbing options.

"Well, sweetie," she said finally, "we're just going to have to unblock you."

5
Margaret

Margaret stepped out of the storage closet, coughing and waving a hand in front of her face. After an exhausting night spent festering about Eddie and the email from his lawyer, she had been at school since six thirty that morning, attacking any chore that might keep her distracted. She had just finished reorganizing the Garden of Happiness hats, T-shirts, and water bottles available for purchase by school families—a task she regretted as soon as she opened the closet door. The room reeked of ammonia, courtesy of the cleaning crew, and a parent volunteer—apparently under the influence of a bottomless triple espresso—had done some feverish, decorative painting in the tiny space. The result was such a stifling spectacle of lush blossoms, robust vegetables, and leering butterflies that Margaret had hesitated to enter without a machete.

She sat on the loveseat in the library corner, took a drink from her water bottle, and pulled out her phone. It was almost nine o'clock—dawn for a college freshman—but she was craving the sound of her daughter's voice.

"Seriously?" Leticia said when she answered.

"Tish?"

"First Dad and now you? This was my one morning to sleep in." Margaret heard her turn on music in the background.

"Your father called you this morning?"

"Yes, and it was awesome waking up to the news that you two are fighting again."

Margaret stood and began pacing around the world peace rug. "He called to tell you that?"

Leticia yawned. "I don't know. Something about you 'confounding his authentic attempts at civility with your usual crushing hostility.' Whatever. *Fighting.*" Margaret pictured her tucking the phone under her chin while she gathered her brown curls into one of the elastics she kept on her wrist.

"Did he happen to tell you what our discussion was about? That he had the audacity to—"

"Ew! No, Mom—I don't even want to know, okay?"

Margaret was quiet for a moment. "It was wrong of your father to upset you with this. Please don't worry about what he said."

"How can I not worry about it? Wait, hang on." Margaret heard voices followed by the *slam* of a door. "Anyway, you guys promised not to be psycho about the divorce, remember?"

"Leticia, no one is being 'psycho,' and we don't need to talk about this. I was only calling to see how you're doing."

"I'm okay, I guess. It rains all the time here," she huffed into the phone. "Sucks."

"So you'll get plenty of use from that rain poncho. And it should fit over your backpack."

"Oh my God, Mom—no one wears rain ponchos." She snorted.

"Oh. Well, do your best to stay dry." Margaret sighed and rubbed at the toe of her loafer with a cleaning cloth. Rather than the warm chat she had hoped for, this call was providing all the emotional solace of a tax audit. "Is your roommate there? How are things on that front?" Leticia had been paired with a dour, hyper-competitive young woman from Baltimore who so far had resisted her various attempts to bond over frozen yogurt. Margaret had met her when she and Eddie—under temporary, excruciating détente—had dropped Leticia off at Reed College. Margaret sized up the young woman immediately and considered telling Leticia how to manage her, but sensed this would only annoy her daughter and said nothing.

"No, she's not here." She paused. "Did you actually throw food at Dad?"

"Oh, for heaven's sake—it was one cookie!"

"A Mint Milano, right?"

"How did you know?"

"You always have those at your school."

Margaret smiled. There was no question in *Leticia's* mind whose school it was.

"Look, Mom, I have to go."

"Oh. Of course."

"So try to be cool about the divorce stuff, okay? I'm already fried here and when you add on the fighting, it's too much."

"Just out of curiosity, did you say the same thing to your father?"

"Mom! I'm trying to stay neutral, but you're making it really difficult."

"All right, all right. I'll do my best. You don't need to worry about us."

"Bye, Mom."

"Love you, sweetheart," Margaret said hurriedly.

"Okay, you, too." Leticia hung up.

Margaret turned and saw Trey, the school secretary, standing in the doorway holding a stainless steel commuter mug and a vinyl Trader Joe's bag covered with tropical flowers. She eyed the bag with distaste. Following a teacher uprising two years prior during which he was accused of eating a rotten pigeon (he claimed it was pickled quail), Trey had been required to confine his lunch sack to a corner of the community refrigerator's lowest shelf in a five-inch square that head teacher Miss Glenda had personally marked off with a Sharpie. "What was that all about?"

Margaret frowned and dropped the phone into her sweater pocket. "You're not supposed to be here today, Trey."

"And yet...I arrive." He popped a pose, toe pointed and nose in the air. "Now, back to my question."

"You realize school doesn't start until next week?" She walked over to the low-slung crafts table and dragged it away from the wall with a loud scrape.

"You should get someone manly to do that." Trey took a noisy slurp from his silver mug. "Like Miss Glenda."

Satisfied with the table's new position, Margaret walked past Trey toward the kitchen.

"Jesus in jackboots," Trey said, getting a good look at her face for the first time, "what happened to you? You look even worse than usual." He reached toward her. "Is that *cover-up?*"

"Stop it, *stop it.*" Margaret swatted his hand away. She knew the makeup had been a mistake—she had no feel for its application—but was determined to erase any residue of the sleepless night Eddie had caused.

"Tell Trey all about it." He followed her into the kitchen. "You know you want to."

Trey had been thirty-four when she hired him shortly after opening the school. He had not appeared to age in the last decade, nor had he updated his oversize wire glasses or revised his uniform of khakis and pastel dress shirts, the effect of which was that he perpetually resembled someone in the background of a grainy bank surveillance tape.

"It's still not clear to me why you're here." She removed a large calendar from its shrink-wrap and hung it on a nail above the counter. Trey watched her, mouth open.

"*You* don't put up the new calendars. *Miss Glenda* puts up the new calendars." He gestured up and down at her. "And you're not wearing a stitch of plaid."

Margaret ripped open the second calendar and hung it on a nail next to the first. This, she knew, was what Trey's "support" felt like, and it was the last thing she needed at the moment. He would continue to stare at her with one eyebrow cocked, unconcerned with generally accepted rules of conduct between employees and employers, until she caved. This was one in an array of infuriating qualities that, while frustrating Margaret on an almost hourly basis, also made him indispensable as the school secretary. No one—not even Margaret—defanged an imperious Westside mom with the ruthless efficiency of a gay man who lacked a social censor.

"I don't feel like talking right now, Trey." She crunched the wrappers into a ball and jammed them into the wastebasket.

"Oh, I know," he said. "You're the strong silent type."

Margaret scooped up a pile of printer paper, pens, and pencils from the counter and walked out of the kitchen toward Trey's office in the front room. "Let me guess," he said, still in pursuit. "Your drunk-kabuki makeup is brought to us by your wasband?"

"My what?"

"The man who *was* your husband. Your *was*band."

They passed into Trey's office and Margaret set down the stack of supplies, then leaned forward and placed her palms on the desk. "Eddie and I are having a difference of opinion on a financial matter pertaining to the divorce," she said, her eyes on the blotter.

"Poor Leticia. No doubt she's being torn in two by mommy and daddy dearest." He whisked a trail of muffin crumbs from the corner of the desk. "It's not enough she's forced to live in the same room with that angry young woman with the Danny Partridge haircut."

Margaret stood up straight. "How do you know about her roommate?"

"Excuse me, but mini-Margaret is a mad texter."

"Leticia *texts* you? I didn't know you two kept in such close touch."

"According to Leticia, I'm the hairy aunt she never had."

"Congratulations on that dubious distinction." Margaret tore open a box of pencils as Trey settled into a chair with his chin in his hands.

"Do I get to hear the nitty-gritty of this 'financial matter?'" he said.

"You do not."

"Fine. I've already invented details that are no doubt more interesting than your dreary, real-life dispute. So what's our next step?"

Margaret threw the empty box into the recycling bin with a *clang*. "I'm going to have to talk with Eddie, obviously, and make him see that he's in the wrong."

Trey looked startled. "What, *in person?*"

"Yes," she ripped open another box. "I believe that's a typical format for these sorts of discussions."

"Allow me to suggest a radical course of action that I know will never occur to you on your own. Have you considered being nice? Furthermore, have you considered doing so via email?"

Margaret scowled. "After everything he's put me through—is *still* putting me through—why would I possibly be nice to that man?"

"I'm just saying—Eddie's not one of your school parents. You might actually have to be pleasant to get what you want."

"I take exception to that," Margaret said. "I am very pleasant with—"

"*Please.*" Trey held up his hand. "I work here, remember? Under no circumstances should you rely on your alleged people skills. No, what this situation calls for is a charming little message in which you tell him that you look forward to working together to reach an amicable resolution. You know, sweet talk the man a little. Yes, he put your heart through the Cuisinart. *However*, for your purposes, the shrewd move is to show a smidge of that vulnerability we both know you'd rather get a poodle perm than own up to. Give him the impression that when he goes to his car, he won't find you crouched in the backseat waiting to filet him with a Garden Weasel."

"That's preposterous. I don't come across that way."

"Once again," he said, pointing at his own face, "not new here. Now, trust me," he stood, took the box from her hands and motioned for her to sit at the desk, "email was *invented* for you. Use my computer and I will go work on the first-day packets in the other room." He stepped out and began to slide the door shut, leaving only his face in view. "And think about this: in your case, being nice also gives you the element of surprise." He raised his eyebrows and made an *O* with his mouth, then slid the door closed with a *thud*.

She opened her email account and stared at the screen. Usually, she ignored Trey's suggestions. After her conversation with Leticia, though, it was clear that Eddie was portraying himself as the reasonable party in the divorce, leaving Margaret to look like the uncooperative shrew in her daughter's eyes. *Two can play the image-management game*, she thought. Margaret knew she would fight Eddie to the end to block his claim to her school, but why not start out by racking up some diplomacy points of her own for her next chat with Leticia? She picked up a pen and tapped it on the desk. The question was, after everything that had happened, could she compose a "nice" email to Eddie?

She had been a senior in college when the rangy man in Levi's cords slid into the seat next to her just as the art history lecture began. She had seen Eddie around, had even had a class with him the year before, but they had never spoken. He was the one with that smile. All those teeth. "How easy life must be with a smile like that," she'd surprised herself by saying.

"Don't you have one just like it?" he asked, turning sideways to get a look at her. No, she explained, her smile did not have the same effect as his. Her smile looked angry and unhappy. Her parents had told her so all her life. "Well, you're in luck," he said, "I can help you with that."

It was Margaret's turn to face him. "Oh, really? And how will you help me? By making me happy?" Her heart thumped wildly in her chest as she surprised herself by forming a wish out loud.

"I was saying I can help you with your smile because I'm going to be a dentist." He moved toward her and spoke against her ear as the professor quieted the room. "On the other hand, dental school sounds like a lot of work. So maybe I *will* just make you happy." As the weeks passed, the universe had begun to shift over and make a place for Margaret where, before, there had been none.

Slowly, she set the pen on the desk and began to type.

Dear Eddie,

I regret losing my temper last night when you visited me at school. I understand that we have several significant issues to settle pertaining to our divorce and I admire your efforts to do so with professionalism and poise. Having slept on our exchange, I hope you will accept my apology and consider working out a revised arrangement with respect to Garden of Happiness. I would certainly be open to altering the allocation of our other assets in an effort to at least partially compensate you for the value of the school. Given an opportunity to talk further about it, I am confident that we can reach an amicable compromise. Perhaps we could meet for dinner at Chez Fong in Malibu one night this week? I still have faith in our lucky restaurant and I hope you do, too.

:-)

M.

Margaret sat back in the chair and dropped her hands in her lap. She was going to throttle Trey. Writing that message had resurrected memories she thought she had purged months—if not years—ago. The scent at the nape of Eddie's neck. The contrast of the soft, brown hair at his wrist and the metal of his watch. The exquisite care in handling that, once reserved for her, was last seen in his attention to his favorite surfboard. These reminiscences didn't fit Eddie today any more than his old powder-blue cords would, but here they were, tormenting her again.

"Let's get this over with," she muttered. She typed in the email address Eddie had created for her personal use years ago and which they still used when communication was unavoidable. She clicked SEND. It took only seconds for an automated reply to appear, informing her that soulsurferdentist@yahoo.com no longer existed. She gasped and slumped into the chair. She stared at the error message, reading it again and again, digesting the fact that he had severed their one remaining means of regular communication.

"Now, I'm no body-language expert," Trey said as Margaret stormed past his work table, "but my intuition is telling me that your message did not achieve its desired result."

"No, Trey. It didn't," she said without looking at him. "Thank you for your misguided advice, but I won't make the mistake of going soft again."

"What are you going to do now?"

"Call my lawyer."

Trey checked the time on his phone. "Hmm, twelve minutes of forced niceness," he called after her as he went back to collating papers. "If it helps you feel any better, I didn't think you'd make it to ten."

6
Ruben

Ruben felt a blade of morning sunlight across his face. He shifted his head on the armrest in another unsuccessful attempt to get comfortable. It was not the first time he'd fallen asleep studying Vince's show, and definitely not the first time he'd woken up wishing he and Deandra had sprung for the premium, fake ultrasuede when they ordered the sofa. Anything would have been better than the stain-resistant, flame-retardant, child-deterrent fabric they had chosen. He felt like he'd spent the night on a cheese grater.

He opened his eyes and saw Deandra dressed for work and standing over him, car keys in hand and purse over her shoulder. "Good morning." His voice was an early-morning croak.

"I tried to get you back into bed around one o'clock this morning, but you were sleeping too deeply, so I just covered you with the blanket."

"Aw, thanks," he said, sitting up and rubbing one of his eyes with the heel of his hand.

"We need to finish our discussion from last night," she said. "I realized this morning that Papa has the perfect expression for this situation."

Oh, dear God, Ruben thought as his father-in-law's face appeared in his mind, long and dour like a paper lantern left out in the rain. Ruben felt certain that Papa's "expressions" were researched and selected with the specific intent of crushing all joy in Ruben's life. "And which expression would that be?"

"Idle hands are the devil's workshop."

"You think I've been idle? That's not a fair assumption just because I don't have a finished script. What about the kids? They don't exactly feed and entertain themselves." Ruben shook his head. "Wow, I feel like a housewife trying to justify what she does all day while the husband is at the office."

"I don't look at it that way, Ruben. We're *partners*, and we're working toward the same goals. Listen, I was up early thinking about this. We need to make some changes."

In Ruben's experience, nothing good ever followed those words. He tugged the blanket up to the hem of his T-shirt. "Okay, hit me."

Deandra pursed her lips before continuing. "If you want something done, give it to someone who's busy."

"Um...*what*?" It sounded like she was quoting more of—

"Papa's expression," she said. "I thought of two more that apply." Her keys jangled as she shifted them to her other hand.

"Awesome." Ruben frowned.

"I understand how your mind works, you know." She reached down and pushed his hair off his forehead. "You think what you do is different from what everyone else does. Like the other people in the escrow office—they talk on the phone and file papers and that's all they'll ever do. You feel sorry for them because they don't know the magic of creating something funny out of nothing, the way you do."

"Well, I wouldn't put it that way," Ruben said, shifting on the sofa.

"And it *is* magic, isn't it, this mysterious ability of yours? That's why you spend so much of your day trying to create the perfect environment to write." Ruben looked away. "And when conditions *aren't* perfect, you figure the muse isn't speaking to you, so you give up and do something else." She watched his face. "Is that close to the truth?"

"You're making fun of me, but you don't understand how hard it is." He stood, adjusted his plaid boxers, and tossed the blanket onto the sofa in a wad.

"I would never make fun of your talent. I'm just trying to help you see that your work is no different than anyone else's—and that's a good thing."

"You're saying that writing a saleable script for a primetime sitcom is as easy as filing a stack of papers?"

Deandra set her purse and keys on the coffee table. "I'm saying that I believe it would help to demystify the process and just get to *work*. Like the rest of us, Ruben. Regular old work, done by regular old mortals."

"Oh, come on," he said with a snort. "It's a little more complicated than that."

"No, I think it's actually quite simple, and I think that's why you're blocked. You're making this project into some kind of quest, when really you should be looking at it as a stack of filing. Sit down, file the papers, move on." Deandra brushed her hands together and smiled at him. "Done."

"This is silly." Ruben walked to the window and looked out between the slats. "I'm not like you, Dee. I don't turn everything into bullet points on a to-do list."

Deandra bristled, but let the comment slide. "Well, it's never too late to start. And I'm going to help by putting lots of items on that to-do list for you."

He turned around. "What are you talking about?"

"Work expands to fill the time allotted," she said. Ruben grimaced at the arrival of expression number two. "If you have more than one project to do, the writing will shrink down to a manageable size and not seem so overwhelming." She walked toward the kitchen and Ruben followed her. "That's how Papa did it when he came here: learn English, find a job, finish school—all at once. He would never have gotten around to starting his company if he'd let himself do those things one at a time."

"So let me get this straight," Ruben said, "you're proposing that I load my schedule with other projects, which will somehow make it easier for me to do the one project I care about?"

"Exactly. Like last year when I chaired a committee at Garden of Happiness and served on the condo board and also took that desktop publishing class. If I'd only been doing one of those things, I wouldn't have accomplished nearly as much." Deandra flipped through a stack of papers next to the phone. "The timing is perfect, too, because school is about to start."

An alarm bell went off in Ruben's head. "What's perfect about that timing?"

"They're looking for parents for this year's committees."

"*Whoa.* Join a *preschool committee*? With those flesh-eating moms you complained about all last year? You're joking, right?" She stopped shuffling papers and looked up at him. Ruben silently conceded that she could not have looked more serious if she were holding a hatchet. "Okay, but a *mommy* committee? There's got to be something else I can do that's more, you know..."

"Masculine?"

"Yes! Masculine."

"No. You are already behind schedule and finding something else will take time that we don't have. Garden of Happiness is the obvious choice—the jobs are all laid out for the taking. Plus, now that I'm back at work, you're the designated butt-kisser at school."

Ruben winced at the thought of having to manufacture small talk with Margaret. "I think this is a bad idea. Margaret hates me."

"Margaret hates everyone." She pulled a sheet of yellow paper from the bottom of the stack and held it out to Ruben. "Welcome to the team."

He did not reach for the paper. "What's that?"

"The list of committees." She prodded him in the chest until he took it. "Take your pick."

She walked back into the living room and scooped her keys off the coffee table. Ruben followed as he skimmed the list. "Come *on*, man, every one of these committees has some kind of flower in the name. Oh, wait," he said dryly, "here's one with 'butterfly.' I stand corrected."

Just then Harris and Lily bolted from their room in their pajamas, bare feet slapping the marble as they ran. "Mommy! Mommy!" they called, slamming into Deandra's legs and wrapping their arms around her. "Are you staying home?" Lily said. "Stay, stay, stay," Harris chanted and squeezed her tighter, then stood on one foot and wrapped a leg around her as well.

"My little clementines, Mommy has to go to work, but I'll be home later, okay?" The twins wailed in protest and clung to Deandra like environmentalists to an endangered redwood. "Nooo!" they chimed. "No work today!" Ruben saw a cloud pass across Deandra's face as she began to disengage from her children while inching toward the foyer. Harris began to cry and, by the puffing of Lily's lips, Ruben could tell she was right behind him.

She needs your help, he thought as Deandra reluctantly made her way to the door with two wailing preschoolers in tow. *And look at you, standing here in your underwear, whining while your wife spends her days away from her children for the sake of your "dream." She deserves better and if you're not careful, she's going to figure that out.*

Ruben began coaxing his children off of his wife's legs. "Hey, Barbie and Ken, who wants French toast? Remember how we cracked the eggs last time? If you go wash your hands and get the stools, I'll let you throw some eggs right in the sink—yeah, baby!"

Deandra raised her eyebrows as the children loosened their grip. "Genius," she said to Ruben.

"That's my name, don't wear it out." Good-byes were exchanged all around and the children raced off toward the kitchen. Deandra left for work and Ruben stood in the foyer, suddenly alone.

"And now, if you'll excuse me," he said to the closed door, "I have to go man up and join a flower committee."

7
Justine

Justine and Greg had always loved their little hillside house—except when they were arguing. There was something about the separateness of the spaces and the way sound seemed to get lost in the peaked skylight that made it impossible to stomp out of a room and toss that last parting shot over the shoulder or launch a snarky retort from kitchen to family room without the other person shouting for the comment to be repeated, making the whole process tedious and unsatisfying. So far, none of their arguments had landed them in marriage counseling, but they *had* looked into hiring an architect.

"Please stop following me," Greg said as Justine trailed him from the bathroom into their bedroom.

"I'm not following you," she said and tossed her hairbrush on the unmade bed. "I came in here to get dressed, same as you. Besides, we need to settle this."

"As far as I'm concerned, it's settled." He pulled a dress shirt from its dry cleaning bag and wrestled with the top button. "This whole troll-family thing is stupid and I don't think we should do it."

"It's *Gnome*. Garden *Gnome*." She took a pair of denim capris from the back of the upholstered chair and stepped into them. "And, yes, it's stupid, but it's part of the program. We've committed to it."

"Correction," he said, holding up a finger, *"you've* committed to it. *I* remain blissfully *un*committed. Like I said, it won't hurt my feelings if you and Emma want to go without me."

Justine threw a pink T-shirt over her head and frowned at him. "You know it doesn't work that way. It's a family thing. Don't you want to make some new family friends?"

Greg pulled on his suit pants. "Between the firm and the neighborhood, I can think of at least three couples with kids that we already see on a regular basis, so...nope. I'm good."

"Oh, come *on*. Why are you giving me such a hard time about this?"

"Why are you taking it so personally?"

"Because. Because I worked very hard to get Emma into this school and I want to do things right."

"I'd say you've done everything right by adding a nice little girl to their roster and paying an entire year's tuition up front." He zipped his fly with finality.

"This is pointless," she said, jamming her feet into her sandals. "I should never try to discuss something with you when you're on your way to court and wearing your giant litigator head." She walked back into the bathroom, squeezed a ribbon of toothpaste onto her toothbrush and began brushing.

"I do not have a giant litigator head!" Greg called from the bedroom.

"Can't hear you!" she lied through a mouthful of minty foam.

Greg appeared in the bathroom doorway, wearing a suit and a frown. "Look, I understand that you went to a lot of trouble to get Emma into Garden of Happiness. I get it. But I think we also have to be careful not to set a bad precedent."

Justine rinsed her mouth and looked at Greg in the mirror. "What do you mean?"

"I mean this school costs a fortune and you've told me about all the volunteer stuff you're going to have to do and now they want *another* slice of our free time—before school has even started?" She opened her mouth to reply but he continued, "So I'm thinking we should find a way to pass on this particular activity. My bet is that Margaret will never know the difference."

"If you'd been at orientation, you'd know that's not the case."

Greg's mouth hardened. "As you know, I was working late last night, which is another reason I'm not keen on spending my free time schmoozing preschoolers."

Emma burst into the bathroom carrying a plastic bag of Cheerios and a sippy cup of milk, some of which was spreading in a moist, oblong splotch across the front of her blue nightgown.

"Daddy, you are fancy!" she said as she watched Greg adjust his tie in the mirror.

"I am indeed, little girl." He leaned down and kissed Emma on the top of her head, then smiled tentatively at Justine. "So can we agree to get out of this thing?"

"I'll try, okay? I don't think it's the right decision, but I'll try." She scooped Emma up and tucked her against her hip.

"Thank you."

Greg walked out of the bathroom and Justine followed. He scooped his keys from the hall tree and picked up the black case he carried to court. "I'm off to do battle."

"All right, well…good luck," Justine said.

"C'mon, don't be mad at me. I have a feeling this whole thing will go away without you having to do anything." He opened the front door and turned to go.

"Hey, what about *my* kiss?" Justine said.

"Oh, right." They exchanged a quick smooch before he started down the steps.

"You'll be home at the regular time tonight?" she called after him.

"I hope so. It might be another late one. I'll call you." He disappeared into the garage.

She tucked Emma's head under her chin and swayed on the top

landing as she watched Greg drive away. What a stupid fight. Of course she should be doing anything she could to get out of the playdate, but not for the reason Greg was thinking. Whether Greg liked the idea or not, she had expected to commit some of their free time to the school. She had *not* expected to spend that time chilling with her old lover. She felt a twist of guilt—another in a series that had started the morning after orientation. She had intended to tell him about Harry that night, but when their phone conversation became all about Simone, she just…hadn't. And now the window on that casual disclosure had closed. If she told him now, it would be obvious that she had delayed, and her hesitation would *mean something*. It was like lunching with a friend and noticing a piece of spinach in her teeth—you either told her about the spinach the moment you noticed it, or you kept it to yourself and tried not to look at it for the rest of the meal. Her being thrown together with Harry had been a shock at first, but now she was beginning to see that it was just a nuisance—one that was not worth making Greg uncomfortable. Harry was her piece of spinach, and she would deal with it herself.

Besides, maybe Greg's prediction was correct. Maybe Bette and Harry wouldn't even follow up to schedule the playdate. *Yeah, right*, she thought as she shut the front door and the phone began to ring.

Two hours later, when Justine and Emma arrived at Ruthie's streamlined, modern house in Venice, Ruthie was already standing in the doorway. Her lemon-colored sundress contrasted with the teal door, two pleasing splashes of color against the spare, gray front wall.

"Hey," Justine said and hugged her friend. "Cute dress."

"Fresh off the rack at Tar-jhay. Is the yellow too much?"

"Never." Justine placed a hand on Emma's shoulder. "Can you say hello to Mrs. Andrews?"

"Hello, Mrs. Andrews," Emma said, clutching the handle of a plastic bucket in one hand and tucking Scooter the turtle to her chest with the other.

"Hi, Emma-Girl," Ruthie said. "Looks like you're ready to get in the sandbox. Calvin and Lucy are ready, too, and while you all play, your mother and I can have a little talk." She shot Justine a stern look.

"What's that for?" Justine followed Ruthie into the house as Emma ran ahead toward the back deck.

"Bring that tray, will you?" Ruthie motioned to a Lucite platter loaded with mini carrots, popcorn, pretzels, and grapes, then took two tall glasses of diet soda from the counter and followed Emma toward the sliding glass door. "We can watch the little monkeys from here." They settled onto a sleek orange sofa by the open door. Just outside, Emma was playing with Ruthie's four-year-old twins in the deck's built-in sand pit, which Ruthie constantly had to defend from local cats seeking a roomy, mid-century-modern litter box.

Justine took a drink of her soda, then started munching a handful of popcorn. When she turned to Ruthie, she found her waiting with arms crossed, her dark-blond braid curving around her shoulder.

"What?" Justine said, her mouth full.

"I see what's going on, you know."

"What are you talking about?" Justine kept chewing.

Ruthie raised a perfectly arched eyebrow at her. "On Pinterest...?"

Justine was drawn to Pinterest the way tornadoes were drawn to mobile home parks. Yes, she should do something more substantive, but who could resist all those colorful little rectangular targets?

"Yeah, I was on there this morning while I was feeding Emma breakfast. Don't tell me you're anti-Pinterest now—you've only had your account for five minutes."

"No, I'm not anti-Pinterest, but—"

"Omigosh, did you see that picture of the cat with the martini and the ski goggles, the one with the caption that says—"

"You're obsessing about him again, aren't you?"

Justine's hand stopped in midair between the popcorn bowl and her mouth. "What? *Who?*"

"You know who. I knew this was going to happen when he showed up at Rainbow of Snootiness or whatever that place is called."

Justine knew Ruthie formed her opinion of the school after reading that supermodel Cienna Chadwick sent her daughter there in *US Magazine*. Justine had ignored her jibes, but now that she'd observed the other parents up close at orientation, she had to admit that the lifestyle of the truly posh Westsider was foreign to her. This was a slice of LA life that she hadn't encountered while she'd been hunkered down in various office buildings, working her way up the promotion ladders at her jobs.

"Harry?" Justine said. "Okay, you lost me. What does he have to do with Pinterest?"

Calvin shot past them and into the kitchen. "What do you need, Cal?" Ruthie called.

"My scoop!"

Ruthie turned back to Justine. "I was on Pinterest this morning, too, and I saw those new pins of yours."

"What about them?"

Ruthie paused, listening to the sounds of drawers being opened and banged shut in the kitchen. "You need help in there, buddy?"

"No, Momma."

"*Please*," she said to Justine. "Adding the Berkeley campanile to your 'Favorite Places' board was one thing. But Sausalito? You hate Sausalito. You always said that place had two things going for it: humidity and seagulls. Then I saw the motorcycle on your 'My Style' board and it all came together. *Harry*. How did it work again—*he* invited you for a romantic weekend, but somehow *you* ended up paying for almost everything? Then you justified it by telling me about some poem he spontaneously scribbled comparing you to 'the flow of the bay.'" She snorted. "It was like watching a horror flick. You rode off with him on that stupid bike and came back a big, frizzy-haired love zombie."

"You're so deluded," Justine said. "First of all, it was 'the *rise* of the bay.' And second, there's no pattern to my pins—they're just things I like." She sipped her soda. "Besides, I hate that guy."

Ruthie leaned toward her. "Do you? Do you really?"

"You know it makes me uncomfortable when you do that repeating thing."

"I thought you hated him, too, but when you told me he was at your school, I heard a little something in your voice, and then—" She became silent and looked off into the distance.

"And then what?" Justine's hand hovered over the grapes.

"Do you hear a sloshing sound?"

Justine squinted and listened. "I do hear something. Definitely wet."

"CALVIN!" Ruthie bellowed, making Justine jump. "You had better not be after that angel fish with Daddy's barbeque tongs again, or you are going to be one unhappy little boy at frozen yogurt time!"

The *slosh*ing noise stopped.

"Anyway," Ruthie continued in her normal voice, "Harry's just always had that crazy hold over you. I know you *think* you hate him. And you *should* hate him. I'm just afraid you *don't* hate him."

Calvin jogged through the room and out the door holding a wooden spoon in one hand and a man's high-top sneaker in the other.

"Well, you don't need to worry because I *do*. Here's the weird thing, though," she shifted on the sofa, "we're going to his house for a playdate."

"*What?*" Ruthie's eyes widened.

"It's this silly school thing. Our families are paired up and they're supposed to have us over for a get-together to welcome us to the school. The wife called this morning, very businesslike, and here's a quote: 'Bring swimsuits.'"

Ruthie's eyelids blinked in a rapid flurry. "I'm sorry, did you just say that you are taking your husband and child into enemy territory to party down poolside with your kryptonite guy? What kind of juice boxes are they serving at this new school of yours?"

"He's not my kryptonite guy," Justine thumped her glass down on the coaster, "and I've already thought about this. Look, this invitation came from Harry's wife; it's legit school business, mom to mom. Besides, it's good that we've been put together in a way because it forces both Harry and me to move on and act normal. We're in the same school and we're going to have to coexist."

Ruthie looked unimpressed. "And you can do that? You can 'coexist'—" she hung air quotes around the word, "—with the man who told you he loved you and then just...*left*? Have you flipped your weave?"

Justine felt her cheeks flush and began wadding her napkin into a ball. "First, we don't know anyone who has a weave. Second, you are watching too many reality shows. And third," she looked at her friend, "what choice do I have?"

"Oh, honey," Ruthie's voice softened, "don't put yourself through this. School hasn't even started yet—just enroll Emma somewhere else."

"God, you sound like Greg." She flopped back against the sofa cushions. "I promised him I'd get out of it."

"Well, why didn't you?"

"I tried, but Bette—"

"Bet?"

"No, *Bette*."

"Whatever. Go on."

"Bette said that Margaret—she's the boss of the school—keeps track of the family playdates. They're mandatory. No exceptions."

"And how did Greg take *that* news?"

"I haven't told him yet."

"Oh, fabulous." Ruthie stood and took their glasses to the kitchen. Justine walked over to the sliding door and watched the children, who seemed to be running some kind of sand hospital, then followed Ruthie.

"So you're determined to go through with this psychotic playtime thing?" Ruthie dropped ice cubes into their glasses.

"I have to admit, I'm curious to see how they live."

"Danger, danger..." Ruthie said in a singsong voice as she poured the soda.

"I'm picturing a jackknifed doublewide next to a sewage treatment plant, but I don't want to get my hopes up."

Ruthie stopped pouring and looked at Justine. "You can joke all you want, but as someone who saw the carnage firsthand, I have to tell you that this is the worst decision you've ever made. And I was there for your wedge haircut."

"I can't believe you're bringing up the Hairtanic."

"I'm serious, Teenie. This isn't grad school anymore and he's not worth the risk."

"Listen, I'm not getting chased out of our first-choice school because I can't handle being in the same room with an old boyfriend. I appreciate your concern, but you can let it go. His voodoo doesn't work on me anymore."

Ruthie shook her head, then ripped open a supersize bag of cheddar-ranch potato chips. "Well, I give ol' Greg a lot of credit. Mac would never stand for socializing with one of my flammable exes, especially on the other guy's turf." She poured the chips into a clear, glass bowl.

Justine felt another twist of guilt. This was the perfect time to confess that Greg didn't know who Harry was, but that would only trigger another love-zombie inquisition. "Mmhmm. Hey, should I carry those out to the other room?" As she grabbed the bowl of chips and bolted from the kitchen, she tried to block out the realization that, for the first time in their history, she had intentionally misled her best friend.

8
Justine

Between her cranky child and crankier husband, Justine wondered if she should have rented a stunt family for their Garden Gnome playdate. This was LA, after all—surely there was an agency that specialized in loaner relatives for ticklish social situations. Based on the drive alone, she would happily have paid to upgrade her current car-mates to more cooperative, playdate-ready models.

"That was your turn right there," Greg said as Justine drove deeper into Mandeville Canyon, a winding enclave of faux-rustic affluence that was classified under their personal, real estate ranking system as "ranchero-swank."

"This is annoying," Justine said. "How did we miss another one?"

"'We?' I didn't realize I was driving, too." He stared out his window.

"Are you going to be a pouty-pants all day? I said I was sorry, okay? I tried, but I could not get us out of this." She nosed the car into a driveway, then threw it in reverse and retraced her route on the two-lane road.

"We had an agreement," he said.

"I said I would do my best, and I did. I *did* warn you that it was mandatory."

"Apparently my definition of 'mandatory' is different from yours."

"I'll remember that the next time I'm supposed to sit through a rubber-chicken dinner at some law-firm event."

He glared at her just as she was looking him up and down. "What?" he said. "What are you looking at?"

"I just think you could have made an effort."

"What do you mean?" He looked down at his black and orange swim trunks, oversize, freebie T-shirt from a legal conference, and plaid flannel shirt. He smoothed the shirt, stopping to scrape at something stuck to its front. "It's a swim party."

"It's not a *costume* swim party," she said dryly.

"So I should have spent an hour performing my ablutions like *you* did? Who are you trying to impress?"

Justine's cheeks turned hot. "I did *not* do that. While you were playing with your phone, I was trying to get Emma into her swimsuit." She glanced over her shoulder at Emma in the backseat and lowered her voice. "She was being impossible."

"See? You're the only one who wants to visit the hobbits."

"OMG, for the last time, it's *gnomes*, okay? Garden *Gnomes*."

"I'm pretty sure you're not supposed to *say* 'O-M-G.' It's not a *word*, Grandma."

"Okay, you and your frickin' fluorescent Crocs are standing on my last nerve."

Emma pressed a button on the toy in her lap and the car was filled for the thirty-seventh time with an electronic melody apparently composed with the intent of shattering the adult optic nerve.

Greg scowled. "Is she really attached to that toy?"

"No, Ted Kaczynski was 'really attached' to his typewriter. She *loves* that toy."

"It's so *irritating*."

"Please, this is nothing. Try it for an hour and a half coming back from the Valley in traffic."

"You should take it away from her after a while."

Justine shot him a look. "Are you new here?"

"I'm just saying—"

"There's the house!" Justine made a sudden right turn and crunched into a circular drive in a spray of gravel, coming to a stop in front of a multi-gabled, Old English home. Emma's toy slid off her lap and under the front seat at full volume, the sound of which was second only to her fire-engine wail of distress. "It's okay, Em. Mommy will get it for you." She put the car in park, then twisted her body around, pawing under the passenger seat while Emma cranked up her protest to a super-treble range known only to professional piccolo players.

Justine retracted into the front seat, rubbing her shoulder. "I don't bend that way."

"Don't you have another toy you can give her?" Greg said.

"No. Maybe it's under my seat. Can you reach behind there and check?"

Greg made a show of leaning back between the two seats. Just as he got his head down to get a better look, Emma thrust her legs out in frustration and caught Greg in the face with her sandaled foot. "Ow!" He sat up with his hand over his eye. Frightened, Emma screamed louder.

"Are you okay?" Justine tried to get a closer look, but he waved her off.

"No, I'm not okay!"

"You don't have to yell," Justine yelled. "You're scaring the baby!"

"The baby started it!"

"It's all right, Emma." Justine tried to sound soothing through clenched teeth. Emma's face was deep red and wet with hot tears. In her right fist, she clutched the ribbon pom-pom that had been attached to her sprout of a ponytail, along with a cluster of curly hairs caught in the elastic. Justine noticed a change in Emma's expression. "No," she breathed.

"You know, my eye really hurts." Greg turned the rearview mirror so he could inspect his face.

"Oh, please don't." Justine reached for her seat belt, eyes still on Emma.

"That foam sandal is harder than it looks." Greg pulled his eyelid back and brought his face within an inch of the mirror. "It could have scratched my cornea."

Justine's shoulders slumped in defeat. "Oh, this is perfect." Emma had stopped screaming, but her face was still red, now for a different reason. "What a freakin' nightmare."

"No, it's okay." Greg flopped back into the passenger seat. "I think it's just a little swollen. It should be—whoa! What is *that*?"

"It's exactly what it smells like. Now let me think for a minute because I can't remember if I put a swim diaper on her before we left the house."

"Well, if you didn't you should floor it because we don't want to go in there with—"

A knocking sound caused all three of them to look toward the side of the car where Bette and Harry stood in the driveway, peering in at them.

"Are we having fun yet?" Bette shouted through the closed windows.

The usual social formalities were postponed as Justine and Greg scrambled to return Emma to a socially acceptable level of freshness. Twenty-seven wipes and three layers of plastic bags later, they reconvened with Bette and Harry in the foyer and everyone tried to act like nothing had happened. Justine wasn't sure which experience would leave her more emotionally scarred—recovering from the aftermath of the deadly swim diaper (which thankfully Emma *had* been wearing) or witnessing the introduction of her husband to her former lover.

"Greg Underwood. How you doin'." Greg grasped Harry's hand, his voice dropping the octave that Justine had noticed all men's voices dropped when introducing themselves.

"Harry Rivers." The two men's forearms visibly flexed as they squared their shoulders to one another. Justine felt like Jane Goodall, peering through the banana leaves at males in their natural habitat, on the lookout for signs of impending poo-flinging or other antisocial behaviors.

"Do people ever call you Hank?"

Justine hoped Bette hadn't seen her wince in reaction to Greg's question. Harry despised the name Hank.

"Only once," Harry said as the two men released their grips.

"Right." Greg wore a tolerant smile as he took in Harry's V-neck tee and low-slung jeans.

"Have any trouble finding the place?" Harry said, stifling a yawn. "Excuse me. Late night last night."

"Nah, piece of cake." Greg crossed his arms and the tolerant smile reappeared.

Oh my God, Justine thought, *it's the passive-aggressive Olympics.* She wasn't sure which offended her more—that Greg wasn't taking her boyfriend seriously or that Harry seemed unimpressed with her husband. She couldn't take another moment of it.

"Thanks for having us!" she blurted.

"What are Gnomes for?" Bette said.

"Great seeing you again," Harry said to Justine and went in for an uncharacteristic air kiss, startling her into stepping on the front paw of Nan Tucket, the family labradoodle.

"I'm so sorry!" she said as the dog yelped and backed away from the group. Emma's chin began to tremble and Justine scooped her up onto her hip. "She's fine, Em, see? Mommy just stepped on her toe, that's all."

"Don't you worry about Nan," Bette said to Emma. "Later she'll steal some food off your mom's plate to even the score." Emma giggled and Bette continued. "Would you like a snack? Because we've got lots of them out back by the pool."

"Let's go to the pool!" Emma clapped her hands. "I want to swim!"

"Swim?" Bette said. "In the *pool*? Where did you get *that* idea?" She gave Emma a gentle poke in the belly. "Come on, then, let's go try this 'swimming' thing." Through the French doors at the rear of the house, Justine saw two young boys in swimsuits playing on the grass near the pool. As Bette ushered them out to the patio, Harry's phone rang and, despite Bette's dirty look, he excused himself to take the call.

Bette introduced her sons, Clayton and Miles, and Justine noticed that, while both boys were hybrids of their parents' looks, Clayton had his father's striking, deep-set eyes. As Justine and Greg began the process of encasing Emma in sunscreen, lip balm, a shiny, pink surf shirt, sunglasses, and a hat, Bette and the boys went to get pool floats from the side yard. Once Emma was impervious to the full spectrum of sunlight, Greg led her into the water while Justine admired the poolside spread of fresh guacamole, a fragrant caprese salad, and dev-iled eggs whose yolks had been piped into their little white bottoms with a pastry tip. When a woman walked out of the house carrying a tray of crudités, Justine had a moment of panic, thinking the event was a potluck and she had forgotten to bring her dish. Then she realized the woman was not another school parent but a professional putting the final touches on the table displays. *A catered playdate*, she thought. *That's not how we roll back in Baja Beverly Hills.*

Bette returned with the boys, who raced across the lawn with the floats, whooping as they leapt into the pool. In the shallows, Emma bobbed daintily on a small, inflatable island like a bullfrog settled on a lily pad. Greg stood alongside her, one hand gripping the float, the other holding his iPhone, which he worked with his thumb. *This is the second time he's checked his emails since we arrived*, Justine thought.

Couldn't he give it a rest while they were with people?

"Don't tell me Junior's still on the phone," Bette said as she crossed the bricks toward Justine. "Rude."

"'Junior?'"

"Harry is nineteen months younger than I am. Doesn't qualify me as a cougar, but it's a change of pace from all the sweet young things who sign on with woolly-eared geezers so they can spend their afternoons shopping at Barneys." She ate a deviled egg in two bites.

Justine took a chip from a glass bowl on the table. "Your place is gorgeous." She turned toward the yard, which extended beyond the brick pool area to a rolling lawn bordered by magnolia and eucalyptus trees. Nestled among them was a bungalow with a Dutch door and a broad skylight. "Is that a guest house?"

"Nope. Harry's studio. That's where the magic happens." With a wink, Bette threw back another egg.

"Ah."

"He's an artist. Sculpture mostly. It's too messy for the house, so we built him his own playroom out here." Bette crossed her arms and studied the bungalow. "He's actually quite good." She seemed lost in thought for a moment, then pulled her attention back to Justine. "You know, better than a person might expect."

"I, um, love the layout of everything." Justine turned back to the main house, remembering its paneled library and sweeping staircase. She tried to reconcile it with Harry's old apartment above the Korean market in Berkeley, filled with repurposed furniture and secondhand kitchenware.

"So have you received the school committee letter yet?" Bette said.

"A couple of days ago. Do you have any recommendations?"

"Doesn't matter. They're all like passing glass."

Justine laughed. "Is that why they have such cute names? To cover the pain?"

"Probably. 'Birthday Butterflies' sounds more appealing than 'Festivities Enforcement Squad.'"

"That bad?"

"You get used to things like having to buy a gift for the school on your kid's birthday."

"Wait, *what*?"

"Don't worry. Within a month you'll be trained like Pavlov's dog—you'll start reaching for your checkbook when you hear the front gate squeak."

"I'm glad Greg's not hearing this."

Bette shrugged. "That's life at a power preschool. There are five kids waiting to take your kid's spot and Margaret has all the leverage because the parents need her recommendation to get into a choice kindergarten. On the upside, Garden of Happiness has a spectacular placement record at the elite schools. Margaret goes to bat for kids all the time, calling her contacts in the admissions departments and lobbying for them to accept her students." She shifted the bowl of irises on the table, adjusting a few of the stalks. "If she thinks you're not completely on board with her school, though, you'll be out in the cold when application time rolls around."

"I guess I figured that once we were in, things would be a little less...Gothic."

"Don't sweat it. Just pick a committee and put your back into it." Her hand hovered over the platter of deviled eggs. "You ever miss your old job?"

"Not even a little."

"You will." Bette gave her a knowing look, then picked up a tortilla chip and bit it in half.

The French door opened with an expensive *whoosh* and Harry appeared, holding a pilsner of beer. "Hey, that took a long time, didn't it?" he said, joining Justine and Bette.

"Well, if it isn't our absentee host." Bette noticed the glass in Harry's hand, then turned and walked toward the pool. "Greg," she called, "would you like some pretentious microbrew?"

"Anyway, I *am* sorry I was gone so long." Harry took a step toward Justine. "We haven't had a chance to talk."

Justine poured herself a glass of lemonade. "Love your place."

"Thanks. Yeah, it's nice, I guess."

"I think any home with eight ottomans qualifies as more than nice."

"You counted my ottomans?" He smiled.

"It's just something I do. And shouldn't it be 'ottomen?'"

Harry scowled. "Really? Is that right?"

"No," she laughed. "I was messing with you."

"Well, anyway, this is just a little spot I like to think of as my—"

"Don't say it!"

"Ottoman empire," he finished with a sweep of his arm.

"Oh," she groaned, "that was terrible."

"Junior," Bette said, walking back toward them, "Greg would like a beer when he gets out of the pool. Can you run get one out of that fancy little fridge of yours?"

"Yeah, okay," Harry said and started toward the house.

"He's always hated nicknames," Bette said, "but I can't resist."

"Hmmm." I wouldn't say *always*, Justine thought, remembering one morning in his apartment when he woke with such raging bedhead that she dubbed him "Animal" after the wild-eyed Muppets drummer. The name stuck, becoming one of those code words that couples used like a secret handshake.

"Top off your lemonade?" Bette held out the pitcher.

"Sure, thanks." As Bette poured, Justine noticed the silver, C-shaped band on her wrist. "Your bracelet—it's very unusual."

"Oh. Yeah. I wear this one a lot." She held her arm out to Justine.

"I like this part here." She turned her hand over and Justine saw a stylized coyote embossed in the silver.

She swallowed hard. "It's lovely."

"Tell Junior. He made it."

Yeah, Justine thought. *I know.*

Harry emerged from the house again just as Greg and Emma approached, wrapped in oversize towels. The boys ignored the rest of the group as they took turns jumping into the far side of the pool, screaming phrases from some TV show before splashing into the water. "Your beverage, sir," Harry said, and handed the beer to Greg.

"Perfect." Greg set his iPhone on the table. "Thanks."

Emma dropped her towel on the patio. "Mommy, Daddy says it's your turn to swim."

"We've been playing pony and Daddy's reins have taken quite a beating." Greg gingerly rubbed one of his ears, which Justine noticed was bright red.

"Come *on!*" Emma tugged at Justine's hand. "Your binkini is under your clothes, remember?"

Justine felt Harry's eyes on her. "Yes, I remember, but first we need to eat lunch, Ladybug. Pick up your towel and I'll make a plate for you."

"But I want to swim!"

"Em…" Greg gave her a stern look. Emma frowned and crossed her arms.

"Go see if you can get the boys to sit still long enough to eat," Bette said with a nod of her head toward Harry.

"Mission: Impossible," Harry said, and headed to the other side of the pool.

As Greg began loading food onto his plate, Justine settled Emma into a chair with a peanut butter and jelly sandwich professionally cut into windows. "I love these leather placemats, Bette. I didn't know Hampton made tableware."

"It's something we're experimenting with," Bette said. "Those are actually prototypes."

"Do you work for Hampton? I didn't know that."

Bette looked up from scooping caprese salad. "Since my father died last year, I *am* Hampton."

"You're Billy Hampton's daughter?"

"That would be me, yes."

"I guess I should have known that."

"Why? It's not like we have tour jackets."

"I thought Hampton was based in New England," Greg said, adding a trio of cherry tomatoes to the Matterhorn of potato salad on his plate.

"That's right, but we're relocating the company to Southern California over the next eighteen months. In the meantime, I live on airplanes and Skype."

"Wouldn't it be easier for you to move back East?" Justine said.

"In some ways, yeah, but I've been here a long time and I'm an LA girl now. Autumn is supposed to smell like brushfires, not apple cider, you know? Besides, Harry would shrivel up and disappear as soon as the weather turned cold. He actually tried living in Chicago years ago." She laughed. "He survived one winter before scampering back to SoCal."

Justine concentrated on poking the straw into Emma's juice box. *Less than a year,* she thought. Harry was back in California only months after leaving and she never knew it. She jammed the straw through the foil seal, sending a stream of chilled apple juice onto Emma's tummy, making her laugh. As she pushed the salad around on her plate, she recalibrated her impression of Harry's and Bette's relationship, and Bette's proprietary tone clicked into place. Harry hadn't simply married Bette—he had married a worldwide luxury brand and the privileges that came with it, including a custom studio for his art. It all made sense. Now that she thought about it, he had hated that dingy apartment above the Korean market.

Junior, she thought with a smile. *God, that must make him crazy.* She'd never seen a woman so immune to his charms. Well, except for the few times Ruthie had been in the mix, but that didn't count. She looked over her shoulder. Bette had disappeared and Harry was standing by the built-in barbecue, talking to Greg. She guessed he must have been on some extended rant about his artistic vision because she hadn't seen such a pained expression on Greg's face since her mother's last birthday, when he had been subjected to an involuntary tour of the Museum of Miniatures.

Justine studied Harry with a cold eye. He was as handsome as ever, but he had an ego the size of a Rose Parade float. And he was high-maintenance—requiring constant strokes to soothe his insecurities. Maybe if she'd been living with those issues for a few years, she'd be calling him "Junior" and sending him to shag beers, too.

"What's funny, Mommy?" Emma said.

"Nothing, little girl. Here, eat the last piece of your sandwich and in a few minutes we'll get in the pool."

For the first time, she was glad they'd been matched up with Bette and Harry. Now that she was seeing him without the soft-focus lens of her memories, she would have no problem dealing with him at school. She would transition him into her himbo dad-friend and go about her business. And if he happened to realize at some point that he had blown it by letting her go all those years ago, well, that would be *his* problem. She was content with her secure, non-egomaniacal husband and Harry had missed his chance.

She stood up from the table and peeled off her T-shirt to reveal a navy-blue bikini top. She had agonized that morning about whether to wear her flirty but challenging two-piece or the buzzkill but low-risk one-piece. Now she was happy she'd gone for the bikini gusto. Sure, she would be ruined if she lost concentration and relaxed her abs, but as long as she maintained focus and kept clenching, she was all right—at least for the eight feet between the table and the pool.

As her shorts fluttered down to her ankles, she heard the ping of a submarine's sonar coming from Greg's phone on the table. She leaned down to get the shorts and saw the text box open on the screen.

> *Are you coming in after playtime? We could use your big brain. :) Simone*

She picked up the phone and read the message again. "You've *got* to be kidding me," she said under her breath.

Greg walked up, rubbing his eyes with his palms. "Dear God. How many hours was I talking to him? *There's* my phone." He noticed the look on Justine's face. "What's wrong?"

She held the phone out for him to see. "Really?"

Greg read the message and shook his head. "I told her I'd be out of pocket until late afternoon." He closed the text box with his thumb. "And I just replied to her email questions half an hour ago." He looked up and set his phone on the table. "Why are you glaring at me?"

"That message just reminds me of how she talks to people at the firm."

"Well, if she's smart, she'll realize she has a lot to prove on this case and she'll focus on helping us through discovery, not sending silly texts."

"Mommy, do you have another baby in your tummy?" Emma pointed a peanut-butter-encrusted finger at Justine's midsection.

Justine snapped to attention and re-clenched her abs. The unwanted mental image of Simone—and her taut belly—poolside at the firm's Palm Springs litigation retreat caused her to suck her stomach even harder against her spine. "Of course not, Ladybug," she said as Greg tried to hide his smile. Justine looked around for Bette and Harry. "Where did they go?"

"Bette is getting more towels and I have no idea where DaVinci 2.0 went. Maybe Bette put him in his crate. And speaking of people disappearing, isn't it about time we packed it in?"

The French doors opened again and Harry walked out wearing nothing but black swim trunks and a light blue towel hanging from his shoulder. He was broader in the chest than he'd been in grad school, with a bit more hair nestled between his pecs, but these were minor points. *Hello, dad-friend.*

"Last one in's a rotten falafel." He smiled at them and tossed the towel on a chair.

"A little bit more 'playtime,'" Justine said to Greg, "then we can go." Taking Emma by the hand, she walked across the bricks toward the pool steps.

Later that night, when the house was quiet and Emma and Greg were asleep, Justine padded barefoot across the wood floor to her dresser. Through the open window, she could hear someone on the sidewalk below—the *jangle* of a dog leash and *crackle* of a transistor radio. Pushing aside a black-and-white wedding photo in a carved wooden frame, she reached for a small pottery box. She lifted the lid and traced the hairline crack where she had glued it years ago after it had slipped from her hand and broken.

She reached into the box, past dried four-leaf clovers, stray whiskers she had saved from her beloved cat, and her old college ID cards, to something hard and cool underneath. She held the metal in her hands, felt it warm to her touch and, in one deft motion, slipped it around her wrist. Through the slats of the shutter, the moonlight glinted on the woven silver and the tiny embossed coyote.

"This is for you, special one," he had said as he turned her arm over and kissed the spot where the two slender sterling fingers almost met. There was moonlight that night, too, pouring through the window of Justine's apartment along with the ever-present aroma of curry from Mrs. Singh's kitchen below.

"Oh, Harry, it's beautiful."

"It's perfect on you." He paused and ran his finger across the coyote, studying it. "I listened to nothing but Miles Davis while I created this. I think it really shows in the piece."

She held his face in her hands and kissed him.

"Come here," he said and pulled her to him. She wrapped her arms around his waist and rested her head on his chest. An old Crowded House song drifted in from the other room. They swayed back and forth on the linoleum as Harry stroked her hair and Justine felt a powerful thrum of hope.

9
Margaret

Margaret caught a glimpse—then another—of her lawyer as he made his way through the colorful crowd on the Venice boardwalk. He wove among the street performers and lumbering tourists with fluid precision, the spokes of his wheelchair flashing in the afternoon sun. She waited until he spotted her, then waved hello.

"Thank you for fitting me into your schedule, Seth," she said as he rolled up next to her.

"Thank *you* for agreeing to the unorthodox location." A thick shock of silver hair flopped onto his forehead. "One of the perks of working on Main Street is my afternoon jaunt to the ocean. I find it rejuvenating." The beach was at its widest where they were walking, but even from the distance, Margaret could see pelicans dive-bomb into the low whitecaps. To the left was a chain of grubby tourist shops with roll-up metal doors, each blaring Top 40 pop, while the right side of the paved walkway was lined with folding tables and makeshift displays of string bracelets, exotic insects preserved in resin, and wood carvings for sale. The crowd seemed to serpentine within itself as bicyclists, rollerbladers, and strollers mixed with pedestrians while everyone dodged the hucksters working their section of the walkway. "Let me know if you'd like to get a henna tattoo." Seth chuckled and Margaret smiled in return, but said nothing. She wished they had met somewhere that did not smell like Eddie's incense. "I never see clients here, but I heard the anxiety in your voicemail and, whenever possible, I prefer to deliver bad news in person."

Margaret stopped walking. "'Bad news?'"

"Eddie's request for an appraisal is a reasonable one, I'm afraid." He circled around to face her.

"You call taking half of a business he showed zero interest in 'reasonable?'"

"His level of interest is not the legal yardstick here. It's a marital asset, plain and simple, just like *his* business."

"He made the decision to pull back from his dental practice when he started pursuing his other interests." Margaret shielded her eyes from the sun. "He kept talking about starting some new venture, but of course nothing ever came of *that*. His business is worthless at this point."

"And thanks to the great state of California, half of that worthless business is yours."

They began moving down the boardwalk again. "Let me understand this. Eddie decides to flake out and become a New-Age surf cliché, lets his business wither, then pockets half the value of my school—the culmination of my life's work in early childhood education—as easy cash on his way out the door?"

"I'm not saying we're going to make it easy for him, but this is not a surprising development." A man approached riding a bicycle and blasting Parliament-Funkadelic from an old-school boom box bungeed to the handlebars. Seth wheeled aside to let the man pass, then swung back into place next to Margaret. "Did you expect he would abandon his claim to that asset?"

"On the contrary, it never occurred to me that he would make the claim in the first place." She slipped her hands in the pockets of her jacket and looked out at the ocean as she walked. "Promises were made."

"In writing?"

Margaret hesitated. "No."

"In that case, if you want to keep the school, you're going to have to buy Eddie out of his half."

"In his dreams," she said, her voice tight.

Seth guided Margaret away from the pedestrian swarm to a grassy area under a cluster of palm trees. "I know how difficult this is."

"I'm not some hysterical housewife, Seth. I don't need you to soothe me." She stared out at the water. "I need you to make this go away."

He took a deep breath. "Allow me to recap, Margaret, if I may. Your home, thanks to the current market, is upside down. Your investment portfolio is respectable, but nothing to make a broker work on Sunday. Your cars are negligible. That leaves the school property, which is worth more than the other assets combined."

Margaret did not respond.

"Therefore, it seems highly unlikely that Eddie would sacrifice his share of the most valuable item in your joint estate for the sake of an understanding that was never memorialized on paper."

A gust of ocean air lifted Margaret's bangs from her face and rattled the dry palm fronds hanging in the trees. "It may be that you don't know Eddie as well as I do."

"Agreed. I learn something new about people every day; it's one of my favorite parts of the job." He clapped his hands once, then rubbed them together. "So I will respond to the other side's email and inform them that there is an agreement in place that excludes Garden of Happiness from the marital estate. I don't like our odds, but I'll hit them as hard as I can."

"Thank you, Seth."

"While I communicate with the other side, however, I must advise you to begin making arrangements to buy out Eddie's interest. If that requires a second mortgage on the school, you should start that process as a contingency. That's the reality of the situation."

"I appreciate your advice, but I'll deal with my own reality for the time being."

Ten minutes later, she was driving toward her gym in Marina del Rey, frowning as she thought back over her conversation with Seth. She could see why Eddie would ignore the inconvenient fact of their verbal agreement, but her own lawyer had to be persuaded to enforce it as well? As usual, it was up to her to find a solution as others flailed uselessly around her.

Eddie had been unimpressed the day they first saw the vacant house through the window of their realtor's tank-like Mercedes. "That's a nonstarter," he said, and began flipping through the stack of MLS descriptions for the next property. Margaret, however, over-looked the sagging roofline and boarded front window. The little house was perfectly positioned on the lot, with room in front for a toddler yard and easy passage around the side that could be closed off for security. She pictured the house after she had updated its facade, replaced the fence, and painted the structure in what would be her signature color scheme: green, yellow and white. "You can turn off the car now," she said, and pulled the door handle. A quick tour confirmed her decision. "This is it," she said to Eddie in the dilapidated kitchen while the realtor took a call on her cellphone in the backyard. She pulled open a cabinet to find a curling, aqua shelf liner and a rusty ant trap.

"We should at least see the other listings." Eddie looked with distaste at the stained sink.

"That would be a waste of time." She took him by the hand and walked out the back door. "See that?" She pointed at a sad, two-story guesthouse at the rear of the yard. "My office will be right up there. And your office is…" she swung her arm toward the third floor of the office building next door, "…right there. We could eat lunch together."

"Well, folks," the realtor said, making her way across the crumbling deck in stiletto booties, "what are we thinking?"

"We need a minute," Margaret said.

"Of course. I'll go check in with my office." Clutching her phone, she disappeared into the house.

"I want to make an offer," Margaret said once the realtor was out of earshot.

"There's plenty of time for that."

Margaret knew she could bend him to get what she wanted, but she would have preferred he show a little enthusiasm. Eddie was chronically easygoing, and it was maddening to her. Even when he had been looking for new office space for his own practice, he had taken such a casual approach that, finally, Margaret could stand it no longer—she narrowed it down to three options and stood with him at the kitchen table as he made the final choice.

"Let's lowball it," she said, watching for his reaction.

"Are you sure you don't want to buy in a less expensive area?"

Margaret scanned the yard again, visualizing a place where she could implement her educational approach—honed over years of teaching—with autonomy. "I'm sure."

"Okay, then," he said, "it's your school. It should be where you want it to be."

"Do you mean that?"

"About it being where you want it to be?"

"No, what you said about it being *my* school."

Eddie laughed. There was the smile again, bookended by crevices that had deepened over the years. "Yes, I mean it."

"Because that's important to me."

"Oh, I *know* it is." He pulled her into a hug. "I promise to keep my grimy paws out of it and not interfere. Does that make you happy?"

"Yes." She pressed her cheek against his collarbone. They stood on the deck, arms around each other, and she considered how smoothly her plan was coming together. It felt like a gift, but gifts made her uneasy.

Margaret shook off the decade-old memory and pulled into a parking space behind the kickboxing gym. She was glad the meeting with the lawyer hadn't interfered with her workout; she was in the mood to punch something. Eager to escape the ripe funk from the adjacent sushi restaurant, she grabbed her bag and hurried to the gym's rear entrance, where she threw open the metal door, stepped into the hallway, and slammed into Eddie. They sprang apart like warring tribesmen who had backed into each other in the underbrush.

"I thought you switched gyms," Margaret said, rubbing the spot where she'd banged her elbow on the doorframe.

"I changed my mind," Eddie said, raising his chin.

"You should put that on your tombstone." She walked past him toward the weight room.

"Did you schedule that appraisal yet?" he called after her.

Margaret whipped around to launch a scorching reply, then remembered her promise to Leticia. She wondered briefly if her daughter's term "psycho" might be open to interpretation, then accepted that she was outgunned by motherhood once again. "I'll be addressing that in the very near future."

"Okay, I'll be in Portland, but my lawyers know how to reach me." He shifted his gym bag on his shoulder, watching as his words hit their mark.

"Portland? You're going to—"

"Yes, to see Leticia. She's having a hard time settling in, you know.

She was hinting that she wanted some dad-time, so I'm flying up for a couple of nights."

"But we said we'd give her space to adjust on her own—to reinforce her self-confidence during the transition."

Eddie shrugged. "I guess I don't agree with your tough-love policy."

"That's not tough love! Tough love is a very specific program of—"

"It sure feels tough to me, but what do I know? Anyway, I don't have time to get into this right now." He reached for the doorknob. "Anything you'd like me to tell your daughter when I see her?"

Margaret wanted to scream, but she was determined to keep things civil. "That won't be necessary. She and I are in constant communication."

A mix of amusement and satisfaction flickered across Eddie's face. "Have it your way." He *thump*ed the door shut as he left.

If there's any justice in the world, your flight will be filled with teething, diarrheic babies, Margaret thought, glaring at the door. As she turned and walked through the weight room, she pictured Eddie and Leticia talking over coffee—Leticia sharing her struggles and Eddie getting to serve as supportive parent. She felt a lump rise in her throat at the thought of precious one-on-one time with Leticia, then remembered the smirk on Eddie's face as he gloated about his travel plans. "Manipulative man-child," she said under her breath. She reached the middle of the gym and threw her bag on the floor.

The gym was long and deep, with a free-weight room in the rear and a front room that looked onto the street. It was filled with workout machines and a full-sized boxing ring stood in the middle. Every available space held speed bags, heavy bags, or punching dummies, the latter of which bore a convenient and remarkable resemblance to Eddie.

"Gloves on, let's go," said Kenny the trainer, who was waiting in the ring in his black sweatshorts and tank top. "I can see you've already killed at least three people this morning, so let's start before the body count gets any higher." He slapped the training pads together with a loud *crack* that blew his sandy, shoulder-length hair away from his face.

"Very funny, Kenny," she said, stuffing her hands in her gloves. She slipped between the ropes and stood in front of him on the canvas.

"All right, give me fours and please don't hurt me," he said, holding the pads out at chest level.

Margaret began punching the pads in sets of four.

"That's it, young goddess!" the trainer cheered.

Margaret stopped punching and dropped her hands. "No."

"What?" he said, still in his stance.

"The encouragement." Margaret shook her head. "I don't like it."

"You don't like *encouragement?*" He withdrew the pads, the muscles in his shoulders rippling beneath his suntanned skin like puppies romping under a blanket. "Who doesn't like that?"

"We've talked about this, Kenny. 'Young goddess' sounds facetious when applied to a woman my age—particularly when it's applied by someone who primarily watches Vin Diesel movies."

"Okay." Kenny looked crushed.

"And while we're on the subject, the same goes for 'ninja vixen.'"

"No fair—that's my best one!"

"No more." She put her fists on her hips. "Let's not have this conversation again."

"Fine." He raised the pads again. "You sure know how to take the fun out of things."

In her three years at the gym, she and Kenny had bickered good-naturedly about everything from workout pants to movie reviews to politics. So when the tears suddenly spilled onto Margaret's cheeks, the only person more surprised than the trainer was Margaret herself.

"Hey, whoa." He reached out, but stopped short of touching her. "Are you all right? I was just kidding."

She opened her mouth to respond, but was horrified to hear a sob escape instead. Then another.

"Shit." Kenny looked around for help, but there were no other women in the gym. Clients from the other room peered around the partition to see what was happening.

"What'd you do to her, dude?" one of them called out.

"She hates my jokes. Now go finish your reps," Kenny barked at them. "You should sit down," he said to Margaret and guided her through the ropes to a wooden bench against the wall. Elbows on her knees, she watched her tears splash onto the black rubber floor as if they belonged to someone else—some strange, unhinged woman whose emotions had gotten the better of her.

The trainer shifted from foot to foot. "I'll go get you a bottled water!" he said and dashed from the room.

Margaret stared at the floor, shaking her head. What were the chances that Kenny would pull a direct quote from her last vacation with Eddie? It was a weeklong trip to Kauai the summer before Leticia's senior year—taken in celebration of their twenty-fifth anniversary. By the fourth day, it had become apparent that they had little to talk about other than Leticia, and the unfamiliar setting only showcased the lulls in their conversations. Adding to the tension, Eddie had loaded their schedule with everything from shamanic sessions to surf lessons with the idea that Margaret would love sharing these experiences with him. After she repeatedly declined to take part in activities she felt were ludicrous or dangerous, Eddie had had enough. "You sure know how to take the fun out of things," he'd said before catching a taxi to the airport and flying home three days early.

She'd heard similar accusations all her life—hurtful comments that, over time, she'd attributed to others feeling threatened by her competency. Hearing it from Eddie, however, left her feeling attacked and confused. Why was he so angry about personality traits she'd had since he met her? And when had parasailing become so damn important?

In the wake of that trip, the friction between Eddie and Margaret blossomed into frequent arguments followed by crushing household silences. As Leticia withdrew from the drama, the family fractured into three individuals who briefly interacted at birthdays and holidays before retreating once again from each other's company. Now, sitting on the wooden bench, Margaret wrestled with the fear that had nagged at her since the failed trip to Kauai: that her family had disintegrated because Eddie and Leticia wanted to distance themselves from Margaret, the terminally un-fun person.

Kenny returned and held the bottle of water out to her like he was handing a suitcase of unmarked bills to an armed kidnapper. He stepped back and watched as she pulled off her gloves and took a drink.

"Why are you staring at me like that?" she said. "Haven't you ever seen someone have an emotional breakdown?"

"Only about a dozen times a day. But I've never seen it happen to *you*. You look like shit, by the way."

"Why, thank you." She took another sip from the bottle.

He shrugged. "You're the one who doesn't want encouragement."

In spite of herself, Margaret smiled. Like a shaft of sunlight through a cloud bank, it glowed for a moment, then disappeared.

10
Justine

The first morning of preschool arrived, and Emma was completely on board with the process as long as it didn't include setting a single Velcro sneaker-clad foot on school grounds. Justine stood with her in front of the yellow door as they watched a small parade of children—each accompanied by one or more parents, guardians, or nannies—pass into the play area. She knew her daughter well enough to know that something was keeping her from walking through the door and that she would share it with her mother only when *she* was ready. Unfortunately, the timeframe for these disclosures could run anywhere from thirty seconds to four months. As the big hand of the all-weather clock swung farther and farther past the six, Justine became increasingly perturbed while Emma settled into a deep, meditative state of stubbornness that would have made a Zen master look like a chain-smoker who'd lost his lighter. Clearly, she was at one with blowing off preschool.

"Here we go, Emma." Justine reached again for the doorknob, which was set six inches above her head, presumably with the goal of foiling the plans of any Garden inhabitant who might be a flight risk. "This is going to be big fun."

"Can I play with Harlan?"

"We just talked about this, Ladybug. Harlan doesn't go to your new school."

"How come?" Emma switched her black Transformers lunch-box—which she chose herself in spite of the girlier models suggested by the sales clerk—from one hand to the other and looked up at her mother.

Justine opened her mouth to answer as a petite woman in stiletto Mary Janes teetered up behind them holding a rhinestone-encrusted iPhone and swinging an enormous embellished handbag from the crook of her arm. She tugged a small girl in lavender UGG boots along behind her.

"I have to have someone who can work Friday nights," the woman said to Justine. Justine looked behind her, thinking the woman must be addressing someone else, but there was no one there. "*Every* Friday night," the woman stressed. "No exceptions."

This kind of bossiness could not go unanswered. "Friday's my night at the dog track," Justine said, returning her look, "but I could work you in every other Tuesday."

The woman flashed a tight smile, then turned her head and tapped the Bluetooth clinging to her ear, indicating she was on the phone. She and her daughter brushed past them and through the yellow door.

"Charmed, I'm sure," Justine said to the closed door.

"I want to play with Harlan," Emma said again with a scowl.

Justine turned back to her daughter. "Harlan's family belongs to the temple at the end of our street, remember? You'll still have lots of playdates with him, but he's going to preschool at the temple."

Emma sighed theatrically. "Harlan's so *lucky*."

Justine squatted and drew Emma toward her, lowering her voice. "You're going to have a great time at Garden of Happiness, Emma. Remember those giant Lego blocks? The really big ones you played with when we visited? They're in there right now, waiting for you to stack them up and push them down the slide." Justine stood and once again took hold of Emma's hand and the two bags of school supplies. "You'll love it once we're in there. I promise."

"But, Mommy?"

Justine stiffened, keeping the focus on their target: the door. "Yes, Emma?"

"What if the other kids are mean?"

Justine's eyes filled with sudden tears. Until now, she had managed to distract herself from her own anxiety about Emma starting school, but this question cut straight through her. She dropped the bags and gathered her daughter into her arms. "Oh, no, baby girl… Why would you think they'd be mean?"

"I don't know them." She scowled. "They're *strangers*."

"Well, they're strangers now, but pretty soon they'll be your friends."

"How do you know?"

Justine blinked hard. How was she ever going to walk away from this place without Emma's little starfish hand in hers?

"What's wrong, Mommy?" Emma rubbed her mother's arm. "Are you afraid the other mommies will be mean, too?"

Justine smiled and smoothed Emma's hair. Of course she was worried that the other mommies would be mean. Hadn't Emma seen the one that just strutted past? Based on her experience so far, Garden of Happiness was shaping up to be junior high all over again. She could handle it, of course, but what about Emma? Was this how it was at all the "good" Westside preschools, or had Justine made a terrible mistake in choosing this one? They wouldn't know the answer until they passed through that door.

"This is a big day for both of us, Emma, did you know that?" Her voice wobbled but she kept going. "We're both starting a new school and we're both going to make lots of new friends."

"If anyone is mean to me, I will kick them in the bahookie." Emma grinned and Justine marveled at her little girl's spirit while acknowledging that the teenage years in their house were going to be absolute murder.

"Emma! You sure are *not* going to kick anyone in the bahookie." *But I like your style,* she silently added and kissed her daughter on the cheek.

Emma pulled away and picked up her lunchbox. "Can we go in now?"

"What are we waiting for?" Justine gathered the bags again, took Emma's hand and, grasping the world's highest doorknob, swung open the door.

Waiting on the other side was the skinniest woman Justine had ever seen outside of a casket. "Welcome to Garden of Happiness," the woman said with the sincerity of a career flight attendant.

They were in the breezeway that ran along the side of the main building. Arranged along the wall was a row of picnic tables with stations to relieve parents of registration packets; earthquake/civil unrest supplies; family photos, which would be placed in the child's cubby for comfort; and checks for the next tuition cycle. Parents could also leave payment for luxury items, like logo-embossed T-shirts and hats, and an extra hour of supervised playtime after school. Behind Justine, the door opened and shut as more students arrived. Emma slipped her arm around her mother's leg as children and grown-ups flowed past them.

The skinny woman shifted her clipboard from one hip to the other and flung her ombre hair behind her shoulder. "Name?"

"Hi. Underwood? Emma Underwood." The woman gripped the clipboard with hands no larger than those of an organ grinder's monkey. She wore chunky, lace-up leather boots, a grommet-covered leather belt, and a snug, camouflage T-shirt with a stylized "D&G" appliquéd in gold vinyl across the bust, the cumulative effect of which was that she looked like she was about to parachute into enemy-designer territory.

"Wait, what?" She looked up and squinted at Justine. "What was the name again?"

"Underwood. Emma Underwood." Justine set her bags down and stuck out her hand. "I'm Justine."

"I'm Zoe Leonard," she said, returning the handshake. "You know, Tarquin's mom?" Zoe paused and Justine wondered if she was supposed to know who Tarquin was. The woman flipped her two-tone waves again. "What group are you in? Soil, Seeds, Sunshine, or Sprinkles?"

"I don't know yet."

"Okay, wait." Zoe flipped some pages. "This list is effed up, excuse my French. I'll be right back." She clomped off toward a doorway, her clipboard hanging at knee level.

It was easy to distinguish the returning students from the new ones. The veterans moved smoothly through the check-in area on their parents' hands and then, reaching the play yard, released their grip and moved toward their toy of choice without a backward glance, like skiers delivered onto a scenic slope by a mechanical lift.

The new children, in contrast, clung to their parents in various forms of distress ranging from silent stoicism to unchained aggression. Justine squeezed Emma's hand and looked down to see her staring open-mouthed at a little boy furiously pummeling his mother's shoulder. They watched as a teacher in her late twenties wearing trim track pants and running shoes quickly moved in on the situation.

"No, no, Navarone." She inserted herself between mother and child and motioned for the mom to stand up. "We mustn't hit Mummy." She flipped her long, white-blond hair over her shoulder and squatted down to the boy's level, continuing in a singsong New Zealand accent. "We never, never hit our Mum, all right?"

The mother stood behind the teacher and rubbed her upper arm as she pleaded with her child. "I know you're mad at me, baby. Maybe you're not ready to start school today, right? Let's think of something else to do instead. What would make you happy?"

"And we're moving away from the hostage situation," Justine said under her breath, propelling Emma farther down the breezeway.

"Okay, *here* you are," Zoe said as she reappeared with her clipboard. "Ella is in the Seeds Group."

"It's Emma." Justine spoke loudly to be heard over the nearby cluster of moms in workout wear having an animated debate on the comparative merits of yoga, Pilates, and something called "Krav Maga."

"Okay. So disaster stuff goes in the purple bin and, after you turn in everything else, there are snacks for transitioning moms in the kitchen." She motioned toward the wooden steps. "You know the drill, right? You hang out in there every day until the teachers tell you your kid is ready to be here without you. Then you get to leave."

"Right," Justine said. "Thanks."

"There's my friend, Emma," Justine heard someone say and turned to see the blond teacher approaching.

"I am so excited to see you!" The teacher knelt next to Emma, never breaking eye contact. "Do you remember me?"

Emma glanced up at her mother and back to the teacher. "I think so."

"Excellent. I am Miss Glenda and I am one of your teachers and this is a very big day, isn't it?"

Emma hugged her lunchbox to her chest. "Yes."

"Did you and your mummy bring a lovely family photograph from home today?"

"Yes," Emma said again.

"Wonderful. That photo will go right in your cubby where you can see it whenever you like. In fact, how would you like to go and see your cubby right now, and you can help me tape your family photo just where you like it?"

Emma thought for a moment. "Can I pick any cubby I want?"

"No, Emma, Miss Margaret has already picked a cubby for you, but I can tell you that it's a very nice one."

"Is it carpeted?"

Miss Glenda looked up at Justine with a puzzled expression. Justine shrugged. "Well, no, none of the cubbies are carpeted."

"Oh." Emma was silent for another moment. "We can see it anyway."

Justine reached into one of the bags at her feet, handed the family photo to Emma, then kissed the top of her head.

"Mommy's not leaving, okay? I'll be here the whole time so if you have a problem—"

"She's not going to have a problem," Miss Glenda said with a firm shake of her head.

"I know, but just in case she needs me—"

"She won't need you. She's going to be just fine, and now it's time to tape up that photo, right, Emma?" Miss Glenda held out her hand.

Emma looked at the hand and then turned to her mother, motioning for her to bend down. When Justine was close enough, Emma threw her arms around her neck. "Bye, Mommy."

Justine's throat closed as she clutched her daughter. "You're such a big girl. You have fun and I'll see you in a little while, okay?"

"Okay." She turned and took Miss Glenda's hand.

Justine wrapped her arms around herself and watched Emma walk off toward the cubby area, marveling at how she looked both too small and too big from across the sandbox. She felt like someone had stolen her pacemaker.

"You look like you could use one of these," said a woman who appeared next to her holding a box of tissues.

"Oh." Justine cleared her throat. "Thanks." She plucked a tissue from the box and dabbed the corners of her eyes.

"First time?" The woman wore a loose, pajama-like outfit and had oddly angled hair that appeared to be under extreme chemical coercion.

"Yes," Justine sighed, still watching Emma. "They've got this separation thing down to a science, right? I mean, it seemed like they did in orientation and I'm kind of counting on that..." She sniffed and wiped her nose.

"Listen, your kid's doing great." Her voice had a nasal edge to it. "We transitioned last year and it took them four days just to pry my kid off my leg. Besides, you're not going anywhere today. You get to hide in the big house, eat snacks, and spy on her the whole time. No worries." She flipped her hand, brushing away the inconvenience that was separation. "Wait until they don't want to *leave* school. *That* makes Mommy feel great. By the way, I'm Willow." She held out her hand and Justine took it, expecting a handshake. Instead she got a quick slide across the palm and a parting squeeze of her fingertips before Willow began adjusting one of the several complicated necklaces that hung from the precipice of her bosom.

"Nice to meet you. I'm Justine Underwood."

Willow dropped the necklaces back onto her chest. "So *you're* Justine Underwood." Justine sensed a shift in Willow's stance. "I've heard all about you."

"No way." Justine smiled. "No one ever hears all about *me*." Her tone was light but she, too, shifted her posture.

"You're in marketing, right? PR?"

"I *was*, in a previous life."

"Fabulous! I need you, I need you. Tell Margaret you're mine." She reached through the neckline of her top and gave her bra strap a yank, anchoring it on her shoulder with a fleshy snap.

Justine looked around, but the hive of activity seemed to have drowned out Willow's outburst. "I'm not sure what you mean."

"You have to be on my committee." Willow wrapped her fingers around Justine's forearm and gave it a tug.

"And what committee is that?" She tried to remember what she had marked on her volunteer form. Maybe she was already on this woman's committee. Maybe she could get off of it.

"Fundraising!" she brayed. "I'm the fundraising chairman. Chairperson. Whatever." She fluttered her hands. "You've *got* to be on my committee."

"I'm just trying to remember what I signed up for on the sheet they mailed out…"

Willow gave a knowing smile. "I get it." She drew Justine closer to the fiberglass scrub sink piled with bars of grayish, misshapen soap and an industrial sized pump-jug of hand sanitizer. "You don't want to overcommit." She lowered her voice. "But think about this. You're new. You're going to need face time with Margaret, especially if—wait—do you have an older kid who's already at a private school?"

"No, just Emma."

Willow's mouth curled into another smile. "Yeah, so you're going to need *major* face time if you want Margaret's help up to the next level, kindergarten-wise. And no committee is more plugged into Margaret than fundraising."

"Well, that makes sense…" Justine peeked around the corner of the building. There was Emma, emerging from the cubby area with Miss Glenda, who pointed toward a table overflowing with craft supplies. Justine saw Emma's eyes light up and felt herself relax a bit. She turned back to Willow. "Sure. I'll be on your committee."

"Fabulous! I'm adding you to my roster ASAP."

"So what do I do?"

"I'll contact you about our first meeting." She turned to walk away. "You're a goddess!" she said over her shoulder as she took the two steps down onto the sand.

After turning in all of Emma's paperwork and supplies, Justine went to the kitchen—official holding pen and designated breakdown area for mommies of new children. Across the deck, she saw Willow talking to Margaret. Something about Willow's double-barreled recruiting tactics left Justine feeling uneasy. She was already protective of those four hours each morning when Emma would be in school. She didn't intend for that precious slice of freedom to be blown on some school committee.

She was not feeling pressure from Greg to go back to work at the firm, or anywhere else, for that matter. Sometimes she wondered if he harbored a secret hope that she would morph into a traditional homemaker—someone who not only handled all of the domestic duties, but was also *into* it. As a Hamburger Helper repeat offender with consistently bloated hampers and cloudy shower doors, she knew this metamorphosis was never going to happen. After years of working at jobs where she was successful but not excited, she had promised herself when she quit the firm that she would not go back to work until she was passionate about something. Lately, she had become fascinated with interior design. Each morning for months she had gotten up before Emma, poured her cup of coffee and scoured the design blogs for inspiration. Now she had her first test project planned out: their bedroom. She couldn't wait to start turning her notes and sketches into reality. She had even looked into the professional design program at UCLA Extension and was considering enrolling in one of the courses in the spring. Hopefully, the admissions department would never find out that her design credits included papering her undergraduate dorm room with Fiorucci angel posters.

As she climbed the steps into the main building, she decided not to worry about her conversation with Willow. She had to join one of the committees anyway and, according to Bette, they were all equally excruciating. How bad could it be?

"Oh my God, who brought *doughnuts?*" The woman's jersey skirt swung from her flat, tan pelvis as she stepped away from the counter and the paper box that sat on it. "Evil!"

It was the fourth time Justine had heard that very exclamation since she had wedged herself into the wooden booth in the corner of the kitchen.

"Maybe I'll just smell them," the woman said. "Smells don't have calories, right?"

Justine opened her paperback copy of *A Confederacy of Dunces* and tried to settle back into reading as two other moms sat down nearby.

"I don't know what we would have done without Margaret," said the mom wearing a cotton tunic and intricately woven sandals.

"Really?" The other mom munched a strawberry and pushed a cluster of dreadlocks off her forehead. "What was going on?"

"Well, Ryan has been co-sleeping with us since he was born, but then he stopped letting my husband in the bed."

"No way."

"Anytime Adam would come near the bed, Ryan would hold up his hand and shout, 'No, Daddy! Only Mommy!'"

"Awkward."

"I know, right? But what are you going to do? We thought maybe he was feeling territorial because we'd changed nannies, but after three weeks on the sofa, Adam's back was really bothering him, so we asked Margaret for advice."

"What did she say?"

"She said we needed to set firmer *boundaries.*"

"Wow."

"She said it was *our* decision where Adam slept and we needed to make that clear to Ryan."

"I would never have thought of that. I would have been worried that I was tampering with some kind of primal sleep rhythm or something."

"That's what I'm saying: genius. She said, 'children need to know they're not in charge—it's a relief to them.'"

"Okay, I need a T-shirt that says that."

"I know, right?"

Justine closed her book and checked her watch. Two and a half hours left in the school day. She wished she could peek in and see how Emma was doing, but the mommies were under strict instructions to stay corralled in the transition area and out of sight of the children. Emma had been escorted in to see Justine once so far, after a tussle with a boy in her group over the possession of an orange watering can.

"You be nice," Justine had said in a low voice as Emma stared back at her with a surly expression.

"We don't tell the children to be nice." Miss Glenda's bottom teeth showed prominently when she spoke. "The notion of niceness confuses them. It's too vague. We can discuss this concept further if you'd like to schedule a time outside of school hours." She whisked Emma out of the main building. The other moms, who had become quiet during Miss Glenda's reprimand, resumed their conversations behind Justine as she stood in the kitchen doorway.

Unable to face the cramped wooden booth again, Justine strolled through the kitchen and out into the short hallway, taking in the flyers, sign-up sheets, photographs, and crafts tacked onto every surface. There were framed photographs of past graduating classes, painted handprint tiles mounted in rows around the tops of the walls, birthday photographs glued to glitter-covered popsicle sticks, and Polaroids covering the kitchen pillar with Sharpie captions that read, "Duke made a pyramid out of Floam today," and "Selena, her daddy, and his Emmy on Share Day."

Justine moved through the building's unoccupied main room toward the front office, running her hand along rows of picture books and feeling the bits of foam and felt on the crafts table. The sounds from the playground mixed with the voices of the moms in the kitchen, forming a soft background hum in the otherwise silent room.

She came to a sprawling display of family photographs on the wall outside the school secretary's door. Soon, Justine's family would be represented here as well, since "candid photograph of entire family" was on the list of materials to be turned in on the first day of school, along with more puzzling items such as cotton gloves and glow sticks. The variety of photos was impressive, verging on competitive, and she began to have second thoughts about the whimsical shot she had submitted that morning of the three of them holding Easter baskets and wearing fuzzy bunny ears. There were families fresh from river rafts, clenched in matching Christmas sweaters, and hanging from trees like Von Trapps. They piloted gondolas, clung to one another on zip line platforms above Costa Rican rainforests, and clustered like backup singers around everyone from Mickey Mouse to Beyoncé. When she saw *his* face in a photo, she told herself she had not been looking for it.

"Well, if it isn't my new school friend, Harry," she said to herself. He was fresh from the surf, swimsuit clinging to his thighs and his arm snug around Bette's waist as Clayton and Miles stood on either side of them. Although the perfect lens flare over his shoulder looked orchestrated, she knew it had been spontaneous. Those kinds of things always happened in photos of Harry. It was one of his more obnoxious qualities.

Justine laid her hands on both sides of the picture. The red craft paper was smooth and dry and, even in the September heat, the cinderblock wall behind it was cool on her palms. She studied the photograph as any woman in her position would—looking for hideous, reptilian features that Bette might have kept hidden from sight during the playdate. She wore a classic, black bikini that revealed neither a hirsute stomach nor any unexpected vestigial appendages, but rather a toned, athletic figure with a sprinkling of freckles across her chest. She looked genuinely happy, her smile bright, relaxed, and confoundingly fang-free. How long ago had this shot been taken? Before she began referring to Harry as "Junior?"

"What are we looking at?"

The man's voice caused Justine to leap away from the photos. Harry had made it halfway across the room without her noticing.

"Geez!" She laid her hand on her chest. "Did the SWAT team lower you in here from the roof or something?"

He laughed. "I can't believe you didn't hear the skirmish in the kitchen when I asked for one of those bottles of water on the counter. Man, those women are *on edge*." He walked over to the photo wall where she had been standing and browsed the pictures, lingering over the shot of his family.

Justine ran a hand through her hair then cleared her throat. "So, I was thinking I'd see Bette here today since Clayton is starting school."

"He's home sick. Bette's with him." With a sudden movement, he turned to face her. "Hey, I have to ask you something."

"Um…okay." For the first time, she noticed what Harry was wearing. A faux-vintage "ironic" T-shirt? *Please*. What was next, a trucker hat? The fact that he could look good in d-bag clothing was just wrong.

"You know what I was thinking about after you were at the house? Remember Tahoe?" His eyebrows rose with the question.

"Oh my *God!*" she blurted in spite of herself. "That trip was insane."

It had been their second adventure together, a budget getaway that relied on internet coupons and two bags of groceries that they bought at Andronico's Park 'N Shop on the way out of town. They called it their no-star weekend—as opposed to five star—and everything went wrong, from her overheated car to his sprained thumb (a casualty of the motel's aggressively withholding vending machine). She had never experienced so much laughter and sex in three straight days in her life. It was after this trip that she arrived at Harry's apartment to find he had cleared out a drawer for her in his dresser. When she opened it and discovered he had covered the bottom with her favorite lavender-scented liner, she was speechless. That was the side of him that Ruthie never knew.

"And those guys at the restaurant," he said, "we almost had them convinced that we'd seen that creature in the lake?"

"That thing was freaky. What was it called again?"

"Tahoe Tessie!" they said in unison.

The hanging door to the front office slid open and a man with a receding hairline and mint-green dress shirt appeared in the doorway. Justine remembered seeing him at orientation, and he hadn't looked any happier that night than he did now.

"At ease, supplicants," he said, and pointed at the manila envelope in Harry's hand. "If those aren't your registration materials, there's going to be a gnomicide."

"Yes, Trey," Harry said in a weary voice and held out the envelope. "Here you go."

"Well, hallelujah. Now I can check your packet off as complete." Trey took the envelope, ignoring Justine. "Someone's been buzzing me on her broom for days looking for this."

"You mean looking for the check inside," Harry corrected him.

"Isn't that what I said?" Trey stepped back into his office and slid the door shut with a *bang*.

"You made a special trip here today just for that?" Justine said.

"Typical Garden shenanigans. Hey, listen, I've been thinking. It must have been a shock for you, you know, seeing me here. I hope you're not feeling…uncomfortable."

Justine crossed her arms. "Why would I be uncomfortable?"

Harry stepped closer. "I mean, no one else knows our history. I feel bad—you having to keep a secret in your marriage because of me." He watched her face as he spoke. "I'd hate to be the cause of any tension between you and George—"

"Greg."

"Right. Greg. Great guy, by the way."

"Yes, he is," Justine said. "And don't worry—you're not causing any tension. You're just another preschool dad. To both of us."

They looked at each other for a moment. "Good to know," Harry said, then pulled a postcard from the back pocket of his jeans. "You should come to my opening. It'll be in this new gallery over on Robertson." He handed her the thick, matte card. "You can bring your stab," he added, calling up their old, joke slang for "boyfriend."

She turned the paper over in her hands as they walked back toward the kitchen. "This looks great. Good for you, Harry."

"Oh, it's nothing. Just the culmination of a lifetime's work, right?" He lowered his voice. "Anyway, I'm glad we talked about keeping our past on the down low. It's probably best if Bette doesn't know that the new mom she's taken under her wing is the woman who broke her husband's heart."

Before Justine could respond, Harry pointed toward the side window where the top of Margaret's head could be seen gliding past. "Oh, great, here she comes. Listen, I'm not up for a lecture on late fees right now so I'm going to duck out the front. Watch out for the flying monkeys."

Ten seconds later, the only evidence that Harry had ever been in the room was the invitation in Justine's hand and the expression of annoyance on her face. Did he just say that she had broken *his* heart? She didn't need his fake emotional charity. "The Crapwizard rides again," she said into the empty room.

"Justine Underwood." Margaret stood in the kitchen doorway in her kilt and loafers, clipboard in hand. "Is there a problem?"

"Not at all. Just stretching my legs and looking at some of the children's artwork." She reached out and poked at a cluster of paint-scarred cotton balls glued to a piece of green construction paper. "So charming."

Margaret stepped into the room. "I'd like to have a word with you about Emma."

"Of course." *Hey, Mother of the Year*, Justine chided herself, *get your head back in the game.*

Margaret fingered a beaded sterling chain draped around her neck with a thick metal loop that held burgundy reading glasses. "Emma Underwood is doing fine so far."

"I'm happy to hear that. Are you calling her by her full name?"

"There are three other Emmas in Seeds, so we have to do something to differentiate them."

"Oh, no, three other Emmas in her group?"

"Popular name. We've got a couple of Emmas in every group—have had for two years now. The sunbonnet names are making recordkeeping a nightmare at the schools."

"'Sunbonnet names'?"

"The old-fashioned sweet names like Emma, Hannah, and Rose. They're coming in waves lately. Between the sunbonnets and the quirky ones, the only way for a child to stand out these days is to be named Susan or Carl."

"Wouldn't it be easier just to call her Emma U.?"

"Under normal circumstances, yes, but we have two Emma U's this year. Then we thought about using the middle initial as well."

"But Emma's middle name is Frances."

"Right."

Justine and Margaret stared at each other while they each silently considered the notion of a preschooler with the handle, "Emma F.U."

"Right," Margaret repeated. "You see our dilemma."

"Okay, well, if she's all right with it then I guess I am, too."

"Excellent. I'm glad that's settled." Margaret motioned toward the doorway. "Walk with me."

The two women returned to the kitchen, where Miss Glenda was dropping orange fish crackers into plastic cups on a tray.

"And here are my brave transitioning mommies," Margaret said, addressing the room. "Please, ladies," she motioned to the counter, "enjoy some snacks."

As Justine moved toward the food, she overheard Margaret speaking to Miss Glenda. "Tell the hospitality committee to coordinate the paper goods next time. Mismatched napkins and cups don't say Garden of Happiness to me."

Margaret looked around the kitchen, then seemed to remember something. "By the way," she said to Justine, "Willow Neff told me that you are her new star on the fundraising committee."

The snacking moms became quiet, all ears tuned to this exchange.

"Oh, I wouldn't say 'star.' I'm just a worker bee." *And I don't even want the job*, she added silently.

"Don't be modest." Margaret saw a teacher wave to her through the doorway and motioned that she was coming. "Co-chairing the school auction is an ambitious undertaking, especially for a mom new to Garden." She walked out of the kitchen, leaving Justine staring at the empty doorway, and the other mommies staring at Justine.

After a moment, Justine took a deep breath and turned on her heel, addressing the kitchen at large. "If anyone needs me, I'll be in the make-believe area," she said, heading for the school's interior. *Making believe that did not just happen.*

11
Ruben

Ruben stood in the flow of parents moving through the Garden of Happiness kitchen and fought the urge to flee. He saw a passing mom giving him an appraising look and self-consciously hitched up his jeans. "Mornin'," he said. "Do you know where I could find—" but the woman walked past in the morning crush.

He noticed a box of doughnuts at the end of the kitchen counter. "Yesss," he said, and plucked a pastry from the assortment. "Well played, Snack Mom."

"The party planner suggested a *Teletubbies* theme," he heard a woman in a cashmere pashmina say to another woman in passing. "I told her I'd call her next time we were planning a party for 1998."

"Have my assistant give you the number of our sleep trainer," a woman with a gold handbag said to a fellow mom. "She got Abigail on track in three nights and we didn't have to do a thing."

This isn't a preschool, it's a staging area for a strike force of ballet-shoe-wearing, studded-handbag-wielding mommy mercenaries.

Where was Margaret? He couldn't leave until he talked to her about joining a committee. Meanwhile, his writing time was ticking away. He checked the doorway again, where he saw one of the few other dads staring at him. He looked fresh from the non-sticky, air-conditioned world of adults, and Ruben could guess what the man was thinking: *What does that guy do all day while I'm out earning the money to pay tuition at this place?*

He had just taken his first bite of doughnut when a woman appeared next to him wearing the kind of boots he usually associated with sword-fighting cats.

"Excuse me," she said, "don't I know you?"

Finally, someone was making an effort to socialize. "Hi, yeah, I think I saw you at drop-off a couple of times last year." He smiled. Actually, he had no idea if he'd seen her because drop-off time was typically spent getting busted for dressing the twins wrong for "T-shirt Tuesday" or forgetting that it was their family's turn to bring organic snacks for Ozone. "I'm Ruben. My kids are—"

"I thought so. You are not a new Garden of Happiness parent. Those doughnuts are for parents in transition. *Exclusively.*" The woman's teeth were so white that Ruben felt the urge to shield his eyes.

"Oh, I...I'm sorry," he stammered. "I guess I thought these were for, you know, *everybody.*"

"No," she said, taking in his Chuck Taylors and bright-green T-shirt with the words "Squirrel Whisperer" across the front. "They're not." Her eyes lingered on the doughnut and it occurred to Ruben that this woman might actually repossess his pastry.

"You must be a snack mom." He nodded toward the box of doughnuts. "Outstanding choice."

The woman straightened her shoulders. "I'm a Hospitality Sprite."

Ruben guffawed then tried to cover it with a cough. "Whoa, inhaled some powdered sugar there."

The woman's eyebrows converged, a motion that seemed to require substantial effort.

Ruben caught sight of Margaret across the kitchen. "Well, nice talkin' to ya," he said and raised the doughnut in salute, then pursued Margaret into the school's main room.

"Um, Margaret?" he said.

She stopped in the library corner and turned to him. "Yes?"

"Hi. Hello, I'm—"

"You're Lily and Harris' dad."

"Yes." He thought he should shake her hand, but he was still holding the doughnut. When he switched it to his other hand, it left both of them sticky with icing. Margaret seemed to have already lost patience.

"How can I help you?" she said.

"Right. My wife says I should—I mean, I would like to join a committee. You know, with the other flowers."

"That's very generous of you. Did you have a particular committee in mind?" By now several moms had gathered around Margaret, waiting for their turn to gain an audience with her.

"I, um—"

"Let me guess," she said. "You would like to join a committee that does boy things, not girl things." The mommies giggled.

"That's pretty much the size of it," he said with a smile.

"You have two options," Margaret said. "There's a group we call the Handy-Daddies. They do small projects around the school such as building bookcases and hanging shelves."

"That sounds good—" Ruben began.

"Full," one of the moms interjected. "That group is full. I know because my husband is on it." She wore black yoga pants and a plunging workout top covered in hot-pink lotus flowers. Her hands cradled a stainless-steel drink cup that read *Namaste Up! –Santa Monica Prestige Yoga.*

"The alternative that seems to be popular with the dads is the Bookworm Bunch," Margaret said. "They're in charge of our library—"

"No room there, either," said another mom, and all heads turned toward the tall woman in a tailored pantsuit and ponytail. "You've got to be ahead of the curve if you want to get into those groups," she said to Ruben.

"Yeah," said a mom in skinny jeans and rhinestone-encrusted flip-flops, "that's where the dads cling to each other for safety."

"I'm assigning you to the Sunflower Committee," Margaret said. "They serve an important function here. I'm sure these moms can fill you in on the details." She moved away to field questions from another cluster of parents.

"Wow," Pantsuit Mom said, "she's never made a dad a Sunflower before." The other women murmured as they closed in around him.

"So..." Ruben said, "what's this Sunflower gig?"

"Basically, you deliver a meal to a Garden of Happiness family that's having some kind of crisis," Yoga Mom said. "You know, to cheer them up."

"Sunflower? Cheerful?" Pantsuit Mom said. "Sound butch enough for you?"

"Just don't forget about food allergies!" one of the moms called out.

"Oh God." Ruben took another bite of his doughnut. "So if someone has a death in the family, I take them a meal."

"Well, not just any death," Yoga Mom said. "It has to be immediate family." The mommies nodded agreement.

"Yeah," another mom spoke up from the edge of the group, "as far as Margaret's concerned, a dead aunt doesn't cut it."

"Oh-*kay*..." Ruben thought for a moment. "Sick kid?"

The mommies considered this. "Seriously sick?" one asked.

"Mmmm, yes. Let's say seriously sick."

"Always," Pantsuit Mom said. "Always if the child is seriously ill."

"Divorce?" Ruben said.

"Not covered," came the quick reply.

"Moving?"

"Nope, that usually just makes everyone jealous," a mom said.

"Unemployment?" Ruben said.

"God, no." Yoga Mom checked over her shoulder and lowered

her voice. "No one ever divulges that. If word gets out, Margaret will put you on her watch list of potential tuition defaulters."

"Should I be writing this down?" he asked.

"Don't bother," Pantsuit Mom waved the question away. "There's a manual. And don't forget about surgery. The immediate family rule applies and, just to be clear, the nanny does *not* count as immediate family no matter how deep the child's attachment issues are. *And*," she paused and looked around at the other mommies, "it has to be *non-elective*." This statement triggered rumblings through the group but Pantsuit Mom stood firm, crossing her arms and pressing her lips together.

Ruben looked around at the women, confused. "I don't get it. What's the big deal?"

Everyone chimed in at once, and the mom next to Ruben explained that Margaret once refused to approve a Sunflower delivery for a certain mom who had undergone a particularly aggressive tummy tuck. Margaret's hard line in this instance remained controversial and still triggered heated debate at Sprinkles Group get-togethers.

"See? It's simple, yet not-so-simple," Yoga Mom said. "And that's why the Sunflowers don't usually take dads. These matters require a feminine touch."

"Oh, yes," he said, "I can feel the TLC."

He looked at the unsmiling women surrounding him. *Sweet mother of Charlie Manson*, he thought, *what a crew.* He realized he had been waiting for someone to start laughing and confess that they had been pulling his leg all along. But there was no laughter. These women were serious as cancer—only the most aggressive forms of which qualified one for a Sunflower delivery.

"Okay, wait," he said and made a timeout *T* with his hands, releasing a flurry of powdered sugar onto the floor. "Just to recap, as long as the family's not milking it, I take them a free pizza and I'm good to go. Right?"

The group threw up its hands and grumbled disapproval. "Pizza?" one of them said. "This is why we should only let them build things," another said as she walked away. The group dispersed, leaving Ruben standing by himself.

"Dude," he said to Ozone, who was nestled under a low table of picture books, "I don't know how you live here."

After taking a second forbidden doughnut from the box in the kitchen, Ruben said good-bye to his children, then burst through the Garden of Happiness gate and onto the sidewalk like a man pursued by the law.

Ruben's mechanical pencil's lead broke. Again. He leaned back in the booth and tossed the pencil onto his new, supposedly lucky notebook. All around him, people were getting their work done—tapping away on screens and keyboards. He'd never trusted laptops. He liked the feel of pencil on paper. Right then, though, he would happily have hooked up to any electronic device—including a microwave—if it would get his script off the starting line.

He rubbed his eyes with his palms. Preschool lasted four hours and barely half of that remained. *Come on, come* on, he thought. *Get in the zone. Be the ball. File the papers.*

He scanned the coffee shop for inspiration. His eyes lingered on a man in a baseball cap and jeans who was staring at his laptop screen with pursed lips—a writer. Ruben felt a surge of envy as the man's fingers flew across his keyboard in a burst of apparent creativity. *He's catching up on emails*, Ruben lied to himself and looked down at his notebook. On the page was a single line: "*Doughnut*

Try This at Home." He had spent so much time staring in frustration at the title of Vince's sitcom that it wouldn't surprise him if he broke out in a rash the next time he encountered it. Below the title was a cloudy, gray oblong, evidence of multiple erasures following multiple false starts.

Frickin' doughnuts. Between Vince's show and the hard-ass Hospitality Sprite, they had become the motif of his day. Deandra was a better man than he was, putting up with those women and all their superiority and rules. Then there was Margaret—that mash-up of Mussolini and Buster Brown. No wonder so many of these kids had night terrors. His kids loved the school, though, and they were miraculously thriving under the Garden of Happiness regime. He almost wished they weren't so happy there so they would have an excuse to leave. It galled him to be kicked around in a school they had to stretch to afford in the first place. What was the big deal about preschool, anyway? Some of these parents acted like their child's entire future hinged on their performance at circle-rug song time. *You think that weak clapping is going to get you into an Ivy League school? Now, try it again from where the wheels on the bus are going 'round and 'round, and this time I want to hear you* sell *it!*

He thought back to his own preschool—a year spent at his parents' church being herded along with thirty other classmates between the muddy play yard with its drifts of dead leaves against the chain link fence, and a classroom decorated with Bible verses and wooden blocks in the shapes of family members. Even now, he could picture exactly what the daddy block looked like, with its bold outline of a suit, hat, and briefcase. In Ruben's play world, the daddy block had a secret life that the rest of the block family knew nothing about. The daddy was a block of intrigue that regularly embarked on dangerous exploits around the classroom. The other children often became frustrated that, just when the block family was sitting down to dinner in the playhouse, Ruben would announce that the daddy block had received word from headquarters of another mission, this one more daring and potentially deadly than the last. At the end of playtime, the daddy block would be discovered by another child and the grim circumstances of his demise—drowned in action in the hand-washing sink, hung by the enemy from the curtain cord, buried in a freak landslide of cushions in the reading corner—would cause the two middle-aged teachers to exchange a concerned glance.

One of his preschool teachers, Mrs. LeGrande, had selected him as her least favorite. He had felt it happen shortly after he started at the school and had accepted it in the way that small children routinely accept as fact things that they know in their hearts to be true: Santa Claus comes down the chimney on Christmas Eve. Mommy and Daddy are divorced. Mrs. LeGrande hates me. He could still remember the teacher's hand clamped onto his elbow, the yellow ridges in her fingernails beneath the clear polish. "There is no excuse for throwing sand, Ruben," she'd said as she frog-marched him across the playground and through the squeaking metal gate. "I just reprimanded you for that ten minutes ago."

It was all so unfair. Had he been throwing sand? Of course he had. He was throwing sand at Monique Freed, the girl he was someday going to marry if he decided not to marry his mom. The injustice came from the fact that two other boys were also throwing it, and the teacher *saw them*. Ruben *saw* her see them. And then he saw her make the decision to punish only him. He never forgot the smell of the clingy white chalk as Mrs. LeGrande directed him to stand with his nose in a circle at the blackboard for the last fifteen minutes of the school day. She hadn't wanted to hear his explanation. Neither had his father after he read the note that Mrs. LeGrande pinned on Ruben's shirt before he went home.

Ruben swirled the coffee in the bottom of his cup and tried to imagine being as angry at one of his own preschool-aged children as his father had been at him all those years ago, but couldn't. The thought of a child at Garden of Happiness being made to spend time with his or her nose stuck in a chalkboard circle was laughable. Litigation would follow, no doubt. If the nose in question belonged to a parent, however, he could see Margaret getting away with it.

He looked down at his notebook again, clearing his mind. He picked up the pencil and bounced it on the spiral binding, then hunched over the page to write a line before it was lost. Then another. For a moment, he glimpsed the story's arc and, this time, it worked. *Yes*, he thought and felt a tingle in his stomach—the same one he got when he knew a joke was about to come together.

"That's what I'm talkin' 'bout," he muttered, his hand gliding across the page.

His cellphone rang, scattering his thoughts like birds spooked off a power line. He raced to capture all of his half-formed ideas. When he glanced at the phone and saw the local area code, he immediately imagined the worst-case scenarios that parents conjure when their children are out of their line of sight. He threw down the pencil and took the call.

"Ruben Daniels?" said the woman on the other end.

"Yeah, this is Ruben." He frowned at the scribbles on the page in front of him.

"Margaret said you'd be able to help me with a little emergency. Is there any way you could take a lunch over to the Farbers before school pick-up time?"

"I'm sorry—who is this?"

"I'm Elaine Yantz. I'm chair of the Sunflower Committee."

"Okay..." Ruben said. There was an unusual sound in the background of the call. Was that a pan flute?

"Time is of the essence, so let me give you the Farbers' address. It's—"

"Um, I know I'm only a trainee Sunflower since I just signed up an hour ago, but isn't this usually more of a dinner thing?"

"Usually, yes, but this family just had a baby and they made special arrangements to receive a lunch rather than a dinner." Ruben heard a sharp sigh through the phone. "I'll spare you the whole nanny/mother-in-law/trophy wife turf-war saga. Suffice to say that dinner is covered. However, the Sunflower who was supposed to deliver lunch today just informed me that she's making an emergency trip to the orthodontist with her sixth grader as we speak. And since I'm calling you from a spa in Ojai, I'm really, *really* hoping I can count on you."

At least I pegged the pan flute, Ruben thought.

He looked down at his page, the nuances of his notes already becoming muddled in his mind. What would the daddy block do? He knew what his own father would have done—ignore the call altogether. He turned to a fresh page and clicked his pencil. "Let's have that address."

"Wonderful. And by the way," Elaine said, "the Farbers have some specific dietary restrictions."

"Elaine, I'd be disappointed if they didn't."

12
Justine

Greg scooted a bite-size piece of pork chop around his plate with his fork, accumulating peas and mashed potatoes on its leading edge like a cow-catcher on a locomotive. "Look, just call this tree person and tell her you never agreed to do the auction." He transferred the bite to his mouth and gave Justine a *ta-da* gesture with his knife and fork as if to say, "Problem solved."

"Her name's Willow and it's not that simple." Justine studied her spoonful of peas. "Margaret's already under the impression I'm doing it."

"So?"

"So I don't want to be the new mom who bailed out of the auction on the first day of school."

"It's not bailing out if you never said you'd do it in the first place."

"Yeah, so now I get to call Willow and have *that* conversation."

"Better than getting jacked up by some pushy committee mom."

"I'm sorry—'jacked up?' You've been binge-watching *CSI* again."

He grinned and nodded. "Man, I love that show." He stabbed his pork chop with his fork and began cutting another bite.

As she watched him saw the meat, which looked about as moist as an acoustic tile, she wished she could motivate herself to become a better cook. She had made several halfhearted attempts since leaving the law firm, but she found the whole process deeply unsatisfying. She had no knack for nuances of taste and was highly suspicious of anyone who could take a dainty slurp from a wooden spoon, squint off into space for a few seconds, and then say something like, "Needs a pinch of cumin." A few years back, Greg's mother had given her a signed cookbook by one of those lush TV hostesses who was always basting something in high-definition on what Justine called "The Food Porn Network." The result was a three-hour culinary assault resulting in a tuna noodle casserole with a hand-toasted breadcrumb topping, which was remarkably similar to fish that had been dragged through a litter box.

"So the pooper did all right today?" Greg's jaw muscles flexed as he worked the meat with his molars.

"Wait." Justine cocked her head toward Emma's door. "Can you hear her?"

Greg froze mid-chew and listened. "Nope," he said finally and resumed eating. "I think she's out."

Justine's shoulders relaxed. "She did fine. She had one problem with a little boy in her group but they worked it out."

"Let me guess—he touched something she thought belonged to her."

"Shocking, right?" Justine stacked her silverware on her plate. "She's your kid for sure." She smiled and carried her plate and glass into the kitchen.

"Good girl," he called after her. "When she turns four, I'll teach her about torts."

When Greg walked into the kitchen carrying his dishes, Justine was standing next to the phone, running her finger down the school roster.

"What are you doing?" he said.

"I want to get this call over with."

"Fo' shizzle." He set his dishes next to the sink and walked out of the kitchen.

"I'm putting parental controls on the television," she called as she dialed the phone. "You're very impressionable."

Willow's home phone rang four times before a woman answered. "Hello!"

"May I please speak with Willow?" Justine raised her voice to be heard over the commotion on Willow's end.

"Who is this?"

"This is Justine Underwood from—"

"*Who?*"

So this is how it feels to be a telemarketer, Justine thought as a child began to howl in the background of the call.

"Oh God, hold on." The woman huffed and turned her mouth away from the receiver. "Concha, she won't eat it when it's hot like that. I said to blow on it, remember? Blow. *So*-plo! *So*-plo!"

Justine had never heard such nasal, terrible Spanish in her life, but Concha must have started puffing because the wailing subsided a bit.

"All right, now *who* is this?" Willow said.

"It's Justine Underwood. We met today at preschool? You asked me to be on the fundraising committee?"

"Oh my GOD!" Willow's voice went from cold lead to warm honey. "I am SO sorry! We're having the mother of all meltdowns over here."

"I'm sorry to hear that. I was calling to talk to you about something Margaret said today."

"Really?" Justine heard a loud crunching sound. Willow was now speaking through what sounded like a mouthful of crackers. "What did she say?"

"Margaret seems to be under the impression that I'm co-chairing the school auction." She waited through some more chews followed by an audible swallow.

"Listen," Willow said, "don't worry about that. Margaret gets things mixed up all the time. You're not co-chairing the auction."

"Oh, thank God! I was so startled when she—"

"You're *chairing* the auction."

"What?"

"And I'm pissed at Margaret for scooping me before I could to tell you myself. Congrats on your coup, new mom!"

"This is a little overwhelming, Willow. It's our first day at the school and we don't even know what's what yet."

"Okay, slow down." Willow's voice became even smoother. "Do you know what a rock star you'll be in Margaret's eyes when you take this on? When recommendation time comes around, you'll be able to write your own ticket. And, with your marketing experience, running our little auction will be a piece of cake, right?"

"I just hadn't planned on doing something this big so soon. Don't get me wrong, I'm happy to be on the committee and do my part, but to run the whole thing all by myself?"

"Stop! Stop right there! I see the problem. This is a misunderstanding. What a relief! Okay, let me explain. Even though you'll have the auction chair title, you will *not* be doing this job alone. You will have a whole committee to help you. You just give assignments and then stand back and let the parents do their thing. You are just the *point person*. The *facilitator*. See the difference? We have parents who help with entertainment, we have dads who take care of all the set up and breakdown, dads who help with kids' art projects—"

"You say there's a dad who helps out with the kids' art projects?"

"God, yes. We have so many talented parents and, believe me, they're all dying to kiss Margaret's patootie. One of our musician dads helped the kids write a song they performed for her on auction night last year. And another dad is a sculptor. He helped the groups make art pieces that we auctioned off. Listen, you will be *amazed* at how much these parents will shell out just for bragging rights and a piece of plywood splattered with glitter-glue."

"What a great idea! Is that dad at school again this year?"

"Let me think…yes. Harry Rivers. He's a Seeds Group dad."

"And these volunteers—would I be in charge of them? Giving them tasks and directing them?"

"Exactly. It's all about delegation! You're a full-time mom, correct?"

"Yes."

"Perfect. You'll be plugged into your new school and Margaret will see what an amazing person you are and the job will be easy-peasy. See? I knew this was just a misunderstanding. Fabulous!"

"Okay, I think this will work out." She didn't want to run the auction, of course, but the opportunity to boss Harry around was too appealing to pass up. He would hate it. It was the perfect storm.

The wail in the background started up again. "Listen, thanks for calling and congratulations, Madame Chair. I'll be in touch about our first meeting. Kiss-hug!" With an electronic *squelch*, the call ended.

"All righty then." Justine dropped the phone back into its charging cradle.

Greg walked out of the guest room, which doubled as a home office, holding a pen and a yellow sticky note. "Did you straighten her out?"

"Pretty much." She began rinsing plates to load in the dishwasher.

"What does 'pretty much' mean?"

"Well, it turns out the job won't be as time-consuming as I thought. It's more of a supervisory position."

"The last time I heard that was when you got roped into running the firm's carpooling program. You ended up working longer hours than the first-year lawyers." He took a piece of bread from the wire basket on the counter and bit into it. "As I recall, that project culminated in your taping a *Scarface* poster to your office door."

There were times when Justine wished she had met Greg somewhere other than at the office.

"Whatever. I needed to set the tone. Who knew everyone would get so competitive about a little carpool contest?" She scraped leftovers from a plate into the trashcan. "Upgraded parking does dark things to people."

"I'm just saying, we've got two years ahead of us at this place. I see no reason for you to take on the school's biggest job on your first day there."

Justine ripped a sheet of aluminum foil off the roll. "It turns out it's going to be a lot more fun than I thought it was."

"Well, as long as you're cool with it. Just don't let them turn you into one of these over-scheduled über-moms we keep hearing about, okay?"

"It's not going to be like that, I—" She was interrupted by the doorbell. "Eight fifteen at night? Really?"

"That must be the messenger," Greg said. "I'm expecting a depo transcript." Before he could make it out of the kitchen, the doorbell rang again, followed by a loud knocking.

"Oh my God," Justine said, "they're going to wake the ladybug!" *And then I will beat them to death with their own femurs*, she thought as she bolted toward Emma's room to close her door. Greg trotted to the front of the house and Justine reached for Emma's doorknob just as she woke up crying. "Aw, it's okay, little girl," she cooed and walked over to the crib to begin The Procedure, Greg's nickname for their Ferber protocol. After five minutes of verbal reassurance and stuffed-animal rearranging, it was safe for Justine to slip out of the room and close the door behind her.

"Frickin' messenger almost took the whole door down," she said before realizing Greg was not in the kitchen. She dumped the last few peas into the sink and, just before she flipped the disposal switch, stopped. Where were those voices coming from? Was Greg giving the messenger a hard time for waking Emma? She looked out the kitchen door toward the front room and heard the voices again. He was talking to a woman, probably Mrs. Reese from across the street who loved to chat while looking at the view from the top of their steps. *Perfect,* Justine thought, *I can finally return her husband's drain snake.* She ducked into the utility room, hoisted the stack of steel coil, and headed toward the entryway. When she opened the front door, she saw Greg leaning against the metal railing next to Simone.

They both turned and Greg gave her a puzzled look. "Is something clogged?" He glanced down at the coil in her hand. "In the yard?"

Simone giggled.

"Oh. Hello," Justine said, ignoring Greg's question. Simone wore an immaculately tailored blue-gray suit that showcased her blue-gray eyes—and her cleavage—beneath professionally arched brows. *No one looks that good at the end of a workday,* Justine thought as she shifted the heavy coil in her hands. *She's like a walking headshot.* Justine looked down to see trails of rust across the front of her sweatpants.

"Greg, you never told me Justine was so handy around the house." Simone crossed her arms and lounged against the rail. "Lucky you."

Greg gave an uncomfortable laugh.

"What brings you to our neighborhood?" Justine said to Simone. "I thought your boyfriend lived up in Bel-Air, right? That elderly gentleman?"

Simone opened her mouth to reply, but Greg interrupted.

"Simone was nice enough to drop off the depo transcript herself." He shot a warning look at Justine. "It was very thoughtful of her."

"Yes, that's very thoughtful," Justine said. "Just a tip for next time, though: if you're going to be a messenger to partners' houses, it's best just to leave the package quietly in case there are children sleeping. I guess you wouldn't know that, though, since it's kind of a *mom* thing."

Simone took her time looking Justine up and down. "You're right about that," she said with a smirk, "I am definitely *not* a mom."

"*Allll* right, well, thanks for dropping this off." Greg pushed the front door open and waved Justine through with the manila envelope before she could reply to Simone. "See you at the office, then," he said before shutting the door.

Justine stalked into the family room with Greg on her heels.

"What was that?" he asked.

"You tell me. Since when do lawyers spend their evenings running messenger errands?"

"I'm sure it was on her way home," he said.

"She lives in the *marina*, Greg. In the opposite direction." She stopped and sniffed the air. "Ew. I can still smell her perfume. What is that, the new Rachel Uchitel? I recognize it from Costco."

"Nice." He took the drain snake from her and she followed him back to the utility room. "She was only taking care of a task," he said as he set the metal coil on the floor next to the washer.

Justine studied his face, remembering his posture on the rail next to Simone. "I think she was rude."

"If you ask me, neither one of you covered yourself in glory on the porch tonight. Then again, when you have the kind of hypnotic effect on women that I have, you get used to ugly scenes like that." He gave her an exaggerated smile.

Justine threw up her hands. "You think you get it, but you don't." She walked back into the kitchen, picked up the sponge, and started scrubbing a plate.

"Come on. I hear what you're saying, but there's nothing to get upset about." Greg spread the newspaper on the island and began scanning it. "Believe me, I know how Simone operates. What she doesn't know is that she's going to work harder on this case than she's worked since passing the bar. By the end of the trial, she's going to hate my guts."

"Mmhmm." Justine wiped the countertop, her back to Greg. "Whatever."

"This isn't worth fighting about." Greg turned the newspaper page.

"I totally agree." Justine walked into the dining room and straightened the chairs, then replaced the painted Italian bowl that sat in the middle of the table when they weren't eating. She loved that bowl. It had been Ruthie's wedding present to them and, with its vibrant colors and elegant silhouette, was her favorite of all the gifts.

"By the way," Greg called from the kitchen, "I told you I have to go to Denver for a depo, right?" She heard him dropping ice cubes into a glass.

"No." *This is classic Greg,* she thought. Now he would act like the fight never happened. She ran her hand across the wavy wooden table top, guiding a pile of crumbs into her palm. The table aggravated her. They had been told by the salesman that it was made out of reclaimed antique lumber from England, only to find out later—when the top began to warp and the store was out of business—that it was in fact made in Mexico with uncured pine.

"It's just one night. I'm going to knock it out while the rest of the team stays here to work on discovery."

"When exactly are you going?"

"The twentieth." She heard a *glugg*ing sound as he filled his glass from the water jug next to the refrigerator.

Justine pictured Harry's postcard sitting on her dresser, the date figured prominently in maroon ink. His show was the same night as Greg's trip.

He shuffled past her in socks on the way to the bedroom. "Maybe you should make plans with a friend or something."

"Yeah." She brushed the crumbs from her hands with a *clapp*ing sound. "Maybe I will."

13
Justine

Justine was suspicious of knitting.

She stood in the Garden of Happiness kitchen with the other transitioning moms, watching the rhythmic finger flicks of a woman knitting a sweater for her son, the heather-blue sleeve lengthening with the smooth progress of beef cranked through a grinder. It wasn't that she was anti-crafting. While pregnant with Emma, she had surprised both Greg and her own mother by taking her work-friend Irene up on her suggestion that they enroll in a quilting class at a shop in Westwood. She discovered she loved working with the pieces of fabric and found the mathematical regularity of creating Emma's baby quilt satisfying, and even soothing. Buoyed by this minor success, she'd decided to try knitting which, it turned out, was the opposite of quilting in the same way that open-heart surgery was the opposite of a shiatsu massage. She finally conceded defeat one night on the sofa when, unleashing a cluster of expletives, she ripped out yet another chain of sad, misshapen stitches. As she gathered the mound of bent yarn in her lap, she became aware that Greg was convulsed with silent laughter next to her—a risky move considering the two sharpened, aluminum prongs in her hands.

On second thought, Justine wasn't sure if it was this woman's knitting prowess in the face of her personal yarn fail that made her uncomfortable, or the information Knitting Mom was sharing with the other mommies about a blog post she'd read called "The Six Signs He's Cheating."

"I'm serious, you guys." She stopped to check a set of perfectly symmetrical stitches. "They're totally normal things you would never think about."

"Such as?" said a woman with tortoiseshell glasses and an artfully mussed bun. The note of urgency in her voice caused the others to turn and look at her. "What? I'm just curious."

"Like he suddenly goes to the ATM a lot, especially in new parts of town," Knitting Mom said. "Or he starts paying a lot of attention to his appearance—working out more, losing weight, fussing with his hair." Justine nibbled a baby carrot and pictured the pair of suit pants draped over the back of the chair in their bedroom—the ones Greg had asked her to have taken in because they were "falling off of him."

"But that's totally reasonable," she said to the group before catching herself.

"Of course," Knitting Mom said, adjusting the sleeve flowing across her lap before resuming production, "but then you read the *comments* on the blog post and, let me tell you, it opens your eyes."

The moms murmured among themselves.

"*Seventy-four* comments from women who said they wished they'd paid more attention to those exact signs. And most of them said their husbands were good guys with no history of cheating."

Justine thought of the stack of ATM receipts Greg had left next to the computer and bit the baby carrot in two. Then again, how much extra time had she spent in the bathroom lately, scrutinizing her brows and minimizing her pores? Had Greg noticed that? She knew the answer to that question was "no" because, well, he was a man. He had, however, commented on the brochure from the local branch of 36-Hour Fitness that she'd left sitting on the kitchen island.

This is stupid, she thought. *Greg's not that guy.* There he was, though, just two nights before, lounging with Simone on the rail of their front porch. They had looked quite comfortable together. That is, until Justine interrupted them.

"Let's start with the fact that you shouldn't take marriage advice from some random blogger," said a mom whom Justine had never heard address the group before. She'd seemed aloof during transition, keeping to herself and wearing a lot of complicated knitwear. Apparently the conversation had moved into her area of expertise, however, because she now seemed compelled to speak from her corner of the booth. "It's all about strategy. First off, the moment you smell trouble, you start interviewing divorce lawyers. I mean the *good* ones—the ones you don't want *him* to be able to hire. Once they've talked with you, they can't represent him because there's a conflict of interest." As she spoke, the kitchen became silent. Even Knitting Mom's needles stopped clicking. "Of course, it goes without saying that you've been keeping your eye on the Ten Year Rule, so if and when it all goes south, you can rely on that eternal silver lining."

A mom in a sky-blue sari raised her hand. "Excuse me, but I keep hearing about this 'Ten Year Rule.' Can you please elaborate on that?"

"That's what I was about to ask," said a mom next to Justine.

"She should teach a class at the Learning Annex," said another.

"The Ten Year Rule? I like to call it 'the light at the end of the tunnel.'" Expert Mom smiled at the room and adjusted the sunglasses perched on top of her head. "It says that once you've been married ten years, you're entitled to alimony *forever*. Unless, of course, you remarry."

As more hands shot up, Justine felt a buzz in her pocket and realized she'd neglected to turn off her phone. She didn't recognize the number but decided to risk breaking the no-phone rule and take the call. She stepped into the unoccupied playroom next to the kitchen and crouched down inside a toddler-sized plastic post office.

"Hello?" she said, keeping her voice down.

"Hey. It's Bette. I was expecting voicemail. Aren't you in transition right now?"

"Oh. Hi, Bette. Yeah. I'm hiding."

"Well, keep your head down because those fink moms will rat you out for a phone infraction the first chance they get."

"Uh, okay." *Bette approaches preschool the way other people approach a CIA extraction,* she thought.

"I'll keep it short and sweet. I am inviting you to lunch, per my obligation as your official Garden Gnome. Are you in?"

Good Lord, Justine thought, *I've received jury summons that were more heartfelt.* "How can I turn down an invitation like that?" she said with a laugh. Bette did not respond. "Yes. Thank you. I am in."

"All right, then. Let me check my availability."

Justine heard papers shuffling in the background. She peeked out the red, plastic window. No teachers in sight, but she would pick a different hiding place next time; the inside of the little post office smelled like bottom.

"Dammit," Bette said. "I can't do it until next month. The first week might work, but I don't have the file with my travel dates." The shuffling sounds stopped. "I'm going to have to email you when I have that information, Justine. I apologize for the inefficiency."

"No worries, we'll figure it out. Thanks for the invite." *The "mandatory" is implied.*

"There you are, Mrs. Underwood." Justine froze at the melodic voice of Miss Glenda.

"Bette, I gotta go," she whispered into the phone. "I've been cheesed." She looked out the window again and there was Miss Glenda in her nylon track pants and spotless white sweatshirt.

"Just where they said you'd be." She scowled. "If you could kindly come out now."

Justine tried to act nonchalant as she crawled out of the miniature building and got to her feet. "Just where *who* said I would be?"

"The other mommies."

"The other mommies *tattled* on me?" Bette was right. She started to put her phone away, but Miss Glenda held up a finger to stop her.

"I'll need you to power off your mobile, please. Completely." She stood blocking the doorway to the kitchen as if she were prepared to wait all day for Justine to comply. Wavering between resentment at being scolded and mortification at being busted, Justine powered off her phone.

Miss Glenda waited until she had Justine's full attention. "Margaret would like to speak with you."

"Is it Emma? Is everything all right?"

"She didn't share the nature of her request with me." Miss Glenda walked into the kitchen with Justine on her heels and began setting out stacks of paper napkins decorated with rainbow-colored turtles. She worked with intensity, as if she were much too high-ranking to monitor Margaret's parent conversations. "She's waiting in her office."

Justine looked around the kitchen at the other mommies who had stopped talking when she entered the room. *Tools,* she thought.

"Dead mom walkin'," she heard one of them say as she stepped out onto the deck.

Justine had never been summoned to Margaret's office, but she couldn't imagine that she or Emma could be in serious trouble *already*. Emma had had another skirmish the previous day—a disagreement with Miss Glenda about sitting crisscross applesauce for the duration of story time—but that wouldn't warrant a private conference with Margaret, would it? At the top landing, the ocean breeze filtered through the branches of the massive willow that stood by the stairs. She knocked on the door, which opened within seconds.

"Yes?" Margaret said.

"Hi, Margaret. Miss Glenda said you wanted to see me?"

Margaret forced a smile with such effort that Justine half-expected to hear a mechanical grind of gears as the corners of her mouth moved upward. "Yes." She released the doorknob and walked toward her desk, motioning for Justine to sit on the denim sofa next to a throw pillow hand-embroidered with the words, "We ♥ Garden of Happiness. Love, The Neff Family."

Margaret opened the bottom drawer of a filing cabinet and started flipping through it. "Is this about Emma?" Justine said.

"Emma Underwood is finding her way," Margaret said, her eyes on the files, "unlike two other children in Seeds who are making life difficult for Miss Glenda." She stopped and gazed out the window. "Occasionally I make exceptions in the admissions process—selections that are contrary to my instincts." She looked at Justine. "I eventually regret it. Every time."

Justine wondered if Margaret were saying this for her benefit. Had Emma been one of her exceptions? Had Justine?

"Here it is." Margaret tugged a thick, green folder out of the drawer. "Willow Neff reminded me that I still had some auction papers up here, so I'm giving them to you directly." She retrieved her reading glasses from the end of their chain and placed them on her nose. "Now that you're our new auction savior, that is," she said with a half smile.

"'Auction savior'?" Justine laughed. "But no pressure, right?"

"The former chair made a commitment to me a year in advance, then failed to live up to it."

"Oh, that's too bad."

"I should have known better than to assign our most important event to an anxious parent. A parent's anxiety always manifests in the child. As soon as I started conveying my auction expectations to this particular mother, the child began to display unacceptable behaviors. Before long, I had to recommend that the family seek counseling to help correct the problem at home. We refer families in need to an excellent therapist here in Santa Monica."

Justine wondered what kind of behaviors they were talking about. "And that didn't help?"

Margaret slammed the file drawer. "The family refused to see the therapist and the situation deteriorated. They're no longer at the school, but in the end, everyone finds their place."

"I see." *This conversation could use a little haunted-mansion organ behind it.*

"It happens." Margaret swiveled toward her computer, scrolled through several documents and clicked her mouse. When the printer started up, she turned back to Justine, making a noticeable effort to perk up. "But I'm sure that's all behind us now that you're at the helm." Justine noticed that Margaret's smile lacked the little eye wrinkles that conveyed sincerity.

"You bet," Justine said. "Once you've convinced six hundred actuaries to do the Macarena in the middle of Universal City Walk, you can pretty much handle any occasion, right?"

"I'm sure you'll find our event much less challenging," Margaret said. "It's very simple, really. There's dinner and dancing, and the silent auction. Last year we had a little over four hundred items—an all-time record and something to shoot for. There's also the live auction, which is always the highlight of the evening. Everyone seems to be auctioning off purebred puppies these days, but I've always dreamed of offering something that none of the other schools have ever had. Maybe a share of a private jet, or a role in a Spielberg film—a small role, of course. Not the lead. Do you have any thoughts on theme?"

"A theme for the event? Uh, not just yet. Still letting the ideas percolate, you know."

Margaret handed her a piece of paper still warm from the printer.

"Here are the fundraising totals from last year's auction." She tapped the number at the bottom of the last column. "That's where we came out in the end—another record. Again, something to shoot for."

Justine glanced over the paper. "Great."

"Of course, what matters most to me is that everyone has a lovely evening. I'm so grateful for my amazing committee parents and their expertise. After all, I'm just an educator. Is everything clear for now?"

"I think so, yes. I'll go through this file and talk details with Willow."

Margaret's phone rang and she picked it up, scowling as she listened. "I'm on my way," she said, then smacked the handset back into its cradle and walked briskly toward the door. "Bring your things. I'll need you to lock up behind you."

Justine grabbed her purse. "Is everything all right?" she asked when she reached the door.

Margaret was already three steps down the flight of stairs. "Our resident supermodel has arrived."

"I don't get it," Justine said, yanking the door shut.

Margaret hit the landing, her kilt swinging as she turned the corner. "Paparazzi."

Justine followed Margaret's path across the deck toward the school entrance and stood next to a paint-splattered easel while Margaret stepped across the threshold and beyond her line of sight. The space above the outdoor enclosure's wall and the yellow door seemed to sparkle, and beyond it she could hear Margaret's voice.

"You are on private property, gentlemen. Step back!"

The shimmer above the wall intensified and the door burst open. Justine shielded her eyes from the flashes, but could not look away from the throng of shouting people. Margaret stood, arms spread, in front of a half-dozen photographers who were taking photos as they yelled over one another.

"Cienna! Over here!"

"Any comment on the divorce rumors?"

"Let's get one with the kid, Cienna!"

A woman and young girl slipped through the yellow door behind Margaret. Within seconds, the door slammed, shutting out the camera flashes that left green circles floating in Justine's vision. She saw Miss Glenda station herself in front of the door as Margaret escorted the blond woman, svelte and polished, past the picnic tables and toward the center of the school. Holding the woman's hand was her daughter who, aside from the size difference, could have passed for her twin. She looked like a replica built on a one-fifth scale.

That's Cienna Chadwick, Justine thought, *the one Ruthie's always talking about.* "They called her 'Chadwitch' when she was on that reality show," Ruthie had said. She had seen the daughter's name on the group roster: Cymphony.

"I'm working with the city to get a permit to build a privacy enclosure in front of the school," Justine could hear Margaret saying as the trio approached. Cienna did not respond.

The two women could not have been more different. Margaret's modified Sandy Duncan haircut, square kilt, and chunky loafers were in stark contrast to Cienna's tousled mane, low-rider jeans, and delicate metallic sandals. Justine noticed that the little girl also wore shiny sandals—a flagrant Garden of Happiness dress-code violation.

Two boys darted by wearing foam animal masks, roaring and chasing each other around the picnic tables. They sped past the easel, knocking it across the walkway and directly into the path of the oncoming supermodel. Cienna and Margaret reached the blocked walkway as Justine stepped forward to return the easel to its spot. "Excuse *us*," Cienna said to Justine with an impatient exhale, her eyes hidden behind expansive sunglasses.

"You're excused," Justine said, and dragged the easel out of the way, its legs scraping shrilly against the concrete. By the time she looked up again, Cienna and her entourage were out of sight.

Justine straightened the paint pots in the easel's tray. "Excuse *us*," she mimicked under her breath with a hiss and tossed a handful of wooden paintbrushes back into their coffee can. She looked up to see Harry smiling at her from under one of the picnic table umbrellas.

"Okay, you have to stop sneaking up on me." She went back to tidying the easel. Why was he always around?

"Who's sneaking? I'm here on official Garden of Happiness business."

"Oh, *really*."

"Check it." He reached into his messenger bag and pulled out a copy of *The Lion and the Little Red Bird*. "One word: storytime."

"I *love* that book." She took it from him and flipped through the pages. "But bad news, bro," she said without looking up, "story time is two words."

"No way."

"Way." She handed the book back to him. "Try not to slosh any of your intellect on the kids, mm-kay?"

"Sure, I'll try not to dumb 'em down too much. Thanks for that. So, are you coming to my show?"

"When is it again?"

"Geez, didn't you read the invitation?"

"Hello?" Justine tapped her temple with a finger. "If I retain everything I read, I might forget our nation's nuclear launch codes. Or how to make Play-Doh on my stovetop."

"It's a week from Thursday," Harry said, a tinge of irritation in his voice.

"Um... I can probably do that if the sitter's available and if Greg gets home from work on time. You know, so he can come with me." She slung her purse over her shoulder. "I'll see what I can do."

"You could come with a friend if the hubs is too busy." He flicked his hair. "Do you ever hear from Ruthie? Are you guys still in touch?"

Yeah, she hates your frickin' guts. "Sure, we're still tight."

"Tell her she's invited, too."

"I'll pass that along." She snapped her fingers. "I just realized I might have a meeting that night. I'm waiting to hear from Willow about it." She watched Harry's smile fade. "I don't know if you heard, but I've been made chair of this year's fundraising auction." *This is where he figures out that I'll be supervising him*, she thought. She mentally rubbed her hands together in anticipation.

"You're kidding, right?"

"No, I'm not kidding."

"I hate to tell you this, but you're screwed." He shook his head. "That Willow, I swear. When it comes to preschool poxes, she's right up there with head lice."

"It can't be that bad," Justine said, her anticipation fading.

"Did you hear what happened to the last person who had that job? Margaret didn't like her ideas and when the woman wouldn't let it go, Margaret kicked her out of the school."

This sounded eerily like the flipside of the story Margaret had told her upstairs, but she shook it off. "C'mon, you just don't want me bossing you around on that art project of yours."

"Are you kidding? I would *love* to be bossed around by you." He grinned. "And speaking of you…" He flipped open the messenger bag again. "Look what I found." He pulled out a worn, leather journal.

Justine's hand went to her mouth. "Oh my God."

"So you remember it," he said.

Of course I remember it, you moron. She breathed out slowly through her nose. "Yes."

"Our everlasting hangman game. We used to take this thing everywhere, even on the cable car in the city. You were so cute, always

nibbling on the tip of the pencil when you were trying to stump me."
He thumbed through the pages, smiling.

"Where did you find it?"

"In some boxes in my garage."

"You kept it all this time?"

He looked up at her, cocking his head to the side. "Of course I did." He stared at her for a moment, then flipped farther through the pages, stopping on one toward the back. "This was the day before I left for Chicago."

"What is it?"

"I made this sketch of you in the margin, see?" He held the journal out to her, but she already knew what she would see on the page.

"Harry Rivers." They both turned to see Margaret motioning from the top of the kitchen steps. "Are you ready to join the reading circle?"

"*Doo*-die calls," he said with exaggerated pronunciation, then slapped the journal shut and held it out to Justine.

"What are you doing?"

"Didn't you see the last page?" His smile was mischievous. "It's your turn."

"Yeah, right."

"Come on." He set the journal on the picnic table. "It'll be fun." He walked away toward the kitchen, leaving her standing beneath the umbrella and wondering if she'd imagined his wink.

14
Margaret

Autumn arrived with the punishing, arid gusts that signaled the beginning of the dry season in Southern California. "The Santa Anas are here," the mommies said to one another as they plucked their T-shirts away from their moist torsos and fanned their faces with the latest edition of the school newsletter, the *Garden of Happiness News Beet*. Blasting down from the mountains without warning, the scorching Santa Ana winds seemed to pull the breath from the body, agitating even the most tranquil of dispositions.

It was Margaret's favorite time of year.

She loved the sensation of her hair whipping away from her cheeks and the fierceness of the heat that shot into the house at night no matter how slightly she cracked the window. While everyone else seemed to be made of clay, melting away as they moved down the sidewalk toward the school, Margaret thrived under the assault.

"What *is* it with you?" Trey said and mopped his forehead with a paper towel from the kitchen roll. "If I didn't know better, I'd say you were made of asbestos. Wait," he said, "*do* I know better?"

Margaret poured boiling water into her oversize mug of oatmeal. "Why are you looking at me like that?" she snapped.

"Hot oatmeal? Really?" He reached for his steel water bottle on the counter and took a long drink from it. "That is only going to fuel speculation among the parents that you are, in fact, Satan."

The kitchen phone began to ring. Margaret stirred her oatmeal and watched Trey as he peeled the wrapper from a piece of string cheese and bit the end off of it, chewing methodically and leaning on the counter with one hand. On the fourth ring he looked at Margaret, who raised her eyebrows and tilted her head toward the phone on the wall.

"Oh, excuse *me*," he said. "I believe the rule is that whoever is closest gets it, but *whatever*." He stomped across the kitchen and picked up the handset. "Garden of Happiness!" he barked through a mouthful of cheese. "*Who*?" he said, then listened, looking up at the ceiling. "Let me see if there's anyone here by that name." He held the handset to his chest and turned to Margaret. "It's for you."

"Oh, for God's sakes, Trey, what's the matter with you?" She reached for the phone. "Who is it?"

"Someone named Seth. He sounds deeply disturbed." He held the handset out to her. "I'd record the call if I were you."

At the sound of her lawyer's name, Margaret withdrew her hand. "I'll take it in your office."

"Oh, really?" Trey said, his eyes narrowing. "I am, shall we say, *intrigued*."

"Just put it on hold."

"Hello, Seth," she said after sliding Trey's door closed behind her.

"That's some receptionist you've got there. I'm guessing you found him through a prison work-release program?"

"If only it were that simple."

"Sorry to call on your work line, but I couldn't reach you on your cell and this is time-sensitive."

"I was hoping the period of silence since our last conversation was a positive sign."

"I'm afraid not. We bought ourselves some time by challenging the other side's position, and believe me, I threw up every roadblock we've got. The bottom line, though, is that your husband's lawyers are immovable on the school being part of the divorce settlement. As I said before, it was a long shot."

Margaret's shoulders sagged and she banged her mug down on Trey's desk, sending a blob of oatmeal over the rim and onto his blotter. "Well, can't you push harder?"

"It's no use. They'll get a judge to rule on it and I guarantee it'll go against us. The legal precedents are solidly on their side."

"That's very disappointing." She sank into Trey's chair.

"And so we press on."

"Bastard," Margaret said under her breath.

"Excuse me?"

"Not directed at you, Seth. I was just reminiscing about Eddie."

"Understood. It's not the first time I've encountered that particular term of endearment in my practice." His voice was warm. "Moving on, the next step is to make financial arrangements to buy Eddie out of the property. We talked about the possibility of your obtaining a second mortgage. Unless, of course, you have another source of funding."

"No," Margaret said. "There's no other source."

"Very well. Have you had a chance to begin securing a second?"

Margaret exhaled loudly. "There's not going to be a second."

"I don't get your meaning, Margaret."

"I *mean*, I will not be able to arrange a second mortgage because I took one out on the school two years ago."

"Hold on—you never told me the school was already leveraged."

"It's none of anyone's business."

"Eddie doesn't know about this, either?"

"Why would he? He's had *nothing* to do with this school. I took out the loan and reinvested it in improvements. That's what business owners are supposed to do."

It was Seth's turn to huff into the phone. "Margaret, you make it difficult for me to do my job when you do not give me all the facts."

"Frankly, Seth, I was expecting you to do your job and make this problem go away without my having to divulge the intimate details of my business."

"I'm your lawyer!" Seth blurted, then became quiet. "Before I end this call, I need to ensure that you grasp the seriousness of your predicament. If you are unable to raise the cash to buy Eddie out of his half of your school, the property will have to be sold and half the proceeds given to him in order to settle the divorce. Therefore, if you do not wish to sell the school property, it's imperative that you secure funding from any source you can."

"Thank you for the dire warning, Seth, but I can assure you I will not allow the school to be sold."

"I hope your confidence is well placed. I'll be in touch."

"Good-bye," she said and hung up. She knew Seth had done all he could, but she was right back where she had started, and it was intolerable. How had she misjudged Eddie to such an extent? It was truly vexing when people failed to live down to her expectations. She should have realized that something was different about him that night when he confronted her in the kitchen. New Eddie had acquired a relentlessness she would not have thought possible, and it had taken a $150 phone call to make her see it. She would not make that mistake again.

"Shit," she said, pushing the sweaty bangs off her forehead as the heat in the office closed in on her. She sank farther into the chair, her stomach churning at the realization that Eddie had pulled it off: she was actually going to have to pay him for the privilege of keeping her school. She pressed the heels of her hands to her eyes as another thought occurred to her—one that she had done her best to avoid until now: where the hell was she going to get that money?

"Margaret?"

She turned to see Cienna Chadwick, Supermodel, in the doorway looking effortlessly breathtaking in skinny jeans and a silk blouse.

"What can I do for you, Cienna?" Margaret said briskly. She was in no mood to tolerate any emotional terrorism by the glitterati. If Cienna wanted preferential treatment on parking or some other school matter, she could take it up with Trey and good luck to her.

"I just..." she began, her voice wobbly. "I mean I wanted to thank you for helping me with Cymphony and her eating." She closed her mouth and shook her head, fanning her eyes with her hand as she teared up. "Your advice. You helped me. A lot." She waved at her face some more as the tears tracked down her flawless cheeks. "Just...*thank you*." She hovered in the doorway and wiped her chin with the back of her hand.

"Oh." Margaret ripped two tissues from a box on the filing cabinet. "Well, here." She handed her the Kleenex. "You're quite welcome. Just a matter of being consistent and following through on consequences at every meal." *Excellent*, Margaret thought. *I knew Cym could do it—and a week earlier than I predicted. Once the parents are under appropriate supervision, the children almost always flourish.*

"You can't imagine what a difference it's made in our house at mealtimes." Cienna somehow made nose-wiping look like the *Sports Illustrated* swimsuit issue.

"I'm very glad to hear it," Margaret said. "Thanks for letting me know your progress."

"Sure," she said with a stuffy laugh as she dabbed at her eyes. "Like I said, I just wanted to say thanks. See you later."

Margaret stood in the doorway and watched Cienna pick her way through the class of children that had spilled into the main room. Once again, her expectations of others had been exceeded. If this trend continued, she was going home early.

She slid the door shut behind her and made her way through the clusters of children and out the kitchen door. The sandy play area was, as always during school hours, controlled chaos. Today the teachers had supervised the digging of a large hole, which had then been filled with water dyed green with food coloring. A small girl stood in the center of the hole in a pink, velour tracksuit with the words "Juicy Couture" spelled out on its front in sequins. She was knee high in the green water, which absorbed farther up her pant legs with each stomp of her foot. *Preschool is for making messes*, Margaret regularly preached to parents. *That is the child's job. If your child doesn't leave school filthy, they're not doing it right.*

As she skirted the play area, she reminded herself not to look up at the office building next door. For almost a decade, she had routinely glanced up at Eddie's office window during her workday to see if she could get a glimpse of him and share the two-fingered wave they had exchanged since college. For the first few years after opening the school, Margaret would feel a little *zing* whenever she caught sight of him in his robin's-egg-blue smock. The color suited him and the smock's boxy shape only enhanced his muscular build. As the years passed, the little *zing* had evolved from somewhat bashful marital lust to a hard shell of possessiveness. When the mothers and teachers commented on the sweetness of their next-door arrangement, Margaret felt a different glow—one that came from knowing she had something others valued, or even coveted.

Toward the end of their marriage, Eddie had kept the window blinds tilted at an angle that obscured the view from campus. The last few times Margaret had looked there, she had seen only the rippled reflection of the play structure and the dull gray of her school's roof. Like a dog discovering an invisible fence, the pain induced by that new boundary had quickly extinguished the habit.

She was halfway across the deck to her office stairs when Trey appeared through a classroom doorway and began speed-walking toward her. "A word, maestro," he said, motioning for her to follow him.

"I don't have time right now, Trey, I have to attend to an urgent matter."

"I'll see your urgent matter and raise you a hissy fit," he said, and swooped into the empty art room.

"Oh, here we go," Margaret said under her breath and reluctantly followed him inside. "What is it?" she said, hands on hips.

"Miss Glenda has informed me that yesterday—after you left and I went to take the donated lunches to the homeless shelter—a woman talked her way through the front gate. She said she had arranged with you to make a visit to the school."

"No one made any arrangement with me."

"*Naturellement*, but you know how flustered these preschool teachers become around a fancy-talking grown-up flashing a business card, the poor dears."

"She left a card?"

Trey pulled a business card from his shirt pocket with a flourish. "She's an appraiser."

"Yes," Margaret said, reading the woman's information.

"She appraised the school."

"Thank you for the clarification, Trey." She turned the card over in her hands and recalled the email from Eddie's lawyers. They expected her to schedule an appraisal, too, so they could average the two and set the market value of the property for the buy out. *It'll be a cold day in Van Nuys before that happens*, she thought, and tore up the card.

"I can tell you're upset," Trey said. "Let me help by firing Miss Glenda myself. It's no trouble."

"What?" Margaret looked up at him. "No! No one's getting fired."

"Drat."

"Here." She deposited the paper shreds in his hand. "Go recycle those. Now, if you'll excuse me—" She started walking toward the door.

"So little Eddie Munster's making a play for the school. Does Leticia know about this?"

Margaret turned to face him again. "Not from me, she doesn't. I'm doing my best to shield her from the details of the divorce, although I don't seem to be able to shield *you* from them."

"When I see dots, I connect them," he said with a shrug. "Besides, it's all pretty simple—you take a second mortgage, you pay off Fast Eddie, and it's all over before Miss Glenda can say 'I don't own tweezers.' What's the big whoop?"

Margaret studied a watercolor of a rather depressed-looking bear drying on the table.

"Oh, no," Trey said. "But wait. You poured a new concrete tricycle yard last year. And you put central air in the classrooms *and* re-roofed the entire campus." His hand flew to his mouth. "You already took out a loan on the school!"

"Sshh!" she said, glancing at the doorway. "Keep your voice down."

"Oh, girlfriend," he said, eyes wide, "poopie just got real."

"No. Poopie is still quite *un*real, thank you very much. And, just so we're clear, you are *not* to share this information with Leticia under any circumstances. Do you understand? She's got enough to worry about with her midterms."

"I can keep a secret."

"No, you can't."

"Fair point, but I will keep *that* one. So what's our next step?"

"*Our* next step? No. *My* next step is to secure the necessary funding to pry Eddie's fingers off my school once and for all—which, naturally, I will find a way to do."

Just then, Willow and Justine passed by the art room in animated discussion, stopping on the deck just outside the classroom door. Margaret and Trey both watched them.

"Guess I know what you'll be doing with this year's auction money," he said in a low voice.

"That's absurd," Margaret said. "You know the auction only brings in a fraction of what I need."

"What I'm *saying* is, every little bit counts. You don't know what's going to happen and, come the revolution, I wouldn't want to be caught trying to find that last twenty-grand of loose change in the bottom of *my* handbag." He *tsk*ed and crossed his arms. "What a year to have a newbie mom running the auction." He nodded toward Justine. "Do you think she gets it?"

"What do you mean?"

"I mean, do you think she understands that her job is to keep you happy by working like a first-generation immigrant to raise as much money as humanly possible?"

"I don't know..." Margaret watched Justine smile and gesture wildly as she chatted with Willow. She thought back to their meeting about the auction. Had Justine's attitude seemed a little casual?

Both women burst out laughing, then walked farther down the deck and out of sight. Trey shook his head.

"All I'm saying is, if I were you, I would be all over her like Crème de la Mer on a reality-show housewife."

"Since I have no idea what you're talking about, I will accept your simile on good faith. And now I really must take care of something upstairs."

"You're going to call that banker of yours for another loan, aren't you?"

"Yes, Trey," she said in a tired voice and walked out of the art room toward the stairs. *More specifically*, she thought as a blast of arid wind tore through the play yard and rocked her back on her heels, *I'm going to call in a favor.*

15
Ruben

When Willow Neff, Garden of Happiness alpha mom, informed Ruben that the fundraising committee meetings were held at Fred Segal, he hoped she was referring to a bar, or at least a deli. This hope evaporated however, when he discovered he would be venturing into the retail epicenter of Westside mom hyper-cool. *Screw it*, he thought, *I'm already the sketchy misfit dad—how much worse can it get?*

Much worse, he realized as he pulled into the parking lot in his Subaru wagon and searched for a space among the gleaming Land Rovers, Mercedes, and Porsches already lining the rows. Walking into the store's tiny cafe, he saw Willow seated in the corner and a semicircle of women who had commandeered what looked like dollhouse tables and chairs to form a growing cluster around her.

How had this happened to him? He had been feeling pretty good about jumping right into his Sunflower duties on the first day of school. When he told Deandra about his committee assignment that night at dinner, however, she was unimpressed.

"It's cool that you signed up so quickly and all, but don't you think you should join a real committee?" She wiped applesauce from Harris' chin with a paper napkin.

"The Sunflowers *are* a real committee. They help people who are, you know, going through transitions…" He shifted in his chair, becoming uncomfortable that he was having this conversation at all. *I am Ruben, Sunflower advocate.*

"I know what the Sunflowers do and that's great. It's just that delivering an occasional grilled Caesar with the dressing on the side to a mom who's hiding out after her boob lift is not what I had in mind." She reached across the table and began cutting Lily's chicken on her plate. "I think fundraising would be a good spot for you."

"Wait," he said, "you hated that group."

"True, but it *is* the most powerful committee at the school. You know Margaret—she likes her money. Plus, all the Hollywoodies are on fundraising, so you could make some useful connections."

Ruben looked down at his plate. He was a terrible networker and he knew it. His most recent attempt was a disastrous conversation at the Improv with a producer during which Ruben somehow found himself on the topic of athlete's foot...and was unable to get off of it. *Athlete's foot.* He still didn't know how it had happened. His mind had simply locked up and the more baffled the man's expression became, the more Ruben pressed on involuntarily...*about a fungus.* His palms dampened at the memory of it.

"Yes," Deandra said with a smile, "you belong on the varsity team with the power moms."

"So that's my goal now—to become a power mom?"

"That's the dream," she said as a spoon full of mashed potatoes flew out of Lily's hands and landed on Ruben's jeans.

And this was the dream come true: sitting with a group of committee-hardened mommies while gripping a six-dollar latte and praying his flimsy pie tin of a chair didn't collapse under him. Unlike the Sunflowers, admission to the fundraising committee required no grasp of subtle procedural rules or distinctions, but rather a simple desire to join the team. "Oh, how I love a man who's not afraid of the F-word!" Willow had burst out when Ruben approached her about it in the kitchen. "Welcome to fundraising—you're in!" Power moms or not, fundraising was the committee equivalent of a sure thing.

"Oh, look, everyone," Willow said as she slapped a brown packet of raw sugar against her palm, "our one and only committee dad is here. Isn't he brave?"

"Hello," Ruben said, feeling the eyes of every woman in the circle on him.

"I'm sorry, what's your name again? I want to say Richard."

"Ruben."

"Right. Introduce yourself, Ruben." Willow's spoon made a metallic *clang* as she stirred the sugar into her coffee.

"I'm, um, I'm a comic." And, as happened every time he told people he was a comedian, they tilted their heads to an assessing angle. He could almost see their thought bubbles: *He doesn't* seem *funny*. Keeping a promise to himself, he added, "I'm also a writer." This appeared more believable to the women, whose heads now tilted in another, more receptive direction.

"Are you a novelist?" said a woman wearing patent leather booties and a Mr. T-worthy array of gold jewelry. "Have you written anything we've heard of?" All heads swiveled from the woman back to Ruben.

He thought of the notebook sitting in his backpack—where he'd written two-thirds of a first draft that he was pretty sure didn't suck and an outline for the rest—and immediately regretted having mentioned writing at all. "No, but I'm working on a TV project right now."

"Good for you," said a woman in a chunky, lavender sweater with stick-straight, platinum hair. "Are you at CAA? You might know my husband there."

"No..."

"Are you at WME, then?" asked another woman. "By the way, guys, they've just shot a pilot based on my last book." The group cooed their congratulations.

"Um, no, I don't actually have an agent yet. But I hope to soon."

The group recoiled, stunned at this blatant admission of non-success. "Oh...well," Willow said, "good on you." She looked around for help in moving on to a new subject. "Claire?" She pointed to a woman who was lovingly peeling the wrapper from a Zone Bar. "Didn't you say you had something to share with the group?"

The moms launched into a discussion about the recent proposal that would require families to purchase their children's artwork before taking it home. Ruben collapsed against the back of his chair, the group's attention off of him at last. He chided himself for not making a better impression, but at least he'd stayed away from the topic of athlete's foot.

An hour later, the continuous stream of non sequiturs had bludgeoned his mind into a near-stupor. Nothing had been planned or decided, and there was no apparent agenda for the meeting. He had gathered, however, that there was a face-off brewing between two of the snack moms in Soil Group, that everyone was scrambling to enroll their kids in swim classes at The Splash Company since they'd hired a half-dozen "delicious" UCLA water polo players as new instructors, and that Margaret's marriage was rumored to be "in a rough patch." Several of the moms expressed surprise at the last item.

"You guys," one of them replied, "haven't you noticed that she's been harsher than usual lately?"

"Is that even possible?" Ruben said, and laughter rippled through the group.

"Oh, snap," said the woman on his right, elbowing him in the arm and giving him a warm smile. Side conversations broke out as the moms speculated about the status of Margaret's relationship.

"Ladies, you know how Margaret is about her private life," Willow said.

"You talk to her more than any of us do, Willow," said a woman a few chairs away.

"I really couldn't say what's going on," Willow replied as she began to root around in a pocket folder covered in a pink leopard-skin pattern.

"*Confirmed*," a mom behind Ruben sang softly.

"Have you seen Eddie lately?" said another. "He looks pretty happy for a man who's supposedly having marital problems." Another mom responded with a knowing look.

"You're a man," said the woman on Ruben's left. "What's your take on it?" She had strawberry-blond hair that she'd twined into two low braids. The mom on her far side leaned in to listen.

"I don't know," Ruben replied. "We're not exactly...buds."

"Oh, come on," Braid Mom said. "Men can totally read other men. Give us your male intuition."

"Well," Ruben said, "I can tell you that I've taken Donnie and Marie there for a couple of their dental appointments—"

The other mom held up her hand to stop him. "I'm sorry...'Donny and Marie?'"

"Our twins. I have nicknames for them. You know, Donny and Marie, Captain & Tenille, Steve & Edye."

"That's funny," said the other women.

"Yes, yes," Braid Mom waved her away. "I want to hear what he thinks about Eddie."

"Right, well, I've taken Peaches and Herb there for a couple of appointments." Ruben glanced around then moved in closer to the two women. "Just between us, I thought he had kind of an attitude, you know? Like he thought he was pretty smooth."

"*Yes*," Braid Mom said, her eyes narrowing.

"Oh, I would *totally* agree with that," the other mom said with a nod. Ruben sat back and considered how easy it had been for him to sell out one of his own. *Sorry, man*, he thought, *all's fair in love, war, and preschool committees.*

"Moving on!" Willow bellowed.

Ruben checked his watch. Once again, his writing time was dribbling away. *This isn't a meeting at all*, he thought, *it's a marathon brunch/gab session.* If he were going to commit to Deandra's plan of infiltrating the power moms, however, he was going to have to embrace the vibe.

"I'm new on the committee, too," said the woman on his right, keeping her voice down.

"Yeah?" Ruben said. "What are you in for?"

The woman smiled. She wore a soft-pink, bateau-neck sweater and small gold hoops. She lifted a legal pad and stack of manila folders from her lap. "I'm chairing this year's auction. My name's Justine." She held out her hand. "I think it's cool you're a comic, by the way."

"Hey, thanks," Ruben said, returning her handshake.

"Excuse me," Braid Mom hissed across Ruben toward Justine. "Did you say you're chairing the auction?"

"Yes, she did," Ruben said, avoiding eye contact with Willow, who was glaring at the talkers.

"Hello," Justine said, giving Braid Mom a little wave.

"*Shh!*" Willow said in Ruben's direction.

The three of them stared silently ahead until Willow turned her attention to another section of the group, then Braid Mom spoke under her breath without turning. "Maybe the new auction mom can convince Willow to make her husband get us a decent emcee this year."

"Who's Willow's husband?" Ruben asked.

"Head of comedy programming at AMC."

"Really?"

"Oh, yes." She made a face. "A real charmer, too."

"Ah, got it." Ruben recalled the lean, brusque dad he'd seen at school with a cellphone welded to his face. This was a man who could make Ruben's career with a wave of his pinky toe. Ruben seized up with insecurity. Admitting in LA that you were born without the schmoozing gene was like admitting you hated sushi or that you listened to Milli Vanilli on your iPhone.

"Okay," Willow said to the group, "one last task before we all get back to our lives." She reached down next to her chair and began wrestling six stationery boxes from a Neiman Marcus shopping bag, thumping them onto the table one by one. "Which one of you angels can take care of our first fundraising mailing?" She looked around the tables as the committee members sprang into evasive action—pulling key chains from handbags, crumpling napkins into empty coffee cups, and studying PDA screens with the intensity of transplant patients awaiting organ donations. "I see. Well, scurry all you want, but the envelopes must be stuffed. Who's going to be my hero?" She looked around the tables again.

"I guess that would be me," Ruben said.

"Fabulous!" Willow squawked. "I can't call you 'goddess,' so I'll call you our official fundraising stud. How's that?"

"Just what I was hoping for." He gathered his things as the room erupted with the sounds of moving chairs.

"Nice going, stud," Justine said.

Willow motioned to Ruben. "Let me show you what I need." She ran her finger down the ends of the boxes and scowled. "Hmm, one of them must have fallen out in my car. Be a doll and wait here a minute."

"Do you want me to get it?"

"Would you?" She pawed through the formidable mustard hand-bag that was collapsed on the table, its contents threatening to dribble out of every stitched-leather orifice. "Silver Benz wagon," she said, holding out an enormous, mink pom-pom key chain and shaking it at him. "You're fabulous."

"Yes, I am," he muttered and pushed through the glass door to the parking lot. Outside, clusters of salespeople on their breaks smoked and showed off their tattoos and luxury eyewear in the late-morning sun. Ruben wove through the incoming customers—expensive-looking women of the sort that would wear a crystal-encrusted Bambi T-shirt without a whiff of irony. Ruben clutched the poufy key chain out of sight and tried to think of a way to make a connection with Willow's husband.

When he returned to the cafe, he found Willow hunched over the corner table, her back to the room and phone pressed against her ear. He could tell she was crying. The only thing worse than Deandra's tears were the tears of a woman he didn't know. At least with Deandra, he'd been around long enough to learn the ground rules: don't ask if she's all right; hugging is acceptable, but only if it's non-sexual; apologize immediately whether you know why she's crying or not; repeat as necessary. An encounter with an unknown crying woman was like trying to defuse a bomb while someone shouted instructions in Eskimo. Since the other committee moms had scattered, however, he had no choice but to approach without backup.

"I'm sorry," he heard Willow say into the phone, "but I'm doing the best I can." Ruben noticed the wad of makeup-smeared napkins in her hand. "Darling, I can fix this, all right? All I need to do is—" Suddenly, her head jerked away from the phone and she looked at the device, stunned. Ruben watched her face crumple as she slowly replaced the phone in her purse. He took a deep breath and forced himself to approach her.

Seeing Ruben, Willow snapped to attention, becoming hyper-animated again. "Here's our fundraising stud," she said with force and sat up straight. She ran her hands across the table, gathering the stray napkins into a clump, which she crunched into a tight ball between her palms.

"Are you all right?" Ruben held the stationery box against his hip like a schoolboy's books.

"Of course." She gave him a fierce smile, as if daring him to conclude differently. Her eyes were ringed with misshapen clouds of mascara.

"I'm just asking because it looked like you were—"

"You found the box." She dropped the napkin ball on the table and clapped her hands twice. "Fabulous. Now, sit here." She pointed at a chair across the table.

Ruben hesitated.

"No, really," Willow said. "*Sit.*"

Ruben sat.

"Wonderful," she said, and took the box, placing it on top of the stack. "This shouldn't take too much of your time, just a few hours." She sniffed noisily and ran a finger under her eye, which left a gray streak toward her temple. "And—oh my God—I just thought of something else! As soon as you've finished this task, I've got another little project for you to do."

"Fabulous!" Ruben said before he could catch himself, then grinned through the scrutinizing look Willow gave him in return.

16
Justine

While Justine couldn't say exactly what effect she was going for as she dressed for Harry's art show, she knew it wouldn't be found in the shopping bag Ruthie had been carrying when she showed up unannounced to "help."

"The light in your bathroom is too harsh," Ruthie said. She stood in front of the mirror with Justine, who was wearing outfit number three from the bag. "It's the combination of an all-white room and a skylight that does it."

"Yes, *that's* why I look like a cross between a cosmonaut and a Bolivian coal miner—all the *sunshine*." Justine frowned at the reflection of the black cargo pants, gray turtleneck, and khaki canvas coat.

"I like this on you." Ruthie turned Justine by the shoulders to see the back of the outfit. "It's relentlessly chic. Almost savage."

"Are we done here?" Justine went to the doorway to peek into the family room and check on Emma.

"It depends. Is that the outfit you're going with?"

"I'm going to say no, considering it would give Stanley Kubrick nightmares. And you've got me wearing *three* jackets. I've already sweated down a cup size."

"Okay, 'cruel chic' is off the list. That leaves 'global' and 'green.'"

"'Global' reminds me of that mannequin in the window at Cost Plus—the one that looks like the United Nations threw up on her." She began peeling off jackets. "Also, I don't think people wear sombreros to art galleries. At least, not after six o'clock."

"All right, then, 'green' it is. That trash-bag tunic is eco-fierce. And, hey, you can tell people your pants are upcycled. Artists love that shit."

"*Sshh!*" Justine looked into the family room again, but Emma was oblivious as she played restaurant on the coffee table with her set of plastic dishes and wooden food. Justine could only hear Emma's side of the conversation, but it sounded like she was refusing to make a substitution for an imaginary customer.

"You're killing me with this stuff." Justine went into the bedroom and Ruthie followed her. "And I know what you're doing, by the way."

"I'm sure I don't know what you're talking about." She rooted around in her shopping bag. "Let me find my copy of *Eastern European Vogue.* I think you'll agree that some of the looks on this fall's runway are quite fetching."

"Ruthie!" Justine said. "This is all very funny but stop trying to make me look bad for Harry's show. I'm going as a *friend.* It's not like I had my tube top and crotchless tights laid out when you got here." She slid open the closet door and flipped through the hangers, shoulders sagging. "Besides, even if I were *trying* to look good, this closet is a wasteland." No matter how creative she tried to be, all signs were pointing to the dreaded remains of her work clothes from law firm days. The only other options were her wedding dress and her mom clothes—an assortment of jeans, shorts and tops that, when considered against the backdrop of a trendy art gallery, morphed into the kind of misshapen rags associated with island castaways.

She pulled two hangers off the pole and held them up for Ruthie. "I'm going to have to go with this—the tragic black slacks and soul-crushing purple blouse." She tossed them across the bed. "Everyone's going to think I'm from Human Resources."

"Well, you know what they say," Ruthie moved a stack of upholstery fabric samples and settled into the chair by the window, "when you feel lousy about yourself, it's not even worth going out."

"Okay, *no one* says that."

"How great would it feel to slip on some sweats, order up some Chinese food, and have a girls' night in? Wait, what else do I have?" She pulled a DVD case from the bag and waved it in the air. "*Dirty Dancing*, hells yeah! No one puts Justine in the corner!"

"My mom's going to be here any minute to watch Emma." Justine stepped into the slacks. "Just come with me. It'll be hilarious—they're going to have food and live music and…we can *mock people*. I know how much you love that."

Ruthie thought about it. "I *do* love the mocking."

"See? It'll be great."

"No way, lady. And you shouldn't be going, either." She stood and began pacing the room. "I'll say it again: kryptonite guy."

Justine groaned. "C'mon, you like art, right?"

"Yes, I do. You, however, do not."

"Hey, I like art." She buttoned the blouse and slipped on her black pumps. "I think Harry would love to see you. Have you thought about that?"

Ruthie's laugh had a hard edge to it. "Not gonna happen."

"Why do you say that? You guys were friends."

"Oh, yeah, my *friend* who smoked your heart down to the filter, then tossed the butt—I mean *your* butt—out the window as he burned rubber out of town."

Justine's face went hot. "No need to sugarcoat it."

"Okay, then. Heed my words, Justine: stay away from him."

"Did you just say 'heed my words'? I think you should know that when you talk like that I picture you with a big wart on your nose, offering an apple to a hotter, younger woman who lives with dwarves."

Ruthie shrugged. "What can I say? We watch a lot of Disney." She followed Justine back into the bathroom. "By the way, I meant to ask earlier, but why do you have a mountain of random crap in the corner of your family room?"

"That would be auction merchandise."

"Parents are already dropping things off at your house?"

"That's nothing—I've already gotten two emails and three voice-mails from Margaret, wanting to know if we have a venue yet and reminding me that she expects one hundred percent participation from parents. And we just had our first committee meeting yesterday."

"Guess you'll be redecorating your bedroom *next* year. I'm sure Greg will be relieved that he gets to keep enjoying the dorm-room/ assisted-living ambiance you've got going in there."

"Very funny. Listen, it's going to take more than a preschool fundraiser to keep me from fixing that room. It was all I could do not to burn that plaid bedspread in effigy this morning."

"I know—instead of that dumb art show, why don't you stay home tonight and show me your design sketches again? I promise to remember the names of the paint chips this time."

Justine set her hairbrush on the counter. "I know you're watching out for me, and I appreciate it. But I've realized something: being at this school with Harry is a gift." Ruthie opened her mouth to speak but Justine kept talking. "Having him show up in my life again has given me a fresh perspective, and now I have true closure on that chapter."

Ruthie's expression softened. "You don't have anything to prove, Teenie. He's an asshole and he hurt you bad. It's as simple as that."

"I'm over all that—really." She leaned toward the mirror and brushed on her mascara. "I'm a different person than I was then. I'm happily married. I'm a mom. He can't mess with me like he used to. But you know what?" Her eyes twinkled as she capped the mascara and dropped it into her makeup tray. "I think he might end up regretting ever letting me go."

Ruthie put her hand on Justine's forearm. "Don't make the mistake of thinking you can win the battle of the head games and teach him some kind of lesson. He knows *exactly* what to do to cripple your defenses and he always has. I'll give him credit—the man has skills. But *you're* not fake like that. Besides, this isn't some contest. This is your family we're talking about."

"Don't you think you're being a little dramatic?" Justine gently pulled her arm away and began applying lip gloss.

"Don't underestimate the power of the time tunnel, Justine. I guarantee Harry hasn't."

Justine rubbed her lips together. "What are you talking about?"

"Look, I can see you've worked hard to convince yourself that you have a handle on the situation, but the fact that you're not the same person anymore is the thing that makes you vulnerable. Harry is not just some guy. He's a good-looking, good-smelling portal back to the days before you ever had to think about things like playdate politics or which pieces of plasticware in your kitchen might be made from toxic chemicals. No one can blame you for getting drawn into the memories of falling in love in your twenties. I get it. It's intoxicating, and Harry can bring that part of your past alive in glorious 3-D."

Justine slowly rolled the lip gloss tube back and forth between her hands.

"It's easy to understand how you could lose sight of his faults when being around him feels like taking a vacation into your old life." She paused. "And that's what Harry's counting on." Ruthie looked up sharply. "He's already trying to lure you into the tunnel, isn't he?"

Justine thought of the hangman journal that Harry had kept all those years. She'd been unable to resist turning through a few of the pages before a rush of sensory memories made her cram it in the back of her dresser drawer, out of sight beneath her special occasion underwear (which she had intentionally not worn that night as evidence to herself that going to the art show was no more significant than going to the dry cleaners). Of course Harry had known the journal would have an effect on her. But if she *knew* he knew, and she was *aware* of it, that meant she was one step ahead of him…right?

"I will take your silence as a yes. I knew it." Ruthie pointed at Justine. "And that is why, on the Serengeti of life, the gazelles do not hang out in the same bars as the cheetahs. Now, what did he do?"

"Grandy!" Emma squealed from the family room, signaling that Justine's mother was peeking through the entryway window as she always did when she came over.

"Saved by the grandma," Justine said with a smile as she moved past Ruthie and out of the bathroom. "Last chance to come with me, sister."

"I'd sooner get my chest waxed."

Forty minutes later, Justine was in the unfamiliar territory of Robertson Boulevard, with its celebutante-infested boutiques and haughty, high-concept home furnishings stores. She approached a small crowd that had spilled out of the gallery doorway and onto the sidewalk. *I'm not doing anything wrong*, she thought. *I'm not sneaking around. I'm friends with his wife and I'm wearing boring underwear*. She moved through the clusters of people and into the gallery, slipping among conversations and clouds of cologne.

"Unless you get the oceanfront bungalow, it's not worth going."

"I'm wait-listed for the crocodile in navy, six to eight weeks."

"No, they're level. They look very natural in that top."

"I'm telling you, every place I've seen under five million is a dump."

"I think my personal assistant is stealing my reality-show concepts."

"Hello."

Justine let the greeting float past her until she realized that the woman behind the massive tree segment serving as the reception desk was addressing her. She was disturbingly pretty—rock-your-faith-test-your-mettle-screw-the-shareholders pretty—with white-blond hair, polar teeth, and legs that seemed to reach her earlobes, all wrapped in a wisp of glistening, white silk. *She's like a super-sexy stalagmite*, Justine thought.

"Oh, hello." Justine started to ask a question, but was interrupted by a man in his twenties wearing a slate-blue sport coat and fedora. He whispered into the receptionist's hair.

"I am *so* sorry," she said and pushed a large, open book toward Justine. "I have to go help with photos." She wiggled her fingers and walked away, leaving Justine quite certain that there was nothing in her underwear drawer—special occasion or otherwise—that could peacefully coexist with a dress that short. She picked up the heavy, sterling pen and surprised herself by signing *Justine Morgan Underwood*. She never used her maiden name. Where had that come from?

She had grown accustomed to the implied context that standing next to Greg gave her in any social situation. Being on her own in the close, noisy crowd made her feel like she had stumbled into some kind of secret lodge meeting for the lethally hip. *Man up*, she thought. *You've got your own identity. You don't always need to be latched on to a stroller or a shopping cart or a husband. Someone you know from college is having an art opening and you're here to cheer him on. It's all quite reasonable, so let out a notch and go pretend you always hang with the arterati on Thursday nights.*

"Would you care for a glass of wine?" said a man behind her.

"Thank God." She smiled at the young cater-waiter/actor in his white dress shirt and black vest and took a glass from the tray.

The gallery was airy, with exposed wooden rafters and sealed concrete floors. She moved through the reception area and passed between the freestanding white walls with an expression that she hoped conveyed an intense appreciation for the arts and not some kind of personality disorder. As she entered another section, she saw the source of the music that floated through the gallery like cigarette smoke: a trio in the corner was playing Jobim next to an oversize bonsai tree. The dark-eyed singer shook a percussion egg with quick flicks of her wrist as she crooned a samba, accompanied on bass, guitar, and drums by three men, each dressed in black pants and purple, silky shirts. *Oh, wonderful,* she thought. *Forget HR—I'm dressed like the fourth backup musician in a Brazilian rent-a-band.* She took another gulp of wine.

Scanning the room for a familiar face, she saw only strangers making their way in the flow from room to room. She still had not gotten a glimpse of Harry, but if turnout were any measure, he was having a great night. Jostling through the crowd, it was obvious that he had moved well beyond his humble beginnings in Berkeley, where he would scratch out sketches and carvings at a battered drafting table while she sat on his lumpy sofa, working on her thesis.

"I feel like I'm circling around something," he would say as he turned a piece of wood over in his hands. "I'm close but it won't reveal itself."

When she entered the next room, her eye was drawn to a large sculpture. She moved toward the piece, which sat on a low pedestal and reached a foot above her head. The figure was sinewy but voluptuous—the warm tones of the wood swirling into soft grays and blacks with small pools of silver that held the light.

"She's something else, isn't she?" said a man who moved to stand next to her. He had bright, boyish eyes and she guessed him to be in his mid-fifties.

"Yes, she's beautiful." She looked at the base for information but found nothing.

"She shows up frequently in his work." The man stepped forward, eyes on the sculpture.

"Really? The same woman?"

"I would say so. I have one of his sketches on the wall of my office. Look at it every day. As soon as I saw this one, I knew it was the same girl. A lost love, I would presume." He shrugged. "Then again, I could be wrong. Art is interpretation, after all."

Right, she thought. *I knew that.* "So you follow his work?"

"For a couple of years now. I find it comforting."

This was not a word she associated with Harry. "Comforting? How so?"

"His pieces convey a theme with which I am quite familiar."

Justine had never considered what the theme of Harry's art might be. Apparently, these were the things people "in the know" said to one another in galleries. She studied the sculpture again and thought back on the other pieces she'd seen, trying to identify the common thread.

"Is it power?" she said. "Or maybe lust?"

The man placed his fingertips on the small of her back and spoke into her ear as if sharing a secret. "No, my dear. It's fear."

There was a sudden commotion and Harry entered the room, grinning and shaking hands as he greeted guests. "Ah, my friend has returned from the ladies' room," the man said, motioning toward the other doorway. "Enjoy the rest of your evening."

"Nice talking to you," she said with a wave.

Justine watched Harry work the room, his dark jeans and linen shirt accentuating the lean, muscular frame underneath as he made his way through the group. *Fear.* She was going to have to think about that. She saw the beautiful receptionist reach up, her hand on

Harry's shoulder, and say something to him. He threw his head back and laughed, then hugged her and went back to his conversation. His eyes lingered on her backside as she walked away. *That* was the Harry she knew.

Justine handed her empty wineglass to a waiter and pulled out her lip gloss. As she watched Harry's progress through the room, she guided the applicator around the curves of her lips, then gently rubbed them together. When she opened her purse again, she saw the light on her phone's screen. Greg was calling.

"Hey, it's me." He did not sound happy.

"How'd the depo go?"

"Oh," he snorted, "it was stupid. The lawyers on the other side are idiots."

"I'm sorry…they're what?" She pressed the phone to her ear as she watched Harry, who had not yet seen her.

"Geez, what's that racket?"

"A Brazilian combo. That heartless girl from Ipanema is up to her old tricks."

"What are you talking about? Where are you?"

"I'm at the gallery opening, remember?"

"Oh, right. The gnome-artist guy."

Justine rolled her eyes.

"I thought you were on the fence about going," he said. "You don't even like art."

"Yes, I do! Why does everyone keep saying that?"

"How's Emma? Your mom's watching her?"

"Yeah, they're both at home right now. She's fine."

"Good. Also, I wanted to let you know that you're going to be getting an email shortly from one of the committee heads at the firm. It's not for several months, but they want us to have a dinner party at our house for some first-year associates—something about them being afraid of the partners and that we need to try to convince them we're human. I know you're not going to be happy about it, but this one's mandatory."

"Hey, now—I like doing social stuff. Remember your thirtieth-birthday karaoke party? And our *Downton Abbey* marathon night with the Altmanns and the Farrells? It's just that when it's some contrived law-firm event, people are reluctant to relax and have fun. Plus, it's a lot of work."

"Well…I have a possible solution for that."

"Okay." She walked around a pillar to try and escape the music.

"Simone has offered to do all the work on the dinner, even down to the flowers. Now, before you say anything, she has really stepped up on this case and I get the feeling she's volunteered to take the burden of the dinner off of you as a way of mending fences. I think it would be nice if we gave her a chance to redeem herself."

"Well, that didn't take long."

"What do you mean?" he said.

"She's barely been on the case a month and she's got you lobbying for her redemption."

"That's ridiculous. She doesn't 'have me' doing anything."

"We've talked about this in the past, remember? You're the one who said you never wanted to be stuck having to rely on her on one of your cases. Suddenly she's the second coming of Matlock?"

"You're reading way too much into this, Justine. She's just trying to be helpful."

"Oh, Greg, you can*not* be that naïve."

"You made it," said Harry, who had walked up behind her. She held up a finger and pointed at her phone.

"You know, it's really hard to hear you," she said. "We'll figure this out when you get home, okay?"

"*Is that your husband?*" Harry mouthed and motioned for her to hand him the phone. She heard Greg's voice in her ear. "Justine? Are you there?"

"Hang on a sec, Greg," she said as Harry flipped his hair and reached for the phone.

"Hey, man," Harry said, "sorry you couldn't make it tonight. You're missing a hell of a party." He glanced around the room, acknowledging smiles and nods from guests. "What's that? Depositions? Oooh, rough."

Justine pictured Greg sitting on the bed in his hotel room, pointing the remote at the television and scowling into the phone. He ranked making small talk somewhere between attending a funeral and lancing a boil.

"Thank you for lending your beautiful wife to my little event. And, listen, we'd love to go out with you two, you know, eat some sushi and shoot a game of pool." He gave Justine a thumbs-up. "Yeah, the women are the social planners. We just do what we're told, right? Okay, sounds good." He ended the call.

"What was *that* all about?" she asked, taking the phone from his hand.

Harry laughed. "What? I'm just being social. *And* reminding him what a spectacular woman he has."

"Speaking of our beloveds, where's Bette? I haven't seen her anywhere."

"Migraine." He waved to someone across the room.

"That sounds miserable."

"She gets them sometimes. She took her meds before I left. Now she'll sleep it off." He looked back at Justine and stepped forward, gathering her into a slow, full-body hug. "I want to thank you for coming tonight. It means the world to me to have you here."

She allowed herself to absorb the familiar, intimate impact of Harry's body for the first time in eight years. "Oh." The nape of his neck smelled exactly as she remembered. On reflex, she breathed in the scent. "Sure." She inhaled again.

"And I want to talk, but I have to take care of a couple things first. *Mmmm.*" He gave her another squeeze and stepped back. "Can you stick around for a while?"

"For a while, I guess." She tucked her hair behind her ear.

"Are you all right? Your face is kind of pink."

"I'm good." She cleared her throat.

"I'll catch up with you a little later."

Justine knew what Ruthie would have said if she had been there, watching Harry glide away among the guests: *Mr. Head Game: The Sequel.*

One aggravating hour later, Justine cruised yet another food station, where she selected a miniature sandwich, bit into it, and immediately deposited the bite into her napkin, folding it closed with a grimace. "Watch out for the yellow ones," she said to the startled couple next to her. She tried to wash the taste from her mouth with some champagne from a glass that had not left her hand since Harry's hug. Justine had hardly seen Harry in the last hour, but each time she had, he had been socializing and motioned for her to wait a little longer.

"Time's up." She banged her champagne flute down on a silver tray and headed for the lobby. She was within sight of the front doors when she heard a nasal voice behind her.

"Justine, you're leaving?"

She turned to see a woman in a tangerine silk pantsuit, a fat slice of turquoise dangling over her bust by a thick, gold chain. "Willow."

"Love the kismet of running into you! You're here alone?"

Justine stifled a yawn. "Yeah, but I don't know why I bothered. I don't even like art."

"Of course you don't. No one who likes art would come to see this infantile crap."

Justine's eyes widened. "You don't like it?" She felt a nasty thrill of disloyalty.

"*Please.*" Willow waved dismissively at the installations around her. "Dreck. Thank God I didn't drag my husband here, I would never have heard the end of it." Without warning, Harry was at their side. "Well, there he is!" Willow said and clapped her hands. "'Garden of Happiness' artistic genius!" She threw her arms in his direction and he tilted toward her in a near-hug.

"Hello, Willow." Justine ignored the knowing look he was shooting her over Willow's shoulder.

"You ladies aren't leaving, are you?" he said.

"I don't ever want to leave! It's too magical!" Willow said. "By the way, have you met our new auction chair?" She gestured toward Justine.

"Yes, but we haven't had a real chat yet," Harry said with another meaningful glance.

The diamonds on Willow's tennis bracelet sparkled in the halogen lights as she pointed across the room at a man in a brown leather jacket. "*There's* someone I've been trying to talk to all night. You're both fabulous—*mwah!*" She blew air kisses and walked away, flipping the tail of her shiny tunic over her rear end as she went.

Justine rubbed her temples.

"What happens now?" Harry said with an expectant smile.

"I ride off into the sunset," Justine said.

"But we haven't had a chance to talk."

"About…?"

"Don't you think we should catch up? Enough about me," he waved at the surroundings, "I want to hear about *your* life."

"Oh, we can always chat at school. Besides, this is *your* big night. It's been enlightening on many levels and I'm happy for you. I really am. I'm even considering not using air quotes around the word 'artist' when I speak of you in the future." She pulled her car keys from her purse. "But it's late. I'll see you around the sandbox." She turned and walked through the tall, wooden doors and onto the sidewalk. He caught up with her, but she kept walking, past the illuminated shop windows and dark doorways.

"That was some speech," he said, smiling.

"Don't do that."

"What?"

"Don't do that meta-conversation thing where you critique what I'm saying before we've finished talking. It makes you sound like a douche."

He burst out laughing. "Okay, so you're mad because I kept you waiting. I'm sorry, okay? Now can you please slow down? I'm about to pull a hammy trying to keep up with you."

Glaring at him, she made a miniscule reduction in her pace.

"Look, if you feel like you have to go home, I should at least walk you to your car."

She pointed down the sidewalk. "I'm right there on the street. You should go back in the gallery. You're going to be missed."

"I'd rather be out here in the shadows with you."

She stopped and faced him. "Okay, what is that? I'm trying to figure out how to be friends with you, Harry. That's why I'm here tonight—to cheer you on as a friend. But all I get are smarmy comments like that one."

"Sweet Justine." He stepped toward her and his boots scratched in the leaves. "I'm not making this any easier, am I?"

"All I know is, every time I look over my shoulder, you're whipping out a vacation memory or a journal or something else from Berkeley. Why?" She started to move away so there would be no chance of smelling him again, but he caught her gently by the wrist and took a step closer.

"This probably sounds like another smarmy comment," he said, "but seeing you that first night at school was really hard for me. I don't know, maybe it'll get easier."

Ruthie was right, she thought. Going to Harry's show had been a very bad idea. She became aware of the warmth radiating from his fingers and looked down at his hand on her skin.

"Things haven't turned out the way I always thought they would."

"Oh, no." She looked up to see him searching her face. "You did *not* just say that." She pulled her arm back and pressed her temples with her fingertips again. "I have to go." She walked to her car without looking back. She heard nothing behind her but the traffic on Robertson Boulevard.

And now she couldn't talk to Ruthie about Harry anymore.

17
Justine

Nothing took the fun out of lunch like the word "mandatory." Or, as Justine was now discovering, the word "Bette."

"I need to wrap this up inside of fifty minutes," Bette said as she slid into the booth across from Justine, dropping her phone and sunglasses on the table and waving for the waitress before they had cracked the menus. She had picked the Century City restaurant—a steakhouse chain known for its artery-packing cheese dip and clientele of urbane young professionals—because it was walking distance from the Hamptons Leather satellite office in one of the high-rise buildings that ringed the shopping center. "I'm Skyping with the East Coast at one o'clock."

Justine noted that Bette's sleek trousers and sueded silk blouse were the perfect counterpoint to the restaurant's surroundings, which featured plenty of wood grain and retro lighting in an attempt to create the atmosphere of a casino run by George Jetson in a redwood forest. She adjusted her peach cotton cardigan and sat up straighter in her leather chair.

Thirty minutes into their Garden Gnome lunch, they had covered the closure of one of Santa Monica's popular birthday party facilities, revisions to the school's late pick-up policy (parents would now be charged one dollar for each minute they were tardy, up from last year's fifty-cent fee), and a detailed account of Bette's blossoming grudge match with her sons' fencing instructor. When Justine had scheduled the lunch with Bette, the timing had seemed ideal. After spending her first post-transition weeks within a short radius of the school, fighting tears each time she saw the empty car seat in the rearview mirror, she had thought a big-girl lunch away from Santa Monica would be a fun distraction. Now she wished she'd planned something more celebratory—like a gyno exam.

"So what's this bullshit I hear about you running the school auction?" Bette signaled the waitress for a coffee refill.

"Well, it just kind of happened."

"Knowing Willow, I can imagine *exactly* how it happened. I blame myself."

"What are you talking about?"

"I should have had your back. I figured Willow would try to harvest you for her committee—but dumping the entire auction on a first-year mom? *Not cool.*"

"That's sweet of you, Bette, but I've done plenty of events before. It'll be fine."

"I'm not questioning your expertise. You're new, though, and you don't know the dirt on the parents yet—the ones you have to suck up to, the ones who hate being sucked up to, the ones who are unhappy at the school and will trash-talk you for sucking up to Margaret, the ones who don't want anyone but *themselves* sucking up to Margaret."

"That's a lot of sucking."

"That's not the half of it. From what I hear, Margaret's kilt is even itchier than usual these days."

"I've heard the same thing, but why?"

"I suspect it's her marriage, but I don't have any hard facts."

"She's a tough boss, huh?"

"No, *I'm* a tough boss. But I've never made a studio head cry." She took a sip of coffee and thought for a moment. "So what's the auction theme this year?"

"I don't know yet. Margaret was asking that, too. We were supposed to discuss it at the first committee meeting, but trying to stay on topic was like herding cats."

Bette looked like she might spit take across the table, but swallowed hard instead. "You don't have a *theme* yet? Sweet Jesus, please tell me you have a venue."

"Well, no. But I've got some ideas."

Bette stared at Justine, unblinking. "Do you have paper and a pen?" she said finally.

"You know, I used to do this stuff for a living, Bette."

"I know that, but you've never done it *here*. Now, paper and pen. Chop-chop."

If Justine hadn't received yet another email from Margaret just an hour before lunch—this one filled with more "suggestions" for auction items she'd like to see donated by particular families—she might have taken exception to Bette's tone, particularly the "chop-chop" part, which felt like one of those things people weren't supposed to say anymore. Instead, she reached for her purse.

"Riviera Country Club. Ask for Jaime in catering. Use my name. You'll want the ballroom, the lobby and the main dining room, with the smaller dining room for staging and security. Tell him you want the same food setup they did for Little Acorn School, but without the prime-rib station. He'll know why."

Justine wrote in her purse notebook as quickly as she could. "Okay, next you need to nail down your big fish before their older kids' schools get all the good loot. We've got a Disney family who'll give a massive movie and poster basket plus premiere tickets. And our Nickelodeon family is still here, too—hit them up for a group tour. Go through your roster, but I know you've also got access to finale tickets for *So You Think You Can Dance*, *The Voice*, and a couple of those cooking shows. You can probably squeeze a little walk-on

TV part from one of the producers around the school. Let's see," she tapped her coffee saucer, "we've got a rock star or two, so there have to be a couple of autographed guitars, tour jackets, the usual. I'd shoot for some kind of backstage package that includes a limo. You got all that?"

"Getting it." Justine turned the page.

"As for the supermodel, last year I know she promised a session with one of her photographer buddies, then at the last minute backed out and donated a bag of clothes from her budget collection that she claims to 'design.'" Bette made a face. "So good luck with that."

"Fantastic."

"Now. Let's talk real estate. The vacation getaways always make bank in the bidding. We've got the Rosenbergs' house in Napa, the Heitzs' villa in Tuscany, the Walkers' pied-a-terre in Paris, and the Smooke-Martinez home in Aspen for starters. They're usually good for a weekend or two. Press for multiple windows of availability— then you can sell it more than once. Oh, and the Traceys will tell you they have access to a chateau in France. Do not believe them. Just smile and say thank you and pretend to write it down. Also, the fancy moms will want you to deal directly with their PAs, so get some guidance from Willow on that before you hit them up for donations."

Justine looked up from writing. "'PAs?'"

"Personal assistants."

"Oh, right."

Bette checked her watch. "Moving on."

Justine glanced across the restaurant just as Simone walked in the door, moving with the kind of carriage typically accessorized with two-dozen roses and a tiara. She wore a honey-colored wrap dress that would make any other woman look like she was shoplifting bananas, but which oozed over Simone's curves like maple syrup. This was why Justine didn't like eating in Century City—at lunchtime, the place was crawling with people from the firm. Simone smiled over her shoulder at the man holding the door for her, which happened to be Greg. Justine's stomach lurched and she swallowed hard.

"Something wrong?" Bette said.

"What? No, nothing. Go on with your list." She tilted her head back down toward her pad, but her eyes were locked on Greg and Simone, who were being led by the hostess to a table across the room. Greg was laughing and talking with his hands, while Simone smiled back at him and tucked her hair behind one ear. Justine checked the door, hoping to see another lawyer from the team arriving to join them, but she knew she was kidding herself. This was a lunch for two.

Bette twisted in her chair to see where Justine was looking and saw them settle into their seats. She watched for a long moment before turning back around. "Ah," she said. "Who's the blow-up doll?"

Justine almost laughed. "An esteemed colleague." She watched them over Bette's shoulder.

"I know you're not asking my opinion, but Greg strikes me as a good guy." She looked down and swirled her coffee in its cup. "They're not all like that, you know."

Justine considered this. "Yeah. I know." She watched Simone laugh and reach across the table, touching Greg on the forearm.

Bette cleared her throat. "That being said, even a man with the best intentions can be susceptible to—"

"Skankstress?"

Bette raised her eyebrows. "Personal friend of yours?"

"Oh, we know each other." She was now openly staring across the restaurant at the other table.

The waitress arrived with the check and Bette gave her a credit card from her wallet, holding it between two fingers like a cigarette. "I've got to get back. I guarantee my whole staff has been on either Vine or Tinder since I walked out the door."

Justine pulled her attention back to Bette. "I'm sorry. Listen, thank you *so much* for lunch and for all the help with the auction."

"Sure thing. And you know I'm good for Hamptons stuff, too—whatever you need. Just let me know."

"I really do appreciate the support." She tucked her notebook and pen back into her purse. "*All* of it."

"No Gnome left behind." Bette signed the credit card slip as her phone began to ring. She checked the screen before rising to give Justine a hug. "I've got to take this, so don't wait on me. Talk soon." She picked up the call and returned Justine's wave as she barked into the phone. "I hope you're calling to tell me those assclowns in merchandising got their shit together."

Justine crossed the room and was standing at Greg and Simone's table before they realized she was coming. "Hi, guys," she said, savoring the shock on their faces.

"Oh, hello," Simone said with a sour look.

"Justine!" Greg scrambled to his feet and hugged her. "What's going on? Why are you at the mall?"

"Lunch with Bette, remember?"

"Oh, right. Forgot about that." He returned to his seat and glanced at Simone.

"I'm not surprised it slipped your mind, honey." Justine moved next to Greg's chair and ran her hand through his hair. "You've been so busy lately."

Greg looked puzzled as her fingertips grazed his forehead. "Uh, yeah. It's pretty busy right now." He pushed his hair back into place. "We were just getting a quick bite. Do you want to join us?"

"That's sweet of you, but I should go; it's almost time to pick up Emma. It's good you're giving Simone a little break, though, poor thing. I see what you were talking about now—she *does* look completely run-down." Justine gave Simone a half frown of fake sympathy.

Greg's mouth fell open. Simone shot him a look that could boil water.

"Gotta go." Justine leaned down, took Greg's face in her hands and gave him a slow, passionate kiss on the mouth. "See you at home tonight," she said, finally pulling away as Greg sat back in his chair, eyes half-closed and cheeks flushed. "And, listen, instead of billing this lunch to the client, why don't you pay for it out of our personal account." She turned to Simone, who was sitting, arms crossed and lips pressed together. "Just a little something from *us* to you," she said, and walked out of the restaurant.

18
Margaret

It was late afternoon and Margaret sat on the denim sofa in her office, wondering if rabbits had armpits. The question had appeared in her mind as she lifted Ozone from his blanket onto her lap, grasping him around the midsection behind his front legs. This was not something Margaret would typically think about, but she was more than content to ponder the enigma of the bunny undercarriage if it would keep her from thinking about the phone call she'd just had with her banker.

"I'm confused, Margaret," Frank had said. "You've already taken out a second mortgage on Garden of Happiness."

"Yes." Margaret stifled a sigh. "I'd like to do it again."

"But you haven't paid off the existing loan."

"Right."

There was a pause on the line before Frank spoke again. "Am I missing something?"

Obviously, thought Margaret. "As I explained, due to personal circumstances, I'm going to need to arrange additional financing." She paused. "Additional financing in order to buy out Edd—my husband." She gulped. "Soon-to-be ex-husband."

"Margaret," Frank began with the delicacy of a man who knew when a conversation was about to go horribly wrong, "I'm afraid I'm unable to help you."

"Is there a problem with my paperwork? I'll admit, I did complete the application in a rush."

"No, your application is fine. It's just that the bank can't extend any more assistance to you in your current circumstances. I'm sorry."

"You can't be serious," Margaret said. "I've banked with you for twenty years. I defy you to find a blemish on my payment record."

"True," he said, "and the bank appreciates your excellent history and values you as a customer. However, the second mortgage you took on your property was a sizeable one and the balance remains significant. We're just not comfortable with a loan of this amount against the remaining equity, especially in the current market."

"Is that right?" she said. "'Not comfortable?'" She reached into the filing cabinet and pulled out a family file. "Do you think I was 'comfortable' when you called last year and asked me to accept your sister's child into my school? A child so high-strung, mind you, that he consumed half a can of Play-Doh during the *interview*?"

"I, uh..." Frank stammered.

"Do you have any idea how much of my staff's time your nephew requires each day? Under normal circumstances, I would never have enrolled him because of his potential to disrupt the system, but for you, I made an exception." She paused. "Because I value my relationship with you, Frank."

In truth, the young boy was one of Margaret's most satisfying developmental interventions and was making great progress in spite of his insufferably narcissistic parents. Margaret was not about to share this information with Frank, however; leverage was leverage, and at this point, she would take any she could get.

"And I very much appreciate that, Margaret. I know Capone can be a handful—"

Margaret winced at the pretentious name and cut him off. "All I'm asking is that you bend the rules for me the way I bent them for you. There has to be some compromise we can reach, wouldn't you agree?"

"I'm sorry, but I can't do that, not for the amount you're requesting. Now, if you wanted to reapply for a smaller amount—one that is more in line with the current equity in the property—we could have a serious discussion about that."

She slowly closed the folder and set it on the desk. Next to it was a small, framed photo Eddie had taken of Margaret as she stood by the front gate on the school's opening day, looking ill at ease, but jubilant.

Frank had been her best option and she knew it.

"Not to overstep," he continued, "but certainly your husband understands that you can't pull half the school's value out of it with its current encumbrances. Now, I'm looking at your profile here, and I see that you have a separate savings account that has been growing steadily for a number of years. It's significantly less than the amount you were hoping to borrow, but were you intending to—"

"That's our daughter's college money," Margaret interrupted. "It's off limits. To both me and my estranged husband." She picked up the folder and jammed it back into the hanging files, then slammed the drawer shut.

"Ah," he said. "Well, as I said, we value our relationship with you, and I'm sorry we were unable to process your application. If you decide to pursue that smaller loan, please don't hesitate to contact me."

"Of course," she said without inflection as she ended the call.

She petted Ozone with force, flattening him across her lap like a fur napkin. Was a spotless payment record worth nothing in this town?

"You come from a large family, Ozone. Don't you have a rich uncle out there somewhere?"

Just then, Trey barged into her office carrying a stack of folders, his hair and shoulders sparkling with drifts of purple glitter. He froze and looked at Margaret, narrowing his eyes. "Were you just talking to that rabbit?"

"Why are you covered in glitter?"

"I don't want to talk about it," he said and stomped to Margaret's desk, trailing a shower of twinkling, purple flakes, "but you can tell Miss Glenda that retaliation will be swift and will burn like a Michael Bolton ballad." He dropped the stack of files on her desk. "Here are the checks for you to sign, an updated printout of your interview appointments, and many other compelling items that you refuse to take from my outbox. You're welcome."

"For the last time, Trey, I put things in *my* outbox for *you* to take. Not the other way around. The rules of office hierarchy are completely lost on you, aren't they?"

"I simply prefer my interpretation of them."

"You should go," she said flatly. "School's been out for an hour."

Instead, Trey pulled a half-eaten packet of pomegranate seeds from his pocket and began digging in it with his index finger. "My roommate's off work today, so he and his girlfriend will be on the Wii, either fake deep-sea diving, fake tennis-playing, or air-guitaring their way through the entire Metallica catalog." He slurped up a few more gelatinous seeds and licked his lips. "If I go home right now, I'll be too tempted to tell him what a bad idea it is to have a girlfriend who's so good at faking things."

"All right," Margaret said with a sigh. "Whatever."

Trey looked up from his seeds. "I've never heard *that* word cross your lips before." He noticed something on the rug underneath the coffee table. "What is the phone doing on the floor?" He slid the seed pouch back in his pocket and studied the room. "Wad of nasty tissues on the table, red-rimmed eyes, palpable malaise," he ticked off, his voice rising. "Jesus in Jheri curls, Margaret, what is going on up here?"

"If you must know, I just learned that my loan application has been turned down."

"*What?* Does that banker not know who we are?"

"Apparently not," she said, stroking Ozone as Trey watched her with obvious concern. "What?" she said finally, glancing up at him.

"So? What do we do now?"

"I really don't know," she murmured and flicked a cedar shaving off the sofa and onto the floor.

"We're losing her, doctor!" He motioned for Margaret to stand. "Let's go."

"Go *where?*"

"I'm walking you to the Armenian market for a Yoo-Hoo." He plucked her keys from the desk and jangled them as he waited. "That should put the snap back in your knee socks."

Margaret blew out a mouthful of air. "I'm not accustomed to being 'managed' by one of my own employees, Trey."

Trey crossed his arms and stared at her, lips pursed.

"All right, I'll go—but only so I can get some peace for the rest of the afternoon." She looked down at Ozone. "What about—"

"Do not even speak of bringing that rodent with us," he said. "What are you going to do, strap him into his Bunny Bjorn?"

"I suppose he's fine here for a few minutes." She set the rabbit on his blanket, allowing Trey to prod her out the door and down the stairs. "Why do they sell Yoo-Hoo at the Armenian market?" she asked as they reached the front gate.

"Because Yoo-Hoo transcends all cultural barriers. Now, go toward the light." He opened the gate and waved her through.

They started walking toward the corner. As they neared the entrance to the office building next door, they saw a man exit the lobby accompanied by a woman in a flowing, multi-colored caftan.

Margaret slowed. "It's Eddie."

Eddie and the woman stopped on the sidewalk, deep in conversation.

"It is indeed," Trey said. "Work it."

"This is the last thing I need right now, Trey." She felt leaden, as if she were moving underwater.

"Watch out, he brought a drag queen," Trey said as they got closer. "God, the worst Shirley MacLaine I've ever seen."

Eddie noticed them when they were only a few feet away, his displeasure evident on his face. "Oh, hello, Margaret." He turned to Trey, the distaste noticeably tripling. "Trey."

"Hello," Margaret said.

"Edward." Trey pursed his lips and gave a curt nod, releasing a light shower of lingering purple glitter onto the front of his shirt. Eddie watched the sparkly bits settle with a disapproving frown.

The woman in the caftan was in her forties, with iridescent eye shadow and an open face. She smelled strongly of essential oil—a scent that fell somewhere between green tea and a wet campfire. She smiled broadly, seemingly oblivious to the tension in the group.

"Oh," Eddie said. "Cassandra, this is my wife, Margaret, and her secretary, Trey."

"Blessings," Cassandra said as she took Margaret's and Trey's hands between hers in turn.

"Hello," Margaret said, quickly withdrawing her hand.

"Administrative assistant," Trey said, shooting Eddie a dirty look.

"Cassandra, could you give us a minute?" Eddie opened the door of the Smart car at the curb. "I need to speak with Margaret."

"Naturally." Cassandra picked her way across the tree roots and into the car.

Margaret watched him shut the door. Something had changed since she'd last seen him. Had he lost a couple of pounds? Gotten a spray tan? Veneers? Whatever it was, there was now a tangible unfamiliarity about her husband that affronted her, hanging in the air between them like an acrid belch.

"Trey," she said, throwing her shoulders back, "do me a favor and pick up some spicy peanuts to go with the Yoo-Hoo."

"Or I can wait while you two chat it out and we can walk together."

"I would prefer you go on without me."

Trey lowered his voice. "But what if the woman with the sideburns is working today? You know she likes you better."

"Oh, for Pete's sake," Eddie said. "Take a hint!"

"On your way," Margaret said with a nod.

"Well, toodles, then. Love the espadrilles!" he said to Eddie, then took off down the sidewalk, elbows pumping.

"They're not espadrilles—they're Toms," Eddie muttered, then turned back to Margaret. "He always was an ass."

"Are you quoting Buddha?"

"Don't start, Margaret."

"Or what? Your mulch-scented girlfriend will see the vein that pops out on your forehead in a very unspiritual way when you get angry?"

"I knew you were going to think that." He glanced at the car. "She's not my girlfriend."

"Please." Margaret crossed her arms. "I don't have time for games. What did you want to talk to me about?"

"Listen, not that I owe you any explanations, but Cassandra is my business partner, all right?"

Margaret dropped her arms. "Your business partner? What business would that be?"

Eddie paused. He seemed to be deliberating on how much to tell her. "We are reconfiguring my dental office for the new practice," he said finally. "That's why we were up there—I was showing her the space so we could make plans."

"What new practice?"

Eddie hesitated again. "Energy healing."

"You can't be serious."

"I knew I shouldn't have shared that with you. Just forget it."

"I wish I could. I thought you'd pushed your New-Age obsession as far as it could go—and now you're sinking money into a farfetched therapy business with someone who looks like she's auditioning for *Godspell?*"

"Well, thank you for bringing up the issue of finances because that's what I wanted to talk with you about." He gave her an unfriendly smile. "It's time to put this school buyout matter to bed."

"Why? So you can throw the money away? I see now why you've been pushing so hard—you got bored with your business and abandoned it and now you're counting on money from my school to start another one."

"I did not abandon my business," he said hotly.

"Just own it, Eddie, all right? If the surf conditions were good or you felt like wandering around the hippie shops on Main, you would have your receptionist cancel your appointments for the day. Did you think that wasn't obvious? Why do you think your patients disappeared? Who wants to open their mouth for a dentist who's phoning it in?"

"Wow, so I'm the villain for wanting to change my life. *That* seems fair. And since we're owning things, it's time you *owned* that you were invited to accompany me on all my explorations. I wanted to do things together, if you recall. That's more than most guys my age would have done. Have you ever thought about that? The other husbands were off watching sports or playing golf—or they were telling their wives they were playing golf when they were really seeing their girlfriends. And what did I want to do? Expand my mind. Learn more about myself and life. But you couldn't be bothered. You were too busy with your precious preschool."

Margaret glared at him, fists clenched at her sides. This was the man who had seen her differently than the rest of the world had—differently than she had seen herself. He was Leticia's father, forever connected to Margaret through human membrane. He was a disappointment, an underachiever who moved through life without the deliberate intent it required. He was her love, her lover, her mate. He had twined around her and nuzzled her open like a jewelry box, then left her toppled and exposed.

"Why did you have to change so much?" she blurted.

Eddie gave a harsh laugh. "Why couldn't you have changed a *little*?" They stared at each other for a moment before Eddie looked away, running a hand through his hair. It was then that Margaret identified the thing that was different about him. He was not wearing his wedding ring.

Trey bounded up to them, a large paper sack in his hand. "What did I miss?" he asked breathlessly, but they both ignored him.

"As I was saying," Eddie said pointedly, "the time has come to settle the matter of the school."

"And as *I've* said before, I need more time."

"That makes no sense. I don't know what's going on with your books, but if you're short on cash, you can always tap into your little army of parents, right? You're always bragging about how you can get anything you want out of them. Well, now's the time."

"I've never characterized them that way!" Margaret said.

Trey set the paper sack on the sidewalk, pulled out a bag of Flamin' Hot Cheetos, and noisily ripped it open.

"Do you mind?" Eddie said, giving Trey a dirty look.

"Oh, all right." He held the bag out to Eddie. "Don't Bogart them."

"You are an imbecile!" Eddie burst.

"Tough talk coming from a swami in Dockers." Trey withdrew the bag.

Eddie set his jaw and turned back to Margaret. "My lawyers are moving forward on the buyout. If you don't comply, the school will be sold and the proceeds split."

"Augh!" She wanted to punch him, just like one of the dummies at the gym that looked so much like him. "That is never going to happen, Eddie. *Never.*"

"I'm done with this conversation." He threw up his hands and began walking toward the car.

"That's right. Slink away, as usual," Margaret called after him.

She started back toward the school as the car pulled away from the curb. Trey seized his grocery sack and caught up with her as she reached the gate. "What's next, monsignor?" he said.

She whirled around to face him. "Would you *please* stop asking me that?" She reached into his bag and took a fistful of Cheetos, then stalked across the front play yard before turning around again. "What's next is this: you are going home and I am going to find a way to pay that man off, even if I have to sell *you* on Craigslist to do it."

Trey's face contorted into what those who knew him would identify as a smile. "She's ba-*ack*," he said in a singsong voice, and followed Margaret through the yellow door.

19
Ruben

"Mommy jokes?" the comic known for his ironic mullet said when Ruben returned to the Comedy Store's green room after his set. "You're doing mom humor now? What the fuck?"

He was flopped onto the upholstered bench that ran the perimeter of the room, the centerpiece of which was a stubby mirrored piano—a relic of the 70s and the cumulative pounds of coke that fueled some of the biggest standups of the day. Tonight, however, it held two sweating bottles of vitamin water and an iPhone in a battered, rubber case.

"Be sensitive, bro," said a comic on the other side of the bench as he adjusted his maroon, pleather jacket. "He might have cramps." He smirked and took a gulp of his Sam Adams.

"Menstrual humor," Ruben said, twisting the cap off a bottled water. "Very high-brow. You should probably stick with your usual masturbation material, don't you think? You know what they say: 'write what you know.'" The mullet comic guffawed and Ruben walked out to find the booker and get his share of the door.

Something about the exchange bothered him. Was *he* "writing what he knew?" Sure, the new bits he had added to his set were inspired by the preschool, but they didn't *define* him. He was still the same guy he'd always been; his current Mr. Mom life was temporary.

It had to be.

When the cigarette-scented man standing near the door handed Ruben a wrinkled envelope, it felt lighter than usual.

"What's up with this, Armando?" Ruben said, fingering the cash inside.

The booker shrugged. "What can I say? Not many people mentioning your name at the door tonight." He scratched the ring of salt-and-pepper hair that sat just above his ears. "Nice set, by the way. My wife would like the chick stuff."

"Uh, thanks." Ruben picked his way through the props scattered backstage and checked out the audience through an opening in the curtain. Scanning the seats, he saw far fewer familiar faces than he usually did at his gigs. God, it was a lot of work, hustling to get people with jobs and families to come out for shows, especially during the week. Drawing the grown-up crowd to the Sunset Strip took relentless marketing, and now that he thought about it, after a busy week with two after-school playdates, snack duty at school, and another fundraising committee mailing to get out, he hadn't gotten around to making an email flier for this show—a first. He searched for Vince in the crowd. Although *Doughnut Try This at Home* was a breakout hit, Vince was still a presence in the clubs. Ruben hoped he hadn't been there that night to see the low turnout.

He watched the current comic from the wings, critiquing her performance. She wasn't doing too bad, he thought, but there was a desperation about her act that seemed to throw off her timing, making Ruben wince. That was the thing about standup—in a club filled with boozy patrons and sidebar conversations, it was a challenge to give your material subtlety. And subtlety, he had discovered, was what he enjoyed most about his writing now that it was beginning—at last—to gel.

His mind was becoming accustomed to the process, dipping into a stream of creativity that seemed to flow each time he opened his notebook. Rather than jot notes and ad-lib the details at the mic, he became absorbed in the process of refining a written passage. Sometimes, if interrupted, he would have to reorient himself to the outside world, as if he had pushed up from the bottom of a swimming pool into the atmosphere of air and noise. There were times when he wondered if he might ultimately find writing more satisfying than standup, but the night's anemic turnout was a blunt reminder that he might be getting ahead of himself. The currency in comedy clubs was the ability to fill the house and if Vince got the impression Ruben's audience appeal was waning, he would lose interest. He searched the audience once more, relieved not to find Vince among the faces. He took his absence as a lucky break and vowed to promote the crap out of his next gig.

"Hey, Ruben, did you see Vince?"

He turned to see Armando on his way to the green room.

"Vince is here?"

"Nah, he's gone now. He was looking for you after you finished your set."

Ruben walked over and lowered his voice. "Hey, did he say anything? Did he like my stuff?"

"What am I, his girlfriend?" Armando disappeared down the dark hallway.

Out on the street, the night air was cool. Ruben stepped onto the sidewalk, turning left toward the parking lot. Across Sunset Boulevard, a crowd snaked into the House of Blues, distorted strains of music drifting across the traffic.

Ruben yawned and checked his watch. Eleven thirty. His body needed sleep, but it always took him a while to come down after a gig. He knew that when he slipped into bed later beside Deandra—after packing the twins' lunches—he would lie there and stare at the red light on the smoke detector, torturing himself over what Vince had wanted to say to him. He wished he could catch some extra sleep the next morning, but he had to get to school early to sell raffle tickets for the auction. He trudged up the ramp to the parking structure, secure in the knowledge that he was the only comic working the strip that night heading home to make peanut-butter-and-banana sandwiches for Elvis and Priscilla.

20
Justine

Confusion. Guilt. Annoyance. Unfocused arousal. These are a few of the many reactions a woman experiences when woken from a romantic dream by a real-world erection belonging to a non-dream-cast-member, and Justine was scrolling through every one of them. She peeked at the blue LED display on her bedside clock. 1:18 a.m. Behind her, Greg's breathing was slow and regular and he made no move to follow up on the firmness he was pressing into the curve of her hip. This led her to believe she was dealing with a rogue appendage looking to scare up some action while the rest of the body dozed, a phenomenon Justine and Ruthie privately referred to as "sleepwanging." Closing her eyes, she tried to ignore the beginnings of a headache and drift off again. She wanted to get back to her dream.

It was one of those plotless, yet deeply stimulating dreams—the kind that reverberated through her the next day and left her spending a little too much time in the supermarket line wondering what the bag boy looked like without his shirt. The star of this dream was not an employee of her local market, however. It was Harry.

They were riding through the Berkeley hills on Harry's motorcycle, but for the first time, she was driving and Harry was behind her. Also, for reasons that made complete sense at the time, they were naked. They rounded the curves of the hills, leaning into the turns as he wrapped himself more tightly around her. Climbing higher, he pressed his lips to her ear, and above the thrum of the engine, she heard him say, "You up?"

Justine's eyes fluttered and focused again on the clock. 1:21. Greg's hand skimmed her hip and settled on her breast. She felt the warmth of his chest against her back. "Yeah." He buried his face in her hair and his breathing became deeper and faster. She started to turn toward him. "No, stay like that," he murmured. His fingers slid down to grasp her hipbone, pulling her into his rhythm. Her body's automatic, chemical response to her husband felt like an admonition. She tried to clear the dream from her mind as she watched the number change on the clock...and change once more.

"Mmloveyou," Greg said afterward, then kissed the back of her head and flopped over to his side of the bed, asleep again. Justine wondered if he had even been completely awake. She could not remember the last time she'd been roused for pre-dawn lovemaking—certainly not since Emma's arrival. And his choice to keep her facing away from him was out of the ordinary; aside from special-occasion variations, Greg was a face-to-face sex guy. In all, their interlude felt a little...uncharacteristic. She lay still and considered this information.

Through the open window, she heard a dog barking somewhere in the neighborhood. She thought she could smell the lemons on the tree, then wondered if she were imagining it. Turning onto her back, the streetlight glowed through the shutters, throwing long, striped shadows that sliced her into illuminated strips and did nothing to help her headache. The mini blinds in her old apartment in Berkeley had created a similar effect. She had a vivid memory of the weightless bands of light falling across Harry's body, flowing along his torso and bending at his waist like a prism. As she reached out and traced one of the rectangles on the sheet, the light touched her wedding rings. She twitched her pinky and flipped the engagement diamond back to the top of her finger as she did unconsciously one hundred times a day.

Greg had been nervous when he proposed to her. It was Christmastime and they had spent the day in the crisp air of Carmel-by-the-Sea, holding hands and wandering through shops draped in pine boughs and twinkling lights. Everywhere they went, they were serenaded by costumed carolers, charmed by glimpses of the sea at the end of each street, or enveloped by the scent of hot, spiced cider. They were having one of those vacations that made life feel like a big present, waiting to be unwrapped.

"I could *so* live here," she'd said and slipped her arm through his.

Greg had smiled. "I'm shocked to hear that." When the smile lasted longer than usual, she asked him what he was thinking.

"Oh, nothing, just working on some holiday plans." He'd looked away and changed the subject.

That night they dressed up and ate at their hotel, a rambling complex scattered along the cliffs above the Pacific, by far the most luxurious place either of them had ever been. Justine wore a black, jersey wrap dress that she'd been saving for a special night out, and black, platform peep toe heels bought especially for the trip. Greg looked handsome and official in his best suit, the one he usually reserved for court. They sat tucked away in a corner of the room near the glowing hearth of a river-rock fireplace. Their steaks were obscene in scale and, even without the soft-focus of the cabernet, the setting—among the rough posts and beams with candles reflecting in the panoramic glass walls—was exquisite. They talked about their dreams and goals and about the future as they hoped it would be.

It wasn't until Greg slipped from his seat and bent next to her on one knee that she realized what was happening. She felt the diners at nearby tables watching them, but she didn't care. Greg held a small, red, leather box in his hand, which he opened to reveal a classic diamond solitaire. Justine's heart beat in her throat.

"Greg, oh my God."

Wobbling slightly in his stance, he kept his eyes focused on hers as he spoke. "I can't imagine my life without you."

It was the perfect thing to say.

Yawning, Justine sat on the edge of the bed and tugged on her blue robe. Sliding her feet into her shearling slippers, she cinched the robe and walked out of the bedroom. There was one activity that never failed to ground her. The house was still as she made her way to her daughter's room.

She pushed the door open and stepped into the glow of the nightlight. Emma was sleeping hard, splayed out in her crib among her favorite stuffed buddies. She was rigorous in her selection of sleep mates; each night's bedtime ritual included a review of the collection that would be in the crib with her, with singsong condolences and a kiss offered to the group she would instead arrange in her comfy story chair for the night.

Good for you for being so selective, Justine thought. She leaned down on the crib rail and rested her chin on her hands. It was difficult to imagine Emma any older than she was. She tried to fast-forward to teenage Emma, studying her face for clues as to what the coming decade would bring, but came up with nothing. It was much easier to conjure up baby Emma, whose pure, round features were still visible, even with the changes brought on by toddlerhood. The thought of Emma with a boyfriend—or a husband—was simply too much for Justine to process.

"I pity the fool who breaks your heart," she said. Emma shifted in her crib with a soft *mew,* her foot appearing under the edge of the aquamarine blanket like a small, shy sea creature. Justine kissed her fingers and pressed them to Emma's sugar-cookie cheek. "Sweet dreams, Super Girl."

She walked out of Emma's room and stood in the hallway, hands on hips. She didn't feel at all sleepy and hated lying in bed only to stare at the ceiling. Pushing her hair from her face, she went into the spare room and sat down at the computer. Four new emails had arrived since she'd gone to bed—all from Margaret.

She was about to open the first message (subject line: *Are we making certain to avoid last year's unfortunate choice of DJ?*) when she shook her head and closed the screen entirely. Auction micro-management could wait until morning. She knew she would have to reply first thing, however, before Margaret began a round of her infamous follow-up calls. "That woman would make Mother Teresa's trigger finger itch," she muttered. She pushed away from the desk and stomped out of the spare room. Now she was not only awake, but aggravated. She tightened her robe and headed for the family room, resigned to watching the all-night knife-selling show until she was sleepy enough to go back to bed.

As she passed her purse on the hall table, she heard an electronic warble. She flipped back the leather flap and saw that her phone was glowing. "If that's Margaret texting me this late at night, I'm going to officially lose it." On the screen was a single text message. She didn't recognize the number, but she knew who'd sent it.

i miss u. animal

She sank onto the curved arm of the sofa, holding the phone away from her but unable to put it down. For a flash, the old Harry was there—the sexy, self-deprecating man she had fallen for that first night on the boat. *Animal.* He had taken himself away...and now he missed her. She read the text again and, to her horror, felt a surge of lust. She jumped up and set the phone on the coffee table, backing away from it with her arms wrapped around her ribs. *That feeling wasn't real,* she told herself. It was just a memory made powerful by loss, like a phantom limb.

How could she have thought she could casually coexist with this man? To Harry, the reminiscences and old inside jokes he brought up to her at school were frivolous souvenirs—a keychain from the World's Tallest Thermometer tossed in a shoebox. To her, they were radioactive material to be kept in lead-lined bunkers. She thought of something Ruthie had once said. "Teenie, it'll never be a fair fight with Harry. You're his Cadillac Ranch...but he's your Chernobyl."

She closed the robe around her neck. She hated the jolt the message had given her—the way it made her marriage suddenly seem fragile. More than that, she hated the fear she felt in the dark, quiet house. Between Greg's unusual choice of a faceless sexual encounter and her own late-night lusting for her former lover, she was beginning to wonder which member of her marriage might be the least trustworthy—a question that a few months ago would have been unthinkable.

"What a bunch of jackasses we are," she said, staring at the phone.

Now she was ready for sleep, if only she could turn off her mind. Snatching the phone from the table, she deleted the message, then padded toward the rear of the house, flinging the phone into her purse as she passed it on the hall table. Ignoring the moonlight streaming into the kitchen, she went straight to the cabinet above the refrigerator, stood on her toes and pulled the bottle of Seagram's off the shelf. Unscrewing the top, she took a large swallow, grimacing as it went down. "God, that's *rough,*" she said, before taking several more gulps. She leaned against the island and closed her eyes, hoping she'd drunk enough to cancel any inflammatory texts, nursery-school neuroses, naked-motorcycle dreams, and oblique lovemaking that might still be on the schedule for the evening.

"Private party?" Greg said behind her, causing her to jump and lose her grip on the bottle.

"Shit," she said as it hit the wood floor, shooting a thick stream of whiskey onto her robe and across her shins. She glared at Greg. *"Really?"*

"I wasn't trying to scare you." He stepped closer in his bare feet, stopping at the edge of the spill. "Do you want help?"

Justine rubbed her eyes as the sticky trails of whiskey dribbled down her ankles and into her fuzzy slippers. "No, I got it," she grumbled.

"What are you doing, anyway? Is something wrong?"

"I can't get back to sleep." She grabbed the roll of paper towels from the holder and spooled off a large wad, tossing the empty tube on the counter. "I'm…stressed out." She dropped the paper towels onto the spill without looking at him, then poked at them with the toe of her slipper.

"Oh, don't tell me it's that stupid auction again."

"It's nothing I can't handle," she snapped.

"It's *preschool.* You shouldn't have to 'handle' anything." He filled a glass with water from the jug in its wooden stand. "I'm just surprised to see you going for the whiskey. You know it makes you puke. Is this one of those cries for help I always hear about in radio commercials—the kind I'm not supposed to ignore?"

"Very funny. I just wanted to make myself go back to sleep and the only other option was that beer that's been in the back of the fridge for four months. I decided I didn't need to be awake *and* burpy."

"Good call." He stood in his boxers and T-shirt, sipping his water and watching her.

"So what's *your* story?" She dropped a soaking ball of paper towels in the trash can under the sink. "You're usually out for good after we make The Love."

"Yeah," he said with an uneasy laugh. "Guess I'm not myself tonight, either."

"Is that why it was different?" She watched his face.

"What do you mean?"

"I don't know. It just kind of felt like you weren't quite...there."

He frowned. "I've got a lot going on, too, you know. This pre-trial work is crushing, and we're nowhere near done."

"Hey, I know you're busy. I was just asking."

"So maybe we're both just having an off night."

They studied each other for a long moment.

"Yeah, that must be it," she said finally. "An off night."

"Let me help you finish wiping the floor and then we can go back to—are you okay?"

Justine clamped her hand over her mouth as her stomach lurched. She jammed the wad of paper towels into Greg's side like a football and sprinted for the bathroom. "I don't want to hear a word about this when I come out," she managed to blurt over her shoulder, then squeezed her lips together as her stomach rolled again.

"Hey, look at us, partying 'til dawn," Greg deadpanned, waving the empty paper-towel tube over his head. "Maybe I should make margaritas."

21
Ruben

Ruben maneuvered the double stroller down the grocery store aisle crowded with weekend shoppers. "Stick cheese, cracker fishies, and tortillas," he said, dropping the items into the grocery cart one by one. "What else?"

Deandra checked her list. "Okay, now we need bread, macaroni and cheese, and milk."

"I'm on it! Let's fly, Fred and Ginger!" He jogged back down the aisle, weaving the stroller around the shopping carts.

"Whee, Daddy!" Lily called as Harris squealed with excitement.

When he returned with the items, he screeched the imaginary brakes and brought the stroller to a sudden stop next to the cart. The twins dissolved in laughter, hanging over the bar that ran across the front of their seats and flapping their arms.

"Wait," Deandra said, "that's not the right brand of macaroni and cheese."

"Oh," he looked at the box, "you know what? I heard this brand was better for them than the Day-glo orange stuff. We had it for lunch a couple of days ago and they dig it."

"But I thought you loved fluorescent foods." She smiled and tossed the package into the cart.

"All right, all right," he said. "I know, but I got into a discussion last week with some of the fundraising moms and it's pretty gross what's *actually* in the stuff I ate when I was little."

She tilted her head and studied his face. "Well, check you out." She rubbed his shoulder. "I think that's sweet."

"*Hello*, that's how we power moms roll," he said, making her laugh. They continued working their way through the store.

"Hey," she said, "do you want me to make those pork rolls you liked so much?"

"The ones with the little rice blobs? Absolutely."

When they reached the meat department, Deandra elbowed Ruben and motioned toward a woman talking over the counter to the butcher. "That mom's in Soil Group," she said. "I can't remember her name."

"It's Babette and don't even get me started," he said. "She's too busy trying to be everyone's real estate agent to notice that her son has serious anger issues." He browsed through a display of cookies as he talked. "Meanwhile, the rest of us have to deal with the fallout when he kicks and throws sand at our kids. From what I've heard, that family is *this close* to getting a mandatory therapy referral from Margaret." He looked up to find Deandra staring at him, her pen frozen above the grocery list. "What?" Ruben said with a shrug, a plastic pack of cookies in each hand.

"Okay, now you really don't sound like yourself."

"Why do you say that?"

"You've never been one to keep up with gossip." She squatted next to the stroller and re-tied Lily's pony tail, which had slipped loose. Then she leaned in and kissed both children on their cheeks with a loud *smooch*.

"I don't 'keep up' with it. It's the same stuff you used to talk about." He paused. "Before."

Deandra stood up, looking puzzled. "But that was different."

"Different how?"

"I'm trying to figure out why it feels that way." She thought for a moment, then winced. "This probably sounds unfair, but I think it's because I'm used to hearing the moms talk like that. But you're a dad, you know? A *guy*."

"Wow. Feeling a little insecure about my manhood right now." He lowered his voice an octave. "When we get home, I'm going to change into my work boots and go *lube* something."

"Yeah, you're right. That's stupid." She shook her head. "I'm sorry."

"I hear that chatter all week, Dee, that's all. It's in my head."

"Yeah, I get it, sweetie. Never mind." She leaned in and squeezed his hand. He caught the scent of her Kors perfume again and breathed it in.

After checking out, they passed the Starbucks stand wedged next to the floral display. "I'll be coffee boy," Ruben said and joined the line. Five minutes later he handed Deandra an extra-hot mocha.

"Mmm, thanks." She took a sip, then pointed at his cup. "Uh-oh, I think you took the wrong one. That says 'nonfat soy latte.'"

Ruben glanced down at his cup. "Nope, I'm good." He took off, pushing the stroller toward the exit.

"Wait a second," he heard Deandra say as she pursued him into the parking lot. "Since when do you drink nonfat soy lattes?" she called over the rattle of wheels on the asphalt.

"What'd you say?" Ruben hollered over his shoulder and sped up.

When she reached the Subaru, Ruben was busy buckling the children into their car seats.

"Ruben," she said, and walked over to the open door.

"Yes, my precious lotus blossom?"

"Don't give me that. You know what I'm talking about. That's why you made me chase you through the parking lot."

"Actually, I wanted to see what that shopping cart could do if you really opened 'er up." He began loading the groceries into the back of the car.

"I'm serious. You're not acting like yourself and it's starting to creep me out."

He stopped and faced her. "What exactly is the issue? Yes, I have changed my regular coffee order. Should I have alerted local authorities?"

She crossed her arms. "So why have you changed to soy?"

Ruben looked uncomfortable. "Why does it matter?"

"Because it's another thing that doesn't feel like you. You are, for lack of a better term, a 'lactose aficionado.'"

It was Ruben's turn to cross his arms. "No."

"'No?'"

"That's right. I'm not telling."

Taken aback, Deandra's arms fell to her sides. "Wha—why not?"

"Because you're just going to give me a hard time again. So forget it." He took the stroller by the handles and stepped on the two red levers near the back wheels, collapsing it forward into an unwieldy bundle. He lifted it into the back of the car, mashing it against the row of grocery bags. "Let's go." They didn't speak again until he had pulled into traffic.

"I won't give you a hard time," she said softly.

Ruben exhaled through his nostrils. "I switched to soy because regular milk makes me bloaty." He regretted saying it the moment he heard it out loud.

Deandra pursed her lips and her eyes went wide.

"And there's the face," Ruben said with a scowl.

"I can't help it. You sound just like one of *them*."

He checked the rearview mirror and saw that the twins were engrossed in their new grocery-store trinkets and paying no attention to grown-up conversation. He pulled the car to the curb and faced his wife. "You have to stop," he said. "This is not cool."

"No, what's 'not cool' is watching my sexy husband turn into a...a soccer mom."

"It's a coffee drink, for Pete's sake."

"It's not just that. It's everything." She picked at the hem of her shirt. "I didn't think getting involved at school would change you so much."

"I haven't changed, Dee, I'm in a new environment. It's part of being a comic—I observe what I see around me and I absorb it, and then it bubbles back up. You know how it works." He shifted the car into park and stomped on the parking break. "I don't understand why you're making such a big deal out of a bunch of nothing."

"I get that you're basically the only dad among all those women. I should have thought of that when I came up with my genius plan." She rolled her eyes. "What's bothering me is that I keep hearing about all your socializing with the school moms, but nothing about your writing. Your script is the real reason you're there, remember?"

There was a time in Ruben's life when he had a temper, when his frustrations would ignite like Roman candles, firing at everyone around him. He hated this aspect of his personality that reminded him so much of his father and he had worked for years to defuse it. Deandra's insinuation, however, took him all the way to the brink of that old feeling. He gripped the steering wheel and stared through the windshield.

Ruben loved this woman. He loved the way she anticipated his thoughts, and that she was strong enough to push past all his jokes and challenge the man behind them in a way no one else ever had. His wife, however, was not perfect. Love or not, Ruben had no illusions about this.

"I am doing," he said in a measured tone, still staring ahead, "exactly what we agreed I would do. I'm doing my committee job. I'm sucking up. I'm also writing. And soon I will meet with Vince and take my shot at moving up to the next level. Then you will be able to quit working for that healthcare hag and get back home to your children." When Deandra did not respond, he continued. "You're not going to have control over every step of this process, Dee. I know that's hard for you, especially after the rough start I had with my writing, but..." He took a deep breath. "You're going to have to trust me."

When Ruben looked back at Deandra, the first thing he saw were the tears splashing onto her hands still folded in her lap. *Shit*, he thought, *now I'm the asshole who made her cry.* Would he ever get the hang of being a husband?

He reached over and touched her leg. "Hey, it's all right, okay? Please don't cry. Whatever I did, I'm sorry."

"You didn't do anything." She sniffed noisily. "The trust thing. It's hard for me, you know? Not because of you—you've been so great, Ruben. It's all me." She wiped at her nose with the back of her hand. "I think I'm too much like my father."

Ruben scrubbed the mental picture of Deandra as her father from his mind so it would not reappear the next time they had sex. "Come on..." he said, "that's not true." He glanced over his shoulder at the twins who were both, miraculously, asleep in their car seats.

"Ruben," she said, "there's something I haven't told you."

Ruben pulled away. *Here it comes*, he thought. *She's out of patience. She needs to make a change. Or worse—she's fallen under the influence of some trollpouch at work who drives a 7-Series BMW and wears Justin Timberlake aftershave.*

"What's the matter with you?" Deandra said, scowling at him.

"Nothing." Ruben shifted in the seat.

"You had the weirdest look on your face just now."

"Never mind that. What's this thing you haven't told me?"

Deandra pulled her long curtain of black hair around in front of her, where it hung to her belt buckle. She twisted it around her wrist, considering her words. "I want to start my own business."

"You want to—"

"I've been thinking about it for a while now, and I know I can do it. I want to run a placement service—a company that connects moms with childcare helpers." She gave him a tentative smile, watching his face for a reaction.

Ruben gathered her into a hug, smiling into the curve of her neck. Then, as he settled sideways in his seat, Deandra told him how the idea had sparked in her mind one day in the bookstore's business section. She began doing research and imagining a new direction for her life once Ruben got his TV job. "I told myself I wouldn't mention it yet, since you're under so much pressure right now." She ran her hand down his cheek, lightly brushing the stubble under his chin with the backs of her fingers. "But watching you work outside your comfort zone has inspired me, sweetie, and I wanted you to know that."

Ruben drove away from the curb, his mind churning. Suddenly, it wasn't enough to be writing a script for Vince. He was dreaming for two now. He heard a familiar voice in his head. "Make it happen!" It was his old boss at the escrow company, barking as he did in every staff meeting. "You gotta open doors!"

By the time they drove through the mechanical gate under their condo building, Ruben had already identified the first door he needed to open. Behind it was Willow's husband.

22
Margaret

It was the Hindenburg of financing plans.

It had taken two days, but Margaret had finally cobbled together a strategy for raising the money to buy Eddie out of Garden of Happiness. She had factored in every possible source of funds, including all of her personal retirement savings, a smaller loan from the bank, a loan from her parents, the collection of an increased school tuition three months earlier than it would customarily be due, and a spectacular revenue from the school's silent auction. Success required unwavering commitment on all fronts, flawless timing, and significant fiscal risk—not to mention Eddie's cooperation in waiting until after the auction to receive his money. The failure of any single component of the scheme would bring its entire delicate structure crashing to earth.

Margaret threw her pencil down on the yellow pad and sat back in her chair. To say she did not relish the prospect of asking her parents for money was an understatement on a par with "vegans are not partial to brisket." Her parents had never seemed to know quite what to make of her—a fact that had troubled her since childhood. She had grown up feeling mostly disconnected from her home life, like a foreign exchange student whose host parents struggled to bridge the culture gap with hot meals, academic praise, and arms-length advice on cultural assimilation. Margaret had sensed her parents' emotional wariness from a young age, just as she sensed that it did not apply to her brother Wayne, who was eight years older and oblivious to anything that fell outside his own shadow. She had grown up thinking her parents' detachment reflected some shortcoming in herself that she would overcome as she got older. As she moved into adulthood, however, she instead realized how much damage parents could thoughtlessly inflict on a child, and she became averse to the discomfort that accompanied interactions with her own.

Her current circumstances, however, overruled her usual resistance. It was time to make the call. She pictured her parents in the immaculate kitchen of their San Diego retirement unit, with its forest of oak cabinetry and baffling milk-cow motif. They would be standing at the breakfast counter in their dazzlingly white walking sneakers, bellowing into the speakerphone as if making a ship-to-shore connection.

She reached for the phone and was about to dial when she glanced out the window and saw Justine on the deck below. She stood with two other moms, holding a paper coffee cup and throwing her head back with laughter. Rather than wave good-bye to their children and leave, the three moms settled onto a bench to continue their conversation, smiling and sipping their coffees as they chatted.

Margaret lowered the phone, her eyes on Justine. This was not a woman who appeared to be consumed with the business of running the biggest fundraiser of the year at the most prestigious preschool in West LA, if not the entire city. On the contrary, she looked to Margaret as though she were primed for a day of shopping, mani-pedis, and lunch with the girls—none of which would move Margaret any closer to the successful execution of her plan. It followed, then, that Justine—like some other parents Margaret had encountered over the years—might have lost sight of just what a privilege it was to be a member of the Garden of Happiness family.

Margaret rolled her chair sideways to the filing cabinet and unlocked the drawer. "Must be nice," she muttered, and began flipping through the student files. Sometimes the parade of pampered parents that streamed through the yellow door each morning was too much to stomach. Did they ever stop and listen to the things they were saying—their supposed "complaints?" Nannies with colds, crowded yoga classes, contractors who set the Italian tile a quarter-inch off in the new master shower. "Princess problems," Leticia had dubbed them with an eye-roll after her first summer helping out in the school's toddler camp when she was in high school. Margaret would have given anything to have had those kinds of "problems" when she was a rookie parent. With two chunks of grad school debt to pay off, Margaret's puny teaching salary, and Eddie's practice not yet off the ground, the last thing she'd had time for was flitting around town in workout wear. As far as she had come since those days, she was not about to let some spoiled dilettante mom jeopardize her plans.

Her fingers moved through the student files a second time, taking extra care as they walked across the bright green tabs. "Underwood, Underwood," she said with each flip until she reached the last student in the alphabet: Siddartha Zuckerman. Emma Underwood's file was not in its place. She picked up the phone and called Trey.

"Yes, commodore?" he answered.

"Did I leave Emma Underwood's file in your office?"

"Indeed you did."

"Can you bring it up, please?"

"*Certainly.* Let me just sweep aside all of the orders from picture day that I was just organizing. May I bring you anything else? Cognac? Extra towels?"

"Oh, for Pete's sake. I'll get it myself—I want to make some tea anyway." She hung up and looked down into the play yard. There, whipping down the metal slide, arms in an ecstatic *V* above her head, was Emma Underwood. She wore pink pants and a fleece top that matched the blue bows on her braids. Flapping in her hand was the morning's art project—a construction-paper jack-o-lantern with multicolored feathers glued to it. How a frivolous mom was raising such a secure, resilient child was beyond Margaret. She watched Emma collapse in giggles at the bottom of the slide. It was time to restore Justine Underwood's sense of urgency.

As she reached the door, she heard an unfamiliar electronic chime. She waited with her hand on the knob and, just when she thought she'd imagined it, it happened again. Walking briskly back to her desk, she saw a flashing bar on the side of her computer screen. As the rhythmic *bloop-bloop* continued, she noticed Leticia's tiny photo in the blinking bar. Her daughter was trying to contact her! Margaret snatched the mouse and began clicking, unsure where to aim. Leticia had given her a quick tutorial on Skype before leaving for school, but none of it was coming back to her now as she raced to connect before the *blooping* stopped. Finally, Leticia's face appeared onscreen, scowling into the camera at point-blank range. Margaret self-consciously adjusted the layers of hair around her face.

"Hello, sweetheart," she shouted toward the computer. Leticia pulled back and her lips began moving, but no sound came out on Margaret's end, prompting another flurry of rapid-fire mouse-clicking. "Hold on, Tish, I'm just working on the volume here!"

Leticia covered her ears and Margaret saw her reach forward and tap her keyboard, then motion for Margaret to do the same. Finally, she noticed the volume adjustment buttons and dialed up the sound just as Leticia appeared to be giving up.

"—my God, MOM!" her voice enveloped the room. Margaret tapped the volume down again.

"I think I've got it now," she said, sitting forward in the chair.

"Wow," Leticia said. "Total Skype fail. That was like teaching Grandma to use AOL. When I was ten."

Margaret hoped the screen's picture was grainy enough to hide the horror that must have swept across her face at this comparison. "Is everything all right?" She leaned toward the monitor, examining Leticia's face for signs of trauma. In spite of the hiccups in the connection, she could see that college already had changed her daughter, from the burgundy-and-blue streaks in her hair to the slightly haughty tilt of her head. The cumulative impact of these subtle shifts in a single, unexpected visual took Margaret's breath away.

"I'm fine, Mom. Geez. Relax." Conversation and laughter could be heard from the hallway outside Leticia's open door.

"Okay, that's good." She reached for her water bottle and took a few swallows. "This is a nice surprise—how's school?"

"Whatever. It's okay, I guess. Sociology is lame, but I love my lit class. Statistics...I don't know." Leticia glanced away from the camera often as she spoke.

"What's that you're wearing? I don't recognize the royal blue."

Leticia looked down at her sweater. "Oh, yeah. It's my roommate's. I just threw it on."

"We talked about what a bad idea it is to share clothes, remember? You're inviting trouble if you start intermingling your possessions."

"Oh my God, Mom, I didn't Skype you for a lecture, okay?"

"Fine." Margaret held up her hands. "I'm happy to talk about any topic of your choice."

"Okay. Then I would like to talk about this financial problem between you and Dad." Her chin rose at the end of the sentence.

Margaret sat up in her chair. "Obviously your father has been talking to you. What has he said, exactly?"

"He said that you're being uncooperative and that it's making it impossible to settle the divorce and move on."

"He said *what*?"

Leticia's expression became more tentative. "He also said your unfairness is causing a financial hardship."

"'A *financial hardship*?'" Margaret reminded herself to keep her composure. "If I didn't know better, I'd say you had taken notes."

"Come on, Mom, I just want to know what's going on."

"Leticia, you've made it clear that you do not want to get involved in the divorce and I have honored that request to the best of my ability. So I'm a little confused that you suddenly want to know the details of our settlement."

"It's just that he made me really nervous, talking about money."

"Nervous in what way?"

"It's hard being away, and I really love my school." She hesitated. "I'm worried that you guys won't be able to pay my tuition," she blurted.

In the tiny inset view in the corner of her screen, Margaret saw her own expression become an incensed grimace. "Of all the manipulative, emotionally stunted—how *dare* he play on your fears to advance his agenda. That self-serving man-baby! We agreed we would not involve you in any of this!"

"Mom!"

"Then again, what's an agreement to Eddie Askew? Nothing!" Margaret ranted. "A verbal convenience of less long-term significance than one of his farts!"

"Mom, stop!" Leticia reached across to her bed, grabbed a stuffed dog, and pulled it to her chest.

"To put your mind at ease, Leticia, your tuition money is right where it's always been—in a separate account that is not affected by the divorce. I can assure you that our understanding regarding those funds is one agreement your father *will* abide by."

Leticia said nothing, snuggling the stuffed dog up to her neck and hugging him harder.

"I apologize for losing my temper, but I am appalled that he would drag you into this—no, more than that—that he would risk upsetting you in order to exert pressure on me. It might interest you to know that the dispute your father is referring to is—"

"I can't deal with this, Mom," Leticia interrupted, reaching toward her keyboard. "I have to go, okay? Bye." She pushed a button and disappeared with an electronic *ping*, leaving Margaret to stare at an empty screen.

23
Justine

Justine looked over her shoulder to make sure Emma was out of earshot, then spoke into her cellphone. "I'm one pair of fauxga pants away from becoming a Westside mom cliché. That is all." She ended the call and put the phone down on the breakfast room table next to her laptop. Ruthie would understand when she got the voicemail. "Fauxga" (a.k.a. fake yoga) was one of their danger words—code for the worst-case scenario West LA mom, whose Namaste-embellished Range Rover occupied two parking spaces at Whole Foods while inside she berated a clerk for being out of soy milk as the slogan on her organic cotton T-shirt directed those around her to practice random acts of kindness. In the past, Justine had observed the fauxga followers from afar—noting the juxtaposition of a pair of Toms shoes with a rose-gold Rolex at Peet's or the "breathe" tattoo on the wrist of the mom who seemed to fill her lungs primarily to give orders via cellphone to her child's nanny. Since becoming auction chair, however, she was finding it increasingly difficult to hold herself apart as an amused observer of this particular slice of mom subculture. To the contrary, she was beginning to worry that she was morphing into one of them.

She peeked around the side of the laptop, abandoning the email she had been writing—part of an extended and contentious three-way debate on the merits of "dusty rose" over "peony" for the table linens at the auction party. Exhibit A sat at the other end of the breakfast table: the most expensive handbag Justine had ever owned, with buttery, pebbled leather, matte, nickel hardware that glowed like moonlight on a Maserati, and rolled-leather shoulder straps as thick as a baby's wrist. She swallowed hard. She'd had the bag for a week and was still in shock that she'd bought it. One minute she was walking through Fred Segal with two other moms after an auction meeting. The next thing she knew, a twenty-something salesman wearing tight, white jeans and a quarter inch of eyeliner was handing her a large shopping bag and shouting over the Ramones blasting from the recessed speakers in the ceiling. "Don't fight it, sugar. Sooner or later Marc Jacobs owns all our asses."

Afterward, she found herself walking alone in the parking lot, blinking in the afternoon sun and slowly becoming aware of three things. First, that in her shopping bag was the most exquisite accessory she would ever own. Second, that it had better be—it had absorbed her entire bedroom-redecorating budget. And, third, that in her retail lather, she had initialed the tiny line on the receipt printout confirming she understood the store's no-returns/store-credit-only policy. There would be no undoing this epic impulse purchase.

This must have been how it happened in Jonestown, she thought bitterly as she idled in her car, leaning into the vent and blasting the air conditioning into her face. Apparently, if you were going to hang out in the village, you could only get away for so long passing the Kool-Aid jug with a polite, "No, thanks, I brought a Snapple from home."

She reached across the table for the handbag she would now be carrying for the rest of her life and which would likely hold her cremated remains into eternity. She hugged the bag to her chest, breathed in the scent of the leather—no doubt hand-oiled on the slopes of Vesuvius by Mensa-member virgins—and wondered what the hell was happening to her. Had there always been an "it" bag-craving beast lurking within, waiting to be released by exposure to an affluent preschool peer group?

That morning she would return to the scene of the crime—Fred Segal—for yet another auction meeting. As the event date neared, the committee assembled every week, with hours of protracted email correspondence, sidebar conversations, and relentless micromanagement by Margaret filling the days and evenings in between. It had been weeks since Greg appeared in the spare bedroom doorway to ask when she would be coming to bed. The new routine was for Justine to tiptoe into their room after midnight, having finally negotiated such daily challenges as listening to the complaints of a parent whose personal balloon artist felt slighted by the Riviera's manager, or dissuading Margaret from pressuring parents by posting a list above the cubbies of families who had not yet RSVP'd to the party. Bette had been right; this job wasn't about event planning—it was about diva wrangling. And Justine was over it.

"Why are you hugging your purse, Mommy?"

Justine opened her eyes and saw Emma standing next to her chair with a quizzical look on her face and a hot-pink sippy cup of milk in her hand. She cleared her throat and put the purse back on the table. "Oh, it just looked so lonely sitting there all by itself. But you know what? I'd rather hug *you*." She gathered Emma into her lap and squeezed her, nuzzling the fine wisps of hair behind her ear. "Let's go get ready for school and make your piggy-tails, little girl. I bet I know which color clippies you'll pick today."

Emma frowned at the mention of school. "Miss Glenda doesn't like me anymore."

"I can't imagine that," Justine said as she closed her laptop. "Who wouldn't like an Emma?"

"It's true! She makes angry eyebrowns at me." She jammed her finger up her nostril.

"Is it when you're doing that?" Justine moved Emma's hand away from her face with a stern look that made Emma giggle.

"No, really! Miss Margaret, too."

Justine's hands became still and she watched her daughter's face. "What do you mean?"

"They look at me and frown a lot." Emma suddenly looked stricken. "And I need to go dookie."

In the charge to the bathroom, their exchange was temporarily forgotten. She did not think of it again until she got the call during her committee meeting. "Emma is fine," Miss Glenda began after identifying herself. For some reason, the phrase had the opposite of its intended effect, making Justine clutch at her throat, certain that something had happened to her daughter. "However, we would appreciate it if you could stop by the school."

Justine's heart thumped as she parked at the curb, eerily deserted in the hours between the frenzied drop-off and pick-up periods. She flipped the latch on the picket gate and hurried toward the kitchen, wondering what could have happened that required her presence.

Had Emma's adjustment to Garden of Happiness not been as successful as it seemed, or was something else going on? She had heard other mothers talk about children who transitioned into the school without incident only to develop "troublesome behaviors" as autumn progressed. There were whispered stories of families who had suffered a change of fortune, suddenly unable to do anything right in the eyes of the school, meaning, of course, the eyes of Margaret. It was common knowledge that, once a family was on this slippery slope, it would not be long before the other children would arrive one morning and find their classmate's cubby empty and their magnetic name badge missing from the "Lettuce Take Turns" board. Justine thought back on Emma's earlier declaration that Miss Glenda and Miss Margaret no longer liked her.

If this turned out to be preschool politics related to Margaret's recent crankiness, she would be making some "angry eyebrowns" of her own.

Emma and Miss Glenda were waiting when Justine hurried up the wooden steps into the kitchen. "Here's Mum," Miss Glenda said to Emma. "I told you she was coming, didn't I?"

Emma sat in the corner bench dinette, where Justine had spent so many hours transitioning at the start of school. "Mama!" she said, holding her arms out to her mother.

"I'm here, Ladybug." She could tell from Emma's splotchy face that she had been crying, but she looked more angry than hurt. Justine slid into the bench next to her and stroked the sweaty hair from her forehead. "What's going on?"

"Emma would like to tell you what happened in the Craft Patch a short while ago," Miss Glenda said.

Emma crossed her arms with a huff. "Messiah wouldn't share the recycling blocks."

Justine stifled a groan. That was one name she would never get used to. "Then what happened?"

"I took them. But it was only to share! I was going to *help* him play with them."

"Did the Messiah—sorry—did the little boy want your help?"

"*No,*" she said with an exaggerated sulk.

"And then…?"

"Miss Glenda made me say sorry and give them back." Emma glowered at the floor in silent contempt of the criminal justice system.

"Maybe you were being bossy with Messiah when you took the blocks. What do you think?"

Emma kept her eyes on the floor. "Messiah was all done."

"It sounds like Messiah was *not* all done."

Emma waved for Justine to bend down toward her, then said in a loud stage whisper, "Mommy, he didn't mind *at all*. He didn't even tell on me. It's *no fair*."

Justine looked over at Miss Glenda, who had been watching Emma silently, her hands clasped in front of her. "Is that...it? Did anything else happen I should know about?"

"No, that is the gist of the incident," Miss Glenda said, clearing her throat. "We felt it was important that Emma hear directly from you that she must resist the urge to take other children's toys out of turn." She looked down and tugged at the zipper of her gray hoodie.

Justine hesitated. She had been called back to school for a dispute over a toy? That didn't make sense. Even Miss Glenda seemed uncomfortable addressing the situation with her usual seamless authority. For the first time, Justine considered what it must be like to work for Margaret, not as a tuition-paying parent on a committee, but as an employee. As she watched Miss Glenda fuss with her zipper, she no longer saw the school's junior enforcer, but a young woman who seemed to be struggling with her role in this "incident" just as much as she and Emma were. Justine didn't know what was going on, but she had a strong feeling it had nothing to do with her daughter.

She stood and held her hands out for Emma to do the same. "We're done here," she said and kissed her on the head. "No more being bossy with other people's toys. Got it?"

"Okay, Mommy."

Miss Glenda broke out of her trance and stepped forward. "I believe Miss Margaret wanted to speak with—"

"We're *done* here, Miss Glenda," Justine repeated. The two women exchanged a look, and although she tried to hide it, Justine could see the relief in Miss Glenda's face as she held her hand out to Emma.

"Come along, then," she said, leading her toward the door. "Let's rejoin your group."

"Bye, Mommy," Emma said with a wave.

Justine waved back. "See you at pick-up, Ladybug." She watched them walk out of the kitchen and down the steps. When she turned to retrieve her purse, Margaret was standing by the refrigerator, clipboard at her side.

"I see you responded to Miss Glenda's call." She seemed flushed and furtive to Justine, as if she had just finished feeding an errant parent to that annoying bunny of hers.

"Of course," she said. "But I'm still not sure why I'm here."

"I'm sorry?"

"A disagreement over a toy? Isn't that just another day at the office for a preschooler?"

"I love it when parents explain children to me," Margaret said under her breath.

"Excuse me?"

In the sandy play yard outside the kitchen door, a girl pushed a wooden fire engine, imitating its siren with a steady wail.

"I assume Miss Glenda shared our concerns with you," Margaret said.

"Not exactly, no."

"We see this occasionally—a delayed reaction to separation. The child pretends to go along with the new routine, but can only keep up the pretense for so long before rebelling. Unfortunately, once rebellious behaviors begin, they can be very difficult to extinguish. I feel sorry for Emma Underwood," Margaret *tsk*ed. "The stress brought on by change is too big for her to process appropriately."

"You feel sorry for *Emma*? On my way in here I saw a kid bite the top off a glue stick and you're focused on *my* daughter's behavior? What I find interesting is that Emma told me just this morning that you and Miss Glenda don't like her anymore, and now I've been called out of an auction meeting for some incident that turns out to be nothing." Behind her, the girl bumped the toy fire engine up the deck stairs and kicked the siren wail up a notch.

Margaret nodded and pursed her lips. "I see. And when your event falls short of its goals, you'll say that our efforts to address your child's behavioral challenges are to blame. I've heard this all before."

Justine shook her head. "Wow. Speaking of behavioral challenges, has it occurred to you that people might actually enjoy serving on these committees if you dialed down the grim reaper management style? We're *volunteers*. We're not digging the Panama Canal here; it's a preschool party."

Margaret worked her jaw forward and backward before replying. "That's the thing with you moms. You flounce in here with your highlights and your skinny jeans and it's all fun and games, isn't it? It's just something else to play at while the husbands are at work."

"Play?" Justine snorted. "I'm pulling longer hours on this event than I did when I worked full time—and I didn't even *want* this job."

"Oh, *please*."

"Whether you give them credit or not, you've got an army of moms here busting their heinies to keep you happy. There's not a vendor within a mile who hasn't been shaken down for an auction donation."

Margaret banged her clipboard down on the counter. "You all think you're safe in your perfect little families and your perfect little lives. You don't take any of this seriously because you're just passing through. Well, let me tell you—this is not a game, and long after you and your child have moved on, I will be here, do you understand? This is *my* school."

Easy there, Captain Queeg, Justine thought.

The girl with the fire truck suddenly stopped wailing. In the ringing silence, Justine saw that Margaret's eyes were bloodshot and that the skin around them looked as fragile as crepe paper. She wondered what had pushed Margaret into the angry desperation that was radiating from her now. Then she remembered the look on

Emma's face during Miss Glenda's reprimand and felt something shift inside her. She stepped toward Margaret and placed her hand on the edge of the counter. "You don't know me or my life. Now, I'm not interested in this personal crisis of yours everyone's talking about—and, yes, everyone *is* talking about it—but if you think calling me in here to pin some bogus psychofluff on my kid is going to intimidate me into raising more money for your school, then *you're* the one playing games."

"Feel better now that you've acted out?" Margaret said.

Justine stared at her for a long moment. "If you'd like someone else to run this thing, I can have all the merchandise on the school's doorstep by the end of the day. That should get some positive buzz going for your big fundraiser." She crossed her arms.

Margaret's mouth settled into a hard line. She took her clipboard from the counter. "I would prefer that the school not suffer an unnecessary disruption as a result of your lack of commitment."

Justine gave a short bark of laughter. "Right. I didn't think you'd take me up on it. Besides, as much as I'd love to have my life back sooner rather than later, I actually *care* about *my* reputation." She looked around the kitchen, blowing out a mouthful of air between her lips with a motorboat sound. "You know, I *do* feel better now that I've acted out." Swinging her purse over her shoulder, she walked out the door and down the wooden steps.

Her hands didn't start shaking until she pulled out her car keys and chirped the driver's side lock. As she gunned the car away from the curb, she jammed in her earpiece and autodialed Greg. When the call rolled to voicemail, she hung up without leaving a message and tried Ruthie. "Come on, come on," she said, tapping the steering wheel as the phone rang in her ear. Already the scene in the kitchen was playing back in her mind. "Dammit," she said, hanging up again when she heard Ruthie's voicemail greeting.

How could she effectively debrief after her preschool trauma if she couldn't get anyone on the phone? She drove toward Century City and Greg's office.

No matter how many times they redecorated, the firm always smelled the same when she stepped off the elevator—a medley of furniture polish and air freshener with a hint of toner. The familiarity was comforting as she waved hello to the receptionist and turned the corner into the suite. It was easy to imagine that it was five years earlier—that she still worked there and was stopping by on her way from a meeting to say hello to Greg, the lawyer she had started dating. He had been a "baby lawyer" at the time, fretting before every court filing, pulling frequent all-nighters, and competing to stay on partnership track. As the months passed, she helped turn his office from a sterile room stacked with banker boxes and black binders into a stylish, sophisticated work space. When he made partner and moved into a larger office, her present to him was the luxurious leather desk chair she knew he coveted and which she had been steadily saving for with each paycheck.

She turned down another mahogany-paneled hall, her footsteps silenced by the thick, tan carpet. Outside Greg's door, his secretary sat at her desk, writing on a sticky note while talking on the phone. "Hey, Denise," Justine said softly as she passed. "Good to see you."

She opened Greg's door, the words spilling out before she was inside. "Oh my God, you are *not* going to believe what just happened at the preschool."

Simone sat behind Greg's desk, nestled into the black leather seat. She wore a sleeveless emerald shell, its matching cardigan discarded across Greg's in-box. On the desk was a grande Starbucks cup with

"*Simone*" scrawled on it in grease pencil. "Sounds gripping," she deadpanned, her fingers still on the keyboard. "Do tell."

Greg's wooden door had a pneumatic arm that eased it shut with a quiet hiss. The device worked slowly, allowing plenty of time for Denise to hear Justine's response out in the hall.

"You're in my husband's chair."

"I'm *working*." Simone resumed typing.

"You can work somewhere else."

Simone looked up at Justine, a slow smile spreading across her face. She ran her hands down the chair's arms. "But this is where Greg expects to find me when he returns."

Justine forced a laugh. "Who are you supposed to be? The poor man's Jessica Rabbit?"

"You make me sad, Justine." Simone swung her hair, which cascaded in chestnut waves down the front of the silk shell. "When you worked here you were cute—at least, in a retro-quirky, Anthropologie way. When did you turn into one of those dowdy housewives pushing a sticky stroller through the food court?"

"Gee, I guess that was about the time you were slithering around on *another* partner's furniture. I believe Greg said it was Mort Stivey? He wasn't sure if Mort came before or after Jerry Weems, but I'm sure you can understand how challenging it is to keep track of your activities around here." Simone's eyes narrowed. "That's why Greg said yes when you asked to work on this case, you know," Justine continued. "He told me he felt sorry for you, since you'd become such a joke at the firm."

Simone's lips curled into another smile. "I love how he talks about me when he's at home."

"That's it," Justine said, dropping her purse in the guest chair and walking around the desk. "Time to go bye-bye."

"What are you doing?" Simone said, looking alarmed.

Justine got behind the chair and began pulling it away from the desk as Simone gripped the arms. "I'm a mom, remember?" she grunted as she yanked the chair off its floor pad and onto the carpet. "This is me sending you to your room."

"Stop that!" Simone jumped up from the chair, steadying herself on her platform pumps. "You're unbalanced." She smoothed her hair.

"You have no idea." Justine stepped around the chair, putting herself between it and Simone. "Now *shoo.*" She flicked her hands, waving Simone toward the door.

Simone snatched a file and her phone from the desk, giving Justine a once-over as she passed. "Nice mom jeans."

"Nice extensions," Justine hissed.

Simone started out the door, then turned back to Justine. "And, just so you know, I didn't ask to be on this case. He came to me." Justine waited for the door to sigh shut before sinking into the still-warm chair behind her.

☀ ☀ ☀

Justine was abusing the flatware, thumping forks and knives onto the placemats with angry tosses when she heard Greg come through the front door. She knew he would come find her before doing anything else. Sure enough, within twenty seconds he was standing across the dining room table from her.

"You manhandled her out of the chair and then you *shooed* her?" He set his briefcase down and pulled off his tie with a *zipp*ing sound. "That's my *workplace*, Justine."

"*Sshh.*" Justine looked through the doorway into the family room, where Emma was pushing her stroller around the coffee table wearing her nightgown and a large cowboy hat. "Not so loud." She motioned for him to follow her into the kitchen, where she picked up a wooden spoon and began stirring a pot of rice on the stove. "I was provoked."

Greg crossed his arms. "'Provoked.'"

"That's right. Provoked on several levels, starting with the fact that she looked quite comfy snuggled up at your desk. In your chair."

"Look, I don't know why she was at my desk. She buzzed me from her office. I told her it wasn't a good time to meet because I had to do an associate review in one of the conference rooms. That's where I was when you showed up unannounced and started rolling furniture around."

"For the record, I called first." Justine replaced the pot's lid and moved to the pan of asparagus. "You know what I think of that woman," she said finally. "I don't trust her. But something she said is bothering me."

"And what's that?"

"Did you seek her out to be on this case? Or did she ask you?"

Greg threw up his hands. "*Geez*, I don't know. Do you have any idea how much I've got bearing down on me right now?"

Justine studied his face. "You told me she asked you."

"Then that must be how it happened. I really don't recall."

"I mean, I understand that there are strategic reasons for having a female associate on the team, but I think you're overlooking other, more qualified candidates. What about that sharp young woman from Yale with the cankles? And there's the one who clerked for the California Supreme Court—the one with the braces. She could remove her headgear for client meetings, right?"

"Nice. Look, we're way past staffing decisions at this point. It is what it is, just like on my other cases. Why are we even talking about this?"

"She said you asked her to work with you."

"Was that before or after you forcibly ejected her from my chair?"

"I don't see how that's relevant."

"Oh, for crying out loud. There's nothing like coming home from a hard day's work to a nice, warm cross-examination." He turned to walk out of the kitchen. "I'm going to go change clothes."

Justine watched him leave. *To be continued,* she thought, gathering the hot pads and salt-and-pepper shakers. As she carried them to the dining room, Emma zoomed by with the stroller. "Someone's here!" she said and disappeared into her room. Justine wondered if "someone" were imaginary, then heard the soft knocking from the entryway.

"Sorry to show up at the witching hour," Ruthie said when Justine opened the door, "but this was my window of opportunity to get out without a kid." She held out an aqua envelope. "I will trade you one kiddie-party invite for your punch bowl. Those are my terms."

"Accepted," Justine said, taking the envelope. "Come on in." Ruthie followed her to the back of the house, where Justine dropped the envelope on the island, then squatted to open a cabinet door. "I think the punch bowl is in here." She pushed past vases and stacks of platters.

"Hey, are you okay?" Ruthie said. "You don't seem to be operating at full sequins-and-unicorns capacity."

"Here it is." Justine maneuvered the punch bowl out of the cabinet and cradled it in her arms. "I'm okay, I guess." She eyed the doorway and lowered her voice. "We are in the midst of a hubbub." She carried the bowl to the sink and began rinsing it. "Remember when I had to do traffic school right after I'd had the stomach flu and the guy next to me ate three liverwurst sandwiches during class? Today made me wish for that day."

"Let me guess—this is somehow related to that godforsaken school auction."

"Well—"

"Hello, Ruthie," Greg said, appearing in the doorway in baggy track pants and an ancient University of Chicago sweatshirt that Justine had yet been unable to convince him to throw out.

"Hey, mister," she said and gave him a hug. "Your woman was just about to tell me how this auction of hers is ruining her life."

"Yeah, somehow Justine has become the school's complimentary 24-hour event-planning hotline," Greg said. "Then there's the warehouse formerly known as our dining room. We can barely pull the chairs out far enough to sit down."

"It'll be over in a few weeks." Justine didn't look up as she dried the bowl with a checkered dishtowel.

"Well, between the auction and the old boyfriend, I'd say you've been a real sport about life in the Garden of Nuisances." Ruthie laughed. "You're a lot more tolerant than Mac would be, that's for sure. He wouldn't be able to resist yanking Harry's chain."

Justine stiffened as Greg shot her a questioning look. "Well," he said, turning back to Ruthie, "you have to respect a man in an Ed Hardy T-shirt, right?"

Ruthie snorted.

"Here you go." Justine pushed the punch bowl onto Ruthie unsmilingly. She could feel Greg watching her.

"Oh." Ruthie wrapped her arms around it. "Okay." The three of them fell into an uncomfortable silence, which Ruthie seemed to be waiting for Justine to break. "Well, gotta go," she said finally.

"I'll walk you out." Justine hustled her from the kitchen as Ruthie called her good-bye to Greg over her shoulder.

"What the hell was that?" Ruthie said as Justine opened the front door. "As the middle schoolers say, 'awkward sauce.'"

"Like I said, not the best day around here, but I'll call you tomorrow. Thanks for the invite."

As she passed Emma's room, she heard her singing "You Are My

Sunshine." She knew there would be an audience of stuffed animals arranged on the changing table, just as she knew Emma would have added a white feather boa as a counterpoint to the cowboy hat.

Greg was waiting when she returned to the kitchen. "So am I to understand," he said, turning the rubber spatula over in his hands, "that you used to date that poser whose house we went to for the playdate from hell?"

Justine began spooning rice into a serving bowl. "It was a long time ago—before I moved back to LA...before I met you."

"And all this time, you never mentioned it." He kept his eyes on the spatula, which he was now gently slapping against his thigh.

"I didn't see the point in talking about it. It was just an annoying coincidence from my past."

"Which you kept secret."

Justine hit her spoon on the rim of the pot and a clump of rice flew off, landing on the floor. "I was embarrassed, okay? All the stuff you and Ruthie were mocking is true—the douchebag clothes, all of it. It's one thing for me to complain to her about having to deal with him; she already knows the story from grad school. But why would I want *you* to know I dated that guy?" They glared at each other until the oven buzzer sounded.

"So you tell me he's just an annoyance and I'm supposed to believe you, but when I tell you Simone is just a co-worker, you don't believe *me*. Do you see the hypocrisy here?"

"Of course I do. The difference is that I was *not* happy when I found out Harry was at our school, but you are *very* happy to bask in Simone's office foreplay."

"Oh, come on." Greg picked up a glass, walked to the freezer, and took a handful of ice from the bin.

"You know the other reason I didn't say anything about Harry?" She opened the oven door again and let it drop. "I didn't want to make you uncomfortable. But when I tell you that Simone makes *me* uncomfortable, you shrug it off." She slipped her hands into oven mitts and pulled a pan of chicken from the oven, closing the door with her foot.

"Wait a minute, you thought *that* guy—excuse me, the '*artiste*'—would make me uncomfortable? Are you kidding? What, am I insecure because I'm not wearing a rubber bracelet with some bullshit affirmation on it?" He laughed and shook his head. "I have exes out there, too, you know. I'm just sorry you didn't like yourself more when you were in grad school."

Justine whirled around to reply, but he cut her off.

"And this Simone obsession is coming from something going on with *you*. When you worked at the firm, she was a joke, but now for some reason you've chosen to see her as a threat. I don't know what's changed your perspective, but that's something you need to think about, Justine. That situation is all about your perception—not anything I've done."

"All right, and while I'm 'thinking about my perspective,'" she tried to make air quotes but was still wearing the oven mitts and so settled for waving her arms at him, "*you* should think about whether you're being completely honest with yourself about the big flirt-whammy she's putting on you. Because you know what? I think you eat it up."

"Oh, give me a break. You can't seriously think—"

"Mommy?" They both turned to see Emma in the doorway with her stroller. She had loaded on the remaining accessories from her dress-up box and now looked like a miniature country-western transvestite. "We're hungry. Except not Angus the anteater. He ate his snack too late and ruined his dinner. He's on a timeout to think about what he did."

Justine and Greg exchanged a look then sprang into action, helping Emma wash her hands, serving up the rest of the food, and getting the meal on the table, all while avoiding each other. Within five minutes, Justine had buckled Emma into her high chair and sat down across from Greg. She stayed focused on Emma, who was happy to have the conversational airtime all to herself for a change. They passed the mealtime asking Emma questions, half-listening to her responses while the unfinished argument hung between them.

Justine was clearing the table when they heard the scrape of the front door deadbolt turning over. Startled, she looked at Greg, who shrugged. They hurried through the family room toward the entryway, arriving just as the door swung open. Justine's mother tried to remove her key, the long, beaded keychain clacking against the door as she struggled. "I don't know why you two don't oil this lock." She stepped away from the door, her tote bag swinging from her elbow. "Would someone like to help me with this?"

"Mom, what are you doing here?" Justine stood next to Greg in the entry archway.

"What do you mean what am I doing here?" she said irritably, rooting through her tote bag. "You asked me to babysit so you could go out for your anniversary dinner and here I am." She looked them both up and down. "Please tell me that's not what you're wearing."

24
Ruben

Ruben positioned his card table for maximum exposure to the stream of mommies flowing through the toddler yard for morning drop-off. He unlocked the small metal cashbox and waited. He needed a distraction—something to do with his hands to calm himself. *Thank God*, he thought when the morning's first cluster of parents came through the gate.

"Raffle tickets!" Ruben called out. "Get your raffle tickets *hee-yah*!"

"Oh, Ruben, you're so funny," said a mom wearing an outfit that looked like a cross between a Japanese schoolgirl and an affluent pilgrim. "I'll take five."

"Thanks, Moira. Oh, and I have Taylor's lunchbox." He counted out the tickets. "She left it at our house the other day."

"You're an angel. I'll text Bonita so she can get it from her cubby at pick-up. And we want to squeeze in a playdate at our place before Thanksgiving, too. We'll talk!"

"Hey, Ruben," called another mom as she passed the table with her daughter in tow. "I'll hit you on the way out, okay?"

"You bet, Lynn," he replied, making change for another mom. "Snazzy fedora, by the way."

"You've got a keeper here, Willow," one of the moms said with a nod toward Ruben. "I think he could sell this group just about anything."

Ruben saw Willow moving through the line with a pleased

expression. "I know, isn't he *fabulous*? Don't even try luring him to your committee—he's mine."

When she reached the front of the line, Ruben turned the cash box so she could see how full it was. "Check it out, boss."

"*Love* it! Love *you*!" She plunked her cash down on the table. "I'll see *you* this afternoon, yes?" She held out her French-tipped fingers to receive the stack of tickets. "The kids can go in the hot tub and you would not *believe* the feast I've ordered. There are only fifteen children coming but we're prepared to feed fifty!"

"Oh, yeah, we'll be there," he said and wondered if he would ever get used to Willow's megaphone delivery. "Wouldn't miss it."

Ruben smiled and tried to ignore the churning in his stomach. Willow's get-together was his opportunity to connect with her husband, and already his nerves were dismantling his confidence. He'd spent most of the previous night fluffing and re-fluffing his pillow while picturing himself committing one social gaffe after another.

He had discovered in his research that every aspiring comic in Los Angeles was panting along in Elliott Neff's wake, each hoping to catch his eye and impress him with their shtick. In an interview with *Los Angeles Magazine*, he complained that he had been assailed with spontaneous standup performances by waiters in restaurants, a washroom attendant at the Four Seasons Beverly Hills and, most memorably, four male nurses at St. John's Medical Center who broke into a choreographed performance of Mel Brooks' "Springtime for Hitler" while Elliott was recovering from gall bladder surgery. The YouTube video of their performance went viral, but Elliott was not amused.

Ruben was intimidated but determined. After all, he wasn't some random stalker-comic. He had a legitimate reason to be at the man's house and he knew his wife through non-Hollywood channels. As long as he didn't accidentally drop a piano on the guy, he ought to be able to at least establish the beginnings of an acquaintance.

"Just be yourself," Deandra had said that morning as she left for work.

"Yeah," he said after their good-bye kiss, "like I'm *that* stupid."

Willow's house was a monument to discomfort. Everywhere Ruben turned, he encountered polished knife-edges of marble, experimental furniture that looked to be made from crowbars, leather stirrups and bridge cables, or a sheer drop past a glass enclosure onto the hillside rocks a hundred feet below. It was an airy contemporary in the hills above Brentwood with what a realtor would call "jetliner views," but Ruben was far too occupied with keeping the twins alive to appreciate the house's selling points.

It was as if the residence had been designed as a preschool-parent endurance test, with hidden steps, an unfenced pool, and an open, freestanding fireplace that was, inexplicably, blazing. Already, parents were crisscrossing the open living room like a Secret Service advance team, shouting terse commands to one another as new dangers were uncovered. "No toddler guard on the powder room's doorknob!" barked one mom. "We've got an unfriendly cat on the ottoman. Do not approach!" announced another.

As usual, Ruben's twins took off in opposite directions before he had set down his daddy supply bag. By the time he corralled them into a relatively risk-free corner, he was so frazzled that he was almost relieved to learn that Elliott would not be at the house that afternoon.

"Oh God, no," said a mom in cargo pants and a camouflage tank top, a tattoo of a colorful sugar skull on her shoulder. "Willow would never schedule one of these when he was going to be at home."

"Have you met him?" another mom asked Ruben, checking the crowd over the top of her enormous smoked sunglasses. "He's *such* an *asshole*."

Ruben didn't pay much attention to this. He already knew Elliott's reputation. *I will have to lure him with my bromantic appeal the next chance I get*, he thought, savoring the fact that, at least for now, he had been spared the encounter.

In the meantime, he had to give Willow credit—she had arranged an impressive get-together for her committee. On the lawn around the hillside pool and spa were clusters of white wooden tables and chairs decorated with Garden of Happiness-themed green and yellow balloons. In a big, plastic tub on the grass were matching goodie bags that included a personalized beach pail for each child. Next to it was another tub overflowing with goggles, inflatable arm floaties, and other pool items that guests might have forgotten to bring. And through the sliding glass door was the kitchen, where the immense island held more than enough food for both grown-ups and children, including a color wheel of sandwich ingredients, from yellow bell peppers to celery to tomatoes.

Forty-five minutes into the party, the children had been pottied, suited, sunscreened, and attached to all manner of inflatable devices, and were bobbing happily in the oversize hot tub like fluorescent vegetables in a vat of minestrone.

"I never thought I'd feel more relaxed with my children in four feet of hot water rather than out of it," Ruben joked to a small group of moms, making sure Willow was not nearby.

"No kidding," Justine said as the moms chuckled. "I say we keep them in there for the rest of the party and go get food in shifts."

"Ruben," another mom said, "did I hear you say you had a show coming up?"

"Yes." He wiped the sweat from his lip and shielded his eyes from the November sun, which was now pounding the side of the house. "At the Laugh Factory on Friday night. It's a big one for me. There's a killer lineup—you should come."

"Yeah, I think I can make that." She stepped away as her cellphone started to ring.

"Hey, Ruben," Justine said, "I'm still on the list to get your email fliers, right?"

"Absolutely. They're going out tonight."

"I'll watch for that, too," said Marta, an African-American mom who owned a catering business and whose house Ruben and the twins visited the previous week. She fanned herself with her hand and slipped on her sunglasses. Ruben looked around for shade, but there was no relief from the sunlight bouncing off the white walls. "Oh, speaking of funny," Marta said with a laugh, "did you guys see that YouTube video that was going around—the one of the baby trying to stay awake in his high chair?"

The moms chimed in as Ruben headed for the kitchen to get waters for the group. The sliding glass door was partway open, and when he reached for the handle, he heard a man's voice inside.

"The fuck is this, Willow? A *kiddie* party?"

"I told you about it, Elliott. It's been planned for weeks. It's my committee." Willow's voice was flat and brittle, the way it had sounded the day Ruben heard her on her cellphone in Fred Segal.

"I do *not* appreciate coming home to watch the game in peace and finding a bunch of squawking moms and kids in my house."

Ruben took a step back from the door, but he couldn't stop listening.

"The game?" Willow said. "Perfect. Concha and I will take snacks into the study for you and I'll make you a drink and—"

"No." Elliott's voice was low and dangerous. "I don't want to watch the game in the study. I want to watch it here." He motioned to the flat-screen television on the wall above the kitchen table. Willow looked helplessly at Concha, whose face telegraphed that she had seen it all before.

"But, darling," Willow said, "the guests will be coming in right there to get food and drinks."

"Not anymore they won't." Elliott pulled out a chair and placed it in front of the glass slider. Then he sat down, snatched the remote from the table and clicked on the television.

"Unbelievable," said a woman behind Ruben. He turned to see that Justine and some of the other moms had drifted over to see what was happening.

"Poor Willow," said a mom. "Yeah, it's not like we're friends or anything, but I feel bad for her," added another, triggering a ripple of murmured agreement.

"We shouldn't be watching this," Ruben said, forgetting that his low voice carried farther than the women's did. Elliott's head snapped around and he saw the audience through the glass door, as did Willow and Concha. Willow's face was a mask of mortification.

"What are you looking at?" Elliott barked. He reached over and slid the glass door shut with a loud *bang*. Ruben felt the women collectively start around him as the glass shuddered. Through the door, Willow's face appeared to be collapsing with humiliation. The only sounds in the air were the delighted screams of the children in the hot tub, happily unaware of the adult drama around them.

"Time to go," said one of the moms, cutting the group's stunned silence. She turned and walked toward the hot tub, picking up her child's towel on the way. "I'm right behind you," said another. Ruben stood rooted to his spot on the patio as a familiar, sick feeling— decades old—moved through him. Through the glass, Elliott sat in the chair, arms crossed, watching the television with the remote on his lap.

Willow approached the door, squeezed around Elliott and let

herself out onto the patio. Her cheeks were flushed and her lips turned down at the corners in a way Ruben would not have thought possible. "Sorry about all that." Everyone except the children stopped what they were doing to observe her, this person who had gone into her home as someone they knew and had come out a deflated stranger. "So," she said, her hands rubbing together like they were under a faucet, "if anyone needs any food or drinks, just let me know and I'll get them, all right?" No one responded. "Here's the thing— it's probably best if no one goes in the house right now." Her chin quivered at the end of this announcement. "But who cares, right? It's more fun out here anyway!"

The group slowly came out of suspended animation, with replies of "Sure, honey," and "Okay, Willow." One by one, though, the children were fished out of the hot tub and wrapped like cocktail weenies in their multi-colored towels, their mothers shushing their protests. Once out of the tub, the children sensed that something was wrong and followed their instructions with eerie, silent cooperation.

The party was over.

Ruben watched Willow move among the guests, going through the motions of picking up stray napkins and straightening chairs. Every few seconds, she gave a nervous glance toward the kitchen door, where Elliott could be seen in his chair watching TV, legs stretched in front of him, arms crossed. Ruben wiped the sweat off his upper lip with the back of his hand again and stared through the glass at the person he had come to impress. His eyes narrowed as he considered the future he would have under this man's authority. He had told himself that, for the sake of his career and his family, this was the first door he needed to face, and now was the time to open it.

"Would you mind keeping an eye on Fred and Ethel in the hot tub for a minute?" Ruben said to Justine, whose daughter was busy digging through the bucket of party favors.

"Sure," she said, pausing before she walked away. "Where are you going?"

"To get a goddamned snack."

He walked to the door and flung it open, not bothering to close it after passing by Elliott and heading to the kitchen island.

Elliott jumped up from his chair. "What the hell do you think you're doing?"

"I think I'm doing turkey and provolone," Ruben said, eyes on the spread of food. "Then again, I've always been powerless over pastrami." He hovered over the display, piling sandwich parts onto a piece of bread on his palm.

"I told Willow to keep you people out."

Ruben slathered on some fancy mustard and placed a second piece of bread on top of his creation. Then he leaned against the island and, looking at Elliott, took a bite of his sandwich. "Willow's busy hosting a party," he said between chews. "Maybe you should come out and tell us yourself."

Elliott's jaw slid forward. "Get out of my house."

He took another bite of his sandwich. "I'm a guest of Willow's." Over Elliott's shoulder he could see that the moms had moved back to the open door where they stood, listening. Suddenly Willow pushed her way through the group and into the kitchen.

"It's all right, Ruben," she said, looking in alarm at her husband, who ignored her.

"No. It's not all right." He set his sandwich on the counter and took a bottle of water from a large, stainless-steel bowl of ice. He twisted off the cap and guzzled half of it.

"I said get out!" The remote in his fist, Elliott took a step toward Ruben.

"What are you gonna do, chief? Mute me?" Ruben wiped his mouth on the back of his hand and smiled. "If they made a remote that could do that, believe me, my wife would already have one."

The men were now three feet apart, Elliott in Armani and Ruben in his beloved army-surplus fatigues and a T-shirt that featured three pieces of bacon dancing with canes and top hats.

"You're a jackass," Elliott said with a sneer. "No, wait, that's not quite right. An *unemployed* jackass."

"Stop it, Elliott," Willow said.

"You're a shrewd judge of human nature," Ruben said and toasted him with his water bottle. "I can see how you've gotten where you are today."

Elliott drew his shoulders back in a preening motion. "Then you know who I am."

Ruben stared at him for a long moment before replying. "I do now." He motioned with his chin at the group of mothers and dripping-wet children crowded into the doorway behind Elliott. "And so does everyone else here."

Elliott turned to face the communal glare radiating from the group of sweaty, hungry people in the doorway.

Marta stepped into the kitchen and pointedly pushed Elliott's chair back under the table. "Who's ready for snacks?" she called, triggering a small stampede of slapping, squeaking rubber-clad feet across the tile floor. The mothers followed, flowing around Elliott like a stream around a boulder and taking Willow with them in their current.

☀ ☀ ☀

A half hour later, Ruben strapped the twins into the car, which was parked on such a steep incline that they looked like two tiny astronauts preparing for a moon shot. As the car made its way down the twisting hill streets, he called Deandra.

"I've been thinking about you," she said. She lowered her voice and Ruben could hear her rolling her chair into the semi-private corner of her cubicle. "How'd it go?"

"I'm sorry, Dee, but you won't be seeing me on AMC anytime soon."

"What do you mean?"

Ruben paused. "Let's just say I was myself."

"Oh-*kay*..."

Ruben told her everything that happened at the party.

"Oh my God," she said when he finished. "Willow is married to your dad."

"Yes, she is." The unwelcome feeling stirred again in his stomach. "So much for networking." He drove in silence a little ways, knowing Deandra was there on the line with him.

"Ruben?"

"Yeah, I'm here."

"I know how hard that was. I'm so proud of you."

Ruben hadn't realized how tense his shoulders were until his wife's words released them. He winked in the rearview mirror at his children. "That's nothing," he said. "Check this out: I finished the script."

25
Margaret

By the time Margaret's doorbell rang in the middle of the afternoon, she had only one cigarette left in the pack of Marlboros. The next-to-last dangled from the corner of her mouth as she crossed the family room on her way from the back patio, where she had spent most of the day rearranging the outdoor furniture, scrubbing the canvas umbrella, and repotting root-bound succulents. This was her first break of the day and, frankly, she would not have said no to a beer.

It was the day before Thanksgiving and school was closed. Margaret had done all the holiday grocery shopping the previous weekend, but that morning she had woken with the idea that she and Leticia should have Thanksgiving dinner outside. She planned to clean out the fire pit and string some of those little white lights in the avocado trees above the table. They could eat in the late afternoon, before the sun got too low. Once the chill settled, they would have pumpkin pie by the fire pit while Leticia told Margaret about life at college. It would be a new tradition—just the two of them. For the first time in months, she found herself charging out of bed and throwing on her old khakis and sneakers with something close to excitement. Without brushing her hair, she jotted a schedule of tasks, then a list of supplies, and left for the store.

The cigarettes had been an impulse purchase. There she was in the checkout line, her store club card in hand and a screaming, boogery child in the cart behind her, when she responded to the cashier's greeting with, "And a pack of Marlboros, please." It was as if she said it every time she bought groceries, when in fact she hadn't held a cigarette since college. On the way home, she looked over to see the red and white pack peeking from her handbag on the passenger seat. It looked like someone else's purse, and she relished the idea that she could so easily exchange her life for a different one. It felt good to misbehave, she realized. No wonder people did it so often.

As she pulled handfuls of dead leaves from the fire pit, she thought about the emails she had traded with Leticia since their disastrous Skype exchange. They seemed to have moved past the episode and, although Leticia would be staying at the house for only a portion of Thanksgiving weekend, Margaret planned to use those two days to shore up their relationship, avoiding all talk of divorce. The thought of having her daughter home after months of living in the silent house made Margaret smile. The doorbell rang again and, as she reached for the knob, the ash from her cigarette broke off, disintegrating on its fall to the dark wood floor.

She opened the door and there stood Eddie in jeans and sneakers, his hands in the pockets of the windbreaker she'd given him for Christmas four years ago. He seemed ready to launch into a prepared statement, but his expression quickly changed to shock.

"I'm busy, Eddie." Margaret stood on the doorjamb, blocking the way into the house.

"You're *smoking*?"

"Don't be an idiot." Squinting, she took a deep, crackling drag on the cigarette, then held it between her fingers as she blew a tight stream of blue smoke up into the porch light. "Of course I'm not smoking."

"Do you have any idea what that does to your teeth? Not to mention your gums?"

"So you *do* recall being a dentist." She tucked the cigarette back into the corner of her mouth.

"You look ridiculous," he said, shaking his head.

"You could have told me that over the phone, but thanks for stopping by." She started to close the door.

"We need to talk, Margaret," he said, stepping forward. "Don't make me invite myself into the house."

"Which you just did, by the way." She stepped out of the doorway for him to pass. "I'm working in the back—we can go out there." They walked through the family room toward the double doors. "I would offer you something but, well, I don't want to."

"Still the consummate hostess," he said dryly.

They walked out and down the wide brick steps onto the patio. Eddie stood by the fire pit, hands still in his pockets, and took in the half-potted plants, boxes of twinkle lights and the broom, rake and scrubbing brushes scattered across the bricks.

"Well, this makes sense now," he said.

"What does?" Margaret picked up her gardening gloves.

"The cleaning assault and all the smoking. You've never been very good at coping with bad news."

Margaret frowned at him. "What bad news?"

"Leticia's call this morning? What else would it be?"

Margaret's heart began to pound. "Is she hurt? What happened?"

"No," Eddie said, looking confused. "She's fine, but didn't she call you, too?"

"If she had, I wouldn't be asking, would I? Just tell me what's going on!"

"What's going *on* is that, according to Leticia, she is very stressed out and cannot handle being down here for Thanksgiving, so she's going to spend it with one of her new friend's families there in Portland."

Margaret gasped. "That can't be true. We have plans. We've discussed them in our emails. I bought twinkle lights…" She looked down into the fire pit.

"You really knew nothing about this?"

Margaret shook her head. She took the cigarette from her mouth and flicked it into the dirt at the edge of the bricks.

"Apparently, she's canceling her trip on the advice of the counselor she's been seeing."

"*Counselor*? What counselor?"

Eddie shrugged. "Some quack at the school that the students talk to about their problems."

Margaret *humph*ed at the hypocrisy of woo-woo Eddie labeling a licensed psychologist a "quack." "And you knew about this? That she was seeing a counselor?"

"I found out two hours ago, all right? News to me as well."

Margaret sank onto the brick steps, her elbows on her knees. This was where she had sat with her arms around Eddie when he got the call that his father had died. Here, too, was where Leticia went to cry after her first boyfriend broke up with her. There were good things, too, that had happened on this patio, in this yard. Birthday parties, barbeques, slow dances. All those things a person thinks will never stop coming, month after month and year after year. But they do stop. And nothing is ever the same again.

"I can't believe this." Margaret dropped her gloves on the ground and wiped her eyes with the back of her hand. "What happened?" She looked up at him. "What have you been saying that made her stay away?"

"What have *I* been saying? Oh, that's rich." He threw up his hands. "I knew you would try to blame me for this."

"Well, aren't you to blame? You're the one who made her anxious about her tuition money!"

"And *you're* the one who had the lovely video meltdown that completely freaked her out!"

"You've been manipulating her all along, Eddie."

"And what's this?" He gestured at Margaret's supplies on the patio. "Fancy little lights? You never went to this much trouble when it was the three of us."

Margaret stared at him. When she felt the tears forming, she looked down at the bricks again. "I wanted to make it special. Can't you understand that?" She struggled to control her voice. "I just—" she gulped. "I just miss her so much." She began to cry.

"I know, Greta," Eddie said, swallowing hard. "I miss her, too."

Margaret slumped farther over her knees. Eddie had not used his nickname for her in years. As she worked to contain her tears, Eddie walked over to a bedroom window, absent-mindedly picking at a flake of paint and looking up into the eaves of the house. When the snuffling subsided, he moved back toward the brick steps.

"She'll shake it off—she's a strong kid," he said. "It's just a tough transition."

"Yes." Margaret wiped her eyes again. "There's a lot of that going around."

He cleared his throat. "Listen, I didn't come over here to talk about Leticia. I'm here because I realized I've been overlooking something." He paced in front of the fire pit. "I've been confused—and angry— trying to figure out why you won't move forward on buying me out of the school. I'm thinking, what's the holdup?"

Margaret, her cheeks now dry, watched him and said nothing.

"And then—*wham!*—it suddenly became clear what was going on."

Margaret's eyebrows shot up. "What was it?" she said with genuine curiosity. "What was going on?"

He paused. "I know this is awkward," Margaret recognized the voice as the one he used to comfort patients before drilling out a cavity, "but I would just like to say that I understand."

"I'm glad one of us does," she said under her breath.

"I can imagine how difficult this is for you, facing the prospect of being a single woman again after so many years. I can see that you might be tempted to delay the inevitable in the hopes that I might, you know, reconsider my decision."

"*Ha!*" she burst.

He held up a hand. "Like I said, this is an uncomfortable conversation, but it's healthy to recognize that we had a good run in our marriage and—"

"You have to stop." Margaret waved him away. "You're killing me."

"What?" he said sharply.

"You can't seriously think I've delayed the settlement because I'm trying to hold *on* to you." She pushed her hair from her forehead. "Would you like me to step off the patio and make more room for your ego?"

"You know, you could be more appreciative of my sensitivity."

"Your '*sensitivity*?' I must have missed that part. And please don't make me listen to any more of your ham-handed attempts to *relate* to me. *God.*" She stood and faced him, crossing her arms. "I want nothing more than to put this divorce behind us."

"I don't know what that lawyer of yours has been telling you, but this is a very simple process. You take a second on the school and then—"

"Eddie. Listen to me. It won't work." Her voice became small. "I've tried."

Eddie massaged his forehead with his fingertips. "Why do I feel like I'm trying to order off a Chinese menu in Swedish?"

Margaret took a deep breath. "I already took out a second. Two years ago. And before you ask what I did with the money, I put every penny of it back into the school. I've got a plan in place and I will raise the money. You can rely on that."

"'I can *rely* on that?'"

"It will work. I just need a little more time."

"Oh, this is fabulous. Thank you for writing the epitaph to our marriage."

"What are you talking about?"

"It's the motif of the last twenty-five years, isn't it? *You* don't need anybody. *You* can do it all by yourself. Did it ever occur to you that when we got married, I expected you to lean on *me* every now and then? But, no, that would never be acceptable—not for the Iron Lady of Santa Monica."

Margaret flinched. "More of your famous 'sensitivity?'"

"I'm sorry, what did you say? I was busy thinking about your secret loan documents."

"Oh, for God's sakes. You'll get the money for your business, Eddie, or for your new girlfriend. Although I'm guessing those two are one and the same." She noticed a twinge of discomfort in his face. "That's what the big panic is, right? You and Miss Xanadu can't wait to open your New Age nail salon or whatever you called it?"

Eddie looked up into the avocado trees. "As it happens, Cassandra and I have dissolved our partnership. We will not be starting a business together."

"Oh, really?"

"I'm not sure that a career in the metaphysical arts is the most strategic move for me at this point in time."

Margaret studied his face. "And what precipitated this development?"

He opened his mouth to reply, then stopped. "Your days of knowing all and controlling all are over," he said finally. "And I'll tell you something else. I never liked my office space. I hated it. I should never have let you railroad me into picking that one when I wanted the suite with the ocean view."

Margaret held out her palms. "Why didn't you just say that? I didn't care which space you leased, but you had to do *something*. If I hadn't stepped in, you would still be sitting at the kitchen table, going nowhere."

"Well," he said with a bitter smile, "I'm going somewhere now, aren't I?"

As they stared at each other, the wind chimes tinkled in an afternoon gust. They were drowned out by the tooth-loosening roar of the neighbor's Harley-Davidson pulling into the driveway, where it idled for a moment before the ignition was cut. "I need the money by December seventh," Eddie spoke into the sudden silence. "All of it." He turned and walked up the stairs to the doors.

"Eddie, wait." Margaret followed him through the doorway. "I need more time. Why don't we say the end of the year?"

"No," he said, not breaking stride. "If it's not done by the seventh, I'll have the agent over there to list it. If necessary, my lawyer and I will accompany her."

"I know my plan will work, but it's complicated." Margaret skittered past the family-room coffee table. "I don't think I can collect the extra tuition I need by then."

"Oh, I'm sure you'll find a way to motivate the parents." He crossed the foyer and reached for the doorknob.

"*Eddie.*"

He took a long breath and turned to face her.

"The things you're saying are true and I'm not proud of them," she said, "but think about what my life is now. Aren't I paying enough of a price already?"

"Believe it or not, my goal is not to crush you, Margaret. My goal is to keep myself from dissolving any further into this marriage than I already have. Heaven help me if I back down again."

"Eddie," she hesitated, "Eddie, I'm begging you. I can't lose my school."

"I understand," he said, turning to go, "I feel exactly the same way about myself." He opened the door and walked out, pulling it shut behind him.

26
Justine

Justine trudged up her front steps, a grocery bag in each hand. "Speaking of auction items," she said into her phone headset, "we have to take that high-colonic gift certificate out of the entertainment category and put it somewhere else. Even if we combine it with the free limo package, I just don't think that's anyone's idea of a good time." She reached the top landing and set the bags down on the rubber doormat. "Then I'll write up descriptions for the new items and email them to you before pick-up time, all right? Thanks a lot, Sabine. Bye." She ended the call and carried the bags into the house, kicking the door shut behind her. "This project *is* a colonic," she muttered on her way to the kitchen.

"Are you talking to me?" Greg said from the dining room. "I hope not, because I heard the word 'colonic.'"

"I thought you had a hearing this morning," she called, unloading the groceries onto the kitchen island.

"It was a quickie," he said. "Thank God, because I have to get this brief written. I thought it would be quieter here than at the office, but I forgot this is the auction command center."

Justine frowned and set a gallon of milk on the refrigerator shelf. "What do you mean?"

"The doorbell has been ringing all morning."

Justine stepped into the dining room. Greg sat at the table in jeans and a T-shirt, his laptop, files, and several thick, black binders spread in front of him. "A delivery?"

He pointed toward the breakfast room around the corner, which had become the auction overflow area from the dining room. Justine walked through and found herself face-to-face with Cienna Chadwick, Supermodel. Or, rather, a larger-than-life cardboard figure of her dressed in what looked like a couture fly-fishing outfit. On the floor next to the figure was an enormous basket of products from the Cienna Chadwick beauty, home, fragrance, and pet care lines, as well as a disturbingly generous number of DVDs of her acting debut—a supporting role in the tepidly received action movie, *Canoe Vengeance*. The basket was wrapped in cellophane and gathered on top in a pouf the size of a German Shepherd. "Wow," she breathed.

She squeezed back into the dining room and stood at the head of the table. "We shall not speak of this."

"Word," Greg said, eyes on his screen.

She returned to the kitchen and opened her laptop on the island, checking her emails in between putting away the rest of the groceries. There were several auction-related messages from Margaret, with whom she had been communicating solely via email in the wake of their bizarre confrontation in the school kitchen. "That's over the top, even for Margaret," Bette had said when Justine related the story to her. "I heard she and Eddie have separated, but I figured she was the type to hunker down and not let it show. I bet Trey knows what else is going on, but getting it out of him would be about as easy as breaking Margaret Thatcher."

"Coffee?" she called to Greg.

"Yes, please." She could tell by the auto-response tone of his voice that he was deep in brief-writing mode. She started the pot and scrolled through the rest of her emails as it brewed, sending quick responses to questions from her committee about arrangements at the Riviera, opening Ruben's flier for his standup show that night at the Laugh Factory, and swallowing hard at the notice from UCLA Extension that the spring design classes were almost full. She thought of the stack of magazines and fabric swatches she had pushed behind her shoes on her closet floor and filed the message under the heading "Future Projects."

She carried two cups of coffee into the dining room, setting one next to Greg's laptop and the other across the table from him. "Thanks," he muttered, his hands poised over the keys.

She retrieved her laptop from the kitchen and sat across from Greg to begin writing up descriptions of the latest auction donations to arrive. "Before I forget," she said as she unwound the computer's power cord, "Celia's birthday party is Sunday. You and Mac can have your old-school foosball rematch."

"Who?" he said as he typed.

Justine's phone *ding*ed in her pocket. She pulled it out and saw a text message on the screen.

> *Hey. Are you going to Ruben's thing tonight? Should be amusing. H.*

No, she thought, *love Ruben, but you're trouble*. She slipped the phone back into her pocket. "*Mac*," she said to Greg. "Husband of my best friend, Ruthie?"

Greg looked up at her and blinked. "Oh, right. Sunday? I'll be out of town."

"On the weekend?" She walked around to the power outlet behind his chair and plugged in the cord.

"Yep. I have to be in Santa Barbara all day to prep a client for a Monday depo. I'll be back late Tuesday night unless it runs into Wednesday." He pulled his calendar up on the screen. "I should give you these other travel dates, too, now that we've got all the scheduling done. I have a lot of trips coming up."

As Justine leaned over to look at his calendar, a blue chat box appeared in the corner of his screen, accompanied by the *jingle* of a bicycle bell.

> *legallysimone: should I pack a swimsuit for santa bar-*
> *bara? ha! ;)*

"And *that's* why her billable hours are low. Too much playin' around." Greg clicked the box shut. "Do you want to write these dates down?" When Justine didn't respond, he turned and saw the look on her face. "What? Oh, not *this* again."

"She's going to Santa Barbara with you?"

"Yes, I've booked us on a wine-tasting tour." He rolled his eyes. "Come on, Justine, she's on the team."

She moved to the other side of the table and gestured at the laptop. "Well, what *was* that?"

"It was a joke. We were taking some heat from the others this morning about our depo being fancy."

"Fancy how?"

"It's at the Four Seasons." His eyes flicked away as he spoke.

"The Four Seasons. In Santa Barbara." She crossed her arms. "Where we've been wanting to go for the last three years?" She tried to banish the mental picture of Simone's flawless body draped alongside Greg's as they reclined by the pool on towels as thick as Monte Cristo sandwiches. "I'm sorry, I don't see the joke."

"We're going to be working our asses off up there. We are not ready for this depo. Not even close. But before I can prep for that, I have to get this brief written and filed." He exhaled sharply. "In summation, the *joke* is that no one on the team will be wearing a swimsuit any time soon, regardless of where we are." He stood and walked out of the room. Justine followed him through the kitchen and out onto the patio, where the bright haze made them both squint.

"I can't believe we're still talking about this." He kicked at a sycamore leaf.

"And I can't believe you still haven't shut her down."

They faced off across Emma's green, turtle-shaped sandbox, a standard feature of family yards throughout Los Angeles. "Look," he said finally, "I don't have time today to hash all this out again and even if I did, the conversation would be pointless because the problem isn't Simone. The problem is your insecurity." Without waiting for a response, he turned toward the house. "I'll finish my brief at the office." He went inside, the French door quivering as it swung shut behind him.

"Are you kidding me with this?" She flopped into one of the patio chairs and let her head fall back onto the chair cushion. Looking up into the clouds, she was suddenly exhausted. All she'd been doing for weeks was arguing and negotiating, with occasional breaks for emotional festering and second-guessing. *This is exactly the kind of thing that drives a person to settle in at a folding table and macramé an owl-shaped plant hanger*, she thought. *It would be worth having those beady, wooden eyes on you all day just to get out of your own head for a while.*

She watched a propeller plane pass overhead, its wings wobbling with a distinctly student-driver air as it began its descent toward Santa Monica Airport. Next door, the gardeners fired up a leaf blower, drowning out the *caws* of the crows who were busy scouting for fast-food trash in the neighbor's construction site. Sitting up, she took her phone from her pocket, pulled up Harry's text message and typed a reply.

yeah. i'm going.

Justine was ready to go when Greg came home from work hours

later. "She's down," she said, nodding toward Emma's door. "There's chicken in the fridge." She adjusted her necklace in the hallway mirror, her purse already on her shoulder.

"I ate at the office."

She saw him take note of the heels she was wearing with her jeans. "Plans tonight?" he said without smiling and dropped a stack of binders into a chair.

"School thing. Kind of a moms' night out." She'd always hated that expression and the mental image it conjured—a mob of haggard housewives desperate for any excuse to change into an unstained pair of stretch pants, comb the applesauce from their hair, and lurch out into the night like the Spanxed undead in search of blender drinks.

"I'll be asleep when you get back," he said. "It's been a long day." He dropped his jacket across the chair and headed for the kitchen.

"See you later," she called, already walking toward the front door, phone in hand.

Within five minutes, she was driving up Doheny toward Sunset Boulevard. She pushed the button to open the sedan's moon roof and felt the cool night air on her skin. A group of twenty-something women—all boots and hair and leather jackets—strutted by on the sidewalk ("carving the pavement," as a Fred Segal shoe salesman had put it) and she realized this was only the second time in six months that she had gone anywhere alone in the evening.

Look at me, she thought, *out after dark like a big girl.* Was this what parenting did to a person—turned them into some kind of anti-vampire who only ventured out in daylight (after a liberal application of sunscreen, of course)? It seemed to her that, in the last few years, Greg's life had retained its shape but hers had taken on a foreign, distorted outline while she was busy looking after other things. She needed to remember who she was before she'd said "I do," before she'd thrown away her business cards, and before she'd taken the jarring amusement-park ride of pregnancy and birth—the one that had sent her stumbling out the other side with emotional vertigo and the lingering suspicion that, in the midst of all the screaming, something had been swiped from her purse. *As of tonight*, she thought as she turned up the volume on the radio, *Mrs. Most-Likely-to-Have-Band-Aids has left the building.*

She made a right onto Sunset, glancing at her phone where it sat in the cup holder. There had been no response from Harry to her single text earlier in the day. Then again, she hadn't expected one. Trading texts in sequence amounted to having a conversation, an activity that was much too ordinary for Harry while also carrying the distasteful burden of commitment. Replying to his text that morning had been Justine's way of telling *herself* she was going to Ruben's show—her way of making it official. She had her own reasons for getting out of the house.

The traffic on Sunset thickened as drivers slowed to gape at the knots of leather-studded hair-band fans outside the Whiskey and the parade of stunning women that Sunset Plaza's cafes attracted the way early-bird dinners attracted AARP cards. As the cars crept from signal to signal, she scrolled through the radio stations, hoping to find a song by someone old enough to have a driver's license. The only other musical option was The Wiggles—Emma's CD that had been in such heavy rotation that the sight of it was enough to set her eyelid twitching. "Finally," she said, the familiar snarl of a P!nk song filling the car as she rolled to a stop for a red light. She glanced at the street sign—the club was only a few blocks away.

A motorcyclist on a black BMW glided past, just missing her side mirror, then positioned himself in front of her car, halfway into the crosswalk. *Rude*, she thought, *but that's a sweet bike.* The driver set a foot on the pavement and Justine cocked her head. "I know that bike," she muttered and sat forward for a better view. "And I know that butt."

She smiled. The Wiggles would not condone what she was thinking, but P!nk definitely would. She slammed the heel of her hand down on her horn, causing the motorcyclist to bounce an inch off his seat. He whipped his head around and, through the helmet's open visor, she saw Harry's eyes clouded with anger.

She gave him a little wave through the windshield. Recognizing her, he rolled his eyes. The light changed, and he pointed with his gloved hand for her to follow him onto a side street, then gunned the bike into a right turn. The noise and congestion of Sunset faded behind her as she followed him, giggling to herself. After a few turns, she pulled up behind him at the crest of a residential street.

He had parked in the shadows, where the canopy of trees blocked the streetlights and intensified the twinkling of the city view. She flicked off her lights as she watched him take off his helmet and set it on the seat, then slipped the car into park, engine running.

She lowered her window as he walked toward the car. "'Sup?" she said with a mischievous smile.

"Spaz." He pulled off his gloves. "You think you're pretty funny, don't you?"

"Why, yes," she said. "Yes, I do."

He tucked the gloves in his jacket pockets, then rested his hands in her open window. She motioned to the motorcycle with her chin. "You kept the bike. I didn't know."

"Too many good memories to give her up," he said with a smile. "You know how it is."

"I can imagine." She wished the helmet had given him some kind of bizarre hair topiary shaped like a dolphin or a pope hat. It hadn't.

"Did you check out the view?" he said, but did not gesture at the spectacular vista they both knew was only steps away.

"Los Angeles, right? Yes, I'm familiar with it."

"Not like this you aren't. I know all these streets and that's the best view on this side of town. Come look, then you can leave your car here and I'll give you a ride to the club—the parking there is really tight."

She glanced at the bike.

"See? You want to."

"What? *No*. Listen, I should get going," she reached for the gearshift.

"All right, but you have to see the view first. Come on, Funny Daddy can wait." He motioned for her to get out of the car.

"Geez." She unclipped her seat belt. "You missed your calling when you went into art instead of sales. I will see your view, and then I need to go." She turned off the engine and the street became suddenly quiet.

"Wait." He leaned down into her window again. "Turn the radio back on."

"Now what?" She turned on the car's ignition and the dash glowed blue as "Slave to Love" played through the speakers.

"Wow," Harry said, "does Roxy Music always remind you of Santa Cruz?"

Low blow, she thought. Santa Cruz had been the most romantic weekend of their relationship, a magical forty-eight hours of staggering through beach cafes and boardwalk shops, giddy with each others' presence, before bolting back to their tiny room, all while maintaining constant skin-to-skin contact. After a weekend of hearing the entire "Avalon" album on repeat—courtesy of the guest on the balcony below their hotel window—it had become the undisputed soundtrack of the trip. There was zero chance she'd forgotten this, and he knew it. "Well, of course it does—" she began and turned toward him. His face was inches from hers, his eyes moving from her hair to her lips. She could smell him again; the expensive soap was new to her, but the musky blend of shampoo and skin was as familiar as her favorite jeans.

"I'm glad it hasn't slipped your mind." His voice had shifted into the luxurious cadence of someone who was about to stretch out for a nap. Or have sex. Justine tried to ignore her body's involuntary tingle of anticipation. She thought she had memorized everything about him, but now she was reminded of the tiny, quarter-moon scar on his chin and the flecks of amber around his pupils. She was hovering there, nerves firing, when he burst out laughing.

"Hey," he said, pulling away and flicking his hair, "do you remember the ginormous chili dog you ate on that trip?" He laughed again. "Man, what a crime scene."

Justine clicked off the ignition and threw open the car door.

"Watch it," Harry said, jumping out of the way.

She stepped out and slammed the door. "Let's get something straight." She jammed a finger in his sternum. "I have never in my life eaten a chili dog. I admit that I have signed my name in spray cheese across a *bowl* of chili, but there were no witnesses."

"Okay, take it easy." Harry held his hands in front of his chest and smiled. "My bad."

"Whatever," she said, standing toe-to-toe with him. "What I want to know is what you were *doing* just then." She poked him again, hard in the pec, right where she knew he would be sore from lifting weights. In front of a mirror, no doubt.

"Ow!" He rubbed his chest. "What are you talking about?"

"*That.*" She pointed at the car window. "That ooze down memory lane you just laid on me. Once a head gamer, always a head gamer, right?"

He frowned. "Hey, this isn't easy for me, either. Have you ever thought about that?"

"Nope." She crossed her arms. "Can't say that I have."

He hesitated before speaking. "Like I said before, I tried to play it off, but seeing you at that stupid school orientation really messed me up."

"Oh, *please*."

"You're not just some girl I dated in grad school, okay? Leaving for Chicago was one of the hardest things I've ever done. Do you have any idea how close I came to moving back?"

Justine's arms fell to her sides. "You never told me you were thinking about that."

He looked down at the pavement. "I wasn't sure what your reaction would be. Whenever we talked, it sounded like you were okay with it all and I thought maybe you had moved on." He gave her a half smile. "No one wants to risk getting rejected, right?"

She stared at him, her mouth half open.

"Sometimes I think that if I had that one decision to do over, my whole life would be exactly where it should be."

Justine gasped and took a backward step. "I can't believe you're saying this." She tried to reconcile his words with her memories. Her mouth hardened. "Let me put that another way: I don't believe what you're saying."

"It was like part of me knew that I was supposed to be with you, but I couldn't handle it. Now that I've had some therapy, I understand myself better."

"And what exactly did you discover about yourself?"

"It's tough for me to admit this, but the thing is," he cleared his throat, "I've always been terrified of my emotions."

"You've always been *what*? Wow, you really had me going there for a minute. Let me guess—was this *online* therapy? Because that sounds like the kind of steaming nugget of wisdom you'd pick up in a chat room."

"I'm serious, Justine."

"After all the mind screws you've done on me, what you should be terrified of right now are *my* emotions." She fought the urge to kick him in the shins.

"It's not like the feelings aren't there, or that I'm faking them," he said. "I just can't handle them, okay? I never could."

"It's so brave of you to share your condition with me, Harry. Tell me, does it qualify you for some kind of special parking placard?"

"Very funny. I just wanted you to understand why—"

"Stop." She closed her eyes and shook her head. "Stop talking." When he was quiet, she opened her eyes and looked at him. "Oh my God. What am I doing here?" She turned to go, but he reached out and pulled her toward him, folding her into his chest as he kissed her. She tilted her head, moving into his lips.

His mouth roamed to her cheek and then he held her face in his hands, touching his forehead to hers. "This is real," he said, and kissed her again. She slipped her hands inside his jacket and spread her fingers on his back, pressing him to her.

She heard her phone ring and squeezed her eyes shut harder. She wasn't going to answer it, but Harry pulled away at the first sound. "You should get that." He stepped backward, gently moving her hands off his waist before releasing them. "Might be *la familia*."

Through the car window, she saw the phone glowing in the cup holder. Without a word, she retrieved it. The missed call was from home. *Let me guess*, she thought, *Greg is making himself a sandwich and wants to know what I've done with the good mustard*. She glanced over at Harry, who was running a hand through his hair. She did not want to be anywhere at that moment but inside his jacket. Her hand faltered as she dialed the code to retrieve the voicemail.

"It's me. Listen, Emma woke up crying, then threw up in her bed. She feels hot and I'm not sure what to give her for that. I could use some help here. Bye." She ended the call, guilt creeping over her as she considered the possibilities. Emma had twice before come down with a nighttime flu that had run its course in twenty-four hours. She hoped this was nothing more than another round of the same bug. She looked at Harry.

"You have to go," he said, zipping his jacket.

"I have to go."

"Are you okay?"

She considered the question. "No."

"Me, neither." He steered her toward the car. "We'll talk about it." She got in and shut the door, and he leaned into the window again. She saw his eyes flick to the dashboard clock. "Drive safe. I'll let you know how Ruben's show goes."

"Okay, sure." She sat with her hands in her lap, staring at the keys dangling from the ignition.

"You are precious," he said with a half smile. When she looked up at him, he reached in and gave the tip of her nose a small tap with his finger, then turned and walked to the motorcycle. She watched him scoop the helmet from the seat and put it on in one smooth motion as he mounted the bike. He roared past her with a quick wave and disappeared around the corner at the bottom of the hill.

When Justine got home she found Emma curled up with Scooter the turtle on the sofa, her hair plastered to her forehead and her eyes droopy. Next to her was Greg, a pile of papers in his lap and Emma's old baby bathtub on the floor by his feet.

"In case she throws up again," he said, seeing Justine's questioning glance.

"There's my Emma." Justine dropped her purse on the coffee

table and knelt in front of the sofa to feel her daughter's face and forearms. "She's a little hot. Not too bad. She threw up just once?" She peered into Emma's eyes as she spoke.

"Yeah, just once," Greg said. "I wasn't sure what to do about her bed."

You mean you didn't want to deal with it. "I'll strip it in a minute." She pushed Emma's hair off her face and smiled at her. "How's my little girl doing? Upset tummy?"

Emma scowled and hugged Scooter. "I barfed!"

"I know, Ladybug." Plucking a tissue from the box on the table, she wiped around Emma's mouth and nose. She felt Greg watching her but did not trust herself to have a real conversation with him. She had driven home in a trance and had not yet begun to process her encounter with Harry.

"Are you getting sick, too?" he said. "Your face is splotchy."

"I had the window down in the car. The air was chilly." She glanced at the papers in his lap. "Get a lot done?"

"Hardly, under the circumstances," he said evenly.

"I guess it's never a good time for Mommy to get out of the house." She straightened the collar of Emma's nightgown and noticed it needed changing. "Emma, how would you like to wear one of Mommy's big, soft T-shirts for sleeping? That could be your new gown for tonight, yes?"

"Oh-*kay*," Emma said, making it clear that, as treats went, this was a lousy one.

Justine scooped her up and she flopped, sweaty and sulky, onto her mother's shoulder. With any luck, the barfing stage had passed. "I'll sleep in her room on the blow-up bed so I can keep an eye on her," she said to Greg as she walked past him.

"All right," he said. "You haven't mentioned moms' night out. How was it?"

Justine swallowed hard, cradling Emma's head as she crossed the room away from Greg. "It had only just started when you called," she said, and disappeared into the bedroom.

27
Ruben

Ruben tapped the seat of his jeans and a stab of panic shot through him. Had he lost the notes for his set? He jammed his hand in the pocket. There they were, thank God, folded in fourths as always when he was going onstage. He had never pulled them out at the mic, had never choked and gone blank while performing, but he was superstitious about having them in his pocket. He always said that in an emergency, he could pull the next joke right through the denim on his rear-end using a standup butt-osmosis developed over scores of shows.

He knew his set cold, but he wasn't taking any chances. In addition to the cheat sheet, he was wearing the lucky boxers (black with fluorescent-green flying saucers) he'd worn when he proposed to Deandra, and a rough bracelet of plastic beads strung on a leather lace that the twins had insisted they tie on his wrist earlier that day when he picked them up from school. His real good luck charm, however, was Deandra herself. She would be out there in the seats, invisible behind the spots, but telegraphing palpable support.

Tonight, his mojo had to be in full effect. Not only was Vince in the audience, but Ruben would be handing off his script to him later that evening. They were having drinks after his set and Ruben needed to kill—to leave the stage on a wave of laughter that would carry him all the way to the bar. He sent up a silent prayer to the comedy gods.

They were twenty minutes out and the comics were pacing the

green room in various states of twitchiness—running through their sets in a low mumble, manically bantering with the others, or ducking out of the room to power-drag cigarettes on the sidewalk. They hadn't been told the lineup yet, but Ruben wasn't optimistic about getting a cherry spot in third, fourth or fifth. It all depended on how many seats he had filled. Although he'd peppered the internet with notices and emails, he'd been doing standup well past the point of drawing friends with the novelty of seeing someone they knew potentially bomb onstage. Deandra had said she'd try to drag a friend or two along from work, but that was never a sure thing. There were at least fifteen comics on the bill. Ruben prayed that enough people mentioned his name at the door to keep him out of the double digits.

His cellphone rang and he stepped into the hallway to answer it.

"Ruben!" Deandra said. "You're not going to believe this." The call had a warped, echoed sound to it.

"Is everything all right? Where are you?"

"I'm in the ladies' room. At work."

"At *work*? What the hell? I thought you were already in the audience."

"I *know*," she said and started to cry. "She—" her voice dropped to a harsh, hiccupping whisper, "—that *hag* won't let me leave."

"What? She can't do that!"

"We're getting reviewed on this project on Monday and we all have to stay tonight until she says it's ready. It's such *crap*!" Ruben's ear was filled with a series of delicate, moist sobs.

"Aw, it's all right," he said, helplessness slicing through him as it did every time he heard her cry.

"But you said Vince was coming—that this was the big one. I should be there." She snorted wetly into the phone.

"Listen, don't worry about it, okay? I've got a huge crowd here." *A white lie for a good cause*, he told himself. "Everything is fine, I promise."

The booker pushed past him and into the green room carrying the piece of paper that Ruben knew would be the lineup. Through the doorway he saw the comics gather around as he started reading from the sheet. "Dee? I have to go now, all right? It's almost time. You guys finish your project so you can come home and I'll call you after my set."

"Well, if you're sure…" she sniffled again.

"Positive."

"Break a leg, Ruben."

"I love you and I'll call you in a while."

By the time Ruben got close enough to hear over the warm-up music reverberating backstage, the booker was on slot number five. He waited through the entire lineup, first hoping to be called, then groaning as the numbers ticked by, and finally puzzling over the fact that he hadn't heard his name at all. The other performers dispersed and Ruben asked to see the list.

"You're in the three slot," the man said, opening the paper again and jabbing a finger at Ruben's name.

"No way!"

The man shrugged. "Way."

"Wait, what's that?" He pointed to the number forty-six written next to his name.

"You brought forty-six people," he said, then refolded the paper with a *crackle* that signaled the end of the question-and-answer period. Stunned, Ruben watched him walk away. *Forty-six people? To see me?* That had to be wrong; he'd never pulled that many in his life. He slipped out of the room and around the corner, finding a spot where he could peek out at the audience. There, filling at least two half-moon rows around the stage, were The Mommies.

He did a double take, but it was no mistake. Glossy as show ponies, they chatted, laughed, and sipped their multi-colored drinks, handbags the size of Volkswagens parked at their feet as the house lights reflected the sheen of their hair. Among the faces were moms that he knew from Willow's party, but there were others, too—women he knew by sight but had never officially met. "My peeps," he said to himself with such a rush of gratitude that, for a horrifying moment, he thought he might cry. But then the lights dimmed and the music boomed and onto the stage bounded the emcee, dreadlocks flying as he howled into the mic. The room exploded in applause and Ruben took one last look before returning to the green room to warm up.

Ruben paced the stage, smiling into the spots, which were as bright as a Cessna's landing lights. He waited until the laughter had crested before moving into the next bit.

"We have these friends—newlyweds. They say they're not ready to have a baby yet. They want to *practice* first." He paused. "So they're getting a *dog*."

A round of anticipatory laughter rolled through the audience.

"Yeah. 'Cause *that's* about the same thing, right? Have you ever tried to put a baby down for the night in a cardboard box with an old towel and a tennis ball? Not only does it not work...it *really* pisses off the baby."

He absorbed another wave of laughter from the crowd.

Ruben was having the set of his life.

He was in the flow, launching his material with a jab, a shrug, a flick of an eyebrow. The joke about the mommy tattoos killed and so did the biker gang versus stroller gang bit. He worked all his favorites: hateful yoga practitioners, people who dressed their dogs like humans, and preschoolers who used air quotes. They came back to him in squawks and hoots of laughter.

"So here's what I told the newlywed couple," he continued. "If you want to know what it's like to have a baby, forget the dog—a dog is not gonna get it done. You're gonna need a *horse*." More laughter. "And here's the ultimate preparation: take your horse to a nice restaurant. Yes! Clippity-clop on in there and watch the faces of the people at the next table as you sit down with your *horse*. 'Don't worry,' you can tell them, 'he won't bother you—he's just about to go down for his *nap*.'"

He slipped the mic back into its stand. "Thank you!" He gave the cheering audience a two-handed wave above his head. "Thanks very much!" He shook hands with the emcee, who grabbed the mic as he walked offstage.

"Give it up for Ruben Daniels!" The audience clapped and yelled, with squeals from the front rows. "Good stuff!"

Ruben returned to the green room to get his things. "You ripped the shit out of that, bro," one of the comics said as he passed.

"Thanks, man." Ruben raised his bottle of water and guzzled half of it. He'd sweated through his T-shirt and his scalp was damp down to his sideburns. He was riding a spike of adrenaline that would keep him up until dawn, but he didn't care.

He pulled his phone from his bag and stepped into the hallway to call Deandra. He saw on the screen that he had missed a call from her ten minutes earlier. She answered on the first ring.

"Hey, how did it go?" Her voice was oddly flat.

"Dee, it was amazing—it was dipped in butter." Another comic walked by and congratulated him. "Hey, thanks," Ruben said then spoke into the phone again. "Check this out—I brought forty-six people tonight! And most of them are moms from the preschool—can you believe that shit?"

"That's great, sweetie."

"I'm meeting Vince now." He slung his bag over his shoulder.

"Are you guys almost done there?"

"I'm on my way home right now."

"Hey, are you all right?" he said, but there was no reply. "Deandra?"

"I got fired." She began crying again.

"She *fired* you? Are you fucking kidding me?"

"She said I wasn't pulling my weight on the project," she hiccupped. "That my lack of commitment was the reason we all had to stay late."

"What a pantload." He paced the hallway as he talked. "Listen, you know what? This is perfect timing."

"Yeah, right."

He laughed. "Yes. The more I think about it, the more perfect it is. I'm glad you're out of there. You hate that job."

"Well, that's true." She blew her nose.

"I'm going to see Vince now and he's going to hook me up with a killer job and you won't have to worry about the Beastress of the Valley any more, all right?"

"But, Ruben—"

"Don't worry about it, okay? I got this." If she'd seen the twelve minutes he'd just had, she'd understand that everything was going to be fine. "I'm serious. That she-creature just did you a favor."

"Well…"

"No worries. I'll call you afterward." He signed off and dropped the phone into his bag, smiling to see his script in the inside pocket.

Vince stood as Ruben approached. They exchanged their usual handshake/backslap before sitting down at a cocktail table.

"Dude," Vince said, smiling, "you are *en fuego*."

"Thanks for catching my set." They ordered their drinks and settled in, analyzing other comics' sets and swapping news about clubs and careers they'd been watching. Finally, they had exchanged enough small talk.

"Hey," Ruben said, "you told me something a while back that made me think."

"Yeah?" Vince took a swallow of his drink. "What was that?"

"That I should write something." He pulled the script from his bag and laid it on the table, careful to avoid the moist drink rings. "You said you'd put it in the right hands if I did."

Vince eyed the script without touching it, then drained the last half inch of his cocktail. "Wow," he said finally. "Look at you."

"I've studied your show—which is *fantastic*, by the way." He nodded toward the script. "I think you'll like this."

"No doubt," Vince said. He leaned back in his chair, clasping his hands in front of him. Ruben noticed for the first time that his friend looked exhausted. He had slicked back his wavy hair, which accentuated the circles under his eyes and the pasty complexion at his temples. "Here's the thing," he said. He took a paper napkin from the table and began twisting it in his fingers as he spoke. "I'm sure your script is super-tight, but I can't hand it off for you."

Ruben waited out a burst of laughter from the showroom before responding. "I don't understand."

"Listen, I know I said I could give your stuff to the right people— and I meant it." He twisted the napkin harder, staring at it, his face blank. "But that was months ago."

"Is everything all right?"

"Let's just say things have changed for me at the show." He tried to get another swallow from his glass, then set it back on the table. "It would not help your cause for me to be the one who recommends your script." He looked directly at Ruben. "Know what I'm saying?"

Ruben flopped back in his chair, stunned. "Yeah," he said. "Yeah, I get it."

Vince looked back down at his hands. Neither spoke. Ruben's rush of adrenaline evaporated, leaving him wasted and limp.

The waitress stopped at their table and Ruben asked for the check.

"I'm sorry I can't help you, man," Vince said, making a visible effort to rouse himself. "Your stuff is great."

"Thanks for saying that." Ruben eyed him. "Are you all right, though?"

"Sure. I mean, fuck, yeah, right? That's how this business is, you know?" He gave Ruben an unconvincing smile. "I got some leads. Something will come through."

Ten minutes later, Ruben was on the street, walking to his car, the untouched script in his bag. Onstage, the show was still going strong, but his part of it was long over. He had managed to stay cool as he said good-bye to Vince, but now the reality of the situation pressed in on him like a wet mattress. He had let them both down, especially Deandra. She'd never been fired in her life and here she was, humiliated at the very same job they'd begged her not to leave the previous year. His TV-writing dream had dissolved and now they were both unemployed.

His phone rang in his bag and he pulled it out. *Of course*, he thought, reading the screen. She wanted to know how it went. The ringing continued, but he couldn't make himself answer it. "Dude, you suck hard," he said to himself, and kept walking.

He got in his car, slammed the door, and reclined the seat until it was flat. He stared up through the moonroof for a long time, past a yellow liquor store sign and into the black sky where he knew the stars were supposed to be. Finally, he cranked the seat back up and turned to the stuffed Elmo one of the twins had strapped into the passenger seat.

"Screwed I am, bro." He paused. "I know you feel me."

He started the car and tapped the gas. He had from Sunset Boulevard to his front door to come up with a plan.

28
Justine

Justine drove past Ruthie's house for the second time, eyeing the few slivers of available curb space and calculating whether she could shoehorn her car into any of them. She loved Ruthie's neighborhood in the cool part of Venice with its quirky shops and bustling restaurants, but parking was, as Ruthie put it, "a real colonoscopy," especially on Sundays when the town was overrun with hordes of fedora-wearing hipsters hell-bent on brunch.

"I hope they're serving something stronger than lemonade at this party," she muttered as she pulled up to the stop sign and flicked her turn signal. She decided to hunt two blocks over, and made the right turn onto another narrow, congested street.

"Celia's house is back there, Mommy," Emma called from the backseat. "We should park on Celia's street for the party."

"*Thank you,*" Justine grumbled. She looked at her daughter in the rear view mirror. Emma wore a deep-pink party dress and matching sweater, which—for reasons she would not divulge—she had accessorized with a stethoscope. On her lap was the birthday present, wrapped in sparkly, blue paper with a green ribbon to coordinate with the party's retro Little Mermaid theme. She watched intently as the houses passed outside her window. Justine knew that look: Emma was ready to party.

Don't take your bad mood out on Emma, she thought. *You have no one but yourself to blame for this miserable weekend.* On second thought, she could also blame Greg, who announced Saturday morning that he would be working at home all day, which meant it would be Justine's job to keep Emma quiet and out of his way as he and his black binders took over the dining room again. It had been a tough rally after a mostly sleepless night spent flopping on the undersize blow-up mattress on Emma's floor, groggily alternating between worrying about Emma's fever and festering over her encounter with Harry and all that it meant or didn't mean. Emma slept through the night, waking bright-eyed at 5:12 a.m. to bounce in her crib and pelt her mother with stuffed animals, the previous night's fever and tummy trouble forgotten. Justine, on the other hand, woke to find her head hanging off the mattress at a right angle and looking, as her mother would say, "like two miles of bad road."

She'd seen her little girl grinning at her through the crib slats and her body tingled with mortification. What had she been thinking up there on that street with Harry? How had she let it happen? It was small comfort knowing she could not have found herself in that situation with anyone but him. And the fact that she kept thinking about that kiss was making her crazy. Every time she replayed the scene in her mind, she felt a delicious flow of sensory memories, followed immediately by a bowel-clenching burst of guilt and shame. By lunchtime, she was desperate to get off the emotional seesaw, and it seemed the only way to do so was to be direct. She texted Harry:

we should have a conversation, yes?

An hour and a half later, she received a reply:

i know, right? will call u. u missed a killer show btw.

She had heard nothing from him since.

In the meantime, her interactions with Greg remained cool and distant, a placeholder for the fight they had not yet finished. They had emerged from their neutral corners that morning just long enough to exchange terse good-byes as he left for Santa Barbara.

"There's a parking place, Mommy!" Emma sang, kicking her feet at the prospect of finally getting down to birthday-party business. Justine angled the car against the curb and checked her phone once more. No new messages. She turned off the engine.

Ruthie's front door was open and they went inside, placing Celia's gift among the others on the hall table. The entryway had been draped in fishing nets and hung with shimmering starfish and sea horses, the effect of which was a mid-century modern house that had plunged to the bottom of the sea. "Sounds like the action is in there," Justine said and guided Emma to the doorway of the family room where a professional kiddie entertainer would doubtless be warming up the crowd. Justine headed to the kitchen to hang out with the other big people, who would be sipping weak theme drinks and engaging in the blood sport of the new millennium: competitive parenting. Having been chastened at the last kiddie party as the parent of a unilingual child by a mommy-and-me group who had just come from their children's "Conjugations Kick Butt!" day camp, she reminded herself not to get pulled into the crazy.

But when she walked into the kitchen, she found no clusters of type-A+ parents—only a disgruntled Ruthie flipping frozen lemonade into the blender with a wooden spoon. She wore a headband mounted with a glitter-splattered cardboard seashell the size of a satellite dish.

"Hey, Mer-Mom," Justine said, giving her a hug.

"I'm so glad you're here," Ruthie said, then eyed Justine. "Oh my God, what happened? You've got Kim Novak written all over you."

Justine poked around in the ingredients on the kitchen counter. "Nothing happened."

"Yeah, right. I can see we're going to have to talk, but I've got to finish making this batch of parent drinks first. I'm calling them 'Safe Sex on the Beach.' Get it? A responsible ocean theme?" She went back to scraping the yellow slush out of the can. "They look delicious, but they taste like something you'd use to flush out a pool filter."

The counter was strewn with paper napkins, bendy straws, sippy cups, and sparkling confetti, all in shades of aqua, navy, and green. Lined up at the end of the bar were crisp, paper favor bags, each bearing a child's name next to a prismatic sticker of a fish.

"Lookin' good, Martha Stewart," Justine said. "But where are all the grown-ups?"

Ruthie shot her a stinkeye and flung the lemonade can into a dangerously full plastic wastebasket against the wall. "I see you haven't checked out the talent yet."

"What do you mean?" she said, and laughed at the scowl on her friend's face.

"Go push your way through the toddlerazzi and see for yourself." She motioned with the spoon and slung a staccato stream of lemon ice across the floor. "I don't think I could describe it if I tried. And when you see my husband, please tell him I'm looking for him because," she yelled toward the doorway, "I need some help in here!"

In the family room, everyone was gathered in front of the lobster-festooned mantle and absorbed in the entertainment, which Justine could not see from where she stood. Even the dads were in the audience, having foregone their usual practice of huddling off in their own groups to discuss codebreaking, animal tracking, and other he-man topics. When Justine made her way to the front of the crowd, she saw why. Next to the fireplace, perched on a fishing-net-draped Eames chair, was Porno Little Mermaid.

She was in her early twenties—a natural redhead with delicate features, a flawless complexion, and a body that would make Hugh

Hefner swallow his tongue. The costume itself was a miracle of engineering, with metallic, blue-green scales starting just below the woman's concave belly and a bikini top made of two sequined seashells that provided about as much strategic coverage as Dixie cups placed on the peaks of the Himalayas.

Justine smiled. *I told Ruthie to go with the puppy theme,* she thought. The children, seasoned by the parade of animated knockouts they saw in their videos on a daily basis, seemed oblivious to the mermaid's earthbound attributes. Instead, they were engrossed in her story-song, which she took care to tell with individual attention to each child seated cross-legged on the floor around her.

Justine spotted Mac among the spellbound dads and fuming moms. In his T-shirt, dad jeans, and man-sandals, he was watching the mermaid's performance while absent-mindedly sipping a pink plastic cup shaped like a conch shell. Justine reached over and touched his shoulder, motioning with her head that he was needed in the kitchen. He nodded and reluctantly moved away from the front row with Justine. As he passed one of the dads, the man gripped him in a bear hug, then pulled back and looked at him. "Dude," he said, "you did a good thing here today," at which point the woman next to him slugged him in the arm. Hard.

Two semi-chaotic hours later, only the sticky and disheveled party diehards remained. As the parents said their good-byes, the children staggered around the back yard, navigating the rapid, rocky descent from Mt. Sucrose. Justine knew as she pushed her in the swing that Emma would be asleep in her car seat before the last buckle was clicked. Dragging a plastic trash bag behind him, Mac walked out of the house and started gathering paper plates and cups.

"Do you need help?" Justine said, giving Emma's swing another push.

"No, thanks, I'm good."

"Is Ruthie around?"

"The lady of the house is in the front yard, haggling over mermaid gratuity." He threw a stack of cake-smeared plates into the trash bag. "And, for the record, it was not my idea to collect singles in that big clam shell during the show. That was one of the other guys."

"Oh, yeah, that was classy with a K," Justine laughed. "By the way, your wife is loaning me a pair of neon hoop earrings and I need to get them before we leave."

"Neon, huh? Subtle."

"It's for our preschool auction this Friday. The theme is 'Decades' and I'm going as the eighties."

"Rad," he deadpanned. "You know, I'm guessing Ruthie will go at least three rounds with that mermaid. You should go on up and get what you need from our room."

"Are you sure?"

"Definitely. Her jewelry box is on the dresser. I'll be here with the kids."

"Thanks, Mac."

He frowned and looked down to see that he had stepped on a cupcake, the bright blue icing oozing up over the sides of his mandal. "I'm hit," he cried in mock agony, rousing Emma into laughter.

The drapes in the bedroom were closed and the faint scent of Jergens lotion hung in the air. The house's sleek, modern aesthetic continued in this room, with the exception of Ruthie's nightstand, which was piled with paperbacks and bottles of nail polish, a basket of magazines next to it on the floor.

The jewelry box was made of dark, rich wood with a brass initial plate in its center. Justine lifted the lid and scanned the velvet interior for neon. She recognized the strand of pearls Mac had given Ruthie on their fifth anniversary, along with several pairs of the drop earrings she favored and an assortment of painted clay and gilded pasta creations known to mothers everywhere. Although they had been best friends for years, Justine felt uncomfortable going through Ruthie's things. *I guess the heirloom neon items are on the bottom layer,* she thought. Carefully, she lifted out the top tray and set it on the dresser, then probed inside the box with a single finger, doing her best to find the earrings without disturbing anything. She moved aside a watch, some bangles and a disturbing poodle-shaped brooch that Ruthie was going to need to explain later. As she leaned in for a better look, she noticed a thick, silver loop. Hooking her finger through it, she lifted it from the box. In the half-light, she could make out the imprint near the bracelet's clasp: Harry's coyote. She frowned and turned the piece over in her hands. It looked like an earlier version of her own bracelet, but why would Ruthie have it?

"My husband is an idiot," Ruthie said from the doorway.

Justine turned to see her standing with a dishtowel in her hands. Ruthie's expression was a mix of pain and sympathy, erasing any hope Justine had that there was an innocent explanation for what she'd found. She held out her hand, the bracelet in her palm. "Why—" her voice croaked and she coughed. "Why do you have this?"

"Oh, honey, I should have—"

"Just tell me why," Justine interrupted.

Ruthie moved into the room. "Let's sit down for a minute." She tossed the dish towel on the bed and motioned to a large, upholstered ottoman under the window.

"I don't need to sit down."

Ruthie closed her eyes and blew out a big breath before speaking. "Teenie," she said finally, "you're my best friend. Best friend ever." Her eyes became shiny with tears. "I wouldn't hurt you for the world."

Justine sat back against the dresser. "Go on."

"It didn't mean anything to me, okay? That's the god's truth."

"*What* didn't mean anything?" She squeezed the bracelet in her hand.

Ruthie's shoulders sagged and she looked down at the carpet. "Harry and I went out for a while."

"You *what?*"

"Briefly. *Very briefly*. It was that summer you went to Belize with your cousins and I had to stay in Berkeley for my internship. By the time you were back up at school, he was three guys ago, you know? He wasn't even worth a mention at that point." Justine shook her head and Ruthie's face contorted. "I'm so sorry. Why don't we just drop it?"

"Oh, I don't think so."

Ruthie chewed on her top lip, then continued. "Like I said, we only went out for a short time. Then, that fall, you said you'd met this guy and I could tell you were really into him, but I had no idea it was Harry. How could I have known? By the time I knew it was the same Harry, you were a goner. I should have told you right then, no matter what." Ruthie began to cry. "But, Teenie, you would have hated me. It would have wrecked our friendship and that would have been just too awful, you know?" She snatched the dish towel off the bed and pressed it to her eyes.

Justine sank farther onto the edge of the dresser. "You could have given me a little more credit than that."

"I see that now," Ruthie said, "but at the time I didn't think I could tell you. And then it was too late. But you have to understand—I was trying to protect our friendship."

"Right," Justine snorted.

"It's true. Besides, I figured the thing with Harry would, you know…"

Justine's eyes narrowed. "You figured the thing with Harry would *what?*"

"It doesn't matter what I thought." Ruthie wrung the dishtowel in her hands. "I should have told you from the start."

"No, it *does* matter. Finish what you were saying."

"I just—I didn't think it would matter because I didn't think it would last very long," she blurted.

"*What?*" Justine almost yelped. "What the hell is that supposed to mean?"

"It's not a match, okay?" Ruthie's words spilled out in a stream. "He's the kind of guy who only wants a girl who will torment him and treat him like shit. That's not you. God, it was so hard to watch you try over and over to give yourself to him. That was the one thing he didn't want, but you couldn't see it because you're not messed up like that." She hung her head. "And by then I couldn't tell you what I knew."

Justine stared at her, stunned.

"But I tried!" Ruthie continued. "I tried to talk him down, to point out how bad he was for you. I was hoping you'd see what was going on before you got hurt any more. I was so happy the day he moved away, I can't even tell you."

"You're quite the guardian angel, aren't you? Lucky me." She made a sour face. "Why would he make the bracelet for you when you only 'briefly dated'?"

"That's the first one," Ruthie said softly.

Justine was silent. She pictured Harry in her old apartment, slipping the bracelet onto her wrist.

Ruthie walked over to the window and opened the drapes, filling the room with harsh afternoon sun. "Apparently, I was the first girl not to swoon under the man's attentions, and he didn't know how to deal with it. Once he knew I'd lost interest, he did everything he could to pull me back in, including *that*." She nodded toward the bracelet. "At first, I thought it was sweet that he was trying so hard to get past the rejection. Then, when he didn't give up, I realized he was actually *getting off* on it," she sneered, "as if he'd discovered he was more excited by a woman *not* wanting him. It was twisted. I cut him off completely." She crossed the room toward Justine. "Do you know what the coyote means—his stupid 'symbol'? It stands for trickster. He knows what he is. Do you see now why I've been trashing him all these years? Your krypto—"

"Don't say it!"

"Okay," Ruthie said, her eyes widening for a moment. "I won't."

"Unbelievable." Justine said, shaking her head. "*This* is your idea of friendship? Through an entire relationship *and* breakup you keep this nasty secret from me? I would *never* treat you like that." She held the bracelet out in front of her. "Why did you keep this?"

"I guess as a reminder," she thought for a moment, "of the first time I misread a man." She paused. "God," she said suddenly, "he's such a fucking *coward*."

Justine's memory clicked at the mention of Harry and fear. Then she remembered the man at Harry's gallery show, talking to her about the sculpture of the beautiful, unattainable woman. Justine had sensed something familiar in the turn of her shoulder and the line of her chin, but hadn't made the connection. The statue was Ruthie—the woman who didn't want him.

In years of dissecting her relationship with Harry, the idea that she was the innocuous sidekick to Ruthie's femme fatale had never occurred to her. She rubbed her eyes with the heels of her hands. She couldn't cry in Ruthie's room, not the way things were now.

"I hope you know how awful it was for me to see you get hurt and not be able to stop it, Teenie."

"Oh, I'm sorry. That must have been torture for you," Justine shot back.

Ruthie nodded slowly. "I deserved that. I did the best I could, though. That's all I've got." She reached out and touched Justine's shoulder, but Justine pulled away from her. "When you told me he was at your school, I got the worst feeling about it. I was sure he'd try to game you again. I should have believed you when you said you weren't the same girl anymore."

The memory of Harry's kiss flashed into Justine's mind. "I think I'm going to be sick," she said, ignoring the irony of a mom tossing her cookies at a kiddie party.

"Just breathe deep," Ruthie said gently.

"I have to go."

"Look, I can put in a movie for Emma and the kids. Let's sit down with a couple of fluorescent drinks and talk this out, all right?"

Justine looked down at the bracelet in her hand. Her entire life felt untrustworthy and the pitying look on Ruthie's face made her want to scream.

"I have to get out of here," she said, moving past Ruthie and flinging the bracelet toward the bed where she heard it slide off and *ding* against the wall. Thudding down the stairs, she ignored Ruthie's calls. *I can never let this happen to Emma*, she thought as she crossed the family room to the back of the house. *I have to teach her to be wise.* She stopped short when she reached the sliding glass door, struck by the realization that she had no clue how to do that.

29
Margaret

If one more person asked Margaret about her Thanksgiving, she was going to beat them to death with a Hello Kitty lunch box. It felt like a month had passed since the holiday, but still everyone talked about it. "Superb!" she had replied with such vehemence to Miss Glenda's casual question that the teacher had uncharacteristically hurried away without asking for details.

Margaret had never felt like such a misplaced person as she had over that long, desperate weekend. Every room in the house seemed to attack her with tender memories until, finally, she grabbed her cardigan and fled down the street. A walk through her neighborhood brought no relief, only a torturous series of family holiday tableaus in the dining room windows of the houses she passed. She spent the rest of the weekend driving around Los Angeles while listening to news radio, and sitting through movies at the mall, staring blindly at the screen.

"Good-bye." Margaret forced a smile and waved to Olivia M. and her mother as they shuffled out, the last child to leave for the day.

"See you tomorrow night at the auction," the mother called. "I donated three pieces of my handmade semiprecious-stone jewelry, you know."

"Yes, thank you, I saw your donation forms. Quite generous of you." She swung the yellow door shut and collapsed against it, clinging to the doorknob at her forehead. Finally they were gone, all of them. She pulled out her cellphone and checked its screen. Still no call from Frank. The last time she had followed up on her loan application, he had given her some flimsy line about the office being backed up because of the holidays. Holidays or not, it was Thursday and in four days—when Eddie's deadline arrived—the issue of loan approval would become moot.

"I'll take care of that," Margaret said, taking the rake from Miss Glenda, who had been doing the end-of-day smoothing of the sandy play area.

"But I always do the raking," Miss Glenda said. "It's my last duty of the day."

"And you are exceptionally good at it." Margaret began raking the sand under the big slide. "But today I would like to do it myself, thank you."

"Fine," she said and trudged off toward the deck. When Margaret had made the last sweep past the swings, she turned to find Trey standing next to her, hands on his hips.

"I know what you're up to," he said. "Burying Eddie in your own play yard is a little obvious, but I suppose there is a certain Disney-circle-of-life aspect to it."

"Did you feed Ozone?" she asked on her way to the storage closet between the classrooms.

"Of course not," he said, following her. "Nor will I be lighting that little Ebola carrier's cigarettes anytime soon."

Margaret put the rake in the closet and locked the door. "It's either feed him or change his shavings before he goes back in his cage."

"*God*," he said. "It's *Sophie's Choice*, but with vermin." He sulked behind her into the main building. "All right, I'll feed the little beast if it will get us out of here."

Margaret's phone rang as she was scooping fresh cedar shavings into the cage. She whipped it out of her pocket before the second ring.

"Margie?"

"Oh, hi, Mother." Margaret's posture drooped, both at her mother's insistence on using the despised nickname and at the letdown that it was not Frank calling with loan-approval news.

"Can you hear us?"

"Make sure that volume is up, Nella," Margaret's father instructed in the background, followed by what sounded like the phone being flayed with a toilet plunger.

"Yes!" Margaret said, jerking the phone away from her ear. "I can hear you fine. Is everything all right?"

"We have some news," her mother said.

"Yes?" Margaret carried the paper sack holding Ozone's soiled shavings out onto the deck toward the back of the school.

"Here's the thing, Margie," her father said. "Hello?"

"I'm here, Dad," Margaret said with a sigh as Ozone darted past her feet to hide under the slide.

"Right. Your mother and I have been talking and we've decided to loan some money to your brother."

"That's nice of you," she said, and unlatched the gate into the alley. "I'm sure Wayne will appreciate your help." She walked to the industrial-size waste bin, lifted its lid, and dropped in the paper bag.

"I don't think she heard you, Burt," her mother said. "Talk closer to the speaker."

"I heard you!" Margaret shrieked into the phone. "Good for Wayne!"

"No, dear," her mother said, "this was a very difficult decision for us, but we're loaning money to your brother *instead* of you."

"Mother," she said, her heart beginning to race as she walked back into the school, "what you just said made no sense."

"Talk to her, Burt."

"Margaret? It's your father again."

"Sweet Jesus," Margaret muttered, looking up at the sky. "Yes, Dad. I am *here*. What's this all about?"

"We hope you can understand that we need to help your brother. You know he's never really hit his stride like you have, but this time it sounds like he's got a business opportunity that could actually pan out and—"

"Dad," Margaret stepped up onto the deck. "Let me make sure I'm understanding this clearly. Are you saying that you are not going to loan me the money we discussed?"

"We're so proud of you, Margie!" her mother said. "It's just that Wayne asked at the same time you did and, well, it seems he needs the help more than you do. I know you understand."

"No." She sat down on the wooden bench. "I do *not* understand. You already agreed to help *me*, remember?"

"You never stop being a parent," her mother said. "We do our best to be fair."

"How is this fair? You've loaned Wayne money for his crackpot schemes how many times—four? Five? They've all failed and he's never paid you back." Margaret placed a hand on her chest and took a deep breath. "And how many times have I asked for help? One time."

"We're not saying no, dear," her mother said, "we're saying it will take a little while."

"Well, how long? I have very little time here, as I explained."

There was muffled conversation as her parents conferred. "Until Wayne's internet marketing business is doing well and he pays us back," her mother continued. "Then you're next. We promise."

"Mother, internet marketing is what he tried last time and he ended up *losing* money, remember?"

"Wayne's confident he's got a winner this time. You should see the slideshow he put on his iApple. Dad and I were very impressed."

"First of all—" Margaret began.

"I know this is a tough one to swallow," her father said, "but the bottom line is that your brother is worse off than you are, so we're going to have to help him first. I know you'll see the logic there once you've had a chance to think it over."

"But, Dad—" she said, her throat closing before she could finish.

"Your mother is on the verge of getting emotional so we're going to hang up now. We can talk again tomorrow if you like."

"We love you, Margie!" her mother said tearfully in the background. "So proud!"

There was another round of banging and several mentions of a red button, then her father's voice said, "Is the damn thing off?" and the line went dead.

Stunned, Margaret lowered the phone to her lap as Miss Glenda approached on the deck in a rapid, crouching walk, peering under every table and chair she passed.

"Is something wrong, Miss Glenda?" Margaret asked in a daze.

"I'm trying to establish the whereabouts of our little friend Ozone."

Margaret gasped and jumped up from the bench. At the end of the deck, she looked around the corner of the building. There, across the trike area, was the alley gate, standing open.

"Oh, *no*." She hurried down the steps, her loafers banging on the wooden treads. She broke into a run, scanning the ground as she went, hoping to get a glimpse of tan-and-white fur.

"Ooo-zone," she heard Miss Glenda calling as she searched the play yard.

Suddenly Trey flew past, his long legs taking surprisingly powerful strides in his khakis and desert boots. She saw him stop in the alley doorway, look both directions, then dash out of sight.

Margaret followed him through the gate with Miss Glenda on her heels. "Check over there," she said, and waved her to the right. Margaret went left and began rooting among the trash bins and alley refuse, peering into corners where a rabbit might hide. "Ozone?" she coaxed. "Come out, Ozone!" Yanking at cans and bending clumps of tall weeds out of her way, she felt the panic building. This was too much; she could not bear one more ounce of loss.

"I see you, you scabrous weasel!" she heard Trey shout down the alley. She saw him, fifty feet away, racing after Ozone, who was hopping at high speed past a row of garages.

Margaret sprinted down the alley toward them. "Get him, Trey!"

"Kind of obvious, thank you!" he screamed then launched himself into an ungainly pounce in front of an open garage, trapping Ozone between his arms as he crouched on the gravel. Margaret saw the bunny go haywire with fear while Trey struggled to get ahold on him.

"I'm coming," she yelled, her leather soles slipping on the tiny pebbles as she tried to get traction.

"Gotcha," Trey said, locking his hands around the rabbit's midsection. He held the frantic bunny's pounding hind legs away from his body and struggled to his knees. Margaret had almost reached him when she saw the taillights of the car in the garage come on.

"Trey, look out!"

The Prius backed out of the garage in a smooth, silent acceleration, the corner of its bumper catching Trey under his right arm and sending him rolling through the gravel with a sickening *oomph*.

Margaret dropped to the ground next to him. "Call 9-1-1," she yelled to Miss Glenda, who reversed course and ran back toward the school gate.

Miraculously, Trey had maintained his grip on Ozone, who was lying across his chest wearing a stunned expression identical to Trey's as they both stared up at the sky.

"Don't move," Margaret said, looking him up and down. "The ambulance is coming." He was scraped and bleeding, but at least his limbs seemed to be pointing in their natural directions.

The driver, a twenty-something man wearing Clark Kent glasses and a vintage cowboy shirt, jumped out of the car and ran over to them. "I didn't see him," he said, blanching at the sight of the blood. "Is he all right?"

"Let's hope so." Margaret kept her eyes on Trey, who was now coming out of his daze.

"Ow," he said loudly, rousing Ozone, who began savagely beating him with his back feet. He tightened his grip on the rabbit and turned his face away from the assault.

"Don't move your neck," Margaret said.

Trey noticed the car five feet away, then looked up at the driver. "A *Prius?*" he howled while trying to point the vibrating bunny away from his body. "I've been racked up by a *hybrid hipster* in *Santa Monica?* The cliché hurts more than my ribs!" He wrestled with the rabbit again. "Ow! Fur bastard!"

"Don't struggle, Trey. You have to stay still!" Margaret helped him get a grip on the rabbit, who began beating both of them. Finally, she heard a siren. "Trey, for Pete's sake, give him to me," she grunted. "The ambulance is here."

"Forget it!" Trey winced as he struggled in the dirt. Margaret now noticed that one of his eyes was beginning to swell shut. "If I'm going down, I'm taking this little fucker with me!"

☼ ☼ ☼

The rest of Margaret's afternoon and evening was spent in a series of molded plastic chairs. After arriving at the emergency room, Trey was given a sedative and his wounds were dressed before he was carted away for a series of tests that proceeded at a glacial pace. During one of the many waiting periods, she walked to the lobby and called Trey's emergency contact—his roommate, Abner.

"That is so *random*," he said. "You know he hates that rabbit, right?"

"It would appear to be mutual," she replied, squinting as the hospital intercom blared above her head.

Later, she sat next to Trey's bed as he dozed, waiting for his test results. She tried to check her emails, but once she had followed Trey's gurney through the double doors to the interior of the hospital, the phone signal had disappeared, leaving only scattered pockets of WiFi reception. She didn't know why she was bothering to look; it wasn't as though her parents were suddenly going to email her that they had changed their minds.

She set the phone on the table and leaned forward with her head in her hands. She had counted on her parents' loan as one of the most reliable legs of her financing plan, but that didn't matter now. There were no more favors to call in, and no more Hail Marys. She was losing her school, and with it the last familiar portion of her identity.

Most likely the property would be bought by a developer and the school razed and replaced with a block of condos. Margaret would have to start over and find a way to reboot her business as a divorced, middle-aged woman. Her staff would scatter and find new jobs, although it was impossible to picture Trey working outside the controlled environment of Garden of Happiness. Her second dysfunctional family was breaking up, just like her first. Resignation settled over her like a shroud.

"Jesus with a Jell-O shot," Trey said, awake and gingerly tugging at the bed sheet. "This hurts like a mofo."

"I'm here, Trey," Margaret said, getting up to stand next to the bed.

"Well, *that* makes it all better, doesn't it?" She handed him his glasses, which sat on his nose at a thirty degree angle when he put them on. "Balls," he said, taking them off again. "That satanic chinchilla owes me a pair of glasses."

"Settle down," Margaret said. "You'll have your restitution."

"And he'd better not cheap out, either. I want Transitions—the ones that turn dark outside."

Margaret studied his face, wondering if the sedative had not yet worn off.

"Is there a *problem*?" he said, pursing his lips.

Nope, she thought, *he's wide awake*. "Trey, while I have a moment, I wanted to thank you for—"

"Do *not* say another word," he said.

"But I need to tell you—"

"I mean it! It was a momentary lapse in judgment that will not be repeated. In fact, you can tell that conniving bunny biotch that from here on out, he's got a target on his back. As soon as I'm back at school, it's kill or be killed!"

Margaret smiled and brushed at a tear.

"What's your problem?" Trey said. "I'd tell you your mascara is going to run, but we both know there's no danger of that."

Margaret hesitated. "My financing plan failed. I have to sell the school."

For once, Trey was speechless, his mouth in a silent *O*.

"But I want you to know there will be severance packages for you and the teachers. I'll use the auction money and any other funds I can gather. And, of course, you will each receive a stellar reference from me." Margaret sighed hard.

"Knock, knock," said a voice behind her as a man in blue scrubs walked in carrying a medical chart. "I'm Dr. Bannerjee. How are you feeling, sir?"

Trey groaned as he shifted in the bed. "I feel like a hooker's hoo-ha after Fleet Week."

Dr. Bannerjee's eyebrows made a break for his hairline, but the rest of his face remained expressionless. "That's because you have two broken ribs. The good news is that, with proper care, you will make a complete recovery." He glanced down at the chart. "Now, I would like to give some instructions to your caregiver." He looked at Margaret. "Would that be you?"

"That'd be me, Doc," said another voice from the doorway. A man in cargo pants and a plaid shirt walked in and stood by the bed. "I'm Abner, his roommate," he said to the doctor, then turned to Trey. "Dude, we are so gonna kick that rabbit's ass."

Margaret's phone glowed and vibrated on the plastic tabletop and she picked it up. Her emails had finally come through, including a message from Frank at the bank.

"Well, what do you know?" she said to herself after reading it. "I suppose I'll file that under 'Too Little Too Late.'"

"News?" Trey asked her.

Margaret looked up at him. "For what it's worth, the bank has approved my loan."

"Bro-fist!" Abner grinned and waited for a celebratory knuckle-le-bump from Margaret, then looked around in confusion as she burst into tears.

30
Auction Night

Justine leaned closer to the mirror in the Riviera's courtesy suite and penciled a beauty mark next to her mouth. She pulled back to study the overall effect. Was it alluring...or would people be telling her all evening that she had chocolate on her face? Did she care at this point? She adjusted the floppy, lace bow tied on top of her head and turned sideways to check the altitude of the cones on her strapless corset dress. With each movement, her cheap bracelets jangled, accompanied by the clacking of the glittering crucifixes swinging from her neck.

More hair spray.

She spritzed and scrunched her hair and studied her reflection. She was supposed to be Madonna, but she felt more like a decomposing extra from "Thriller."

"What*ever*," she said, then snapped up the room key from the counter and walked out of the bathroom. Maybe she looked like an overage wannabe playing 80s dress-up, but the party rooms downstairs looked spectacular. She had been at the club since seven o'clock that morning, hanging decorations, organizing auction items, and supervising the arrangement of tables and food stations. Arriving with her in caravan, the fleet of committee moms had descended on the Riviera in a caffeine-fueled, fine-fragrance-scented mass, unleashing a whirlwind of pre-party activity that continued nonstop throughout the day. They transformed the club's lobby and ballroom into a series of decade-themed environments, finishing just in time for Justine to rush upstairs and change into her outfit. With a half hour until the event kickoff, she still had a list of last-minute tasks.

She clicked the door shut and walked quickly down the hall in her lace tights and high-heeled granny booties. Under normal circumstances, her costume would have made her a little self-conscious, but after the week she'd had, it felt good to be someone else.

"Teenie, come *on*," Ruthie had said in her most recent voicemail. "I'm running out of ways to apologize. Don't make me stand in your front yard and play a Peter Gabriel song on my boom box—that's not a good look for a mother of three. Call me!"

For the first time in their friendship, Justine was not returning Ruthie's calls. Her revelation about Harry had changed everything, and although there was a part of her that could accept her explanation, she still had not recovered from the discovery of that bracelet. Each time she had the impulse to talk to Ruthie, she remembered all over again that none of their conversations had been what they seemed, and she would put down the phone, chilled by the feeling that her best friend was as much a stranger to her as Harry's sculpture. It was as if a huge chunk of her personal history had been wiped out in the span of one inappropriate mermaid party. And it didn't help that everything Ruthie had said about Harry—and about Justine—had been true, even truer than Ruthie knew. No, that made it worse. Because now that she knew the truth, she was going to have to deal with it—which of course meant returning Ruthie's call and figuring out how to forgive her—an activity that sounded troublingly close to personal growth. And personal growth was the last thing Justine needed during auction week.

Also trending on the unwanted-truth watch list was Greg, whose trip to Santa Barbara had stretched into a series of extensions, with each excuse sounding more flimsy than the last. Since his nightly phone calls were brief and monopolized by Emma, Justine had learned of the most recent delay in an oddly businesslike email early Thursday morning.

We've added another depo to our list for this trip. The witness lives in San Luis Obispo but has agreed to come to Santa Barbara, so we'll do it here starting at noon today. If all goes smoothly, I should be home by Friday afternoon, but no guarantees.

No guarantees, she thought. *No shit.*

The elevator *ding*ed and she stepped out into the lobby—the designated 70s area. It looked fantastic, with strategically placed lava-lamps, a spot lit disco ball, and orange shag rug in front of the reception table. Already working her station behind the table was Bette, staking out a non-disco beachhead in her Stevie Nicks outfit, complete with a cloud of weapons-grade patchouli that hovered over the spread of nametags and raffle tickets like mustard gas.

"Wow," Justine managed to say before stifling a cough.

"I know." Bette waved her hand in front of her face. "Smells like flea bomb. My assistant at work soaked me with it—thought she was helping. She is so fired. And get this." She held her arms out and turned slowly on her platform, suede boots. "This is what forty pounds of cotton scarves looks like. I don't know how Stevie Nicks even walked in this rig. I feel like I'm wearing a king-size comforter."

"Well, you look great," Justine said, her eyes beginning to burn and tear.

"Where's Greg? Is he here yet?" Bette adjusted the stream of tulle that hung from the back of her white top hat.

Justine hesitated. "He might not be able to make it. He's been working crazy hours for weeks now." She pictured the invitation propped on the kitchen island. She'd surprised herself by leaving it out for him that morning, then had rushed out of the house before changing her mind.

"Yeah, Junior's running late. I knew he'd try to weenie out of it, but I told him tonight was non-negotiable."

Justine's smile remained plastered on her face. She had not heard from Harry since their text exchange the morning after the kiss. She pictured him crouching in his backyard studio, hiding from his so-called "feelings." And here she was, making small talk with his wife, who had been nothing but good to Justine in her own crusty way. Justine erupted into a coughing fit and waved her good-byes to Bette. *Breathe*, she told herself as she fled the reception area. She'd seen that on a bumper sticker on the way to the club that morning. She'd also seen one that said "Simplify," a concept that at the moment struck her as, well, complicated.

The ballroom glowed with jewel-tone spotlights that bounced off the shimmering stars hanging from the ceiling and bathed the space in overlapping colors. Throughout the room, tables were spread with auction items ready for bidding. Along the wall of windows, a series of small-plates food stations was being stocked, while the room reverberated with the sounds of the DJ's mic check and the *crash* of ice being scooped into tubs at the bars. Justine saw her committee volunteers moving among the auction displays in the 50s, 60s, 80s, and 90s sections of the room, making last-minute adjustments to the decorations and placing pens next to all the bid sheets. *Raffle-ticket bowl,* she thought, suddenly remembering that she hadn't yet put it on the reception table in the lobby. She turned to go to the back room and get the container.

"Auction goddess!" Willow blared and flounced toward Justine, her stiff poodle skirt swinging with every step like a mission bell. "Will you look at this?" She gestured around the ballroom.

"It does look pretty great, doesn't it?" Justine said. "And I like your outfit. Very *Grease*."

"I'm a hybrid." She held her arms out, the multicolor spots bouncing off her pink satin jacket. "I'm Sandy from the waist down and Rizzo from the waist up, get it? I was going to be all Rizzo, but there was no way this ass was getting into those pedal pushers. But enough about me! Will you just look at what you've done with this event? You. Are. Amazing, material girl." Willow patted Justine's bare shoulder with each word.

"Thanks for that, but the real credit goes to our intrepid band of auction moms. I'm serious, give those women a couple folding chairs and a sleeve of Ritz crackers, and they'll give you a royal wedding."

"Well, whoever did it, I hope it pulls Margaret out of her funk. The woman has been impossible for the last month."

"I don't think I'd limit that phenomenon to a thirty-day period," Justine said as she straightened a Missoni poncho on its display. Although her professional pride and allegiance to her committee members hadn't allowed her to slack off on her auction duties despite the falling-out with Margaret, her goal for the evening was to have as little contact with her as possible.

"Oh my God," Willow said, and pointed toward the ballroom's entrance.

Justine followed her finger and saw a woman standing stiffly in the doorway. She was dressed as 60s Cher in striped bell-bottoms, a fur vest, and a long, black wig. It took her a second to realize it was Margaret. "Dear Lord," she breathed, "I did not see *that* coming."

"I have to go tell her how fabulous she looks," Willow said, swinging off in Margaret's direction.

"And that's my cue to fetch the raffle bowl." Justine headed away from the door and toward the dance floor.

As Justine rounded the stage, she heard Willow bellow across the ballroom. "Oh my God, Margaret, will you look at this place? Can I pick an auction chair or what?"

If I spend any more time in that bathroom, Margaret thought as she made her way across the lobby, *people are going to start tipping me.* It was forty-five minutes into the party and already she had slipped away three times to close herself in one of the stalls and cry into a wad of tissue torn from the roll. The event was an obvious success, from the capacity turnout to the record number of auction items, but each glimpse of a full bid sheet or fish bowl overflowing with hot pink raffle tickets was a tease—a bitter reminder to Margaret of all she was losing. She forced a smile and moved through the crowd of rowdy, costumed parents—giddy that they were out for the evening unencumbered by strollers, diaper bags, and, most of all, children. Even Cienna Chadwick, Supermodel, was chatting with mere mortals in her shiny 80s leotard and headband, which channeled Olivia Newton-John's "Let's Get Physical" video.

On her way to the ballroom, Margaret saw the teachers, who had coordinated their costumes as 90s grunge rockers. They were a muted rainbow of wrinkled plaid as they giggled and posed for photos in their mussed hair and Doc Martens. Even Miss Glenda mugged along with them. They were oblivious to the fact that in a short while, Margaret would be announcing that the school they'd helped build would likely not exist by spring break. And, in a few weeks, she would be writing their reference letters.

"Margaret," they called as they leaned against one another, their eyelids at half-mast, "Dude!"

The lump rose in Margaret's throat again and she darted to the ladies' room and into a stall, banging the door shut behind her. Sinking onto the toilet lid, she covered her face with her hands in a fresh round of sobs. She wanted to pull into the garage at school knowing that Trey and Miss Glenda would be bickering about the smell in the refrigerator. She wanted to walk into her family room and see Leticia sprawled out with a bag of chips, her phone pressed to her cheek. And, she admitted to herself, she wanted to look out the back door and see Eddie on the patio, waxing the surfboard he'd balanced on two chairs as a thread of smoke drifted from the stick of incense he'd poked into a nearby planter. She didn't recognize her life without these things, but whether she was ready or not, life was lurching forward without them.

Leaning over to pull more tissue off the roll, the long, black hair of her wig swung down across her face. *Stupid costume*, she thought and angrily batted it out of her eyes. The week before, she had stopped at a costume shop on Wilshire with the intention of buying one of those party-pooper T-shirts with the word "costume" printed across the front. In the end, she had reached for the Cher outfit that hung on the wall in its plastic bag. When she was little, she had watched *The Sonny & Cher Show* each week, sitting cross-legged on the carpet in front of the TV, mesmerized by the spectacle of the opening number. As she left the store, she had hoped that small, bright bubble of memory might help her through the difficult evening ahead.

Another miscalculation, she thought, and walked out of the stall. Not only was the costume scratchy and the wig hot and slippery, but she had chosen an outfit that inherently begged the question, "Where's Sonny?" That was what parents had been asking her all night, reminding her again and again that she was no longer half of a pair as everyone else seemed to be. In hindsight, she shouldn't have come as Cher; she should have come as Dirty Harry.

In the mirror above the sinks, she tilted her wig until her bangs were straight, then dabbed her eyes once more. Tossing the tissue through the hole in the marble countertop, she swung the nylon hair behind her shoulder. "At least I got you, babe," she said to her reflection. As she reached for the door, her cellphone rang.

She stepped into the lounge portion of the restroom—an auxiliary area filled with mirrors, upholstered stools, and scattered gilt bowls of pungent potpourri—and answered the call. "Tish?"

"Hi, Mom."

"Is everything all right?"

"Yeah, I guess so. I don't know."

"What is it, sweetheart?"

"Thanksgiving blew."

"I'll tell you something," Margaret said, "Thanksgiving blew here, too."

Leticia gave a small laugh. "I wish I had come home."

Two women entered the ladies' room and Margaret moved to the corner of the lounge. "So do I."

"So, anyway, I hope you won't be mad, but I used my emergency credit card and booked a flight home tomorrow for a three-day weekend."

"Did you really? That would be wonderful. But won't that mean you'll miss class on Monday?"

"It's okay, I can study on the plane. Besides, this trip counts as school in a way because I want to talk to you about my major."

"What about it?"

"I've been thinking and I'm pretty sure I want to major in education. Or get my bachelor's in psychology then my master's in education, you know? I mean, I've always thought it was so cool the way you understand how little kids work and you help clueless parents figure out what they're supposed to do and all that. I want to talk to you about how you did it when you were starting out. Who knows? Maybe I'll end up running my own school someday."

Before she could stifle herself, Margaret yelped into the phone.

"Mom, was that you? Are you okay?"

Margaret snuffled and dabbed at her nose.

"Are you *crying*?"

"I'm okay," Margaret said. "I'm sorry. It's not you."

"What's going on there?"

"Leticia, you would be an extraordinary educator and I can't tell you how proud it makes me that you are interested in the field." She blew out a big breath of air. "It's just that I don't think I'm the best person to give you advice."

"What are you talking about? You're the perfect person."

Margaret slumped onto one of the floral ottomans. "We've— *I've*—been trying to shield you from some of the consequences of the divorce, one of which concerns Garden of Happiness."

"Yeah...?" Leticia said in a low voice.

"It's a convoluted series of events, but the upshot is that I've learned that my skills with respect to understanding and managing people are not what I thought they were."

"You're not making any sense. Are you okay?"

Margaret checked over her shoulder before continuing. "Leticia, I have to sell my school," she blurted, then gulped out a small sob.

"*What*? What are you talking about?"

"It's part of the settlement with your father," she snuffled. "Everything gets split in half and I have to buy him out..." She pulled a tissue from her fringed handbag and blew her nose. "I'm sorry, I can't go into it all. I'm at the silent auction right now."

"I can't believe that," Leticia said softly.

"I can't, either," Margaret said, "but now I have to."

They were both quiet for a moment.

"You know what, Mom? That's great."

"What?" Margaret scowled into the phone.

"I said that's great."

"I don't think you understand, Tish."

"I just read this article about how your life runs in ten-year cycles. That's how long you've had the Garden, right?"

"Approximately..."

"See? That's perfect. It's time for a big change, so you should embrace it. It's all good."

Margaret looked up at the ceiling. "I appreciate the pep talk, but you have no idea what I'm facing here."

Leticia gasped into the phone. "I just realized—my trip down this weekend was meant to be! You'll give me advice and I'll give *you* advice, get it?"

Margaret could not help but smile. "That's very sweet."

"We'll talk it out. Like I said, it's all good."

"I'm glad you're coming home," Margaret said.

"I'll text you my flight time. Wait—you know how to receive texts, right?"

"Very funny."

Leticia laughed. "Bye, Mom."

"Be safe!" Margaret said. "Love you."

"Love you, too," Leticia said.

Margaret dropped the phone into her purse. She wasn't sure what she thought of the ten-year-cycle theory, but her daughter was coming home the next day, and she had to agree with her on one point: the visit felt meant to be.

As she walked toward the door, the dread enveloped her again. Not only would she be stepping onstage shortly to announce her failure to the people who had trusted her with their jobs and their children, but she needed to personally apologize to Justine for her recent, desperate behavior. She had been trying to talk with her all evening, but each time Margaret caught sight of her, Justine would slip away before she could cross the room. Margaret didn't blame Justine for avoiding her, but she was determined to make amends. It was time to track her down.

She flung open the ladies' room door, which swung partway before striking something with a fleshy *thud*.

"Ow, dammit!" she heard a woman say. Margaret stepped out and the door glided shut to reveal Justine rubbing her upper arm. "*Seriously?*" she said, glaring at Margaret before walking away.

"I'm—Justine!—I'm sorry," she stammered, but Justine had already disappeared into the crowded lobby.

Suddenly, Margaret was enveloped by an intense, peculiar odor. She turned to see Bette standing next to her, a half-drained martini in her hand. "What?" Bette said crankily before taking another gulp of her drink.

Justine banged through the Riviera's front door and turned right, making her way down the walk and into the shadows at the edge of the club's front lawn. She needed to regroup and do a last-minute cone check before going onstage to run the live portion of the auction and introduce Margaret.

Margaret. Her encounter by the ladies' room had been the first time she'd seen her up close all evening. Her eyes had been red and puffy and it crossed Justine's mind that she had been crying in the bathroom, but that couldn't be right. Then she remembered her earlier eye-watering experience in the lobby and it all made sense: the patchouli body count continued to climb.

She pushed aside a stack of bracelets and checked her watch. The party was nearly over and Greg wasn't coming. She wished she hadn't left the invitation out on the counter at home. When the night was over, it would be one more humiliating reminder that Greg was somewhere else, with Simone. She wondered if there was a bumper sticker out on the LA freeways somewhere with the perfect advice for her particular situation. She had no idea what that advice might be, but she hoped it included lots of profanity.

It was a cloudless night and, in spite of the glow of the lights that peppered the Riviera's drive, she could make out a few stars in the sky. She rolled her neck in and breathed deeply, rubbing her arms against the chill. It would be over soon. When she turned to go back into the club, she saw Harry walking toward her.

His three-piece suit glowed white in the driveway lights, the black, open-necked shirt and gold chain becoming visible when he was just a few feet away. He had blown and sprayed his hair to look like John Travolta's, and he walked with extra swagger. He was working it.

"Look at you," he said when he reached her on the sidewalk. "You know, I always thought 80s Madonna was hot, but that outfit suits you even better."

Justine made a halfhearted attempt to stifle a snort of laughter.

Harry frowned. "Did I say something funny?"

"Not intentionally," she said, still smiling.

"Now you've got me paranoid," he said, checking himself over. "I thought I looked pretty good in this."

Justine laughed again.

"Okay, that's enough. Tell me what's so funny."

She adjusted her array of crucifixes. "I never realized how seriously you take yourself."

"What are you talking about?"

Justine pursed her lips. "Here's the thing: you have no irony." She crossed her arms. "You, sir, are without jest."

"What? How can you say that? I have tons of jest!"

Justine shook her head. "Nope. Sorry. I don't know how I missed that before. It's simply not there."

Harry's eyes narrowed. "Oh, I get it. You're mad because I haven't called you since, you know, the other night. Okay." He nodded. "You're right. My bad. I wanted to call you, but I've been buried in this new project…" Justine raised her eyebrows and waited.

"All done?" she said finally.

Harry looked wary. "Uh…yes?"

"Great. So I've been thinking about your art show and the pieces I saw there and something has been bugging me. There's a word that's been on the tip of my tongue but I haven't quite been able to name it."

It was Harry's turn to cross his arms. "Oh, really?"

"Yeah, but seeing you tonight has filled in the blank for me. Well, that and talking with Ruthie."

Harry's arms fell to his sides and Justine saw a flicker of pain in his eyes. "Ruthie? You talked with her about me?"

"Oh, just the way your art has evolved over the years." She paused. "Or hasn't."

"What the hell is that supposed to mean?"

"Take this piece, for example." She removed her silver bracelet from the jumble on her arm and held it up in the light. "Comparing Ruthie's bracelet to mine really brought things into focus for me, Harry. I finally found that word I'd been searching for—the one that captures your body of work."

"Oh, really?" he said with a sneer. "And what's that?"

"Derivative," she said, and dropped the bracelet into his breast pocket. "Oh, and Crapwizard. I guess that's two words, isn't it? *My bad.*" She gave the pocket a pat as he set his jaw, his face darkening. *No comeback*, she thought and turned to go. *Finally.*

Her shoes scratched on the pavement as she made her way from the shadows toward the lights of the club. She wanted to find the DJ and make a request. There had to be a song about a girl who had discovered that what she thought was a broken heart was nothing more than emotional indigestion from the romantic equivalent of a bad burrito. With any luck, the song would have a brain-melting guitar solo.

"Stomach flu" was a phrase that gave pause to even the most fearless preschool parent. Ruben and the twins had managed to elude the latest outbreak at Garden of Happiness, but Deandra had not been so lucky.

She lay back against the sofa cushions and draped her arm across her eyes. "God, I can't believe how fast this came on. I'm so sorry, I know you wanted to go tonight."

"Hmmm?" Ruben's voice was muffled against the carpet where he lay on the floor behind the sofa.

"I said I'm sorry we're having to miss the auction party."

"No worries." He flattened his cheek against the rug and squinted into the dusty space beneath the toy box. His notebook was not there. "This is *super* not happening," he said under his breath. How could he have lost it *again*? When he'd realized the day before that it wasn't in his messenger bag, he'd looked everywhere, even scouring the Laugh Factory green room in the middle of the afternoon in case it had fallen out at his last gig. The thought of never recovering all those pages of work—all that time—made him almost as sick as Deandra.

"Ruben, what are you doing back there?"

He stood and hitched up his jeans. "I can't find my notebook. And please don't say 'again.'"

"I wasn't going to say that." She was quiet for a moment. "You have your script, right? It's not lost?"

"No, I have the script." He stared down at the carpet.

"Okay, I'm not trying to be sassy here, but can't you just get a new notebook then?"

Ruben let his chin drop onto his chest. "Dee, my novel's in that notebook."

Deandra's eyes went wide. "Your *novel*?"

"It wasn't finished, but I'd gotten a good start. Plus my outline was in there and my notes…" He groaned and flopped on the end of the sofa by her feet.

"I'm sorry. Your *novel*?"

He rubbed her leg. "Yeah, I know. I hadn't told anyone about it yet. I just had this idea for a story and started playing with it and before I knew it, I had some chapters. I wanted to see if I could write the whole thing, you know? Then I could just lay it on you and say, 'Hey, check out my novel.' Does that make sense?"

"Sure, I get it. Wow, a whole book. That's really something." She gave him a sympathetic smile. "Where have you not looked yet?"

Ruben groaned again. "That's the thing—I've looked everywhere. I think it's gone for good this time."

"Don't say that. We'll find it." She shifted on the sofa and swallowed hard.

"Oh, no." Ruben gently lifted Deandra's feet from his lap as he stood up. "I don't want you worrying about that. Right now we need to get you better. You've got a business to start, remember? Time is money, lady. No slackin'." He smiled and pointed toward the dining room, where he had helped her arrange a desk, file cabinet and new lamp in front of the window—her own home office. "Pretty soon that phone will be ringing nonstop with crabby women wanting you to find them the perfect nanny. You know, with a little buttering up, I just might refer you to my network of power-mommy friends."

"Please don't say butter." She moved around on the sofa again, pulling the blanket up to her chin. "Look, I love my new office, but I don't feel right about the timing of all this. If I hadn't gotten fired, you wouldn't be going back to a job you hated."

"I didn't hate it," he said. "I wanted to try something else." He paused. "And now I have."

"Oh, Ruben, you can't abandon your dream just because the thing with Vince didn't happen."

"I don't feel like I've abandoned anything. I just feel...different. Besides, I'm lucky to get my job back." *Very lucky*, he thought. He hadn't wanted to worry Deandra, but it had taken two days for his old manager at the escrow company to get back to him with a firm yes—two days of near-panic as he scoured employment websites and ran through worst-case scenarios that zeroed out their savings. He gathered an armful of toys and stuffed animals that the twins had scattered before going to bed. When he looked up, she was still watching him, her eyebrows knit.

"I'm serious," he said. "The timing is fine. This is going to work out great."

He propped two of the twins' stuffed animals on the bookshelf and deposited the rest in the wooden toy box before heading to the kitchen. As he took a glass from one of the cabinets, he noticed the drawer under the counter where the phone sat. Why hadn't he thought of that before? He opened it and found takeout menus, appliance manuals, receipts, and a fistful of chip clips—but no notebook. He ran his hands through his hair and wondered if he could have missed it under one of the car seats. Once Deandra was asleep, he would go down to the garage and look again.

He returned to the living room and set an iced drink in front of Deandra.

"What's that?" she said.

"Ginger ale. That's what my mom always gave me when I was sick. You're supposed to sip it." He noticed the expression on Deandra's face. "Why are you looking at me like that? You're going to barf again, aren't you?"

She reached up and took his hand. "Thank you for taking such great care of me, Ruben."

He kissed the top of her head. "You bet," he said into her silky strands.

"I'm serious. Being with the children, working on your writing— it's changed you." She squeezed his fingers. "This may sound weird, but I'm proud of you. I mean, I've always been proud of you, but there's something about you right now, it's…"

"Aw, Dee, you don't need to cry."

She looked up at him, her eyes shiny. Suddenly the corners of her mouth turned down, little beads of sweat appearing on her upper lip. "Okay, *now* I have to barf."

"I'm on it!" He helped her up and escorted her to the bathroom, where he was secretly relieved when she motioned for him not to accompany her farther. He shut the door just as he heard her get sick. "Stomach flu," he said to himself as he picked up the twins' windbreakers and hung them in the hall closet. "That's how they get ya."

The phone rang and he answered it in the kitchen, tucking it under his ear as he thumbed through a pile of catalogs that he'd already checked twice. "Oh my God, Ruben. It's Willow," she yelled over the voices and music in the background. "Where *are* you?"

"Hey, Willow. Deandra's sick so we're having to miss the party."

"Let me guess—stomach flu. That school is one foul Petri dish right now, am I right?" A burst of cheers erupted in Ruben's ear.

"Sorry I had to bail on selling raffle tickets tonight," he said.

"Screw raffle tickets. Listen, I was planning to talk with you in person tonight, but when you didn't show, I thought I'd better call you."

Here it comes, he thought, *another fundraising job*. He had been putting off breaking the news to her that he wouldn't be available for committee chores anymore.

"I have something that belongs to you," she said.

Ruben pressed the phone harder against his ear. "You do?"

"A spiral notebook."

"Oh my God—you *found* it?" Ruben grinned and collapsed against the counter with relief.

"It was sitting on the shelf above the cubbies so I scooped it up."

"Yeah, baby! Okay, I have no idea how it got there but I don't care. Thank you *so much*, Willow."

"Don't thank me yet. Here's the thing." She paused. "I read it."

Ruben's arm froze mid fist pump. "You read my notebook?"

"I know, I'm out of bounds and you feel violated, yada yada yada. Let me ask you this. Are you writing a novel?"

Ruben considered his answer as he re-stacked the catalogs. "Yes," he said cautiously.

"Fabulous," Willow said, "because I have to tell you, it's really good."

"Really? You think so?" His face burned at the thought of Willow reading the beginnings of a story he hadn't even shared with his wife. But she *had* read it, and she thought it was good.

"Yes, I do think so. You've got something here."

"Wow. Thanks, Willow." He unscrewed the top from a sippy cup and poured a dribble of milk down the sink.

"How soon will it be finished?" she asked.

"Um...honestly? I have no idea."

"Say it with me: As. Soon. As. Possible. Got it?"

"Okay, I'm lost. What are you talking about?"

"Look," she said, "not many people know this, but I have a connection or two in the publishing world. I know just the person who would want to see this. But you have to *finish* it, all right? As in, *yesterday*."

"Are you serious? You wouldn't kid me, would you?"

"Ruben, I do not *kid*. I *effuse*. There's a difference. Now get to work. I'll be in touch."

"Willow?" he said before she hung up. "You're a goddess!"

There was no response on the line and Ruben thought she might already have gone or, worse, he had offended her. Finally, she spoke. "You're welcome," she said softly and ended the call.

He stared at the phone. Yes, he was holding it. It was real. Willow had, in fact, offered to put his novel—*his novel*—in professional hands. She thought it was good. No, *really* good. He plopped the phone into its cradle, his mind racing. He would write in the evenings, after work. Or maybe early in the mornings. He could block out some time on the weekends, too. And they would need a second laptop now, of course. He walked through the living room toward the hall, trying to organize the thoughts bubbling through him. Finally, after months, he had great news for Deandra. Yes, things would be more hectic than expected, but they could handle it.

"Hey, Dee? You all right?" He listened at the door. "Wait 'til you hear what just happened. Willow found my notebook." He waited again. "Should I come in?"

The door swung open and there she was, hair piled on top of her head and her small, bare feet engulfed in the shaggy bathroom rug. "This is unbelievable," she said.

"You haven't even heard the good part yet." He stopped. "Wait, why is it unbelievable?"

She brought her hand from behind her back and held out a small, white stick. "I'm pregnant."

"You're...wait—how did you know to...?" He pointed at the pregnancy test. "Something about it didn't feel like stomach flu," she said, watching his face.

"Oh my God." He looked down at the little stick. "Oh, Dee."

"I *know*," she said, and set the test on the counter.

He reached out and held both of her hands. "But...this wasn't when we planned to—"

"True."

Ruben looked down at her tummy, then back to her face. "But we *were* going to—"

"Yes, of course. In another year or two."

They lingered in the doorway, staring at each other.

Deandra licked her lips. "So...how is this going to—"

"We'll figure it out," Ruben said.

"Yes," she said, nodding slowly. "Okay."

"Things happen when they're supposed to happen."

Deandra tilted her head to one side. "Did my dad say that?"

"No." Ruben gathered her to his chest. "I did."

It was time. Margaret crossed the lobby, her bell-bottoms banging against her ankles with every reluctant step. The parents, emboldened by their costumes and the open bar, called out to her in passing.

"Yo, Silkwood!"

"Loved you in *Moonstruck*!"

She responded with little half waves of recognition, numbed by anticipation of the inevitable, her mind ahead of her, already onstage. She became aware of a commotion at the lobby entrance and allowed herself to be drawn with the crowd of curious parents toward the door. As she approached the knot of onlookers, they folded her in, passing her to the front of the crowd with soft nudges on her elbows.

"Better late than never," a dad dressed as Billy Idol said as he made room for her to pass.

"Oh my God, this is genius!" squealed a mom dressed as Jackie Kennedy as Margaret reached the center of the circle.

There, glaring out from under his bobbed wig, was Trey. In his fuzzy vest and paisley puffy shirt, he made a convincing—if tall—Sonny Bono. When Margaret stepped out of the knot of parents, he looked her up and down and his expression darkened further.

"Well, this is a revolting development," he said.

One of the parents burst out laughing. "You mean you two didn't plan this?"

"Of course we didn't!" they said in unison, causing more laughter.

Margaret noticed Trey leaning heavily on the door handle. "For heaven's sake," she said, moving toward him, "what are you doing here? You should be resting at home."

"Back!" he said, and batted her away. "I'm perfectly capable!" He shuffled forward, doing his best to stand straight, and the crowd moved back to make room. Just then the lobby lights dimmed three times, signaling that the live auction was about to start. The parents began to disperse toward the ballroom. "Lookin' good, Trey!" one of the dads called over his shoulder. "You *go*, Sonny!" said another.

"These people could make Gandhi buy a handgun." Trey gritted his teeth and started walking with short, tense steps.

"Here," Margaret said, "take my arm."

He glanced at her with disdain. "I think I'll pass." He straightened his shoulders and continued shuffling.

They slowly crossed the lobby as the parents streamed ahead. "We'll find you a seat inside," she said. "I have to go onstage."

"Jesus in a jumpsuit, it looks like a Liberace piñata exploded in here," Trey said when they entered the ballroom. Margaret guided him to an empty table where he refused to sit, but stood gripping the back of a chair as Margaret stared at the far end of the room. The stage was surrounded by a crowd of parents and Margaret saw Justine speaking with the DJ, a clump of note cards in her hand. Any moment now, she would walk to the mic and begin the presentation.

When Margaret turned back to Trey, he held out a white envelope for her to take.

"Is it too late to contribute to the cause?"

"I appreciate the gesture," she said with a weak smile, "but, as you know, that's not necessary at this point." She looked back toward the stage where Justine was signaling to the DJ with a slashing motion across her throat.

"Excuse me, Miss Scarlet? Perhaps you could stop wringing your hankie long enough to open the damn envelope?" Trey poked her in the arm with it.

"Fine," she said and snatched it from his hand. She ripped open the flap and pulled out a single slip of paper. It was a certified check. Her hand shook as she blinked at the number of zeroes in the amount.

"Trey—" She looked from the check to his face and back again. "I don't know what to say. This has to be your life savings."

"To be replaced by my tastefully epic insurance settlement, which my deranged Chihuahua of a lawyer is finalizing as we speak."

"Well, that's wonderful and I thank you, obviously. *Thank you.* But I can't let you do that. You have better uses for your windfall than loaning it to me." She replaced the check in the torn envelope as she blinked back tears.

"Ha! Ow, don't make me laugh!" He clutched his middle. "Get over yourself, sister. I'm no banker, but you've got 'default' written all over you." He pointed at the check. "Hello? That's not a loan. That's an *investment.*"

Margaret stared at him.

"Partner," he added, emphasizing the word with a tilt of his head.

"*'Partner'?*" The music stopped and the microphone squawked with feedback.

He shrugged. "Until I can think of a more regal title, hopefully one that comes with a signet ring for parents to kiss."

A partner, she thought, her mind racing. Garden of Happiness would survive, but it would not be her school anymore. It would be *theirs*.

"Welcome, everyone, and thanks for coming tonight…" Justine's amplified voice cut through the ballroom.

"Two minutes, Ms. Bono," Willow said with a grin as she passed by on her way toward the stage. Margaret watched her disappear into the crowd of rowdy, clapping parents. At the edge of the group were the teachers, clustered together for selfies as Justine began the introductions. Margaret turned back to Trey, swinging her wig-hair behind her shoulder. "Thank you," she said, her voice cracking, and held out her hand. "Partner."

"Margaret Askew!" Justine's voice boomed across the ballroom as Trey grasped her hand and shook it.

"Well, I guess that's that," he said, smoothing his faux-fur vest.

"Right." She looked down at her patent leather go-go boots. *It's over*, she thought. *It's over and it's just beginning.*

"I believe you're supposed to address the rabble now." Trey nodded at the crowd across the room.

Margaret straightened her shoulders and sniffed loudly. "I don't usually get nervous at these things, but tonight I'm feeling a little emotional." She turned and began walking toward the stage.

"Don't go soft on me now, woman!" Trey called after her. "You have no idea what a bitch I'm going to be to work with!"

When she reached the crowd, the parents once again folded her in, passing her among them with smiles and pats as she moved through the multicolored lights and onto the stage.

:☀: :☀: :☀:

Justine stood shoeless by a long auction table, surveying the ballroom.

The concrete floor was cold through her lace tights, her cones were chafing, and there was a dull thudding behind her eyes—a reminder of the Zima she had consumed in an unfortunate burst of sentimentality while trapped in the party's 90s zone. With a sigh, she gathered the unused bid sheets, crumpled napkins, and plastic cups, and sorted them into the containers she'd dragged from the bar. Then she reached down, grabbed a handful of the decorative, silver table cover and ripped it off with a savage fling, sending a shower of star-shaped confetti into the air. "Huzzah," she said flatly.

As the last guests trickled into the lobby to collect their auction merchandise before leaving, a half-dozen volunteers fanned out through the empty ballroom to break down the party. In a small side room, several moms were gathered around a folding table, sorting through the winning bid amounts and tallying up the night's receipts. Justine could have flopped out on a sofa to wait for the final total, but the thought of being idle made her uncomfortable. She was ready to put the night out of her misery, even if it meant sweeping the ballroom floor herself.

"This one goes out to the Garden of Happiness auction mamas," the DJ cheesed into the mic. Donna Summer's "She Works Hard for the Money" blasted from the speakers, prompting a round of groans from the women scattered through the room. Justine dragged her collection bins to the next table and began gathering more trash.

"Justine."

She turned to see Margaret standing behind her. *Dammit,* Justine thought, *leave it to Cher to have ninja stealth skills.* "If you're looking for the dad dressed as Greg Allman, he left with Cyndi Lauper twenty minutes ago."

Margaret ignored the joke. "May I speak with you?"

Justine threw a handful of cups into the recycling bin with a clatter. "Okay."

"I, um…" Margaret began. "I owe you an apology."

"Really. An apology for what?" Margaret wore a weirdly energized expression—the same one she'd had earlier when Justine introduced her to the crowd. For one awful moment, Justine had thought Margaret might break down and cry right on the stage.

"I've been facing some...challenges these past few months. I wish I could say that I haven't been myself lately, but the truth is that I've been *too much* myself. At least, that's what I'm coming to learn." She swallowed. "You took some of the brunt of my difficulties and I'm sorry for that. My behavior was inappropriate."

"I'm not the only one who took the brunt of it, Margaret." Justine pictured Emma's face during the toy incident in the school kitchen and felt a fresh jolt of anger.

Margaret nodded. "I'm afraid Emma Under—"

"It's *Emma*," Justine interrupted. "Just plain Emma."

"Right. *Emma*. I'm afraid she may have felt the tension of the past few weeks as well. I take full responsibility." She slipped off her Cher wig and let it hang from her fingers at her side. "That never should have happened."

"What exactly *did* happen?"

The corner of Margaret's mouth turned up, but there was a deep sadness in her eyes. "Let's just say I have met the enemy, and the enemy is me. Does that make any sense?"

She had unknowingly summed up the mental conversation Justine had been having with herself as she cleaned. "I think I might know what you mean."

"In any event," Margaret said, "I want you to know that things are going to be different after winter break."

"Yes, they will. We won't be returning to Garden of Happiness."

Margaret was silent for a moment. "I wish you'd reconsider," she said finally. "And I don't say that because tonight is shaping up to be our most successful auction to date."

"No, it's the right decision to go. For all of us."

"Well. You will be missed."

"Oh, I'm pretty sure that's not true," Justine said with a smile, "but thanks anyway." She turned and walked away, dragging the trash bins behind her. She reached the ballroom entrance just as Greg appeared in the doorway.

"I'm really late, aren't I?" His cheeks were flushed like he had been running.

"Yeah," she said, surprised and still gripping the trash cans. "It's over." The song ended and someone turned the lights all the way up, leaving the room stripped of mood.

"Fun party?" Greg stepped into the ballroom and looked around. He wore beige dress slacks with a tan sport coat and periwinkle T-shirt.

"Yeah, I guess so," she said, studying his outfit and wondering why he was dressed like a pediatrician's waiting room. "Made some money. No shots fired. All good."

"That's great," he said, nodding.

"Yep." She heard Ruthie's voice in her head. *Awkward sauce.*

"You need help with anything?"

She dropped the handles of the trash bins. "I didn't think you were coming."

"I didn't think I was, either."

They watched each other for a long time. She felt peculiar not being able to decode her husband's expression; she thought she had seen them all.

"So what changed your mind?"

He licked his lower lip and glanced around the room again. "Things in Santa Barbara got…weird."

Justine's tummy flopped. She waited for him to continue.

"I always figured Simone's reputation was mostly exaggerations circulated by the secretaries. Sure, she was a flirt, but I never took any of that seriously—I was immune to it." Jamming his hands in his pockets, he stared off into a corner of the ballroom. "Or maybe I just told myself I was." He exhaled loudly. "Anyway, turns out she took it *very* seriously."

"Go on," Justine said, raising her chin.

"There's a half day of the depo left. It's an easy one, so Keith can finish it tomorrow without me."

"And Simone?" She watched his face.

"At some point tonight, she'll realize that I'm gone," he said, still looking past her.

"That's a carefully worded sentence."

"It feels like we've been both choosing our words carefully for months." He faced her again. "Would you say that's true?"

Justine's bracelets banged together as she pushed the hair out of her eyes. "Simone has got to go. Off the case, off…all of it."

"Already taken care of. I've got someone taking her place starting Monday." He paused. "But you've got to quit that school."

"I agree."

He took a step toward her. "And that includes the people in it."

"Already taken care of."

"Really?" he said, genuine surprise overtaking his game face.

"Yeah. Really."

He relaxed a bit and a new thought seemed to occur to him. "You think Emma will be upset about changing schools?"

"Actually, I think she was a little relieved not to be going back after the way things have been the last few weeks. And also, I told her you'd buy her a pony."

"Excellent parenting," he said with a chuckle. A busboy pushed a load of dishes past them on a rattling cart, the sound bouncing off the concrete floor.

"I miss how we used to be," she said when it was quiet again. "You know what I mean? I wish we could get some of that back."

"I was thinking the same thing. Maybe we can work on that?"

"I'd like to. But..."

He scowled. "'But?'"

"Only if you never wear that outfit again."

"Hey," he tugged at his lapels. "This is my 80s getup. I'm Miami Vice."

"You realize that's a TV show, not a person, right?"

"And check *this* out." He pulled up his pant leg to show a bare ankle above his shoe.

"Wow. It's like you *are* Don Johnson."

"I was inspired by the invitation you left for me." He smiled. "And speaking of clothes, I've never seen you wear *that* before." He inspected her bustier dress. "You look very...pointy."

She smiled in return. "Hey now, is that a preview of the new sexy talk?" She wasn't sure what would happen next, but she knew Greg was not the kind of guy to sweep her into some big romantic embrace.

"I kind of like you in that dress," he said, wrapping his hands around her waist and pulling her toward him.

Then again, she'd been wrong before.

Acknowledgments

Writing a novel, then rewriting it, then stomping off to stew awhile before taking another shot at it, then returning to it only to call into question your entire pathetic existence before settling in for the real rewrites, well, it can leave you yearning for the reassurance and inspiration that quality, normal humans have to offer—if you're lucky enough to know a few of them. I owe a great deal to some people I feel very blessed to have in my life, both personally and professionally.

I am enormously grateful to Katherine Fausset at Curtis Brown, Ltd. for embracing and championing this book, for believing in me, and for being a damn wise and lovely person all the way around. Huge thanks as well to everyone at Full Fathom Five, including the fantastic Samantha Streger and the wonderful Jane Arbogast, whose email about my manuscript made me do the ugly-cry and who "gets" this book in the way every writer dreams an editor will. And many thanks to Kim Dower at Kim-from-L.A. and Lucinda Blumenfeld at Lucinda Literary—the most dynamic, committed, and charming publicists in the business.

Special, heartfelt thanks to Lynn Hightower, whose sage and sassy counsel not only took this book to the next level while revolutionizing the way I look at storytelling, but who has also kept my real-life feet on solid ground in more ways than I can say. I count myself incredibly fortunate to call her both my mentor and my friend.

Huge thanks to the talented friends and colleagues who took time from their busy lives to read, discuss, and support this project, including Emily Altmann, Lisa Doctor, Kerry Karsian, Lindsay Lang, Jenny Lawson, Helen Reese, Lisa Rae Rosenberg, Mare Smooke, Dean Stackel, Kim Stern, Mia Von Sadovszky, and Melanda Woo. And boundless, loving gratitude to Dori Hairrell Andrunas, who tirelessly supports everything I do, unfailingly pulls me back from the brink, and gently schools me every day in what it means to be a real friend. *Thank you.*

Lastly, and most of all, thank you to Madison and Henry for somehow teaching me exactly what I needed to learn in life right from the moment we met. You amaze me each and every day with your deep souls, huge hearts, and sharp wits. To me, you are the definition of love and I'm so proud to be your mom.

About the Author

Anna Lefler is a novelist, comedy writer, and the author of *The Chicktionary: From A-Line to Z-Snap, The Words Every Woman Should Know,* which *The Chicago Tribune* called "a wry celebration of modern femininity." She was a staff writer on the Nickelodeon/NickMom TV show *Parental Discretion with Stefanie Wilder-Taylor,* where she also served as an on-camera performer. Anna is a two-time faculty member of the Erma Bombeck Writers' Workshop and her humorous essays have appeared on Salon.com, *McSweeney's Internet Tendency,* and *The Big Jewel.* She has performed standup comedy in clubs around Los Angeles, including the Hollywood Improv and the Comedy Store. Anna lives in Los Angeles with her two children, whom she regularly embarrasses.

Visit Anna on her website,
www.annalefler.com

CPSIA information can be obtained
at www.ICGtesting.com
Printed in the USA
FSOW02n0844190915
11147FS